WORD OF WAR

TERENCE STRONG

WORD OF WAR

SILVER FOX
PRESS
United Kingdom

First published in Great Britain by Silver Fox Press, 2017

This hardback edition first published 2017

1 3 5 7 9 10 8 6 4 2

SILVER FOX PRESS

Lodge Drove, Salisbury, Wiltshire, England
silverfoxpress@gmx.com

A CIP catalogue record for this book is available from the British Library
ISBN: 978-1-9998305-0-2

Printed and bound by CMP Ltd, Poole, Dorset

IN MEMORY

Marie Colvin

Sue Lloyd Roberts

Prologue

THE PROTECTOR

Timeline: Baghdad, April, 2008

He stepped out of the air-conditioned cool of the airliner into the broiling heat of Baghdad International Airport. And back into the nightmare.

His heart quickened the moment he smelled the musky desert air. And again, when he was surrounded by the chatter of Arabic voices in the underground Arrivals Lounge.

The clamour and bustle set him on edge, the closeness of people. Anyone could be concealing a weapon, anyone wearing a corset of high-explosives and nails beneath their robes. Even a pregnant woman or child standing next to you could be a walking bomb. That was it, you never knew. Until it was too late.

No longer in the British military, Royce was being met by a senior member of the civilian security company for which he now worked. As a "newbie", he was initially treated more like a client than a member of staff.

A tall, taciturn Geordie with ginger hair had been allocated to "Meet and Greet", a task to which he wasn't most obviously suited. The man wore chinos and an oversized casual shirt with the Magpies' team badge on the breast pocket.

'Hello, sir, my name is Geordie,' he said in a heavy accent, without a hint of irony or humour. He also spoke with the rapidity of a machine-gun. 'I'm Team Leader of our call sign Kilo Five. If you've retrieved your luggage, just follow me.'

With a day sack on his shoulder and towing a wheeled pilot's case, Royce walked with his new team leader to the underground carpark. The unexpected sound of a moped backfiring made him jump. Oddly that snapped him out of the funk he'd been in, back to reality. Reality Royce could deal with, blind fear and flashbacks he couldn't.

'We're a three-vehicle convoy,' Geordie continued as they approached the tired-looking Merc saloons. 'All B6 armoured. Lucky we could manage that on today's roster. Wasn't expecting one man down with an appendix and you coming in so quick.'

'Nor was I,' Royce replied. 'I was on holiday in Cyprus when I got the text from Head Office. I diverted straight here. The paperwork hasn't even caught up yet.'

Geordie grunted. 'First rotation with the company?' he asked. When Royce nodded, the man raised an eyebrow. 'Know anyone here?'

'Stefan Seeff. South African. We were in Afghanistan.'

'The lion-shagger?' Geordie paused for a beat. 'Yeah, he's alright.'

Geordie curtly introduced Royce to the rest of the team. They were all British and all worked for IAP in London. International Asset Protection had offices in Canary Wharf and was run by a former SAS major, dealing with advisory military contracts at governmental level.

The team dispersed to its allocated vehicles. Geordie opened the boot of the Merc in the middle of the three and extracted a body-armour vest. 'Dump your luggage in here and put this on please.'

Royce followed the instructions while Geordie stripped off his own top to reveal a cutaway T-shirt over a wiry and freckled body. He strapped on his belted firearm holster and armoured vest, while still rattling on, 'I'll be traveling in front with our driver.' He pulled his Magpies' shirt back on and opened the rear passenger door. 'Wear your seat-belt at all times. Doors will remain locked, controlled by our driver. Should there be a mechanical failure or we stop for any other reason, don't attempt to open the door or leave unless told to do so by me or another team member. You will be cross-decked to another vehicle which will pull alongside.'

Seemingly without pausing for breath, the man continued as Royce climbed in, 'There's a first aid kit on the floor next to you should it be needed. Usual travel time to the Green Zone is twenty minutes. At any Entry Control Point or other checks stay in the car and take instructions from me.' He dumped a NATO-style ballistic helmet in Royce's lap. 'Keep that to hand at all times. Welcome back to Baghdad.'

As soon as Geordie fell into his seat with his Heckler & Koch MP5 short across his lap, the driver started the engine. They followed the first Merc slowly out through the inner perimeter cordon manned by the Iraqi Police, over the flyover to the outer cordon, which was controlled by the US military.

Once past the ramps, they were running the gauntlet of the ten mile, six-lane expressway – known as "Route Irish" by the occupying Allies – to the city. To the Iraqis themselves it was called, less prosaically, simply as "Death Street".

'Any trouble so far today?' Royce asked.

'Not today,' Geordie replied. 'But there was a shooting on this route yesterday and two IEDs. A lot of dead and injured. Bad shit.'

Royce stared out of the bullet-proof window. 'Seems it'll never end.'

'Keeps us in business,' Geordie replied flatly.

The lead driver of their small cortège seemed to know his stuff. He veered away from roadside police observation platforms, which insurgents with machine-guns or suicide bombers liked to occupy in cars with tinted windows. Royce noted he also kept well clear of a small American military convoy they passed, which made an inviting target, and was obviously suspicious of one particular stretch of newly-laid concrete. The terrorists were known to have posed as repair crews to bury daisy-chained artillery shells to be detonated by electronic garage-door openers or mobile phones.

'Home sweet home,' Geordie breathed as they finally cleared

Checkpoint Three and entered the relative safety of the Green Zone, next to the mighty Tigris River.

The whole district was surrounded by towering concrete blast walls and protected by the United States' war-machine. This was the administrative and military heart of the Coalition, which had invaded Iraq and overthrown its despotic dictator, Saddam Hussein.

What Royce knew, which was never mentioned in the heavily-guarded American Embassy, was that the man himself had actually started his notorious political life as a trained assassin for the CIA. And a failed one at that.

The neighbourhood of the Green Zone was also the traditional home of the nation's political elite with its fine houses and exclusive hotels. There had been no shootings or suicide-bombings around the Zone for several weeks. In that troubled land it had almost become a Camelot or *Shangri-la*. Foreign military personnel and aid workers swam in the hotel pools, celebrity chefs were flown in to cook and singers to sing for the loaded opportunists.

Everyone was living in a dream, a bubble. That's how it felt and that's what they actually called it, "The Bubble". Business thrived, people made money. Lots of money. Millions. Dollars, euros, pounds, roubles, yen. The booze flowed. People got rich, got careless.

Then that Easter, like all bubbles, it burst. Everything changed overnight. Shi'ite insurgents of the Mahdi Army, led by the radical cleric Moqtada al-Sadr, opened up with mortars, rocket-propelled grenades and Katyusha rockets from the Sadr City area of east Baghdad.

The sumptuous Baghdad Palace Hotel received a direct hit on its famous ballroom. Luckily it was empty at the time and only one staff member suffered a minor injury. However, as a result of the damage, several planned exhibitions, conferences and other corporate events had to be cancelled or transferred to other venues at short notice.

It was the evening after the attack that James Royce found himself striding down the luxuriously-carpeted corridor on the third floor of the hotel, a couple of minutes before eight o'clock, the time of the scheduled first meeting with his new client.

Precise time-keeping was one of Royce's traits from a former life spent in the British Royal Marine Commandos. Another was smartness. He was dressed inconspicuously in a beige tropical jacket, slacks and a white-and-blue striped shirt.

He was clean-shaven and tanned from years spent outdoors, his eyes a flinty green grey mix in colour. Like the North Sea, he used to joke. His tawny hair was just now in need of a trim.

Royce was accompanied by Geordie. For good reason, American security in the Green Zone was strict to the point of paranoia. It would take a day or two at least before his biometrics were taken, his paperwork processed and ID badge issued. And if you weren't badged you didn't exist, didn't pack a firearm, didn't go anywhere or do anything without being escorted by someone who was.

There was a big, crew-cropped American seated farther along the corridor, a Glock sub-machine gun resting ostentatiously on his lap. He stood up as the two men approached.

'This is James Royce,' Geordie introduced. 'He's on your list.'

The American nodded, gnawed on his chewing gum, and smiled. 'Sure, Maynard's expecting him.' He studied Royce for a moment . 'So you're the replacement?'

Royce glanced along the empty corridor. 'Would seem so.'

'Call me when they're done,' Geordie said, turning on his heel, 'and I'll collect him.'

Still smiling, like he was in on some secret joke, the American indicated the door opposite. 'That's Maynard's room. Number Thirty Six. Be my guest. By the by, my name's Abe.'

The former Royal Marine stepped forward and rapped on the polished wooden door. On the other side, he heard a female voice curse. He caught the words, 'Christ, is that the time already?' The words were followed by shuffling footsteps coming towards the door. It opened cautiously, inch by inch.

She was taller than he'd been expecting, with a stylish bob-cut of marmalade hair. Her skin was milky white with dark stains of tiredness around her eyes. She had full lips and a ready, impish smile.

'You Royce?'

He nodded. 'Yes. For Mr Maynard Price. GEOcom. He's expecting me.'

Behind him, he heard the American security man guffaw. The woman shook her head. 'Ignore Abe, he's an ass. Yes, I am he.'

Royce lifted an eyebrow. 'Pardon?'

Her blue eyes were smiling mischievously although her lips weren't. She stepped back and threw open the door in an extravagant gesture for him to enter. She was slim, wearing a dressing-gown in jade-coloured satin. It showed a glimpse of cleavage. Her reading spectacles were parked up on her head like an Alice band.

'*I* am Maynard Price,' she announced. Her voice had the deep and throaty tone of someone who smoked and drank a little more than the recommended limits of the health fascists. 'My grandmother's middle name, handed down. Useful for opening doors in Arab countries where we females are considered a sub-species.'

Royce frowned. 'But you are -' He hesitated.

'Yes, I'm Chief Exec of GEOcom. Mid-East Div. Specialising in high tech cell-phone networks for remote regions.' She grinned at him. 'Chief Exec, yeah, so I must be doing something right, yes?'

'I'm sorry for the misunderstanding, ma'm.' He closed the door behind him. 'I was parachuted in, so to speak. The paperwork hasn't caught up with me yet.'

She studied him closely and frowned. 'I had asked for an American to replace Chuck – if possible.'

'It wasn't possible.' Royce gave a wolfish smile. 'I'm sorry, but GEOcom's security contract is with IAP, a British firm. American contractors like Chuck and Abe are in the minority with us.'

The smile moved from her eyes to her lips for the first time. 'Of course, IAP must have been cheaper.' She hesitated. 'I also asked for someone who didn't have an appendix.'

'Ah yes, poor Chuck,' Royce replied. 'Unexpected that. I had mine checked out before I left the UK. It's fine.'

A flicker of a grin suggested that she appreciated the joke. 'Have you worked with Abe before?'

'No. But I'm sure we'll get on fine.'

'Alternate shifts. Twelve hours on, twelve hours off. But then Geordie will no doubt explain the drill.' She led the way through from the ante-chamber into the sumptuously appointed reception room. There were marble columns, glitzy mirrors and gold fittings. She indicated the L-shaped brown suede sofa. 'Shall we take a seat?'

'Sure, Mrs Price.'

'Miss. Call me May.' He nodded as she sat opposite him and gracefully furled her legs. She dropped her spectacles down from her forehead onto her nose and began reading from a sheath of paper. 'Your details, sorta CV?'

'Jeez,' she added. 'Protector's Details. Protector? Why does this company put that? It makes you all sound like own brand condoms from Wal-mart.'

'Most firms refer to us as operators. But then, that's what we are,' he replied drily. 'Close protection.'

She chuckled. 'Quite so. I'm very aware how dangerous working in this part of the world can be. But security arrangements are made between our companies, of course, way above our heads. It's why I like to know my protection operators personally. Because I know my life – and ultimately my company's success – may depend on them.'

'Of course.'

'Can I ask you a question or two?'

'Fire away, ma'm.'

'So am I right you're quite new to this?'

'Close Protection? A year of specialist training.'

'And before that, the SBS? The Royal Navy, what's that?'

'You've heard of the SAS? The British SAS?'

Maynard frowned. 'Of course, military nutters, like our SEALs.'

Royce said, 'Well the SBS – the Special Boat Service –is like the SAS but with webbed feet.'

Maynard laughed out loud. 'Oh God, really?'

'I served here, in Iraq. Mostly down south around Basra.'

'Then you left the British military. Why?'

Royce shrugged. 'Circumstances. The time was right to move on.'

Maynard was perceptive. 'I'm guessing it was a bit more than that. I know when someone's being economical with the truth.'

Royce said, 'I don't want to get into politics and personal opinions.'

'Because it's against company policy?' Her eyes narrowed. 'But *I'm* your client and I'm asking you directly. Our respective board members won't be here with us if we're ever being shot at, will they? So please tell me.'

Royce took a deep breath, he really didn't need this. After a beat he said, 'Iraq has been an illegal war, and badly managed. A total disaster.'

'In what way?'

Royce said, 'Saddam's army and police force were totally disbanded because they were Ba'athist. The US left their entire Military Police Division back home in the States. So the local mosques had to bring in people simply to enforce traffic control. It created a huge vacuum that invited its Iranian neighbours and the jihadists to fill. The whole thing was a monumental cock-up.' He hesitated, and added, 'Pardon me.'

'But you're back here, in Iraq,' she pointed out.

He smiled at her. 'At least now, May, I'm being paid the going rate.'

She glanced down at her notes. 'Age 42. Married?'

'Once. It lasted three years, no kids. She wasn't military-wife material,' he said matter-of-factly, adding, 'I was never there and I didn't exactly play the faithful husband, I'm afraid.'

Maynard's eyes narrowed again. 'So run me through your professional career.'

He shrugged, hating this sort of stuff. 'Academically, I was middle of the road at school. Good at Sports and at English because I liked reading. Okay with arithmetic rather than maths. My father was a Royal

Marine and I followed him. I served in the first Gulf War in Iraq – and the second. Then Afghanistan. That was enough.'

She arched a quizzical eyebrow. 'You're not a great fan of politicians?'

'You might say that.'

'No bad thing,' Maynard rejoined. 'And I like someone who can think for himself, independently.'

'And your assignment here?' Royce asked.

She gave a small chuckle. 'You would not believe how few employees ask me that, or even care.' Her eyes opened wide. 'Would you mind awfully pouring me a drink?'

'Of course.'

'So English. You could be my butler.'

'I don't think so.'

'I'm joking.'

'I'm not. What would you like?'

'Just a bourbon and ice. The cabinet is over there. Get something for yourself. '

He returned with her glass and a tumbler with sparkling water, lime and ice for himself. 'Your assignment?' he reminded.

'Ah yes,' she said, accepting the glass. 'I'm in Baghdad to win a lucrative mobile phone contract. My company should have the edge because we have hi-tech solutions for communications in remote areas. But I have rivals from outfits in both Sunni and Shi'ite business communities here, not to mention Israel. Bribery and other dirty tricks are not unheard of. There are also Dutch and German contenders.'

'And the bombing of the ballroom,' Royce said. 'It's meant the planned Comms Expo and conference has been cancelled.'

'Quite so.'

'An unfortunate accident.'

Maynard pulled a face. 'If indeed it was an accident.'

Royce frowned. 'What do you mean?'

She shook her head. 'No matter. One can get paranoid in this neck of the woods. It's been good to have met you, Mr Royce – Oh that is a bit formal.'

'James,' Royce said, 'Or Rollo, my nickname in the Marines.'

'Oh, I get it.' Maynard smiled. 'Like the posh car. ...Anyway, I'm sure we'll get on fine. When will you be able to start?'

'Apparently it'll take a few days before badging's complete and I'm actually on the job.'

There was an intense glitter in those electric blue eyes, Royce noticed. 'I look forward to it,' she said. He shook the slender, offered hand and left.

The noise and heat of the hotel bar downstairs hit him like a wall. What was it about war-zones around the world, he wondered? They were like magnets to opportunists, rogues and adventure-seekers in equal measure. No matter how desperate and bloody the fighting, the number of dead and injured civilians, the political, media, commercial and military circus was forever in town. Whatever the shortages of medicines, food and water for general populations, there was never any such shortage of alcohol or tobacco or sex.

He squeezed his way through the crowd, knowing he'd find his friend Stefan somewhere here at the centre of the action.

Just turned thirty, the South African called Seeff had served with him in the British Army in Afghanistan and had since lured him into the "The Circuit", as it was known, a lucrative market of ex-military personnel who specialised in the dark art of "close protection". However it was a vocation that had exploded from almost nowhere and standards were very varied and very often left wanting.

Royce found Seeff at one end of the spectacularly large, round rosewood bar with its saffron marble top. Two attractive, fresh-faced young women sat on barstools beside him. One blonde and one auburn, they both wore the emblazoned T-shirt and jeans uniform of the numerous charities and NGOs operating in the country. In fact Geordie had already pointed them out to him holding hands in the lobby.

'I went to that Thai massage parlour,' Seeff was saying, grinning as he always was. 'You know, the one on the next block. Sells herbs. Run by Mr Ping.'

The athletic blonde woman with no make-up nodded. 'I know it.'

'Well, I have this really fantastic massage. Swedish hot-stone or some such. I feel great.' He paused. 'The girl pops out and Mr Ping puts his head round the door. He winks and says, "Hey, Misser Stefan, you like Happy Ending, eh?"'

Seeff added to his rapt audience, 'My mind's racing. Happy Ending? I suddenly realise what he means. "Oh, ah! How much extra will that be?" I ask. Mr Ping looks sorta affronted and shakes his head. "Ah, no charge, no extra. All part of service."'

The auburn aid-worker in a tight blue T-shirt leaned forward, her voice husky and low. 'What happened next, Stefan?'

'Well, I'm waiting and thinking, will it be the gorgeous Li-Li who gave me the massage. Or maybe the sexy receptionist who eyed me up when I came in.' He drew breath. 'For ten minutes I wait. Suddenly the door opens and Mr Ping peers in. "Happy Ending over now, sir," He says, "You finish yet?"'

Neither of the women laughed. Royce decided to rescue his friend. 'Stef, pal, how are you? Great to see you again.'

Seeff's eyes widened and his jaw dropped. 'Yubbah dubbah doo!' he exclaimed. 'Hi, Rollo! When the hell d'you fly in?'

'Earlier this afternoon. I did email you.'

'Internet's crap here. Besides I've been working all day.' He dropped down off his barstool, glancing at the women on each side of him. 'Keep the seat warm for me, ladies. This is my best mate, Rollo. We'll be back in a minute.'

He ushered Royce away from them, farther down the bar where drinkers were queuing to be served. 'What you want, boss? They've actually got your Żubrowka vodka – and tonic?'

'Just a beer, Stef, thanks. Need to keep a clear head.'

Seeff grinned. 'New boy syndrome, eh?' he said, and squeezed himself into the front of the queue. Ever popular, he was quickly served by one of the barmen and returned with two tall glasses of lager.

'How are you finding it?' Royce asked.

'A fuck sight better than Kabul, that's for sure. At least this place is in the 21st century – well, sort of.' He took a gulp of beer. 'And what about your new client, Mr Price, have you met him yet?'

Royce's green eyes hardened into the seaman's thousand-yard stare he was renowned for. 'You bastard, Stef,' he challenged. 'You knew Maynard was a woman.'

Seeff laughed and shrugged. 'Bit of a standing joke with the lads here, sorry. Thought you might throw a fit if you knew it was babysitting a woman.'

Royce sampled his beer. 'Why would I?'

Seeff shrugged. 'They can be tricky to handle in CP. Don't always like being told what to do, especially ones like her. A bit of a ball-breaker, I hear.'

'She seems fine, charming,' Royce said. 'Knows what she wants. Respect, even if she is a Yank.'

The South African suddenly realised that a good-looking Australian construction exec was chatting up his two latest targets. 'Shit, we'd better get back. Those two are hot.'

Royce nodded. 'Known them long?'

It was just turned nine o'clock. 'All evening,' Seeff said.

'Have you spent a lot on them?'

'Enough. They like their cocktails.'

'D'you know their names?'

'Of course.'

'Martina and Billy-Jean?' Royce suggested.

Seeff didn't get it. 'No, Sue and the blonde is Morag.'

Royce grinned. 'I want to come out, Stef, to you, my bestest mate. I know that, of all people, you will understand.'

Seeff was confused. 'What?'

'That I am a lesbian.'

That threw Seeff for a second. 'Come again?'

'I only fancy women, Stef. And your two lady-friends, Sue and Morag don't fancy me. Or, more importantly, you.'

The blood drained from Seeff's face as the penny dropped.

Royce said, 'Seems to me like the age-old story of expectation over experience.' He gave a half-grin.

Seeff's knuckles clenched white, pulling away from Royce's restraining grip. 'Spent a fuckin' hundred on them…'

'Oh, I know Sue and Morag,' Maynard said. 'Lovely girls. Fearless, too, in the work they do. Not sure either of them want a rich sugar daddy.'

It was four weeks' since his return to Baghdad and Royce now felt he knew his client well enough to recount the anecdote. 'I don't think Stefan would ever fit that bill anyway. Although *he's* still convinced he could *cure* them.'

They were seated on the suede sofa in her suite, Maynard wanting to conduct her own assessment of his first month's service. It wasn't conventional, but it was typical Maynard Price. She liked people to like working for her.

The hotel air-conditioning had broken down and she had suggested that Royce might like to remove his jacket. He was more than happy to, also taking off the Czech CZ85 9mm automatic pistol and Gould & Goodrich holster that made him feel like a Prohibition-era gangster. He placed them on the coffee table.

Maynard laughed lightly, 'I don't ever see Stefan becoming a sugar daddy, either. He's even hit on me a couple of times in the bar.'

'I'm sorry.'

'Don't be. I was sort of flattered.' She took her glass of bourbon from the coffee table and sipped at it. 'I'm certainly a bit older than him. That must make me a "milf" in modern parlance. Or is that a cougar?'

'Definitely more a cougar,' Royce said. Then he thought better of it, adding, 'If you don't mind me saying?'

'Of course, not. I asked you.' She took another sip of her drink. 'I love my job, James, but it can be difficult, confusing – and a bit lonely – as a woman operating in the Middle East.'

'I'm sure,' Royce added, nursing his mineral water, ice and lemon.

'I have to dress in a business suit,' she said, indicating the tobacco linen number she was wearing, 'with trousers and a jacket long enough to cover my ass. Low heeled pumps and no more than a hint of mascara. And a hijab, of course. Otherwise Arab men are convinced I'm a hooker or will happily jump into bed with them to seal a deal. I've even been seriously propositioned by Heads of State.'

Royce nodded. 'That I can believe,' he said. He knew the Middle East well enough.

'And if I relax at the bar here at the hotel with my own kind, I get pounced on by every chancer from the military, media or construction.' She smiled and touched his wrist. 'That's why it's been good to have you here, James. To have a civilised drink and meal, and a sensible, fun conversation.'

'That's been my pleasure, ma'm.'

'If only you stopped calling me that.'

'Old habits – ma'm.' He grinned. 'Sorry, May.'

Her candid blue eyes seemed to draw him in. 'How's it been for you? First close-protection assignment and all that.'

'It's been good. Better than I expected.'

'You're very serious.'

'It's a serious business.'

'I always do what you tell me,' she said and stopped.

He realised that she hadn't removed her hand from his wrist. She went on, 'I'll be finished here in a couple of days. Hopefully with a contract signed. Then it'll be on to Tel Aviv for a spell. I want to ask your company to let you and Abe come with me if possible. Are you up for that or do I have to have a new CP man?'

Was he up for it? "Close Protection" was new to him, but he'd landed on his feet. He couldn't have asked for a better client. Maynard

Price was savvy, witty and sharp. He knew she was three years' older than him but she had the fit body of many women half her age. She was a vegetarian and practised Pilates. Was he up for it? If he didn't know himself better, he'd have believed he could be falling for her.

His hand wrapped around her hand, gently easing his fingers between hers. It was subtle but the message was unmistakable. 'I'd be happy to look after you, May, anywhere,' he confirmed. 'Can I ask if you think you will clinch the deal here?'

She considered for a moment, deciding what was safe to say. 'Finally it's between GEOcom and a Sunni outfit here. My researchers in Baltimore say some extremist cleric called Ibrahim al-Samarrai is involved with them. They think he'll milk the contract to buy arms.'

Royce frowned. He knew that name, could see it in his mind's eye on the Rogue's Gallery of Most Wanted in the Ops Room. Suddenly it came back to him. 'Aka al-Baghdadi.'

'Who?'

'His nom de guerre, al-Baghdadi,' he repeated. 'A local bad boy, nothing to worry about...'

As his voice trailed off he realised she was hardly listening to him. Her eyes were tightly focussed on his, flickering occasionally to his mouth, then back again. There was a light in those eyes, a challenge, daring him. He knew it, she knew it. A twist of a smile played momentarily on her lips. Now they both knew it.

He made his decision in that split second. One hand closed over hers like a clam-shell, his other grasped her hair, clawing her head back to expose her arched throat. He closed his teeth around it, biting her flesh gently until she hurt.

She pushed him away, deliberately keeping up the pretence. 'Fuck me, James!' she protested, but her blows lacked strength or anger.

'Shut up,' he ordered, scooping her up in his arms and carrying her towards the bedroom. Buttons popped off her shirt as she struggled fiercely, clawing at his face.

Although he felt the blood trickle from his cheek, he knew she was playing tigers. He threw her onto the mattress with considerable force. The bedhead cracked against the wall, chipping the paintwork.

She gasped for air. 'Bastard!'

'Bitch!' he replied.

His mouth fell on hers, kissing and biting. She dug her fingers into his back, becoming aware that he was now ripping the jacket from her shoulders. Shaking herself free, she found he'd already torn away her expensive chiffon shirt, snapped her bra. One breast fell free, its nipple pink and angry.

'Don't fucking touch me!' she warned as his teeth closed on it slowly and decisively.

That was how it went for the next half hour or so. A fight, a battle between two animals. Each hurt and tested the other, attacked and counter-attacked with as much tenderness as ferocity. He'd recount later, one day, that it had been a fierce struggle with no casualties, and both of them the winners.

She bit his ear and squeezed his balls until she knew it hurt. 'Fuck me doggy,' she hissed in his ear.

He grabbed her waist, none too gently, aware how narrow it was, feeling her ribs under his fingertips. She was on her knees, her ginger bob-cut now a soft muddle as he pressed her face into the pillow. There was no resistance. His left hand found the smooth, tight sag of her belly and dug in deep, forcing her back against him. A low slow whimper escaped her lips. Then she cried out, her voice masking the muffled sound of the explosion outside. Neither were aware of the slight tremble of the building.

His personal radio handset crackled into life. It was on the floor, buried in the pile of his discarded clothes, the sound muffled and indistinct.

'Leave it,' she gasped.

He was tempted. 'It could be important.'

'No, it won't be,' she said decisively and pushed herself hard back onto him. 'Finish me off, for God's sake.'

The next couple of minutes were lost in a violent frenzy of pain and pleasure, the two of them entwined in the tangle of sheets. Then his radio started transmitting again. 'Tango Two Alpha, this is Tango Two Bravo -'

This time he did not hesitate. He swung his legs off the bed, snatched up the radio and stood naked with it to his ear.

'Rollo, it's Stef. Did you hear the bomb outside the hotel?'

'What? No.'

'Really? Never mind, we think it was a suicide bomber. A small blast.'

Royce relaxed. 'Anyone hurt?'

At that moment the Green Zone sirens kicked in, their eerie wailing noise alerting the citizens that they were under terror attack.

'Only the bomber, but that's not the point,' Seeff continued. *'We think it was a diversion. A bunch of gunmen have broken in. We're going into lock-down.'*

'Where are they?'

'Heading up the stair-well.'

'Shit!' He tossed the radio on the floor, grabbed his trunks and pulled them on. As he did he heard the commotion outside the door of the suite in the next room. That is where he'd left his Czech-made automatic and its holster, on the coffee table.

'GET IN THE BATHROOM!' he yelled back, over his shoulder. 'LOCK YOURSELF IN!'

As he raced into the lounge, a hail of bullets punched its way around the security lock of the front door and through the small ante-room to deflect like demented fireflies in all directions. The door crashed open as he dived for the coffee-table. Four or five dark-clad Iraqis wearing ski-masks burst in, shooting indiscriminately. They were through the ante-room, then into the main reception area. One round shattered the mirror above the mock fireplace and another hit the ornate chandelier, showering crystals of broken glass like rain.

Royce slid to a halt on the Persian rug, reaching for the automatic pistol he'd abandoned on the coffee-table. He fumbled to release it from its holster, remembering suddenly that the two magazines of live ammunition were in his jacket pocket on the sofa.

As he dived to find them, struggling to get them out and loaded, the seconds seemed to expand into minutes in his head. He expected the rounds of death to thud into him at any moment, his life to be extinguished without warning.

It was then that he realised that the terrorists had no real interest in him. While one stood by the door, carrying an AK47 at the ready, the others went straight for the bedroom.

Maynard never reached the safety of the bathroom door. Her alabaster body was studded instantly with bullet holes that ripped into her vital organs. The beautiful, slender and naked body twitched and convulsed on the floor for several long seconds before it finally stopped.

Her killers seemed mesmerised, frozen as they watched the result of what they had just done.

Royce finally snapped the magazine into the butt of his automatic. The man on the door appeared to focus on him for the first time, swung round the AK47. Royce knew then he'd lost. He was a trigger-squeeze too late. He was staring down the barrel of death.

But the first shot fired came from the stair-well in the hotel corridor. It hit the gunman on the door in the back of his head, punching out an exit hole in his face. As the man collapsed, Seeff stepped into the room, his gun still smoking.

'HOSTILES RIGHT! RIGHT!' Royce yelled in warning. As he shouted, he aimed at Maynard's killers himself and opened up. The four men were clustered together in the bedroom and it was a turkey-shoot. Royce fired in a frenzy of barely-controlled anger, round after round after round.

Then, suddenly, nothing. With a flick of the wrist, he ejected the magazine, pumped in the second and then shot them all again.

The bedroom was hazy with smoke and stank of cordite. He felt Seeff's restraining hand on his shoulder. 'Okay, mate, steady on. You can't kill a dead man twice.'

1

'TAKE US TO YOUR LEADER'

Timeline: March 2011

The two Chinook helicopters came in fast and low, line astern.

They approached the inky coastline of Libya at an oblique angle, to minimise the distinctive dull thud of the twin rotors being carried inland by the breeze. Below them in the darkness, the surface of the Mediterranean was creamed into a fluorescent froth by each forty tons downdraught of thrust.

James Royce leaned forward between the pilot and co-pilot to get a clearer view through the cockpit windscreen. As the adrenalin flowed, he found his heart beating in time with the powerful Textron Lycoming engines.

Royce stretched out his arm and jabbed his finger towards the array of lights on the ground up ahead and to their right.

The pilot was wearing night-vision goggles. He nodded. 'Benghazi,' he confirmed over the intercom.

It was Libya's second city after the capital Tripoli, which was situated some four hundred miles to the west. Benghazi was the stronghold of the rebel army trying to overthrow the tyrannical regime of Colonel

Muammar Gaddafi. The forces of both sides were battling it out back and forth along the coast road between the two cities.

Up ahead, the first Special Forces' Chinook HC2A of the elite Royal Air Force 7 Squadron gained some height before it passed over the shoreline. It was pitch-black below, and remote. Yet there were still tiny firefly flashes which Royce assumed were small arms being aimed at them by startled individuals. The entire country was expectant, nervous, and almost everyone in it seemed to be armed.

The lead helicopter carried two armoured Range Rovers and six members of E Squadron, Special Air Service Regiment. That load pushed the Chinook to the very limit of its lift capability. The men were a mix of very experienced serving and re-contracted former members of various British Special Forces. It included the recently formed Special Reconnaissance Regiment and the SF Support Group, as well as the Special Boat Service of the Royal Marines.

It was with this unit that Royce had served until seven years' earlier, when he had left for Civvy Street and life on the lucrative "Close Protection" circuit, body-guarding in Iraq, Afghanistan and other of the world's hotspots. He had been near to retiring with a small fortune of savings and investments when his South African pal, Stefan Seeff, had persuaded him to join him and take a final one-year Ministry of Defence contract, serving with the newly-created E Squadron of the SAS.

Technically E Squadron wasn't even part of the main Regiment or its two Territorial Army counterparts. It was a thing of myth and legend, a sort of non-criminal "Dirty Dozen" that could have been dreamt up by Hollywood.

Royce had liked the idea of having both SBS *and* SAS on his CV, and even quite fancied one last stint of the military life that he had always enjoyed so much.

That, he had quickly realised, was a big mistake.

E Squadron may have been the enthusiastic subject of much rumour and speculation within the military world, but he soon found himself referring to them with Seeff as the "Walk-On-Water Brigade". The unit was formed to be at the direct disposal of the Director of Special Forces and the Secret Intelligence Service, more commonly known as MI6.

The problem was they were all, like Royce himself, veterans who had seen everything and done everything, and thought they could get away with anything. Frankly, he considered many to be complacent and over the hill. A lot were semi-retired. They had all worked for different "cap badges" with different methods of operation, never together, and were often in conflict with each other as old military rivals. And they thought they knew it all.

This covert mission was a typical example. Since the British Embassy had closed down earlier in the year, the purpose of it was to transport the MI6 lead spook, Mat Asquith, and his number two, Huggins, into Libya to establish contact with the rebels' National Transitional Council. The two men were being protected by six E Squadron members led by a tall and somewhat arrogant Scottish officer calling himself Major Hamish McDougall, whom none of the men could recall having met before.

The second Chinook, carrying Team B, was back-up in case the first ran into any serious trouble during the initial landing phase of the operation.

Its first job was to provide top cover, maintaining height so, if required, the loadmasters could provide withering counter-fire from the six-barrelled 5.56mm Mini-guns located in the hatches behind the flight-deck. If all went smoothly, the first helicopter would rapidly disgorge its passengers and vehicles, after which the rôles of the Chinooks would be reversed.

Apart from the crew, the only other passengers in Team B, apart from Royce and his oppo Stefan Seeff, were two further MI6 experts.

If things went wrong on the landing-zone, it was the job of Royce and Seeff to try and help as many of the main party to escape back onto the second giant helicopter, bringing the two Range Rovers with them if possible.

However, should all go to plan, the smaller support team would go off on a separate mission of its own to the capital Tripoli in the west of the country.

Nevertheless, as Royce had pointed out at the planning stage, there was no real need for all this provocative and dangerous cloak-and-dagger stuff with noisy and conspicuous helicopters that could so easily go wrong. Dozens of reporters and TV crews were pouring over the border from Egypt to cover the conflict, or flying into one of the airports. Colonel Gaddafi was even inviting the world's media to come and see "the truth" of the terrorist uprising for itself. It would have been far easier and safer to slip into the country with them, posing as reporters or TV news execs.

His suggestion had, however, been swiftly overruled by Major McDougall and seconded by Mat Asquith of MI6. As a humble former green beret Special Boat Service "cabbage hat", his naval infantry opinion counted for little amongst the majority of former "brown jobs" – or army personnel.

Now Royce returned the intercom headset to the co-pilot, left the flight deck and made his way back to where the two RAF loadmasters, Seeff and his own two MI6 spooks were strapped into their seats.

At least the two MI6 officers who he and Seeff were "minding" had agreed with Royce's own misgivings about the way the mission was being conducted.

Ollie Parsons was a grammar-school boy from the wrong side of the tracks in Peckham and not overly popular with his elitist fellow spooks at their Vauxhall Cross headquarters. Neither was Iain Tremain, a softly-spoken former Special Forces and intelligence officer on secondment from Australia. Both, like Royce himself and Seeff, were clearly considered as outsiders by those in charge of the main party.

Royce edged past Parsons to his own seat. Parsons' heavy build looked twice its normal size in the bulky blue bullet-vest. He had an intercom set clamped to his shaven head and balanced a combat helmet on his lap. The plump face was pale and damp with perspiration. Apprehension showed in his eyes, magnified through the heavy spectacle lenses.

Sitting down and replacing his own intercom headset, Royce said, 'We're just crossing the coast now, Ollie.'

Parsons, who was seated next to his MI6 companion Tremain, nodded his understanding.

'I reckon ETA in about five,' Royce added, glancing down at the gold Breitling Chronomat watch he wore on his right wrist. He didn't mention the sporadic pot shots he'd seen being taken at the forward Chinook. There was no need to alarm Parsons unnecessarily.

On Royce's other side, Seeff was grinning with unconcealed excitement at the prospects of the kind of action he missed since serving with the British Army in Afghanistan. 'This is stellar stuff,' he enthused. 'Can't wait.'

Royce gave him a withering look. 'Mad,' he said.

'I'm an adrenalin junkie,' Seeff confessed with a light laugh. 'You know that, Rollo.'

His older friend grunted dismissively. 'I'm allergic to adrenalin.'

The Chinook began to veer repeatedly from left to right and back again, to throw off anyone aiming a weapon from the ground. Then it dropped height suddenly and began jinking again.

Their landing zone was some eighteen miles south of Benghazi. It was a field in the middle of the thirty-seven thousand acre estate belonging to Farmco. Apart from the small dusty village of Al-Khadra, it was remote, flat and utterly black.

A small, single green light flashed from its midst.

'Cleared to land,' the pilot's voice intoned in Royce's earphones.

It had been the signal from their agent on the ground. He was a farm manager known to them only as Tom. Apparently he was a Welshman and a former soldier, who was what MI6 liked to term an "along-sider". That is, he was an expat civilian willing to help his country without necessarily seeking any financial or other reward.

Royce turned to Seeff. 'Let's go.'

The twin helicopter mission was what was known as a standard "Mutual SAR operation" – for search-and-rescue – whereby each aircraft and crew looked after the other.

Both Royce and Seeff stood, removed their intercom headsets and strapped on plain dark British Army helmets with night vision optics. Their choice of weapons for close-protection duties were slightly different from those of a more formal combat rôle, favouring ease of concealment over brute force and firepower. Royce and Seeff were already dressed in black and belt orders that carried large pouches for equipment and ammunition, and Swiss-made .38 Sig Sauer P230 automatics. As they made a final check on their 9mm stockless MP5K sub-machine guns, the rear ramp yawned open and warm air swirled into the cargo hold.

Two RAF loadmasters manned the heavy duty M60 tail machine-gun on the ramp and one of the Mini-guns situated in the side hatch mounting immediately behind the flight deck. The helicopter hovered, all its lights off.

Up ahead, the lead Chinook landed swiftly with a jolt. Four heavily-armed minders of E Squadron spilled out in a defensive semi-circle around its rear ramp. Overhead the twin rotors kept turning slowly, ready for a quick getaway if things went pear-shaped. Disturbed soil churned into a fog of red dust. Their two MI6 passengers followed.

The loadmasters worked at lightning speed to unshackle the heavily-loaded Range Rovers so that the remaining two SAS soldiers could drive them down the ramp and into the field. Royce timed it. Barely three minutes, impressive.

Almost immediately the pilot began winding up the rotors again. The giant helicopter lifted rapidly to a height where it could provide top cover for the second Chinook, which came down rapidly. It landed some fifty metres from where the main party were gathering around the Range Rovers.

The ramp had barely touched the ground when Royce and Seeff

were ducking and running into the miasma of disturbed dust. They
fanned out to the right and left, leaving the Chinook's two gunners with
a clear forward field of fire. Then the two SAS men threw themselves
to the ground, bringing their MP5s to bear on the green signal light in
the utter blackness that indicated the position of the agent called Tom.

Parsons and Tremain followed, helping the loadmasters form a pile
of their luggage and equipment bags. Then, suddenly, the helicopter
was up and gone, following the first. As the deafening noise ebbed
away they were slowly swallowed by a silence that was stunning in its
intensity. It almost hurt their ears as they listened for some sound. The
air was hot and humid, maybe in the low thirties. Somewhere in the
distant darkness, a dog barked.

Through Royce's image-intensifying night goggles, a ghostly tableau
of men and vehicles was displayed in a blurry green and white image
before him: two armoured Range Rovers with a defensive circle of
armed soldiers to his right and, some hundred metres in front, the
solitary figure of the man called Tom. He was standing next to a blue
Toyota pick-up.

Putting away his signal lamp, Tom climbed into the cab and drove
across the stretch of field to meet the main group.

As he jumped down from the pick-up, Royce could see he was
slim, fresh-faced and in his early forties. He wore chinos and a body-
warmer over a check shirt. Major McDougall rose to his feet from the
prone position, lowered his weapon, and pushed aside his night-vision
goggles. 'I'm Hamish,' he said. 'Good to meet you.'

'Tom', the other man confirmed in a light Welsh accent. 'Glad you
got here okay.'

McDougall turned to Asquith. 'This is our Foreign Office chief,' he
introduced.

Asquith shook Tom's hand. 'Call me Mat,' the MI6 officer said
before introducing the small, bespectacled man next to him who was
known as Huggins. 'This is Toby, who is working with me. I'd like to
thank you for everything you've done for HMG.'

Agent Tom looked slightly embarrassed. 'The least I could do. Libya is a great country, a lovely people. They need to be freed from this tyrant. But it won't be easy.'

'Yes, yes,' Asquith replied tetchily. 'I understand all that. Now we need to make contact with the NTC at the earliest opportunity.'

'I realise you do, Mat, but it's a bit more complicated than that. Hard to know exactly who's who in Benghazi at the moment. A number of rebel groups are vying for control.'

As the two men continued their conversation, Royce and Seeff left their defensive positions to join Ollie Parsons and Iain Tremain next to their pile of kit and equipment bags.

Parsons watched the main group talking with agent Tom. 'Let's get over there and find out what's going on.' He turned to Royce. 'You okay with that, Rollo?'

Royce nodded. 'Fine. No sign of trouble. Looks like we've got away with it.'

'Good,' Parsons replied. 'I don't want Mat making any knee-jerk decisions. He can be a bit impetuous.'

Tremain gave a lazy smile. 'Even if he is our chief.'

The affable Parsons grinned. 'Technically,' he acknowledged. '*Only* technically.'

'And *we* don't trust McHaggis,' Seeff added, referring to the E Squadron commander. 'He may think he's the dog's knob, but he's as much use as a chocolate tea pot.'

'That'll do,' Royce chided. 'McDougall speaks very highly of you.'

'Yeah, I bet he does.'

As the four men crossed the field to the main group, Mat Asquith was asking, 'So we'll stay at the farm until daylight?'

'That's best, I think,' Tom replied. 'The locals can get very trigger happy at night and are easily spooked. Everyone's paranoid about Gaddafi's militias and special forces.'

'And try to contact the Transitional Council in the morning?' McDougall pressed.

Tom said, 'I suggest just two of you come into town with me – unarmed – in the farm truck. I'm well-known and respected. We'll talk to various influential people I know. Find out the latest.' He noticed the doubtful expression on McDougall's face. 'I certainly wouldn't advise going into Benghazi mob-handed.'

'If that's your view,' Asquith conceded.

'There's a room on the farm your lads can use,' Tom added. 'There are a couple of phones and whiteboards so you can make a temporary ops centre. I've put it out of bounds to the farm-workers.'

Parsons was impressed. He understood Tom was known to the Foreign Office as a temporary civilian "consular warden" for Britons still in the country. 'We really appreciate what you've done for us, Tom,' he said.

Asquith grunted. 'Oh, this is Ollie, by the way. He's only the sort of Foreign Office B Team. Secondary mission stuff.'

'Thanks for that, Mat,' Parsons murmured. 'Certainly lets me know where I stand in the pecking order.'

Tom smiled politely, pretending not to have noticed the animosity between the two MI6 men. He quickly changed the subject and indicated the two Range Rovers. 'You're a bit short on transport, I see.'

Parsons grinned awkwardly. 'That's the problem with being the B Team.'

'Then you'd best bring your kit and come in the Toyota with me. The sooner we get out of here the better.'

'We'll get in the Range Rovers and follow you,' Major McDougall said and turned away.

It was then that Royce noticed the young lad. He was standing by the open door of the pick-up, staring in bewilderment at all the activity. Aged about twelve or thirteen, he wore a grubby *dishdasha* shirt over a pair of frayed jeans.

'And who's this?' Royce asked.

'Er, what?' Tom was thrown for a moment. 'Oh, this is Tareg. He's staying with his uncle here on the farm. It's safer than with his family in Benghazi.'

Asquith was clearly annoyed. 'What's he doing *here*? He could compromise the entire operation.'

'I nearly ran him over when I left the farm HQ,' Tom explained. 'He'd been woken by the noise of shooting in the suburbs and went out to watch the fireworks, so to speak. I didn't want him running into you lot and getting shot by mistake.'

'Wise move,' Parsons agreed and smiled at the boy. 'Hallo, Tareg. *Kayf halik*?'

'*Al humdillilah*,' Tareg replied shyly, then translated immediately, 'I am fine. And I speak the English from my school.'

Parsons was genuinely surprised. 'So you do, Tareg. Very good. I think your English is better than my Arabic.'

The boy ignored that, something clearly worrying him. 'I see you come in the big helicopters. You are British soldiers, yes? You fight in Iraq and Afghanistan? Now you come to help us?'

'Not exactly soldiers,' Parsons answered awkwardly. The child was certainly well-informed and not at all hostile. He added, 'But we *are* here to try and help.'

Tareg inclined his head. 'They were Chinook helicopters, yes? *British* Chinooks? My country only has two. They are big and so beautiful. I see them in my comic. I want a plastic model kit one day. But it is very expensive.'

While Parsons talked to Tareg, Tremain helped Royce and Seeff load their kit into the open back of the pick-up.

Royce viewed the two Range Rovers stuffed with the eight members of the main group and all their supplies, ready to go.

'I'll get in with you, if that's okay,' Royce said while Seeff joined Parsons and Tremain in the back of the pick-up.

Royce squeezed in beside Tareg as Tom started the engine. The Toyota led the little convoy back onto the cinder track. The farm manager knew the route so well he didn't need to use his headlights, relying on ambient starlight. The flat, almost featureless landscape was criss-crossed with ruler-straight tracks.

'Only a couple of miles to HQ,' Tom said. 'Then we'll be sound. Snug as a bug.'

Royce nodded. 'How long you been working here?'

'Only six months. Smashing job. Very experimental with new irrigation techniques and strains of wheat. The Guide is very keen on leading the desert world in agriculture. He actually visited once.'

That threw Royce for a second. 'The Guide? Oh, you mean Gaddafi?'

Tom chuckled. 'He does have one or two redeeming features – believe it or not.'

The boy had been listening. 'My father hates our Leader. I think most people do. This is why we are fighting him – to be free.'

'And what's your father do for a living?' Royce asked.

'He is a fisherman.' Big brown eyes blinked apologetically beneath the neat fringe of hair. 'But he does not have a boat at the moment.'

'Confiscated by the authorities,' Tom added. 'Fish wasn't the only cargo he carried. Tareg's dad is known as "Sinbad" in the expat community. He's a bit of a fixer, if you know what I mean? Nice guy, very personable. Anything you want, he'll get it for you – at a price.'

'Useful,' Royce said thoughtfully.

'And is your mission the same as Mat's?' Tom asked. 'He said you were Team B.'

Royce shook his head. 'Now we've arrived safely, we'll head for Tripoli. I'd like to meet up with a man called Charlie. I believe you know him?'

'Chingford Charlie? Certainly do. He's the one who got me involved in all this, helping you lot. He's an old Libya hand, well-in with the regime. Must be in his late seventies now, but still sharp as a razor. Knows everyone. I met him at an agricultural trade fair in Tunisia about four months' ago and he kept in touch.' The farm manager glanced sideways at his passenger. 'I suppose he must be one of yours?'

Royce was evasive. 'Not my department, Tom. Stefan and I are just the baby-sitters. You'd have to ask Mat.'

The boy had been staring at Royce deep in thought, thinking hard. 'Mr James, can I ask you a question?'

'Of course.'

'You and the other men dressed in black...? Are you from the British SAS?'

That caught Royce off guard. How did an Arab kid on a remote farm guess that? But, then, didn't boys all around the world know about such things? He hesitated before he replied. 'Tareg, you must understand that I cannot answer that question. The answer is so secret that even I don't know what it is.'

The lad thought for a moment, then nodded sagely. 'Then it is a secret that is safe with me, Mr James.'

'Nearly there,' Tom said.

Up ahead the dark shape of a compound wall came into view. Lights showed from inside some functional, single-storey buildings. They drove through the open compound gates into the gravelled staging yard.

It was then that the torch beam was shone directly in their eyes.

Momentarily blinded, Tom hit the brakes. Royce snatched up the MP5 from his lap.

'Put that thing away!' the farm manager hissed.

Suddenly they were surrounded by angry farm workers and local villagers. Some appeared to be armed with carbines, probably deserters from Gaddafi's army; others carried staves and pickaxe handles. It didn't look good.

2

BRIGHT SPARK

One of the farm workers surrounding them banged his fist on the front of the Toyota pick-up. He was scruffily-dressed, tall and thin with wild hair escaping from beneath a badly-tied turban.

'Uncle Ali!' Tareg cried in alarm.

The man appeared to be carrying a World War Two vintage rifle. It was a British .303 Lee Enfield that could possibly have seen action at El Alamein.

'Let me handle this!' Tom snapped. 'Most of these people are my workers.'

'Over to you,' Royce said and threw open his door. In such situations he preferred to make direct eye contact with aggressors.

He climbed out, leaving his main weapon behind under his seat. Immediately he was confronted with a villager pointing a Luger pistol. The SAS man smiled back at him with a calmness he did not feel.

Tom wound down his window. 'What's going on, Ali?' he demanded in Arabic.

Fear and panic burned in the eyes of the group leader. 'Militia guards in the village hear helicopters. They are loud and flying low. People wake from their sleep. Dogs are barking. There is much noise from the farm, then all is silent. Then noise again.'

'Nothing to worry about,' Tom replied easily.

'Do not take us for fools. Who are these people in your truck and following you in two cars?'

'Oh, yes, I should have warned you,' Tom explained apologetically. His acting ability could have won him a soap opera part. 'A new team of managers for the project – they flew in by private helicopter because all the air flights are booked up for weeks.'

A sneer spread over Ali's face. 'I don't think so. They are Gaddafi commandos. Come to murder us in our beds. *You*, Mr Tom, are a traitor!'

Royce had managed to follow most of the conversation. Trying to weigh up the odds if things didn't calm down, he looked back at the two Range Rovers behind him. All the doors had been flung open and six burly E Squadron heavies were spread out with sub-machine guns at the ready. He shook his head in disbelief.

Of course what they should have done was thrown their vehicles into reverse, turned rapidly and sped away with the MI6 men they were supposed to be guarding. But this was not a team of close protection specialists. As it was they were now more likely to create carnage in a shoot-out that no one was going to win.

'For God's sake, Hamish!' Royce shouted, 'put those bloody weapons away before you get everyone killed!'

Major McDougall hesitated, then shouted something. The pointing weapons were reluctantly lowered.

But Ali wasn't giving ground. 'Get out of the truck, Mr Tom! Now!'

'Stay put!' Royce countermanded.

Tom ignored the instruction and opened his door. He was immediately grabbed by Ali and pulled into the grappling clutches of the other villagers.

'I am now the area militia commander here,' Ali announced proudly. 'I am appointed yesterday. I have catch my first traitor who is sneaking in with Gaddafi commandos. You will all die!'

'NO!' Tareg screamed suddenly. 'You are wrong!'

Ali did a double take. 'Nephew, what are you doing here?'

The boy scrambled out. 'I am helping Mr Tom – because these are secret soldiers from England. They come to help us.'

'Rubbish, child,' Ali countered. 'They are Gaddafi killer squads from Sirte! All dressed in black! We will be well-rewarded for their capture.'

Tareg protested, 'But they come in British Chinook helicopters!'

Ali wasn't interested. 'What in Allah's name is a Chinook helicopter, boy?'

'It is a *British* helicopter! Believe me, uncle!'

Tom added quickly, 'That is true. These people are British embassy staff and their bodyguards. They have come to talk to leaders of the Transitional Council.'

Ali guffawed. 'A minute ago they are a new management team! You lie to us – by your own admission! I am arresting them. If you are right, then these are foreign mercenaries – whichever side they are on. It is our militia's first victory.' His men cheered.

The accidental shot from the .303 shut everyone up immediately. The E Squadron men by the Range Rovers raised their weapons again.

Ollie Parsons dropped from the Toyota's rear to stand beside the driver's door in front of Tareg's uncle. Tremain passed him down a couple of paper packages.

'What's this?' the militia leader demanded.

'*Salam aleykum*,' Parsons replied in his best Arabic. 'Ali, isn't it? Four hundred cigarettes. Rothmans. A present to the rebel forces of Libya from the Queen of England.'

Ali stared at them. 'Queen of England?' he echoed.

'A personal gift from Her Majesty to the rebels of Benghazi,' Parsons confirmed. As Ali examined the package, the MI6 man added, 'Let us go inside and talk. In the morning you can take us to your leaders. I am sure they will be very pleased you have brought us safely to them.'

Asquith had made his way forward from the Range Rovers. 'What's going on, Ollie?' he demanded.

Parsons switched to English. 'I'm talking with this charming if slightly excitable local militia leader. I'm trying to explain why we're here and to stop this turning into a fucking major international incident.'

Sensing that the atmosphere had relaxed a little, Tom made a suggestion in Arabic. 'Ali, first let us offer our guests proper Libyan hospitality, some breakfast and tea.'

Ali nodded reluctantly. 'Very well. But only after these mercenaries hand over all their weapons and equipment to us. Come daylight we take them to Benghazi.'

Asquith strained to hear the Libyan's mumbled words and translate them. 'Surrender our weapons? No way.'

'Keep calm, Mat,' Royce urged. 'They're scared and trigger happy. But we can hardly shoot up a bunch of farmhands and then expect a welcome from the rebel leaders. Let's negotiate to meet them halfway – with no bloodshed to try and explain away.' Royce was tempted to remind him "I told you so" at the planning meetings but he kept his mouth zipped.

Asquith realised he was out of options. 'We're not handing over personal firearms. Never.'

Royce nodded. 'Of course.'

With Tom's assistance, he began a long and heated debate with Ali until it was finally agreed that all the members of the team could keep their personal weapons, provided they remained holstered. In return their captors would not threaten or raise their guns or all deals were off. It was an unhappy and uneasy compromise.

Royce finally beckoned Major McDougall and his five E Squadron minders to explain the arrangement. They looked decidedly unhappy as they trudged into the farm building, dumping their main weapons in a pile outside the door, under Ali's triumphant gaze. Major McDougall scowled at Royce as he dropped his MP5.

Within minutes Tom had organised some of his kitchen staff members from within the militia to make coffee, tea and cook eggs and tomatoes on toast for their unexpected guests around a communal table. Meanwhile Ali organised a few of his neighbours to trawl through the sacks of ammunition, radio equipment and multiple passports taken from the Range Rovers.

It was then that Royce realised they had been so engrossed in their findings that they had for the moment overlooked his own team's equipment, which had been left in the back of the Toyota. Without thinking, Tom had parked it back in the management garages beside the admin block and padlocked the doors.

An idea began to form in Royce's mind. He wandered over to Tareg who was noisily sucking a banana milkshake through a straw. 'Thank you for your help back there, for explaining who we are to your uncle.'

'That is my pleasure, Mr James. I hope I didn't give away any secrets.'

'You didn't. Tell me, where does your family live in Benghazi?'

'In the Old Quarter, near the Fish Market. It is just a flat, but we have a small courtyard with an old olive tree.'

'If we could meet him, do you think your father would be willing to help us?'

The big brown eyes blinked. 'But, of course. I can take you to meet him.'

'Your family sent you here for safety, Tareg,' Royce reminded.

'That is my mother's idea. And I think it is not so safe here after all, yes? It is boring me.'

Royce thought for a moment. 'What does the name Tareg mean? D'you know?'

The boy grinned. 'My grandmother says it means manly, a person who stands his ground.'

'Really?' Royce shared his good humour. 'I thought it meant Bright Spark.'

'Me?'

'You are a Bright Spark.' The boy liked that and laughed aloud. Royce left him and joined Tom who was standing, drinking a mug of coffee.

'I'm sorry about what's happened, James,' Tom said. 'I really didn't expect it.'

'It wasn't your fault,' Royce replied. 'Our lot were stupid to think they'd pull it off with no one noticing.'

Tom shrugged. 'Well, I understand there are still *some* commercial flights coming into Benina Airport. That might have been a less conspicuous way of doing things – although Gaddafi's forces *are* trying to encircle Benghazi.'

'When we drive into town,' Royce said, 'can you take us four and Tareg in your Toyota pick-up?'

The farm manager drained his coffee. 'Sure, we'll have to make up a convoy. Your mates in their Range Rovers. Then Ali and the militia lads will probably take our farm Nissan pick-up with all the confiscated kit.'

Royce lowered his voice. 'Not quite all. Our stuff's still in the back of the Toyota.'

Tom's jaw dropped. 'Oh, God, of course, it must be. I hadn't realised.'

'That's fine, Tom.' Royce glanced at Ali and his friends still rummaging through the mountain of rucksacks and canvas bags. 'Hopefully they won't realise either. So can you try to get us at the *back* of the convoy?'

'I can try. What you up to?'

'As Mat told you, we're Team B. We have a different mission.'

Ali wandered over to them, happily smoking a cigarette. It wasn't a Rothman's. 'My commander in Benghazi will be pleased with what we have found today, Mr James,' he said in Arabic. His voice was slightly slurred.

Royce said quickly to Tom, 'I'll explain in a minute.'

'Maybe I will be promoted already,' Ali continued.

'You deserve to be,' Royce replied with a straight face.

'And my commander can decide whether you are mercenaries of Gaddafi or the Queen of England.'

'Excellent. We all look forward to meeting him very much. Thank you for all you have done, Ali.'

'It is my pleasure, Mr James.'

Some thirty minutes later the eastern sky began to lighten and birds started to sing. When Tom reversed the blue Toyota pick-up out of its garage, the bergens and bags in the rear had already been covered over with hessian sacks. Royce lifted Tareg up over the tailgate before following. Once joined by Seeff, Parsons and Tremain, the plan was set.

Meanwhile the six E Squadron members and the two MI6 officers had got into the two now empty Range Rovers.

The vehicles were joined by a dirty red Nissan truck, driven by Ali and overloaded with scruffy militiamen and their spoils of war. It came chugging into the staging yard, noisily belching clouds of smoke. Ali beeped his horn triumphantly.

Tom wound down the window of his Toyota. 'You lead the way, Ali. We'll keep the Range Rovers in the middle, and I'll come up the rear.'

Ali waved, gave a thumbs-up and put his foot down, heading for the compound gates.

The small convoy trundled its way along the main road towards the city. There was little traffic on the highway until the jagged grey skyline of modern towers and ancient minarets and domes came into view, overlooked by the green hills of the *jebel*.

Then the signs of war began coming thick and fast. Blackened craters from bombs and artillery shells pocked the sandy roadside scrub like acne. Telegraph poles leant at crazy angles with spaghetti tangles of wire hanging from them. Burnt-out shells of battle tanks stood alongside the skeletal remains of wrecked automobiles. Groups of hastily-formed civilian militias stood alongside army deserters in uniformed green, now fighting together against a common enemy. They stood around the heat of makeshift braziers, eating bread, drinking coffee from paper cups, and smoking. All were unkempt, unwashed and unshaven. And all were nervous, waiting. Asking themselves when Gaddafi would make the next move in his fight to take back the city from the people who had become his enemy?

A dazzling light caught Royce's attention. At a roadside tyre shop, oxyacetylene-torches sparked and fizzed energetically as workers soldered the spigot mountings of anti-aircraft guns to the body pans of pick-up trucks. These were the ubiquitous improvised weapons-platforms of the amateur warriors. Known as "technicals", they carried everything from AA and heavy machine-guns to various sizes of mortars and multiple rocket launchers.

Suddenly, all eyes turned skyward. Two dark delta shapes circled momentarily below the cloud before disappearing again. Gaddafi's air force was on a recce mission. Someone on the ground fancied his chances with a loud, wasted half-belt of ammunition. At least the useless, ear-splitting gesture made everyone feel better.

The city outskirts were full of people going about their business and shopping in the markets. Despite the fighting, the place was still very busy. The hypnotic call to morning prayers of a *muezzin* floated magically over the houses from a nearby mosque.

Before their rapidly-planned departure back in Britain, Royce had advised the members of his sub-team to bring items of clothing that would help them blend in with the local population. These weren't disguises like wigs and false beards, but items like cheap cotton over-shirts, baseball caps or T-shirts with Arabic slogans, and waistcoats. All were available over the Internet. As they entered the suburbs of Benghazi, each man now raided his personal bergen for the items he had brought. Parsons made the most artistic effort with a *dishdasha* shirt and an embroidered cap, whilst Royce himself made do with a baseball hat and a blue *shamagh*. It was the most useful part of his wardrobe, which he took with him wherever he went in the world. Tareg watched the quick-change transformation of the four men with undisguised amusement.

Soon they were nearing the harbour and the beginning of the corniche that ran parallel to the Mediterranean shore.

'*Hinaa!*' Tareg called suddenly. 'We are here!'

Royce banged his fist on the cab roof. Tom responded immediately, pulling over and stopping beside the pavement. Meanwhile, the rest of the convoy carried on unaware that the Toyota had fallen behind. Tareg jumped out with Royce and Seeff, helping them to receive the bergens and black canvas bags handed down by Parsons and Tremain.

The job complete, Royce walked to the cab window. 'Thanks for everything, Tom.'

Their friend pulled a tight smile. 'Sorry things didn't work out better.'

Royce nodded. 'Maybe they will from now on.'

'I'll tell 'em you just jumped ship in a traffic jam.'

'Asquith and McDougall will be furious,' Seeff said with a grin.

Tom replied, 'I think they'll have enough on their plate than to be worrying about you lot.'

'You take care,' Royce said. With a wave, Tom shoved the gear into first and pushed his way out into the stream of vehicles. Cars tooted in protest.

Ollie Parsons was in his element, shouldering his rucksack and clamping a hand on the prayer cap that threatened to blow off into the fumes and dust of the passing traffic. 'Team B is on its way!' he proclaimed cheerily.

Weighed down with their bergens and canvas bags, the team followed Tareg and disappeared into the narrow streets of the Old Quarter.

3

WARZONE

The two cars sped out of Benghazi city, west along the Mediterranean coast road towards the capital Tripoli.

Clouds of dust trailed behind them as they passed milling crowds of rebels with their converted pick-up "technicals", mounted with anti-aircraft guns and rocket launchers. Occasionally there would be an old Soviet-era tank, liberated from Colonel Gaddafi's army, clanking along. There were many green-uniformed deserters in evidence too, smoking and sharing cans of soft drinks with the rebels.

James Royce was driving the lead vehicle with Ollie Parsons by his side. The scruffily-dressed Arab in the back, snaggle-toothed with a disconcerting wall-eye, was young Tareg's father. He was fondly known to the British expat community as "Sinbad". As a renowned fixer he had certainly done Royce's team proud.

Not only had he and his wife offered the escaped Team B sanctuary in their cramped flat in the Old Quarter, Sinbad had located vehicles for them and kept them up to date with the fate of the main group.

That news was not so good. The story of an SAS mission fiasco in Libya with members of MI6 had soon gone viral on the social media networks and was being reported world-wide by newspapers and television. With Britain's recent history of catastrophic involvement in the Muslim countries of Iraq and Afghanistan still hanging over it, the rebel leadership in Benghazi wanted to be seen as being masters of its own uprising.

Mat Asquith and Major McDougall's team were summarily dispatched to the Royal Navy frigate *HMS Cumberland*, which happened to be in port at the time to give support to the rebels. It was assumed that helper Tom had gone with them. However, the mission's two armoured Range Rovers, communications equipment and weaponry did not go with them.

Once Parsons had clearance by satellite phone from the so-called "Legoland" headquarters of MI6 by the River Thames in London, they set about planning their original part of the mission as though nothing had happened. Royce shed no tears that they didn't have an in-country Ops Centre that would have inevitably been run under Major McDougall's command.

Annoyingly, Sinbad had been unable to buy back the impounded Range Rovers despite the wad of dollar notes entrusted to him by Parsons. The two were apparently commandeered by the rebel hierarchy.

Several days later their fixer had, however, managed to acquire the high-spec but aging armoured Land Cruiser that Royce was now driving. It had a beefed up engine, more powerful brakes and shock-absorbers, and run-flat tyres. It also had a lot of rust. The air-conditioning and internal intercom systems didn't work. Sinbad reckoned it may have once belonged to someone high up in the Gaddafi regime. It had probably been security-rated a high B6/7 in its time.

The second car, now being driven some hundred metres behind them by South African-born Stefan Seeff, was a more modern and nippy B4-rated armoured VW Golf. His passengers were Iain Tremain and Sinbad's son, Tareg. All four team members had a Motorola T8 short-range radio link between them.

They flashed past more and more civilian vehicles that had been pressed into service with the rebels. It was clear they'd seen some heavy action. Dusty, dented and shrapnel-scarred with bullet-shattered

windows, it would be a miracle if half of them still started when the
ignition keys were turned. A handful of ex-army main battle tanks
and armoured cars were also pulled over at the side of the road. All
faced defiantly west, towards the next large city of Sirte – Gaddafi's
birthplace and his biggest stronghold of support.

'I do see your point, Rollo,' Parsons acknowledged with some
reluctance. 'We could be in big trouble if we try to drive directly along
the coast to Tripoli.'

There was a ghost of a smile on Royce's unshaven face. 'Suicidal
is the word you're looking for, Ollie. We'd be between a rock and a
hard place.' He meant between the advancing Gaddafi forces and the
retreating rebels. 'Even the BBC won't be able to save us.'

He was referring to the big "TV" signs in white insulation tape on
the front doors and bonnets of their vehicles. Although their cover was
as a team from the famous BBC radio World Service, they'd adopted
the familiar two letters for more instant recognition.

Only three days' earlier, the rebels had been forced back by
overwhelming government forces from the threshold of Sirte at the
coastal town of Bin Jawad. The remaining loyal Gaddafi troops were
now reinforced by experienced and ruthless mercenaries hired in from
Sudan, Chad, Algeria and Nigeria to replace the increasing number of
deserting soldiers.

The merciless onslaught had chased the shambolic rebel army back
towards its own base of Benghazi. Reports were that they were trying
to make a stand at the oil town of Ra's Lanuf.

Royce realised that the small groups of rebels, dressed in a mix-
and-match of jeans, T-shirts and camo jackets, who were chatting and
smoking by their vehicles, had experienced real bloody combat and
defeat for the first time. He could see it in their eyes as they constantly
looked at the sky for signs of Gaddafi's fighter-bombers. Knowing
they would come, just not knowing when.

Royce added, 'Even taking the scenic route to Tripoli won't be
without its risks.' The plan was to take a long dog-leg route south into

the desert, parallel to the coast, to avoid Sirte before emerging on the coast again near to the capital itself. 'We'll be passing close to Gaddafi's birth village of Qasr Abu Hadi just to our north. And the local airport. I can't believe either won't have some government defences.'

Sinbad had been listening carefully. 'Ah, yes, my English friends,' he said. 'Where our Brother Leader was born to the devil's whore in a goat-skin tent! And that is the village where he should have stayed.' It was an unusually angry outburst from the Libyan who always seemed to have a smile on his face. 'Gaddafi always looks after his own tribe, his own village, to keep them loyal to him. Sirte is Libya's *real* capital city. Everybody know that.'

While they continued along the coast road no one paid them any special attention. They'd seen one or two other media teams, presumably having crossed the border from Egypt, parked up and doing pieces to camera. It was nothing remarkable as the unfolding events in North Africa made world headline news.

Coming in the opposite direction were increasing numbers of open-topped trucks that were being used as makeshift ambulances. They were returning from the front carrying wounded rebels who had been hastily bandaged. Royce imagined the hospital in Benghazi would be stretched to breaking point. Another lorry chugged past them, loaded with dead bodies. Far ahead black smoke smudged the pale blue sky and artillery rounds like thunder followed close behind pulses of explosive light on the horizon.

As they continued, Royce intoned his running commentary of observations into the throat mike of his Motorola walkie-talkie. His words were relayed back to the following Golf. He observed the state of traffic, any potential problems or threats, noting tracks, streets or alleyways that they could escape to if suddenly faced with an emergency. Even an unexpected traffic jam could leave them exposed on an open road. Rather than remain stationary like sitting ducks for nervous or inquisitive rebels or a Libyan air force strike, it was better to take cover until the road was clear again.

Finally Parsons, who had the road map spread out on his lap, chipped in, 'Next left, Rollo.'

As they flashed past the bullet-riddled signpost for Hūn, Royce repeated the instruction for the benefit of Seeff driving behind them.

Soon they had left the buildings and frenzied traffic activity of the coastal strip behind them. It was swapped for a two-lane strip of sandy tarmac that meandered into the upper reaches of the Sahara Desert. It was achingly empty. There were no people and no vehicles. It was just a flat, slightly undulating moonscape broken only by the occasional patch of scrub or wild grass. The only dead ground was provided by a few dried-up *wadis* that might flash flood in the downpours of the rainy season.

Royce drove at a steady sixty miles an hour. They had departed early from Benghazi to allow plenty of time for the long diversion, in order to avoid the savage fighting at Sirte. But driving in these conditions was itself dangerously mesmerising. Trying to follow the single dotted white line on the sand-dusted tarmac was tiring on the eyes and it would be easy to miss an unexpected pothole until it was too late.

It felt strange to think that exactly seventy years earlier, during the Second World War, the armies of Britain and Germany had been locked in deadly battle on these very desert landscapes between Libya and Egypt. Famously, it had become the turning point of British fortunes. Royce found his mind wandering, and forced himself to concentrate.

After some forty-five minutes, he announced abruptly, 'Something coming.'

The sound of his voice breaking the prolonged silence was a shock. Parsons leaned forward, squinting through his thick spectacles. 'What is it?'

'Something big,' Royce added. 'Just look at that dust cloud. My guess is it's a convoy.'

'But whose?' Parsons asked. 'Gaddafi or the rebels?'

'Could be either, or civilian.' Royce then said, 'Stefan, do you read me?'

'Yes, boss.'

'Whatever's coming the other way, we just keep going, right? Nice and steady. Whatever happens, should you have to get out of your car, do so alone – and let Iain take the wheel. If the shit really hits the fan, use the shorts.'

He was referring to the stockless AK47 assault rifle that each car carried. When the rebels back at the farm had disarmed the team of its main weapons, they had missed the extra personal kit and side-arms garaged away on Tom's pick-up. That included Royce's favoured automatic, a Czech-made CZ85 that was based on the 9mm Browning. It was reliable and deadly accurate. He kept it hidden in a Gould & Goodrich holster beneath the flap of the heavy-duty blue bullet vest he was wearing.

'Roger that,' Seeff confirmed. There was no hint of concern in his voice, if anything the opposite.

Royce grunted, concentrating on the approaching column of vehicles. At its head was a four-wheeled armoured personnel carrier. An Italian APC, he knew. He recognised it, wracked his brains.

'A Fiat double six one one six,' Seeff said.

'Smart arse,' Royce replied. 'Are you also a train spotter?'

'Fuck off.'

There were a dozen of them, additional soldiers sitting on top. They were followed by heavy tank transporters with flatbed trailers. Each carried an old Soviet-made T72 main battle tank. They'd never seen combat, fresh out of bubble-wrap with 125mm smoothbore barrels boasting their masculine pride. These were Gaddafi reinforcements heading for Benghazi. Royce wound down his window and waved. Parsons did likewise, grinning widely.

Troops on the APCs waved back, saw the TV stickers and shouted enthusiastically. A few fired shots in the air.

'Pillocks,' Seeff muttered over the net.

'That was lucky,' Royce breathed.

In the next twenty minutes only two other vehicles passed in the opposite direction. The approach of both got heart-rates pounding and adrenalin pumping, but one turned out to be a livestock lorry full of goats and the other a taxi.

But it was the jet fighters that really spooked them. They were two French-built Mirages flying very low, one just above the road and his wingman behind but a little higher. At first Royce thought he was seeing spots before his eyes. What were indistinct specks on the horizon suddenly transformed, growing into menacing shapes as they rocketed above the road.

The words: 'Aircraft approaching!' had barely left his lips before they screamed overhead, one immediately after the other, drowning out all other noise.

'God,' gasped a shocked Parsons, turning in his seat to follow their trail. 'Were they Libyan?'

'I think so,' Royce replied tightly.

'They might mistake us for rebels.'

Royce nodded. 'Hopefully they'll respect the TV signage. But I wouldn't bet on it.'

'They're climbing now,' Parsons reported. 'Banking. Up to about two thousand, I reckon.'

Iain Tremain's voice came on the net, observing from the Golf. *'One Mirage coming back to take a look.'* His distinctive Tasmanian drawl was clipped, giving away his military background. *'He's slowed up to take an eyeball. Second is giving top cover in case we're hostile.'*

The first Mirage made its cautious low pass about a quarter mile south of the road, looking for any obvious signs of weapons on the vehicles. The second was loitering high above it, protecting his oppo.

'Prepare to abandon vehicles,' Royce snapped. 'There are drainage ditches on both sides of the road just here. Looks like a small culvert ahead. Make for that.'

'I'll give covering fire with my AK,' Seeff offered selflessly.

'Roger,' Royce acknowledged.

But the first Mirage pilot seemed satisfied with the two civilian vehicles carrying large "TV" signs and turned in a wide circle. The two paired up again in the far distance and reset their course towards Benghazi and the column of Gaddafi's reinforcements.

'That's sufficient excitement for one day,' Parsons muttered. 'Enough to make me take up the fags again.'

Royce wouldn't have disagreed. He'd cut down his small cigar habit to just an occasional celebratory treat. And not being targeted by a Libyan jet suddenly seemed like a damned good cause for celebration.

More endless winding road, its definition blurred with eddies of sand. The airless heat was suffocating without functional air-conditioning. Mile followed mile of featureless landscape. The mind just longed for sight of a tree, a pylon, a house, or even a billboard. There was nothing.

Twenty minutes later, Royce's sense of elation after escaping the encounter with the Libyan jets died as quickly as it had come.

'Road block,' he announced and lifted his foot from the accelerator.

Parsons tapped the map with his pencil. 'At the crossroads. Sirte to the north.'

'Bastard Gaddafi village just up road here,' Sinbad reminded helpfully, his bushy joke-shop eyebrows in a frown.

'And the airport, of course,' Parsons added.

Seeff's voice came over the net. *'How you want to play this, boss?'*

The four-wheeled armoured car was parked sideways across the road, blocking the best part of both lanes. It was an aging Portuguese-built Bravia Chaimite from the sixties. Classified as "light" it may have been, but ramming it was not an option. And its manned 20mm cannon pointing straight at them reinforced their lack of choices.

'You hang back, Stefan, and give covering fire if needed,' Royce said. 'Time to test our cover.'

'Roger,' Seeff replied as Royce began moving forward again towards the road block. As the Land Cruiser drew closer, he could make out another vehicle, a small command car parked by the side of the road and two brown canvas tents to house the detachment of soldiers. A cluster of aerials glistened above one of them. A collapsible table and half a dozen plastic chairs stood in front of the tents.

Four uniformed soldiers appeared to be eating their lunch. They looked up as the gunner in the turret of the APC alerted them. The officer rose to his feet and strolled out onto the tarmac. Two of the troops picked up their carbines from the table and followed him, still munching on their food.

When he was some forty metres from them, Royce stopped. 'Get into my seat, Ollie. If the shit hits the fan, do a Y-turn. That's the easiest. Keep calm and don't panic. Stefan will give you covering fire. Then hightail it down the road. These clowns won't be able to catch up.'

Parsons looked ashen. 'I was shit in training.'

'You only had an hour at it,' Royce replied kindly. 'But you'll be fine.'

The Libyan officer beckoned. Royce opened the glove box and extracted the clear water-proof bag that contained their two passports and Sinbad's identity card. He also took a pack of Rothmans from the dashboard sill.

'Wish me luck,' he said and swung open the door.

'Break a leg,' Parsons replied and moved into the driver's seat. He and those in the VW would be able to listen to Royce's conversation with the soldiers on his open radio.

Forcing the warmest smile he could manage, Royce approached the soldiers. '*Sabah al-kher*,' he said.

The officer was tall and thin with a gaunt face that sported an untidy goatee beard. He did not respond to the polite greeting, just regarded Royce with hard raisin eyes.

Royce tried again. '*Inta bititkalem inglizi?*'

'*Aywa*,' the Libya replied with seeming reluctance. 'I speak a little English.'

'Ah, good,' Royce said. In situations like this he liked to read people's eyes and let them read his. It was one reason he never wore sunglasses.

He added politely, 'I am sure it is better than my Arabic.'

The man nodded toward the Land Cruiser. 'You are TV?'

'Media actually. BBC radio. World Service.'

For the first time there was a slight expression of interest on the man's face. 'You are a reporter?'

'My client is a BBC reporter. I am just his security advisor.'

The officer almost smiled. 'He is afraid he may be shot?'

'It's my job to see that he isn't. Libya is a dangerous country at the moment.'

'Yes,' the man agreed, 'until we crush the terrorists in Benghazi.' He indicated the plastic package in Royce's hand. 'Your passports?'

Royce handed them over. They were genuine but with fake identities. 'There are also letters of accreditation from the BBC.'

The officer took his time examining everything. At this remote outpost, the arrival of the two cars was probably the most exciting event that had occurred in recent days. 'There are no visas or visa stamps.'

'That is because we came over the border from Egypt. There were no checkpoints.'

'There are always checkpoints.'

'Not on the route we came.'

'So you have no visas?' he repeated.

Royce sensed the officer was enjoying this. 'Obviously.' Then he played his trump card. 'But we do have a letter from your Ministry of Information.'

The officer unfolded the sheet of A4 official regime headed paper. It was written in Arabic 'To Whom It May Concern' confirming that the carrier was a journalist travelling with the government's permission. 'It is a photocopy.'

'It was issued in London,' Royce replied. 'I believe there was a lot of demand for them. Your government is anxious for the World Service to report the truth.'

'About the terrorists in Benghazi?'

'Of course.'

For the first time Royce sensed he might be winning. He took out the packet of Rothman's and placed one between his lips. 'Would you like one?'

The officer's eyes narrowed but, after a moment's hesitation, he plucked a cigarette and accepted the flame from Royce's lighter. He drew a deep lungful of smoke before examining Sinbad's Identity Card.

'Who is this man?'

'He is our fixer. Helps us arrange interviews, find things, get us around.'

'He is not Government media minder.' It was a statement, not a question.

Royce said, 'No doubt we'll be given an official minder when we arrive in Tripoli.'

'And this is the man in question?' The officer inclined his head.

As he turned around, Royce's heart sank. Sinbad was walking across the stretch of road from the Land Cruiser. He was carrying a brown paper bag, plucking cookies from it, and popping them into his mouth.

'*Salam aleyhum!*' he greeted, and continued in Arabic, 'I wonder if I can help translate?'

'There is no need,' the officer said in his native language. 'You live in Benghazi?'

'I was born there.'

'So you support the terrorists?'

Sinbad looked affronted. 'I spit on their graves. I love our Brother Leader. I read a page from his *Green Book* every night before I go to sleep.'

'Really?' The officer appeared genuinely surprised that the man from the rebel heartland should be such an avid follower of Gaddafi's book of political philosophy.

As Royce winced at the obvious piss-take, Sinbad continued with happy enthusiasm, 'You are from Sirte?'

'Yes.'

'I thought I recognised the accent,' Sinbad said. 'My nephew lives there.' He changed tack, proffering the bag of cookies. 'Perhaps my boss could interview you for the famous World Service of the BBC?'

The man took one of the cookies. 'I don't think so.'

'Home-made by my dear wife.' Sinbad offered the cookies to the other soldiers, who snatched at them eagerly.

'Very nice. Very tasty. Unusual flavour.'

One of the soldiers, who had remained at the table to finish his lunch, walked across to them. He was carrying a clipboard. 'Sir! I've just realised. That Land Cruiser is on the list.'

Royce frowned. 'What list is that?'

The officer took the clipboard from the soldier. 'Stolen vehicles,' he replied. He studied the clipboard then squinted at the Land Cruiser. 'It is the same registration number. Reported stolen from Tobruk.'

'There must be some mistake,' Sinbad protested. He offered the paper bag again.

Absently the officer took another cookie. 'No mistake, my friend. It is a government department car.'

'Those crooks in Benghazi!' Sinbad raged. 'Death to those terrorists. I bought it in good faith.'

'It doesn't look in very good condition,' the officer conceded as he continued chewing.

While wondering how he was going to crucify Sinbad, Royce had a sudden thought. 'Can we return it to the right department when we get to Tripoli?'

It occurred to him that the officer had mellowed somewhat. He actually had a smile on his face. 'That is a good idea, my friend. I will write down an address for you.' The officer hesitated for a moment. 'And... as you are from the BBC World Service and have a letter from the Ministry of Information, I shall stamp your passports with a visa. I officially welcome you to the Libyan Arab State of the People – the *Jamahiriya.*'

The officer was as good as his word. Everybody's passport in both cars was stamped. It wasn't the usual £150 blue jumbo sticker issued in London, but a neat, modest and old-fashioned ink visa stamp.

Half an hour later they were all able to resume their journey. In fact it had been hard to break away without giving offence. The tense stand-off almost turned into a party. Parsons decided to persuade the officer to answer a few simple questions, allowing him to say how the people loved their leader Gaddafi and how the Libyan Armed Forces would soon defeat the terrorists in the east of the country. It was a strictly party-line response, but at least it gave the MI6 operator a chance to get a real interview on tape – supposedly for the BBC World Service – which would help support his cover.

They drove on through the afternoon, eventually re-joining the Mediterranean coast road near the city of Misrata. Dusk was encroaching as they reached the outskirts of Tripoli itself. The eastern area of the city around Tjourna was a rebel-held area, but the men manning the check-points there were friendly enough and welcoming to British journalist teams. Other government roadblocks near the city centre were more hostile, but the letters from the Ministry of Information and the team's newly-acquired visas did the trick and the two cars were allowed safe passage.

However, their arrival at the plush Rixos Hotel was a disaster. It was the official five-star "media hotel" and it was filled to bursting with journalists and TV film crews from all around the world. Moreover it was controlled by an army of Gaddafi "minders". It was their job to provide transport for organised trips and escort reporters, wherever they went, to ensure they filmed and wrote only about what the regime wanted them to see. There was also a picket of them outside to make sure no one escaped to do their own thing.

Their rooms had been booked ahead from London by MI6 administrators posing as the BBC. But when Royce scouted ahead and checked at reception there was no record of the booking. More importantly, there were no available spare rooms either.

It was suggested by the receptionist that his party try the even more opulent five-star Corinthia nearer the coast, which was the official media "overflow" hotel. But, before she could call one of the minders to assist him, Royce slipped away through the kitchen area and out through an emergency exit to avoid the armed officials guarding the car park.

He crossed the large roundabout outside and rejoined the two cars waiting for him in a side street. His team were gathered on the pavement, talking quietly in the shadows. Now quite hungry, they were demolishing the last of Sinbad's cookies.

Their fixer offered Royce one as he was explaining the mix-up over the hotel bookings.

Parsons raised his eyes to the heavens. 'Typical of those muppets at Legoland.'

'Might not be their fault,' Royce said. 'We'd have been down as a no show. And, to be fair, it's all pretty manic on the hotel front desk.'

'Could be a good thing,' Tremain decided. 'If it's a media circus and swarming with Gaddafi's boys, the Corinthia could suit us better.'

Sinbad and his son were leaning against the Land Cruiser drinking from cans of lemonade. 'Please, sir,' Sinbad said, 'there is another place. It is owned by a cousin of mine.'

Royce glared. 'The same cousin who sold you this stolen car?'

'No, no, and I am sorry about that.' He shook his head vehemently. 'I will never trust that man again.'

'This is a proper hotel?' Royce asked and bit into the cookie.

'Yes, it is nice place. Not far from here. Not as smart as Rixos. There are some journalists there already. It is much cheaper, you save much money. And there are few Gaddafi men there.'

'Why's that?'

'Because my cousin hates them. Gives them a bad time and makes them pay for everything.'

'Could be just the ticket,' Seeff said, eating the final cookie and screwing up the paper bag.

Sinbad took out an ancient mobile phone from his ornate waistcoat.

'Oh, Allah cries! There is no network signal again.' He dropped it back in his pocket. 'I will take you there.'

'Why not,' Royce decided. 'If there are rooms, it might suit us better than the Corinthia.' He licked his lips. 'Odd taste to these cookies. Nice enough, but…'

Seeff nodded. 'I recognise the flavour. No wonder those Gaddafi soldiers at the checkpoint suddenly became our best friends. Off their faces…'

'What?' Parsons asked, bewildered.

Sinbad giggled. 'As you say, there is not only one way to skin cat.'

Tareg clearly understood the joke.

'Marijuana brownies,' Seeff explained.

4

GOLDEN PALMS

Jo Brampton was waiting for him, seated on a faded wicker sofa in the hotel reception lounge.

Half-hidden behind a dying rubber plant, she could keep an eye on the revolving glass doors for any surprise arrival of minders from the Ministry of Information. They didn't often frequent the Golden Palms but, she reasoned, it would be typical if they pitched up tonight of all nights.

From that position, she could also see the stainless steel gates of the two wheezing lifts, from one of which her American close-protection man should have emerged ten minutes earlier.

She was killing time while she waited, trying to write a poem. It was something she had loved to do as a teenager, but it was an art that she'd lost since she left her boarding school in 1994 at the age of eighteen.

Her life now was all about being a journalist or war correspondent on the frontline. Reporting from regions of conflict around the world, telling the tragic truth, the inhumanity, and digging out the facts that others wanted to keep hidden. At least that was how she saw it.

WORD OF WAR

I hear there's word of war in foreign parts,

Of broken bodies and bleeding hearts,
Lives destroyed and cities wrecked.
Truth suspended, because no one knows
Lies are the ammunition of both sides
Someone must dig to find
Where facts and corpses hide...

That was as far as she'd got. Rubbish. She struck it through with her pencil and put her notepad away. It was no good, she just could not concentrate. This was the most exciting time of her life. After school, she'd failed as a ballerina because she was too tall and had two left feet, according to her teacher. And she'd failed in the army because she kept closing her eyes when she fired a gun.

It wasn't until she'd followed her Russian father's journalistic footsteps and managed to land a job on a local Cornish rag at the age of twenty-five that a career of any sort had started to take shape. Moving to London she worked on high-end fashion magazines, and hated it.

With a diplomat father who'd defected from the former Soviet Union – and a mother who was a beautiful Iranian novelist – she knew a lot about the world and its politics. It fascinated her. She wrote freelance articles for a number of magazines. "Bram", as she'd become known in the editorial department, had a dream to be another Kate Adie or Marie Colvin, Sue Lloyd Roberts or a Christina Lamb.

Then, the previous year, Brampton had finally got her big break. Her outrageous prima ballerina friend from her teens, Anoushka, had introduced her to her latest in a long production-line of lovers.

Russ Carver was the editor of a struggling weekly redtop, the *Sunday News*. He was looking for someone who could write and also had a keen knowledge and understanding of world affairs. He also wanted someone who came cheap and didn't mind making the tea.

'Dammit,' she said aloud, glancing at her watch. 'Where the hell is Bud?'

Despite its wobbly circulation and crappy offices – actually just off Fleet Street that barely had a newspaper still based there – the *News* still punched above its weight. That was mostly down to Carver's experience and dogged hard-nosed professionalism – and his network of contacts. Brampton could hardly believe her luck in landing personal interviews with both the creepy beanpole Assad of Syria and President Mubarak of Egypt. She'd also started a meeting with the petulant "Bibi" Netanyahu of Israel, but he had walked out on her when she'd started echoing her own father's views on the plight of Palestinians in Gaza.

Dammit, Brampton decided in a flash of ill-temper, she had waited quite long enough.

Picking up her shoulder bag, she marched across to the rattan-covered front desk, her pumps clacking on the polished tile floor. But she'd timed it badly, and had to wait because new arrivals from a Japanese TV channel were signing in.

Impatiently she lit a Balkan Sobranie from her slim-line cigarette case. As she exhaled she caught sight of herself in the one of the mirrored columns. What a mess, she thought. Her hair was its usual untamed riot of black curls; why hadn't she taken the trouble to tie it back? She was no fan of make-up, hardly needing it with her dark features. But she could at least have applied some mascara to make herself presentable. She'd clearly had the time after all, because now she was just hanging around for Bud. At least she couldn't fault her own dress sense, black skinny jeans and a tailor-fitted, plain white blouse with a deep collar. It was finished off with a *hijab* in colourful Florentine silk, that she wore tied loosely around her shoulders, and a fresh flower behind her left ear.

That was a signature look she had adopted from her late mother, who had been born to Persian aristocracy. A good dress sense was one thing she had learned from her time on the fashion mags.

The queue of Japanese was shortening.

She sighed, and that was when she saw him. He hadn't used the revolving glass entrance, but had slipped through one of the regular side doors. She estimated he was in his late thirties or early forties, about six feet tall, and slim. For a moment she thought he might be a Libyan because he was unshaven and tanned and had a blue *shamag* scarf tucked into the canvas travel vest he was wearing. But his hair appeared tawny and she thought his eyes were probably green, although it was difficult to be certain from that distance.

Whatever their colour, his eyes were certainly alert and watchful. He clearly had a knack of blending in as he paused and looked around, assessing his new surroundings. His eyes met hers momentarily, clocked her she was sure. He moved like a panther now, smooth and effortless, towards the reception desk where she stood.

Suddenly the last of the Japanese TV crew moved away with his luggage and Brampton was able to step forward.

'Can I help?' The receptionist wore a uniformed skirt and blazer and a colour-matched purple *hijab*. Her extravagant make-up would have passed muster on a film-set for Cleopatra.

'I'm waiting for my friend,' Brampton said quickly, aware that the new arrival was just behind her. 'Mr Bud Ambrose in Room 306. Would it be possible to call him, tell him I'm here and waiting?'

'Of course, madam.' The woman picked up the desk phone. 'And your name is?

'Jo Brampton.'

At that moment the darkly-suited duty manager joined the receptionist. 'Yes, sir? How may I help?'

'My party is from the BBC World Service,' Royce said. 'I wonder if you have some spare accommodation? Your hotel was recommended by Mr Mohamed Ayman from Benghazi.'

'Ah!' The manager's response wasn't quite as enthusiastic as Royce had been expecting. 'Cousin Sinbad. Well, not *my* cousin. It is how he is known. He and our owner are distant second cousins. Is he trying to offer you a special price?'

Royce shook his head, although Sinbad had said he could arrange a deal. 'Not at all.'

'The BBC World Service, eh? Let's see what we can do...' He consulted the open book on the desk. 'How many are you?'

'We're a total party of six.'

'All our rooms are twins.'

'Three rooms would be good.'

The manager shook his head. 'I am afraid I can only manage two, but they *are* en suite.'

'Preferably together on the same floor?' Royce pressed. 'Top floor at the back of the hotel?'

'Alas no, sir. I have one room on the fifth and one on the third. One at the back and one at the front.'

From a professional point-of-view that was far from excellent for Royce. Front rooms with a street view might be great for happy holiday-makers, but not in a war zone with rebels and government forces shooting at each other. A risk of fire or attack favoured a close-to-roof location and he certainly didn't want their team spread over several floors.

'That's a shame,' Royce said, but it didn't look like he had much of an option. It was a case of accept what was on offer or go to the Corinthia, which would be crawling with Gaddafi's minders.

Aware of the disappointment in his voice, Brampton said on impulse, 'You could swap with my room on the third, if you like.'

Royce looked at her, took in the smoky brown eyes and hair as black as coal dust. 'I couldn't possibly.'

She smiled tersely. 'That's fine. I don't like it much. It overlooks the rubbish bins at the back and the generator makes a racket.'

'You're safer where you are at the back,' Royce insisted.

Brampton looked pained. 'I'd prefer better light and to see what's going on outside.'

The manager looked relieved. 'If you're both in agreement, I'll have the porters switch your effects around later this evening. About nine o'clock. Would that suit?'

'I should be back by then,' Brampton said, wondering if she'd ever get out of the hotel in the first place.

Royce said, 'You're most kind. Thank you..?'

'Jo Brampton. People call me Bram.'

'James.'

As she reached for the offered hand, the receptionist suddenly replaced the desk phone on its cradle, 'I'm afraid there's no answer from Mr Ambrose. It's just going on ringing.'

It was then that Brampton saw him. 'Oh, it's okay. Here he is now.'

Royce turned his head.

There was no missing Bud Ambrose. Ambrose was Texas personified. He stood some six feet six in his Chukka boots and Royce could believe he'd been chiselled out of a lump of Texan lava rock. He had a clean-shaven, defiant jaw, an iron-filing haircut and straight features. His eyes were hidden behind wraparound sunglasses although the sun had already set. Olive-coloured cargo trousers and stretched T-shirt covered his muscle-bound frame. No one was going to mess lightly with this strutting man mountain. The only thing missing was a huge Desert Eagle automatic strapped ostentatiously to his hip. Royce got the distinct impression he probably enjoyed a regular diet of steroids, burgers and cola.

Ambrose totally dwarfed the slender strawberry blonde standing next to him in a bleached denim skirt and linen sports jacket. Royce vaguely recognised her from news reports watched in hotel bedroom televisions in Bagdad and Kabul. Was she on Sky? CNN? Even al-Jazeera? He thought she looked a little flushed. Breathless, her hair unkempt.

'Bud, where the hell have you been?' Brampton demanded. 'Do you know what the time is?'

'Sure I do, little lady. Don't get your pantyhose in a twist.'

Brampton's eyes narrowed. 'And don't patronise me, Bud. We were supposed to be at the meeting ten minutes ago.'

The expression of indifference on his face didn't alter. 'I'm sure the Secretary for Utilities will wait. They're not exactly queuing up to interview him and he wants the coverage... I was just giving Miss Starr here some security tips. Do you know Miss Starr – from TV-Global?'

Brampton bit her tongue. 'Yes, Bud, Rachel and I know each other, thank you.'

Starr blushed deeply. 'Oh, I'm so sorry, Bram, I had no idea you were waiting for Bud -'

'You weren't to know,' Brampton cut in. She turned on her heel and glared at the big American. 'But Bud did, didn't he, Bud?'

Ambrose raised his hand in a mock gesture of surrender. 'Yeah, yeah. I'm sorry. Got a bit carried away...'

Starr nudged him. 'That's enough, big boy.'

'I'm *not* interested in your bizarre mating rituals,' Brampton snapped. 'Let's go.'

She stormed off towards the front door leaving Ambrose to stride after her.

Starr noticed Royce watching the two of them. 'Are you in the security game, too?'

'Close protection,' he confirmed. 'Is it that obvious?'

'You guys are all the same.'

'I don't think so,' he muttered and turned to the manager. 'I'll be back shortly with my clients.'

With that he slipped back out of the building to where the Land Cruiser and VW waited. They drove into the hotel's secure car-park where Royce tipped the armed security guards to keep a special eye on their two vehicles. The four-man MI6 and SAS team loaded themselves down with their personal bergens and black canvas equipment bags, while Sinbad and Tareg shared a holdall and carried the team's large medical case.

As they crossed the floor, Parsons veered towards the elevator doors. 'No, Ollie, no lifts,' Royce said. 'Electricity is unreliable at best. A lift is the last place you want to get trapped.'

'Stairs?' Parsons looked horrified. 'You said we're on the third floor.'

'No, you and Iain will share the room on the fifth. 507.'

'*What?*'

'It's the safest place,' Royce replied. 'Trust me. Stefan and I will double up with Sinbad and Tareg on the third, 305. At about 2100 hours we'll change rooms to 310 at the back.'

The conversation petered out as they entered the concrete stairwell and began the long climb. Seeff broke off at the third floor with Sinbad and his son, while Royce helped Parsons and Tremain haul their luggage to the fifth.

Once they were settled, he led them back down the stairwell to the third floor and the plastic-veneered door to room 305. There, the rest of the team had temporarily dumped their kit and were chilling out with cans of lukewarm soft drinks from the dead mini-bar.

The air-conditioning unit had terminal emphysema and Royce switched it off. At least the flooring tiles were cooling and the bedding looked clean if a bit faded and threadbare. He pushed open the creaking double doors onto a small balcony that overlooked the street. Personally he much preferred humid night air to refrigerated chill any day. He glanced across the street which was fairly busy with traffic. Buildings on the other side looked empty. Some showed signs of heavy mortar or artillery damage, with collapsed walls and brick debris; others had their stucco rendering riddled with bullet holes.

He shut the heavy green velvet curtains. 'Don't anyone stand near the windows with the lights on,' he warned. 'There could be snipers in the derelict houses opposite – Gaddafi's lot or the rebels, who knows? Only needs one to get bored or to be high on weed.' He took a deep breath. 'Anyway, we'll be switching with the woman in room 310 opposite around nine o'clock. Her name's Jo Brampton. Meanwhile I suggest you plug in your radios, computers and anything else that needs recharging while the power's working. Make that your routine, your first job every evening.'

He added, 'That reminds me...'He pulled out the TAG Heuer Android smartphone from the pocket of his cargo trousers. 'Wonder of wonders. A two bar signal.'

Parson's eyes lit up. 'Fantastic!' He was delighted. Having managed to get through to Chingford Charlie from Sinbad's flat before they'd left Benghazi, he had told his "agent" that he hoped they could meet as soon as possible when they arrived in Tripoli. The Thuraya network, operating out of the United Arab Emirates, used a satellite system to communicate with the remotest of places. But earlier in the desert there appeared to have been some local atmospheric interference. 'Can you call Charlie, Rollo? Get him to come here.'

Royce glanced at his watch. 'He may not want to. It's getting on and he's an old man.'

'Be persuasive.'

Scrolling up the short contact list to Chingford's code name, Royce called. 'Charlie? It's James. We spoke the other day.'

'Yes, yes.' The estuary accent had long ago been eroded and replaced with pseudo Eton tones. 'Where are you, dear boy?'

'In Tripoli. Where are you?'

'At the Corinthia, enjoying a meal and a fine bottle of claret,' came the reply. 'The Rixos is full and I gather they're now putting journos in here.'

'We've just arrived at the Golden Palms.'

'What? My God! How did you end up in that place?'

'Long story,' Royce replied. 'Any chance you could come over in a taxi?'

There was a brief hesitation. 'Ah, yes, well, obviously I've opened a tab here in the restaurant.'

Royce said, 'Pay it and we'll reimburse. After your cheese and biscuits, of course.'

'And the taxi?'

'Naturally.'

The deal was done. Royce left the rest of the team to unwind, after advising them to always be ready to depart at a moment's notice in any unexpected emergency. He reconnoitred the two stairways that led to the flat roof and discovered a metal fire-escape ladder that offered a route to the roof of an adjoining warehouse. From his vantage point on the hotel roof, he decided on two emergency "assembly points" – one at the front and a second at the rear – for use if the building came under sustained attack and the team became separated.

Shortly before nine he met up with an angry Jo Brampton who was back at the hotel after her interview with a Gaddafi government minister had to be cut short because she had arrived so late. Between them, they supervised the swap of rooms on the third floor, the hotel staff assisting in the changeover.

Before leaving her in the new room at the front, Royce advised, 'Don't stand in front of the window, offering a silhouette. If you have to, move the electric light nearer to the outer wall.'

Brampton frowned. 'Are you talking about pervs?'

'No, snipers.'

'I've got a bodyguard. He didn't say anything about that.'

'Bud?'

'Yes.'

'Fair enough. Just a friendly word.'

Royce found Sinbad and his son in their new room sitting on one of the beds and playing Zamma, a type of North African checkers.

'Stefan goes downstairs,' Sinbad said. 'Better we stay here.'

'Okay,' Royce said. 'You two have the beds. Stefan and I can use the floor. We've got kip mats and sleeping bags.'

'If you are sure, Mr James.'

'That's fine. I'll see you later.'

He went downstairs to find the reception area buzzing with people and excited chatter. It seemed to be the usual frontline mix of media types, including TV crews and modern age Internet bloggers, dodgy dealers, smugglers and quick-buck wheeler-dealers and, very likely, Gaddafi regime spies.

'Over here, Rollo!' Parsons called from a small group gathered on fake zebra-skin sofas surrounding a glass-topped coffee table with an ornate hubble-bubble pipe at its centre. The MI6 man was examining a street map of Tripoli with Tremain, while Seeff was engaged in a conversation with Jo Brampton and her American minder. Everyone appeared to be drinking orange juice from tall glasses loaded with fruit cocktail.

They looked up as he approached them. 'Hi, guys,' Royce greeted. 'Just one quick operational note. If anything happens unexpectedly, like we get shelled or attacked, we'll have our own assembly-points outside, so we can find each other in the chaos. The swimming-pool bar at the back and the watch-keeper's hut by the car park gate at the front.'

'Right,' Seeff acknowledged.

'Good thinking,' added Tremain.

Ambrose laughed. 'Hey, man, are you for real?'

Seeff turned on him. 'He's for real, Buzz.'

The American scowled. 'The name's Bud.'

'Sorry, Buzz.'

'Are you including us?' Brampton asked. It suddenly sounded like a good idea.

Royce shrugged. 'If you want. It's up to you. Have your own assembly point where you like.'

She turned to Ambrose. 'What do you think, Bud?'

The American lay back on the sofa. 'I think our friend should chill out. Try a Gaddafi Sunrise.'

Royce raised an eyebrow.

Seeff raised his glass of orange juice and fruit. 'A Gaddafi Sunrise. Orange juice, fruit and a secret ingredient.'

'I'm guessing vodka,' Brampton added.

Tremain drawled, 'I'm guessing industrial grade anti-freeze.'

'Or there's the new Rebel's Benghazi Bombshell,' Ambrose said, lifting his tumbler. 'I reckon Red Bull and vodka!'

'Keep your voice down,' Seeff warned. 'Don't spoil a good thing, Buzz.'

'Bud.'

Over Ambrose's shoulder, Royce noticed the arrival of an elderly man at the revolving door. He could have wandered in from the pages of a Somerset Maugham novel. He was instantly recognisable from the photograph in the file back in London.

Chingford Charlie was tall, although slightly stooped with age, his broad shoulders covered by a crumpled linen jacket and blue Oxford-weave shirt which sported a club tie. He removed his straw Fedora before addressing the doorman Farouk, whom he appeared to know. The genial Farouk, in his matching fez and red waistcoat, pointed in the direction of the zebra-skin sofas; then he discreetly accepted the note that was pressed into his palm.

Chingford was always smiling, Royce was to learn. He had a lightly tanned, clean-shaven face and a full head of groomed white hair. His eyes were sharp and blue, always moving, ever alert. Paying particular attention to the females, Royce decided, studying them with distinctly creepy concentration.

Royce stepped forward to meet him. 'I'm James. We spoke on the phone.'

Chingford's handshake was very strong, as if trying to test the other man's mettle. 'Do call me Charlie, old chap. Glad you all made it here in one piece.' He glanced around to check no one was within earshot. 'Just a shame you turned up in such a blaze of publicity. 'Hasn't helped our relations with the rebels at all. They want this to be *their* revolution, not part of some British colonial plot to grab Libya's oil.'

5

REBELLION? WHAT REBELLION?

'It was not my plan, I assure you,' Royce replied flatly.

Chingford regarded him carefully. ''You Regiment?'

'Technically,' Royce answered. 'As we speak, but not historically.'

'Riddles,' Chingford decided with a degree of irritation. 'So historically you were with..?'

'The paddling frogs.'

It was a reference to the unofficial Special Boat Service emblem of a parachuting frog and crossed paddles.

'Ah, a cabbage hat.' But there was little warmth in Chingford's eyes as he smiled. 'I was Regiment once, in the Stone Age. I left in '62 after three years. Got involved in the oil industry, security adviser. Ended up here as their oil industry was first expanding. Met Muammar Gaddafi after the revolution in '69 when he set up his Muslim republic. He was very handsome in his day, very dashing and charismatic.' Chingford paused, thinking back. 'Of course, he also had a darker side.'

'You became friends?' Royce asked.

Chingford shook his head. 'That's putting it too strongly. We developed a relationship, a trust. He had an oil industry and I advised him on its security. That contract allowed me to develop my business in the Middle East, basing myself in Malta. What Gaddafi didn't know was every time I returned to Britain, I'd visit old chums in Hereford or at Century House, as it was then.'

Royce understood. 'The old MI6 headquarters in London,' he confirmed.

'They were troubled times,' Chingford said. 'I did my best to steer Gaddafi in the right direction, but he was always as stubborn as a fucking camel – if you'll forgive my language.'

Noticing that Brampton and Ambrose were now heading for the restaurant, Royce grabbed the moment to have some words in private. He said to Chingford, 'Come and meet our manager, Ollie.'

'The one you're baby-sitting?' Chingford asked. 'He's my London link. And an Australian called Iain.'

'Tasmanian,' Royce corrected. 'A subtle difference.'

Parsons and Tremain were in flippant conversation with Seeff when they saw the two men approaching and stood up to greet the new arrival. 'Ah, I see you've discovered the secret delights of the Gaddafi Sunrise,' Chingford observed.

'Would you care for one?' Parsons offered.

'Was Mohamed a Muslim?'

As they all sat down, Parsons beckoned the waiter. When the man had gone he said, 'Nice to put a face to the name, Charlie. And Chingford is your real name, I believe?'

'Born and bred there,' Chingford explained. 'Got the nickname, so changed it by deed-poll for a bet one day.'

Royce interjected. 'By the way, Charlie, you should know that Ollie and Iain are from the BBC World Service.'

Chingford smiled again. 'Of course they are. Now tell me, what happened to my good friend Tom?'

'Ah, yes,' Parsons replied, looking slightly embarrassed. 'I gather he's returned safely to the UK for a spot of home leave.'

'Nice to know,' Chingford said, hardly bothering to conceal his sarcasm. 'As his career in Libya is pretty much buggered now. An excellent fellow, by the way. Before he assisted your lot, I got him to help organise an RAF mission by Hercules in the desert. They rescued some hundred and fifty oil-workers.'

'It was an SBS mission,' Royce reminded pointedly.

The waiter arrived with another round of popular "non-alcoholic" cocktails.

'So who would you like to interview for your radio programmes?' Chingford asked, raising his tumbler of orange juice.

'Oh, I think you know that, Charlie,' Parsons replied, happily matching the other man's smile. 'People who can see *both* sides to this unfolding story.'

Chingford interlaced his fingers to form an arch. 'The problem we have with that is the top tiers of the administration are mostly Gaddafi family members. Seven of his sons, a daughter and various in-laws. Unless the ship is clearly sinking, *they* are not going to see *both* sides. You also have to consider what vile retribution the Colonel's regime will undoubtedly visit on any traitors. They'll certainly consider *themselves* before they think of talking to *you*, let alone openly change allegiance. Gaddafi's number two General Younis resigned last month and he sacked his right-hand man Abdullah Senussi a few days' ago – for brutality against the protesters, can you believe?'

'So who do you have in mind?' Parsons asked.

'Let me see. It'll be ones who *aren't* family. The defence minister, but he isn't going to accept defeat yet. Head of the Revolutionary Committees or Head of the External Intelligence…No, I still don't see any of them…'

Parsons was suddenly impatient. 'So you think there is no hope of turning anyone?'

Chingford raised his hand in protest. 'Not at all. I'm suggesting that you look at the second tier,' he answered. 'People with special power and influence. People who may be looking for a safe way out, a way to feather their nests for an uncertain future.'

'Initially we'd settle for a radio interview.' Tremain reminded them of the modus operandi. 'Maybe drop a hint or two. See what's picked up.'

'I get it. Very wise,' Chingford replied. 'Don't underestimate the Arabs, especially those in power. They are very smart and very crafty. Most of them will be one step ahead of you all the way. In fact, I am thinking of one in particular.'

'And who would that be?' Parsons pressed.

'A very close personal friend of the Colonel,' Chingford replied, 'and his private security adviser. His name is Nazal Abu.'

Tremain was quick off the mark. 'He's on our radar. Department of Protocol. A senior position, I recall. He's actually a Qatari sheikh, but is regarded here as a regime loyalist.'

'True,' Chingford confirmed. 'Bit of a dark horse, enigmatic. He's been friends with Gaddafi for years, they're very close, but very different. Nazal is also very dangerous, a plotter and a planner.'

'Plotting and planning what?' Parsons pushed.

'Nazal's from a very rich family of devout Islamists.' Chingford said the words wearily. 'It's a miracle he never took holy orders. He hates all things American and he's obsessed with the Caliphate thing – a radical Muslim empire to run the Middle East or more.'

Parsons said, 'Didn't think Gaddafi was into all that?'

'Only half-heartedly, I'd say,' Chingford replied. 'Gaddafi's more into his own personality cult. I think Nazal once hoped his friend would be the great figurehead to lead the Caliphate…but he's probably given up on the idea by now.'

'So is Nazal connected with al-Qaeda and the like?' Parsons asked.

Chingford nodded. 'Almost certainly, but he'd never tell me that. Although we're closer than you might imagine – friends for twenty years – we still have a great divide between us. I'm still the infidel.'

The waiter arrived with a large tray of drinks.

When he'd gone, Chingford added, 'Nazal is connected with the Muslim Brotherhood in Egypt and all the other movements in this so-called "Arab Spring". I wouldn't be surprised to learn he's been helping to orchestrate it – creating power vacuums that he and his followers can exploit.'

'What about the Department of Protocol he runs?' Royce asked.

'Bit of a misnomer that,' Chingford replied. 'More like the Department of Deviance and Sexual Affairs.' He chuckled at his own joke, before continuing. 'Gaddafi uses sex as a power tool, for his own pleasure and for the control of others. He has a prodigious appetite for sex, girls or boys, women or men. When he's off his face on cocaine and Viagra, he doesn't care. Fuelled up, he'll happily fuck four people a day. I've seen him do it.'

Royce asked, 'Does Nazal actually run the Department?'

Chingford shook his head. 'Nazal sits on its governing committee. He's Gaddafi's personal eyes and ears, if you like, and he'll make sure the Guide's orders are carried out. And how.'

Parsons frowned. 'I don't quite follow.'

'Gaddafi controls his own regime largely through the Department of Protocol,' Chingford lowered his voice so that his audience had to strain to hear his whispered explanation. 'His fellow ministers, civil servants, diplomats and military officers all live in fear that their wives and daughters will be seized by him. Mostly women – but sometimes men – will be abused and then subjected to blackmail. To bend them to his will. This is an old-fashioned Arab culture. No one will ever talk about it.'

'I didn't quite realise that,' Tremain admitted.

Chingford added. 'It also extends to the wives of visiting heads of state and monarchs, especially those from Africa. He lures them with gifts of jewellery and money. He is charming, they are flattered. While their husbands are taken to inspect oil-fields or factories or hospitals by Libyan officials, Gaddafi will give their spouses whisky and drugs – cocaine or rohypnol – and then fuck them. It is videoed for blackmail. In part it is like the pagan rites of eating your opponents' heart and liver to steal his strength. Gaddafi just doesn't care if the husbands know or not. Because it works either way for him.'

Tremain said, 'We also have a name of Mabrouka on our files.'

'Provided by me, I expect.' Chingford gave a self-satisfied smile. 'She's known behind her back as Gaddafi's whore-in-chief. A plump and smug little woman who always dresses in plain clothes and a black veil. She started off as a victim like all the others. Then she realised she could turn it around to her own advantage. Do what she was told, then play Gaddafi at his own game by finding him younger, more attractive females and coercing them to give themselves to their Guide and his cohorts.

'Haven't seen her around recently. I wouldn't be surprised to find she's already fled to Paris, holed up in Fouquet's or some equally exotic hotel until she knows which direction this revolution is going.

'Mabrouka has risen to be responsible for the Department's recruitment of schoolgirls and University students – as well as members of the armed forces. Nearly half of Libyan soldiers are women.'

Seeff grinned widely at that. 'Including Gaddafi's famous bodyguards.'

'Ah,' Chingford said. 'The Amazons. Mabrouka has taught them what they can achieve if they apply themselves and sell their souls to Gaddafi, his sons and their friends. One in particular has virtually taken over from Mabrouka within the Amazons. Acts as her Number Two.'

'Who's that?' Parsons asked.

'Well, she calls herself Princess Ayana. Claims to be a part of Somalian tribal royalty.' Chingford laughed. 'I certainly wouldn't argue with her! Stands over six feet in her socks. Gorgeous-looking, but hard as nails.'

'What exactly does she do?' Royce asked.

'Well, she's a captain in the Amazons,' Chingford replied. 'Graduated from the Military Academy for Women. She's a favourite of both Gaddafi himself and Nazal Abu. Nowadays she virtually runs the Colonel's harem. She's learned a lot from Mabrouka.'

'Where is this harem?' Seeff asked with enthusiasm.

'Mainly underground within Gaddafi's fortified compound here in

Tripoli.'

Parsons nodded. 'You mean the Bab al-Azizia citadel?'

Chingford said, 'The one you really want to ask about all this, *she* is the one to talk to...' He indicated across the lobby to where a tall, slim woman in her early-thirties was leaving the restaurant alone. He added, 'Sharp young thing, working for the *Sunday News*. Jo Brampton.'

'Really?' Parsons murmured thoughtfully. 'We were talking to her earlier.'

'Well, she's trying to line up an interview with Princess Ayana,' Chingford said. 'Following up a lead I gave her.'

Brampton caught Chingford's eye, waved and sauntered across. He rose to his feet and kissed her on the cheek.

'Hi, Charlie.'

'Hallo, Jo. And how's my sexy scribe?'

'Still learning.'

'Fast, I bet.' He sidled up to her. "Got a kiss for your old Uncle Charlie?'

She gave him a peck on his whiskery cheek, removed his straying hand from her backside, and turned to the others. 'Hi, guys.'

'You were quick in the restaurant,' Parsons observed. 'Nothing you liked?'

'Not that, just power problems again tonight. No hot food in the kitchen, so just a spot of salad.'

'No Ambrose?' Seeff asked.

'He's just met a group of fellow Yanks. No stopping him. They're out-doing each other on stories.'

As Brampton sat down and lit a Sobranie, Chingford said, 'I was just telling Ollie here how you are reeling in Princess Ayana for an interview.'

Brampton scowled. 'That's very naughty of you, Charlie,' she scolded. 'We journalists have to be very independent and protective of our little scoops. Otherwise where would we be?'

Parsons said, 'It's my fault, Bram. Been putting Charlie under pressure for a lead.'

'You're BBC World Service, right?' she asked.

'For my sins. So any crumbs from your table...'

'Well, Ollie,' she replied with an edge to her voice. 'It's a bit premature, as she and I have only met briefly. Not done a proper interview yet. She is somewhat busy just now, as you might imagine. But if I get a story out, I'll happily pass on my lead.'

Royce laughed, 'You mean *after* your story's published in the *Sunday News*.'

She held his gaze for a moment. 'Oh, I do so like bright men.'

Always trying to score a point, Seeff chipped in with, '*We* are really very hard to find, that's true.'

'Anyway,' Parsons said, 'I'd be grateful of any little nuggets. We're not front end of the news, so there's no great hurry.'

'I promise I won't forget,' she replied.

The next day started early for Royce and Seeff.

Before breakfast they ran a full vehicle check on the Land Cruiser and the VW for fuel, air, water and lubrication. However unlikely the prospect, they routinely checked for the attachment of any bombs.

Then the two men explored the streets immediately surrounding the Golden Palms hotel, getting their bearings. A fairly wide and dusty two-lane carriageway ran past the front car-park, skirted by occasional shaggy palms. Beyond that, the neighbourhood of narrow streets comprised mostly two or three-storey apartment buildings squeezed together with a handful of individual, middle-class villas dividing them. There was a scattering of small cafés, offering street food and strong breakfast coffee. While some shopkeepers were opening for the morning trade, others had kept their metal shutters firmly locked.

Royce was aware that, for a country in the throes of revolution, it was eerily quiet, totally unlike the bedlam they had left behind in Benghazi.

Seeff sensed it too. 'People are expecting trouble,' he said. 'I can feel it in the air.'

They returned to join Parsons and Tremain for breakfast in the hotel restaurant. The power was back on in the kitchen and Royce indulged in scrambled egg, followed by his favourite fig jam on toast, washed down with French chicory coffee.

Tremain remained in their fifth floor room, which was to serve as a temporary ops centre, manning his radio and the satellite phone while the others were out exploring the city.

Using Sinbad and his son as guides, they toured as much of the city as they could in the two cars, making copious notes that would later be transferred onto simplified maps with reference points. They were fortunate that, unlike most of the media at the Golden Palms, they had their own transport and didn't have to rely on local taxi-drivers. Every fifteen minutes, Royce radioed in to the Ops Room to confirm their position and status. If there was any emergency, Tremain would at least have a clue of where to start looking for them.

There appeared to be far less traffic on the streets than usual, according to Sinbad, possibly because there were rumours of petrol shortages. Royce and Seeff took the opportunity to top-up their tanks and spare jerry-cans while the filling stations were still operating normally.

The only outward sign of conflict was at the eastern end of Tripoli in the township of Tjoura. It was a known area of anti-Gaddafi resentment, not least because it contained his very unpopular nuclear research facility. The roads were lined with Libyan Army tanks, armoured personnel carriers and trucks. Yet the streets were otherwise deserted. Tension hung in the air like a pending thunder storm, almost tangible.

An armed soldier flagged them down, looked at their visas and accreditation letters, and absently waved them on. His mind was on other things.

Parsons said, 'Let's take in Green Square on the way back to the hotel.'

Royce obliged, following Sinbad's highly erratic directions. The major landmark had originally been built as the colonial Piazza Italia, before it became the Independence under the Libyan monarchy and then Green Square after Gaddafi seized power.

'Ah,' Parsons said, 'at last! I was starting to believe there was no rebellion in Tripoli.'

'Looks like a demonstration,' Royce agreed, slowing up and pulling in to the side of the square.

Only a few days' earlier the square had been teeming with crowds of rebels, who were ruthlessly dispersed by Gaddafi government snipers firing from the rooftops. Live ammunition claimed several lives and injured many others. Now the crowd was smaller, perhaps only a few dozen people. They were chanting and carrying green flags and banners while foreign TV crews filmed them.

Suddenly Royce said, 'It's a pro-Gaddafi rally.'

Sinbad leaned forward from the back. 'And it is fake. Look!' He jabbed his finger.

A nondescript white van had pulled onto the pavement and soldiers were handing out placards and flags to the growing number of supporters who were disembarking from nearby buses. Another soldier was directing them where to go.

Parsons had seen enough. 'Let's get back.'

Once they had returned, Royce and Seeff spent the rest of the afternoon putting together "Spotted Maps" of Tripoli as a result of their trip around the city. These were highly simplified and stylistic maps similar to those famously used for the London Underground. Different roads were given simple numbers, letters or colours. Locations were allocated encrypted "references" that could be used in radio communications between cars and the Ops Centre. Numbered coloured stickers were used for road junctions. That enabled positions to be given over the radio as, for example, "I am between Red 5 and 6, and approaching Yellow 16" rather than complex street names and map co-ordinates. Not only did it simplify everything visually, it also prevented giving away locations over telephones or unsecured radio nets.

With the job done and photocopies made for everyone in the team, including Sinbad and Tareg, the two men went downstairs to the reception lounge.

They found the place in turmoil.

Gaddafi's minders had arrived in force. They were all men in smart suits and open necked shirts, but bulging armpits indicated some were packing hardware. It was as if the regime had suddenly discovered a nest of rats that was out of their control. Their spokesman was a short, balding man who had an irritated manner which even his fluent English couldn't hide.

As Royce and Seeff joined the two MI6 men at the zebra-skin sofas, the spokesman was addressing the audience of rebellious media hacks, most of whom had already sunk a couple of Gaddafi Sunrises. 'I must insist that you do not venture out again tonight,' he said, using extravagant hand gestures. 'It is for your own safety. If you are seen on the streets it will only incite violence amongst these people.'

'What people?' challenged a lone female voice.

Royce glanced sideways to where Jo Brampton was standing beside Bud Ambrose. She was wearing a light suede waistcoat over what he now realised was her simple signature blouse look. Her colourful silk scarf was worn over her hair as a *hijab*.

'Why, the rebels and *al-Qaeda* trouble makers, of course,' the spokesman replied. 'They are just looking for any excuse to riot and cause wanton mayhem.'

Royce wondered if, given her dark features, the spokesman thought she was from one of the Middle East newspapers. 'I've been out on the streets today,' Brampton replied. 'They are very quiet. There are no rebels. Everyone is hiding indoors.'

'Our Brother Guide's people are not hiding,' the spokesman retorted. 'They are just being careful. They do not want to provoke the rebels. You journalists of the world should learn by their example.'

'Perhaps,' Brampton replied defiantly, 'they are hiding indoors because they are afraid if they venture onto their own streets they will be shot by Government snipers again?'

'Attagirl!' Seeff murmured with a grin.

The spokesman turned away from her. 'That is a wicked lie put out by the rebels in Benghazi, who never even saw what happened. People in Tripoli, who are sane and not terrorists, love what our Brother Leader has done for our country.' He raised his hands in the manner of an imploring evangelist. 'That is why tomorrow we are laying on air-conditioned coaches for you. They are to take you to the city of Sirte to see just how popular our Brother Leader is amongst ordinary patriotic people. My men are setting up a desk in the foyer to take a note of your names and media organisations for the trip tomorrow. Make sure you have your seat booked. There will be refreshments provided.'

'Think we might pass on that!' someone from Turkish television news called out.

The spokesman paused. 'Of course, no one remaining here will be allowed out tomorrow without a Government advisor to help you. And they are in high demand at present – at the Rixos.'

'So we're going nowhere,' Ambrose grunted, his words sounding slightly slurred.

Brampton looked across the table to Royce as she let her *hijab* drop back down onto her shoulders. 'You know what this is all about, James?'

He smiled faintly. 'What d'you mean?'

'After Friday prayers tomorrow,' she replied, 'it'll all kick off. They're expecting big trouble here in Tripoli tomorrow. That's why they're bussing all the media big boys out to Sirte.'

'Gaddafi's birthplace,' Royce said.

'While the media's watching all Gaddafi's supporters parading in Sirte, the real story will be here.'

She dropped her shoulder bag onto one of the sofas and slipped off her waistcoat. 'It's hot in here. The fans aren't working.'

Royce said, 'There've been problems with the generator all day. Can I get you a drink?'

'Just fizzy water and fresh lemon juice would be nice. Thank you.'

As Royce beckoned the waiter and ordered two of the same, Ambrose joined them. He was unsteady on his feet and sat down heavily. 'You're looking especially gorgeous tonight, lady.' He was staring closely at her breasts. 'Nice to see the little girls want to play.'

Brampton was taken aback. 'For God's sake, Bud, are you drunk?'

'Might have had a couple of Sunrises. I can still see what I can see. You'd win a wet T-shirt compo with no water, no problem!'

Royce reached across and placed his hand on the American's forearm. 'Why don't you wind your neck in, Bud, there's a good boy.'

While Brampton hastily pulled her waistcoat back on, Seeff intervened swiftly to defuse the situation. 'Hey, Buzz, why don't you and I go and get a bite to eat in the restaurant. We can exchange yarns from Kabul. Don't want to keep upsetting your boss now, d'you?'

Ambrose shrugged. 'Yeah, okay. I just fancy a camel steak and fries,' he muttered as Seeff helped him to his feet and led him away.

'I'm sorry about that,' Royce said.

'No need for you to apologise,' Brampton answered, brushing a stray twist of hair from her forehead. 'I've got used to it since I was young. It's my own fault. I hate those T-shirt bras, worse than body armour.'

Royce said, 'It's still no excuse.'

'Has he gone?' the woman's voice asked from behind the nearby glass pillar. Royce thought he detected a slight New Zealand accent.

'You're safe,' Brampton confirmed. 'Stefan's taken him to supper – on a short leash.'

Rachel Starr from TV-Global stepped out from behind the pillar and sat down with them. 'I can't believe what he said to you. I certainly made a mistake getting involved with him. Thought he was a bit of a hunk at first. He's been pestering me all evening. Had to hide in the Ladies.'

'He'll be gone for a good half-hour,' Brampton said. 'Hopefully he'll go to bed then. I'll need him up and ready tomorrow morning.'

'Are you going to Sirte on the coach?' Starr asked.

'No, are you?'

'I thought I might as well if we're not allowed out on our own in Tripoli.'

'What does your own security guy say?' Brampton asked. 'The Frenchman.'

'His name's Yves,' Starr replied. 'He's ex-French Foreign Legion. Nothing frightens him. He'll do whatever I ask.'

'The thing is,' Brampton began, lowering her voice. 'When trouble starts big time here, all the media will be high and dry in Sirte.'

Starr frowned. 'But we won't be allowed out.'

For the first time Royce noticed a small scar like a dimple on Brampton's right cheek, that deepened when she smiled. 'Where there's a will.' She tapped the side of her nose. 'Besides, I've heard that trusted Libyan minders are thin on the ground and they're very stretched. Several have defected to the rebels. Most will be needed at the Rixos and the Corinthia tomorrow, so they'll hardly bother with the overflow media dregs like us.'

Royce had been listening carefully. 'May I suggest you don't flag yourself up as troublemakers to the Gaddafi minders.'

Brampton turned to him. 'I'm sorry?'

'Go and book yourselves on for the coach trip now. At the last minute tomorrow, don't turn up. Get Ambrose and Yves to leave polite excuses on your behalf. Migraine etcetera. They won't have time to go looking for you, but they won't be too alarmed either.'

'That's cool,' Starr said.

'I just hope it works,' Brampton replied, 'because I've got my interview with Princess Ayana tomorrow.'

Royce's suggested ploy worked. Three coaches pulled up outside a foyer packed with journalists and TV news crews at seven-thirty. It was bedlam as everyone fought for a seat. Ambrose and Starr's French guardian made excuses to Gaddafi's minders for their respective clients, one with "ladies' problems" and the other with a terrible migraine.

Only one plump and elderly armed minder was left to guard the front entrance of the Golden Palms. He parked himself on a plastic patio chair by the door and settled in for a long shift with a copy of the *al-Jadida* weekly. He would bark angrily at anyone who ventured near the revolving doors.

The man was unaware that eight people were lingering expectantly over pots of coffee in the restaurant, awaiting word by radio from Royce, who was reading a trashy paperback in the foyer. At ten o'clock the minder made his way to the Gents' to relieve himself. He had barely closed the door behind him when there was a rush towards the hotel entrance. With Tremain again remaining behind to man their Ops Room, Royce's group headed to the car park; Brampton and Starr made their way towards the nearby rank of black-and-white taxis with their respective close protection men.

Ollie Parsons had a mission for the day. It was to have a meeting with a senior military figure who had been "groomed" by an MI6 junior culture minister at the British Embassy. With rank of brigadier, Cinti Hassan was considered to be a Gaddafi loyalist, although he had let it be known he would consider jumping ship with his wife and family for the right inducements.

Cinti was apparently in charge of a vast walled compound in Zawiya that housed everything that might be needed for an escape from the country by Gaddafi and his inner coterie. Technically part of 32 Brigade, it secreted rows and rows of vehicles, warehouses of weapons, missiles and ammunition, and storage tanks of fuel.

Although the town was only some thirty miles west of Tripoli on the coastal route to adjoining Tunisia, there were many checkpoints along the road. The place was of strategic importance because it hosted two vast oil refineries and had recently become a battlefield between rebels and Gaddafi troops. Most of the traffic was coming the other way, civilians trying to escape the recent fighting.

At the first few army road blocks, their two cars were waved through with scarcely a second glance at visas and permission papers. But as they got closer to the outer suburbs of Zawiya, they came under more intense scrutiny. Sinbad changed vehicles to travel in the first with Royce and did most of the talking. The words "BBC World Service" seemed to carry a lot of persuasive weight with the solemn-faced soldiers. Even Sinbad's engaging charm rarely brought a smile to any of their faces.

On the outskirts Parsons made another call to Cinti Hassan and confirmed the RV. The team's satellite Thuraya mobile phones nearly always worked, but they couldn't guarantee others on terrestrial networks would be able to call them back.

They found themselves in the town centre and, from having experienced almost deserted streets, they were now surrounded now by a sea of moving humanity. Martyrs' Square was milling with thousands of people. Mostly they were young, wearing T-shirts and jeans in the clammy afternoon heat. The old Libyan tricolour was being waved. These were the rebels. Somehow they'd retaken the town, yet very few of them appeared to be armed.

As Royce drove slowly past, the student rebels waved and shouted on seeing the "TV" signs on the vehicle's bonnet and doors. Royce located the side street they were looking for and then escorted Parsons to his secret RV. It was a lowly café, where Cinti was waiting for them in a back room.

The man , a handsome fifty-year old, was clearly uncomfortable in his surroundings. He glared at the café owner and the café owner glared back, as he wiped down the tables.

Cinti dare not wear his brigadier's uniform for their meeting. But even the immaculately-pressed white *dishdasha* could not disguise his distinctive military bearing, his smartly-hedged, dense grey hair and formal beard. He was clearly from local noble Arab stock, from Sirte where Gaddafi had grown up, but on a totally different social level.

Cinti's father had been a land-owner. His son had been educated in Eton and France, had historical family investments in America. As a smart young officer in the Libyan Army, Cinti had been savvy enough to declare allegiance to Gaddafi. His success and promotion would be assured.

And Gaddafi had sealed the deal by anally fucking Cinti's wife after drugging her and plying her with alcohol and gifts of extravagant jewellery. A record of her pain and pleasure was secretly filmed on tape for posterity. And guarantee of Cinti's perpetual allegiance.

Parsons knew all this because it was duly recorded on Chingford Charlie's file at Vauxhall Cross. Their agent had been a personal witness, sitting behind a two-way mirror, laughing and quaffing champagne with Gaddafi's closest friends while the woman was violated.

Parsons made no mention that he was aware of anything untoward as he emphasised to Cinti how important it was for him to stay committed to Parsons' plan.

'Hassan, I do so appreciate your worries just now.'

Cinti glanced towards the door, concerned the café owner may be close enough to overhear. 'I do not worry if I leave now. I have told my wife and my children to pack. I have decided. I am ready to leave. Maybe you land a Royal Navy helicopter for us, I can give you a safe landing-zone. I will tell you everything.'

Parsons smiled. 'You've already told us everything, Hassan. That's why we are friends.'

Cinti shook his head. 'It is over for Gaddafi. I need out now before it is discovered that I help you. My fellow officers are not stupid. They see things, have suspicions.'

Parsons reassured the man by closing his palm over Cinti's fist that was clenched on the table. 'We need you to hold firm, Hassan. Because we know that *you* are the tipping point, and only you. When the regime is finished, Gaddafi himself or one of his sons will come here and we will know it's the end. Your outfit is his last resort, his final reserve. To fight a last stand or to flee. Either way, we need you here – in place to stop him. That is why we are paying you.'

'I want to leave.'

'We need you here until the end.'

'Your man from the embassy promised -'

'I'm sure he didn't. That's not how it works. We *need* you *here* – in situ.' Parsons relaxed his expression and forced a smile. 'Don't worry, old son. You and your family will be safe. We'll look after you.'

Royce was waiting outside as Parsons left the café minus a wad of dollar notes and a satellite mobile phone so that their "agent" could be safely and reliably contacted again in the future.

The return journey was even slower than the one to get there. Government troops had been reinforced on the roadblocks, clearly under orders to lock-down Zawiya and contain its rebellious inhabitants. Everyone leaving was under suspicion and was questioned intently. Guns were pointed, threats made. Gaddafi loyalists were increasingly nervous. Royce's team were well treated as "invited media" compared to fleeing Libyans who had their cars and contents ransacked and scattered across the road during the frenetic searches for weapons or army deserters.

The fast tropical twilight was closing in over the cityscape as they reached Tripoli.

There was no Gaddafi minder on the door now, but they were met at the hotel entrance by Rachel Starr from TV-Global. She was distraught. 'James, is she with you?'

'Sorry?' He was confused. 'Who?'

'Bram. Is she with you?'

'No. You set off together with her this morning. We've been in Zawiya all day.'

'You haven't heard then? Bram was right. There was trouble in Tjoura in the eastern suburbs. Rebels took to the streets in their hundreds after Friday prayers. The army used tear-gas and snipers. Dozens were killed.'

'You got separated?' Royce guessed.

The small blonde nodded. 'Yes. But I thought she should be back here by now.'

'Don't panic,' Seeff said soothingly. 'That one can look after herself _'

'Oh, my God!' Starr could see over the South African's shoulder.

Royce turned. Brampton was limping in through the revolving doors. She'd lost a shoe and her clothes were covered in blood, some of it glued to and dripping from her matted black hair.

'Help!' she called plaintively. 'Can somebody help me? Bud has been shot.'

6

HAREM MISTRESS

Bud Ambrose was outside in a battered Mercedes taxi.

Royce opened the rear door to find the man sprawled across the cracked leather seats. He was unconscious with his mouth open and blood pulsing from a stomach wound. The driver stood nearby, screaming in Arabic and gesticulating wildly.

'I tried lifting him out,' Brampton gasped. 'He's too heavy.'

'What happened to him?'

'We were at a roadblock. Bud got into an argument, flashed that gun of his and the soldier just shot him. Point blank.'

'What sort of weapon – rifle or pistol?'

'An automatic. A 9mm, I think.'

Royce got one foot inside the taxi and leaned forward. As he tried to check the American's breathing and pulse, he said, 'A low-velocity round, but still bad enough. He needs a hospital – now.'

The driver appeared to understand that. 'No, no!' he said in broken English. 'I not take him! Too dangerous! Get him out my taxi!'

Seeff arrived on the scene. 'Need a hand, Rollo?

'Let's get Bud indoors,' Royce said. 'Trauma injury. Gunshot to the stomach.'

'Our medical kit's just in the foyer,' the South African reminded.

The two men struggled to get Ambrose out of the car and up the hotel steps while Brampton thrust a handful of dinar notes into the taxi-driver's outstretched palm.

Once through the doors, they laid the American out on the marble floor in a secluded alcove and raised his feet on cushions to keep the man's blood supply around his vital organs. Seeff dragged over their main medical bergen from where he'd dumped it by the entrance. He unzipped it. Rachel Starr and assorted members of the press pack gathered around. Irritatingly video cameras were raised and photo flashlights started popping. Someone was actually doing a piece to camera, using the dramatic scene as a backdrop.

Royce snapped on a pair of thin examination gloves and began a preliminary check of the entry and exit wounds

'Will he be alright?' Brampton pressed.

'If we can get him to a hospital fast, he might survive.'

Seeff slapped the American's cheeks gently but firmly. 'C'mon, Buzz, wakey-wakey. Speak to me.'

Royce hastily applied QuikClot granules to soak up the blood and stabilise the wounds before applying adhesive bandages.

Parsons turned to Brampton. 'How'd all this happen?'

'At a road block,' she replied. 'I was on my way to interview Princess Ayana.'

Parsons' interest was obvious. 'But you didn't actually make it?'

'No, she's probably still waiting for me to turn up.'

Seeff was still trying to rouse Ambrose. 'C'mon, Buzz, open your eyes. Speak to me.'

At last the American's eyes flickered open. His lips were parched, a word drying up before it left his mouth. 'Stef..?'

'Thank God,' Brampton breathed.

'Yeah,' Seeff said enthusiastically. 'It's Stefan, your South African chum. Your best mate.'

'Wa...Water.'

'Just wet your mouth, mate,' Seeff said, unscrewing the cap of his water bottle. 'Don't drink it.'

Parsons watched on as Royce completed his initial task, giving the American a syrette shot of morphine. 'James, I can take Bud to the hospital with Stefan. We'll use the Land Cruiser.'

Royce stood up. 'What? I should be doing that.'

'Stefan's a trained medic, just like you. We'll be fine.' He smiled his winning smile. 'I need a favour.'

'What's that?'

'Take the VW. Drive Bram to her meeting with Princess Ayana. Keep an eye on her.'

Royce glared at him. 'I trust you are joking?'

'I've never been more serious.'

'There's been fighting on the streets all afternoon.' Royce tilted his head, listening. 'And unless those are cars backfiring, it's still going on. Bud's been shot. No one should be going outside until morning. I'll do the hospital run with Stefan – but only because Bud's condition is life-threatening.'

The smile on Parson's face faded quickly. 'You'll take Bram to her appointment, because that is an order.'

Brampton suddenly realised what they were talking about. 'No, Ollie, that's too much of an imposition. I've already decided to take a taxi. I know one of the drivers on the rank.'

Rachel Starr overheard her. 'You can't do it, Bram,' she warned. 'That would be madness.'

'It's a bad idea,' Royce agreed.

'James will take you,' Parsons insisted.

She turned on him. 'I don't want him to. Bud nearly got us both killed today. I don't *need* a bodyguard. I'm a press reporter, we manage perfectly well around the world without these macho heavies.'

'And more of us are getting killed and injured,' Starr added. 'Don't look a gift horse in the mouth, Bram. This place is dangerous.'

Royce changed his mind. 'If Stefan's taking care of Bud, I'd be happy to help. Where are you meeting Princess Ayana?'

'She's at a villa in the New City district,' Brampton replied. 'Just to the east of Green Square.'

Royce recalled their thorough recce and mapping of the capital. 'So not *so* new,' he said. 'Developed in the Italian colonial era.'

'Are you sure you don't mind?' Brampton asked.

'Positive. Just give me a second.' He got on the walkie-talkie to Tremain. 'Iain, there've been a couple of developments. I want you to stay in the Ops Room a bit longer. Ollie and Stefan are taking Bud Ambrose to the hospital. He's got a bad stomach wound. I'm going with Bram to an interview she's got lined up.' He gave him the address and switched off.

As Seeff and Parsons set about getting Ambrose out to the car, Royce turned to Brampton. 'You lost a shoe. Can you go and get something sensible for your feet. Not high heels or sandals.'

She gave him a bemused look. 'I'll see what I can do.'

When she'd gone, Royce turned to Parsons. 'I don't understand you, Ollie. Bram may be a good journalist, but she's not part of our team.'

Parsons had the smile of a man who knew what others didn't. 'That's what both you and she think, James. I'll explain when we have a moment.'

Royce was waiting for her with Sinbad, who he had decided might be useful to join them on their mission. But the man had also brought his son Tareg with him.

When Royce protested, Sinbad replied, 'The boy is getting bored stuck in our room. He needs to see our country and know what is happening. You are sounding like his mother.'

Just after Parsons and Seeff had left with Ambrose, Brampton returned wearing a black leather biker jacket, jingling with zips and chains, scarf, black denim drainpipes and aggressive storm-trooper boots.

'Better?' she asked mischievously, pointing to her feet..

'You look very scary lady,' Sinbad offered.

Royce couldn't resist a smile. 'I wouldn't want to cross you,' he agreed.

She replied flatly, 'So, perfect for the mean streets of Tripoli.'

On their way to the parked VW, Royce discovered that the black leather wasn't just for show. Brampton did actually share his enthusiasm for motorcycles. She owned a Triumph back in London, while he was waiting for his early retirement later that year before deciding which bike to invest in.

He threw the ignition on the VW. To his surprise it stuttered and stalled. He tried again. Again the engine tried to come alive, croaked, and failed.

Brampton cursed. 'Oh, of all things!'

'It was fine earlier,' Royce said. 'She's been sweet as a nut.'

'The dust,' Sinbad declared. 'Always it is the dust. Allah's little joke on us. The fine sand gets everywhere.'

Royce tried again. Again the engine spluttered, and then fired. There were a couple of uneven beats and then it settled into a rhythm.

'See,' Tareg said. 'Allah is smiling on us tonight.'

Under her breath, Brampton said, 'Sure, now that He's had his laugh at our expense.'

The streets of Tripoli were now almost deserted, but not quite. As they followed Sinbad's directions, every now and again they came across groups of civilians, mostly young, lurking in the shadows or on street corners. Sometimes rifles were in evidence, sometimes even rocket launchers. These were rebel fighters probing the strength of government defences in the city. Some districts were pro-Gaddafi, others anti.

Brampton wore her headscarf and sat in the back with Tareg while Royce drove, trying to follow Sinbad's haphazard directions from the front passenger seat.

They took another corner and ran straight into an army roadblock. There were armoured personnel carriers parked sideways-on to form a chicane. The soldiers were unkempt and unshaven in uniforms that looked as if they hadn't been washed in weeks. They appeared very on edge.

'This is where Bud and I were stopped.' Brampton peered out the window. 'Where he was shot.'

'Can you see the soldier who shot him?'

'I don't think so.'

Royce radioed an update of their position and the developing situation to Tremain back in the Ops Room.

As the VW slowed gently to a halt, a Libyan lieutenant rapped on the driver's window.

'I deal with this,' Sinbad announced and leapt from the car, waving a piece of paper. As the soldier stepped back to listen to what he was saying, Royce wound down his window.

He just managed to follow the exchange in Arabic. 'We are from the BBC World Service,' Sinbad was saying. 'We are going to interview an important Government person.'

'Who?'

'It is a secret.'

'No one goes out of hotels without escort from Ministry of Information.'

'I am Ministry of Information.' He again waved his sheet of paper.

'You?'

'Yes. You can telephone my boss if you don't believe me.'

'Won't the office be closed?'

'Probably.'

Two more cars had joined the queue behind them. The lieutenant peered into the vehicle, then lost patience. 'You can go.'

Smiling widely, Sinbad scrambled back into his seat and Royce pressed down on the gas, thankful to be on their way.

'What's that paper you have?' he asked.

Sinbad waved it in front of him. 'A letter of authority from Ministry of Information. ID. I am official minder for the media.'

'It's a photocopy.'

'Yes. So?'

'The picture – it isn't you.'

'It is before I shave off my beard.'

Tareg piped up from the back. 'My Dad is Bright Spark – just like his son.'

Their shared humour was short-lived.

They were entering a small square. A barricade of wrecked cars, old bedsteads, wooden pallets, corrugated iron and lorry tyres extended across it with "technical" pick-up conversions mounted with heavy machine guns guarding each end. Some backstreet seamstresses were making a small fortune because the old pre-Gaddafi tricolour was flying from broomsticks and any other makeshift flagpole that the rebels could find. Young fighters were everywhere, mostly wearing T-shirts and jeans, but many sporting bandanas that gave them a look of piratical uniformity. One or two wore remnants of army fatigues, suggesting a strong number of defectors. This time most of the men were armed, although a lot did not look too familiar with the weapons they carried. There was the occasional motorcycle bone dome in evidence, but no one enjoyed the luxury of the flak jackets and helmets that were available to Royce's team.

One man in black trousers and a white shirt stepped forward, raising his left hand in a signal for them to stop. In his right he held a lowered AK47.

'I'll handle this one,' Royce said, winding down the window.

The man had a neat haircut and short trimmed beard. '*Salam.*'

'D'you speak English?' Royce asked.

'A little. I am a doctor.' He indicated the big "TV" marker on the bonnet. 'You are television crew?'

'BBC,' Royce replied. 'We have an appointment for an interview in the New City district.'

'It may be dangerous,' the man replied. 'There is much fighting in Tripoli tonight.'

'Will you allow us to risk it?'

'But, of course. The story of our struggle must be told.'

Brampton leaned forward from the rear of the car. 'Doctor, would you allow me to interview you on our return in an hour or so?'

'But, of course. When you pass through next time, just ask for Dr Jaralla.' The soft brown eyes hardened a fraction. 'But this is now the front-line. We do not know where the nearest Government troops are. We are sending out scouts.'

Royce said, 'They're about three blocks from the direction we've just come.'

'Are they heavily equipped?'

'A couple of APCs.'

Dr Jaralla looked relieved. 'We can deal with them. No tanks?'

'No tanks,' Royce assured. 'Unless they were waiting for reinforcements.'

'You go now.' The doctor stepped back to wave them through. 'I will see you later, Mr BBC.'

They drove through the narrow gap in the barricade and on into the New City district. The villa was fairly easy to locate, set back from the main dusty thoroughfare. Its faded pink compound walls were topped with terracotta tiles and then spoiled by spirals of razor wire. There was nobody about as Brampton climbed out and pressed the intercom by the steel double gates. She answered the harsh female voice, 'Hallo, it's Jo Brampton here. I'm late for an appointment with Princess Ayana. Please offer my most sincere apologies.'

'Wait,' the voice snapped back.

Brampton returned to the VW as the automatic gates in front of them slid open. Two armed female soldiers were standing inside, dressed in distinctive green and black camouflaged fatigues and dark *hijab* headdresses. Neither smiled and both carried AK47s. They looked as though they knew how to use them. One beckoned Royce to drive in and onto the short, palm-fringed drive, which led to an Italian colonial-style villa. There were ornate arches, wrought-iron balconies for many of the rooms and a distinctive stone balustrade surrounding the flat roof.

Another female soldier, petite with a cheerful face and welcoming smile, trotted down the stone-tiled steps to greet them. 'Hallo, you are Jo Brampton?'

They shook hands. Brampton said, 'I am *so* sorry. We were sent back at a roadblock. I tried calling but -'

'I think the phones are down. Never mind.' She looked at Royce and the others. 'And these people are…?'

'My minder James and Sinbad is an– er – Ministry of Information escort.'

'Really?'

'And his son.'

'Little Sinbad?' Another laugh. 'That is fine. My name is Amal. Please follow me.'

She led the way up the steps, through glossy spray-painted double doors and into a marble-floored corridor lit by exquisite glass drop chandeliers. One of the many side doors opened onto a large reception room filled with dusty rubber plants and leather club chairs formed in a circle around a rosewood coffee table. The place smelled of stale air and dust.

Amal showed them in. 'Make yourselves comfortable while I tell Ayana you have arrived. I think she is taking a shower.'

She returned minutes later and promised to bring back refreshments for the others, after first leading Brampton down the corridor towards a door at the far end.

Steam was clearing as they entered the luxurious bathroom with gleaming beige and jade marble slab-tiles, engraved mirrors and gold-plated taps.

A very cultured voice came from behind the glass front of the large shower unit. 'Miss Brampton, I shall be with you in a moment. Take a seat.' It was English spoken with a distinctly Italian accent.

'No hurry,' Brampton replied absently. 'I am so sorry to be late.'

Almost suffocating in the humidity, she slipped off her leather jacket before sitting on the fitted wooden bench.

Ayana emerged wrapped in only a thick white towel. It emphasised the sharp contrast with her ebony skin that gleamed in the bathroom spotlights. She was tall, almost six feet, and exquisitely beautiful. Her hair was even darker than Brampton's; it had been straightened with tongs and was now pinned up.

Brampton took in the honed arms and legs of someone who worked-out hard and regularly. The woman's cheekbones were high and her dark eyes fathomless.

Her handshake was bone-crushingly strong. 'So you are Jo Brampton from the *Sunday News* in the UK?'

'Yes.' Brampton set up the small tape-recorder beside her on the bench. 'I hope it is alright to use this? I want to be accurate.'

'It is fine,' Ayana replied. 'I am told your car has "TV" written on it.'

'We had to borrow it from another media outfit,' Brampton explained. She added with a straight face, 'Ours is a very popular Sunday tabloid.'

'I haven't heard of it.'

'You soon will with scoops like this.'

Ayana threw back her head and laughed loudly. 'Very good! Mr Chingford said you had a sense of humour. But also that you are practical...So you have the money?'

Brampton dipped into her shoulder bag and extracted a clear plastic envelope. 'Three hundred US dollars.' She placed it on the bench beside her. 'And there could be more if we talk more. I am also freelance, so we can have other arrangements, too.'

'And my interview will be unattributed – as we agreed?'

'If you agree, your revelations will be those of "a member of the Colonel's trusted inner circle". No other hint as to your job or gender.'

'That is fine.'

'You are not concerned about repercussions?' Brampton asked.

'You see what is happening all over North Africa,' Ayana replied. 'Our Leader Guide thinks he will survive, I do not. He is totally delusional, his mind addled with cocaine and other drugs. I am making plans. I do not intend to be here when his regime falls.'

'You will go home?'

Ayana stared at her as though she was mad. 'Home? I have no home. I was born in Somalia. Yes, I have friends in England and Italy, but no family or place to live. I am on my own.'

'But your roots are in Somalia,' Brampton echoed. 'You wouldn't want to return?'

Ayana sighed and Brampton thought she could read the pain of the memories etched in the expression on the woman's face. 'My father was a tribal chief, a warlord,' she said slowly. 'He was a very violent man, who drove my mother to madness. He beat her frequently. Some believe the meaning of Somalia is *soo maal*. That is translated as "go and milk". That gave my mother the crazy notion that women should milk their men to keep them peaceable. To drain them of their testosterone, of their natural male aggression. It is what my sister and I were taught to do from an early age without question. My father, my brother, indeed any male who visited the house. Milk them like a cow.' She smiled thinly and corrected herself. 'Or rather bull.'

'That's horrible,' Brampton said.

Ayana almost seemed to delight in the reaction her words generated. 'We had a *lot* of visitors. Yet my mother believed her theory worked, my father beat her less frequently.'

Brampton raised an eyebrow and asked, 'So how did you end up here?'

'My father visited Tripoli on some sort of diplomatic mission with other Somalian leaders in 1999. I had just turned sixteen and he took me along with him. I met Muammar Gaddafi. He was charming, old and handsome in a gnarled sort of way.' She shut her eyes momentarily, remembering. 'Everyone revered him. To me he seemed like a god. He told me to call him Papa.'

'And did you?'

'Of course.' Ayana seemed surprised she had even asked. 'I hated my own father.'

'What happened?'

'What always happens when Muammar takes a shine to you.' She sighed. 'My father was paid off and left for Somalia without me. The people from the Department of Protocol collected me from the hotel where we were staying. It was a very smart and luxurious car with smoked glass windows.

'That evening his harem people had me showered and shaved and given expensive white underwear. I was taken to his underground boudoir where he was waiting for me, naked, sprawled on a bed with silk sheets.'

'Just like that?'

'Just like that,' Ayana answered. 'I knew exactly what to do and had no hesitation. I remember the look on his face. Shock almost, pleasant surprise. Nowadays, we have to instruct the girls, show them porn videos. I was quickly one of his favourites, because I would do anything he asked. And quickly I learned because of that I could get anything *I* wanted from him.'

'Such as?'

Ayana shrugged. 'The best private tutors to make up for my poor childhood education. Then college at Cheltenham in England and finishing school in Milan. I returned here and worked with Madame Mabrouka, the chief procurer for his harem. I learned a lot from her, how to manipulate Muammar Gaddafi himself, how to work his system. To do whatever he wanted, or his sons…but always for the rewards that *I* wanted.'

'You also went to the Military Academy for Women?' Brampton pressed.

'Of course. I wanted to be one of his elite personal guard. The Amazons, as foreigners like to mock. I needed to know how the military worked, and how to make myself strong, how to defend myself.'

'I was a soldier once,' Brampton offered on impulse.

Ayana hesitated, looking her up and down. 'I can believe that.'

'For a few years. I wanted to join Special Forces, but I failed selection.'

'Shame.' After a thoughtful pause, Ayana said, 'He would like you.'

'Who would?'

'Gaddafi, he would like you.' Ayana looked her up and down again. 'He would like those. Forgive me, I notice…You wear a soft bra?'

'I'm only small. Thirty four A.'

Ayana laughed. 'Your nipples are not prominent like mine, but they are very alert. Sensitive.'

Brampton was taken aback, reminded suddenly of Bud's drunken outburst at the hotel.

Ayana unknotted the towel at her chest and let it slide slowly to her ankles. It was like unveiling a statue in flawless black marble. Brampton found herself staring, mersmerised. 'You see,' Ayana said, 'provocative. Maumer is never happier than when tormenting them.'

'You don't mind?'

'I have learned to like it.' Ayana realised she had to explain more. 'It is an exquisite, erotic pain. Here slaves are taught to associate that pain with pleasure, like training an animal.'

Brampton was reminded of her outrageous Russian ballerina friend Anoushka, who loved to shock. The journalist's eyes were drawn to the large silver stud in Ayana's navel, a cut diamond surrounded by glittering smaller stones.

'That's beautiful,' Brampton murmured.

'A personal gift from President Mugabe of Zimbabwe,' Ayana replied flatly. 'And ask no more.'

With that, she stepped behind a screen and pulled down the smartly-ironed battle fatigues that had been draped over the top of it.

The voice asked abruptly, 'You want to meet Gaddafi?'

That threw Brampton for a second. She hesitated. 'Yes, of course. Who wouldn't?'

'What would you *do* for a story, Miss Brampton? How far would *you* go to get what you want?'

Brampton realised it was a wind-up. 'I suspect not as far as you would.'

Ayana enjoyed that and laughed. 'When I next see Muammar, I will ask him if he will give you an interview…a special favour for me.'

'Thank you.'

'And I will tell you what you will find when you meet him,' Ayana continued from behind the screen. 'He is no longer handsome, but he still has great charm. He has a wife called Safia, whom he hardly ever sees nowadays. He smokes Marlboro Lights and Slims. He regularly snorts cocaine and has several Viagra tablets every day, way above the prescribed limits.'

'So his legendary virility isn't natural?' Brampton asked.

'It has a little help from Mr Pfizer, I believe.' Ayana reappeared, wearing her uniform, doing up the buttons of her shirt. 'But I believe he would still do well without it. Oh, and he has a loathing of black underwear, but then he can be intrigued by girls who dare to defy him.'

'Does he like music?'

'His favourite is a Tunisian singer called Nawal Ghachem. He loves her voice and will have his harem girls dance naked in front of him to her songs. You will notice that he has never allowed any entertainer to become a major celebrity here during his entire rule of this country. He would see that as a threat.'

'How many girls does he have in this harem of his?'

'It varies. Sometimes up to a couple of dozen, some in training, some away on holiday or at college.' Ayana paused. 'He is very distracted at the moment, of course. Some girls have been sent home to their villages or abroad.'

'He expects to be defeated by the rebels?'

Ayana laughed. 'I don't think that has *ever* crossed his mind – ' She hesitated. 'I am thinking, perhaps you would like to meet a lady of his harem?'

'Where?'

'Here. In our basement.'

'In your villa?'

'Actually, this is not *my* villa.' Ayana smiled. 'It belongs to Nazal Abu.'

'*Really?*'

'Ah, you have heard of him?'

'Of course, he is Colonel Gaddafi's personal security advisor.'

'And his closest and most trusted friend,' Ayana added. 'He is also in overall charge of this aspect of Muammar's private life. Mr Nazal has someone in our cellar, someone I am training to serve our dear Guide Leader properly.'

'I'd like to meet her very much,' Brampton replied.

Ayana stroked her chin. 'Before I take you downstairs, I think another three hundred dollars would be fair.'

7

SLIPPING THE LEASH

'Nice,' Ayana observed as Brampton picked up her black leather jacket from the seat in the bathroom. 'You have dark tastes.'

'Meaning?'

Ayana smiled. 'Leather and chains.'

'Just fashion,' Brampton replied, mildly irritated at any insinuation. 'I have a motorcycle back in London.'

'That is cool.'

Following Ayana into the corridor, Brampton was aware of the distant noise. 'Gunfire,' she murmured. 'Quite close.'

'The rebels will be testing the army's front line,' Ayana replied, unbothered. 'Looking for weaknesses.'

'What's that noise? Howling?'

'Just the dogs in the backyard,' Ayana replied. 'Pharoah and Cerberus. Huge Tosa Inus. But gunfire or thunder turns them into puppies. Just like most men.'

She turned right down a short passageway. At the end was a closed, metal-studded timber door with a heavy-duty key in the lock.

At that moment the front door of the house swung open and the petite soldier called Amal rushed in. 'Ayana, it is Mr Nazal returned,' she said in Arabic.

The princess looked more irritated than concerned. 'He said he wouldn't be back tonight.'

Amal giggled. 'Typical man, you can never trust them.' She looked back out of the main door. 'He is getting out of the car now.'

Ayana turned to Brampton. 'That door leads to the basement. When you come out, be sure to lock the door after you.'

'What about Mr Nazal? Will he mind me talking to someone in the cellar.'

'He won't know.' She indicated the locked door. 'Go now. I will keep Abu distracted.'

Turning sharply on her heel, Ayana strode down the corridor to greet the middle-aged Arab at the door. He was tall and handsome, impeccably dressed in a suit of silver grey silk that blended perfectly with his shock of white hair and distinguished inky black eyebrows and goatee beard.

While Ayana was throwing her arms around his neck and showering him with kisses, Brampton turned the key in the cellar door and slipped inside and into darkness. She felt around the cool brick walls with her fingers until she found a light switch. When she threw it, a single bulb flickered on down below. It illuminated the wooden steps leading down and a single camp-bed in the circle of light.

A teenaged girl sat on the edge of the mattress wearing a red satin dressing-gown, her hands bound together with plastic ties behind her back. Brampton was shocked to see that she had been blindfolded. Her long black hair was straggly and unwashed.

She looked up, aware that someone had turned the light on. There was alarm in her voice as she asked a question in Arabic. 'Hallo, who is that?'

Brampton began to descend the steps. 'Don't worry,' she replied, her pronunciation less than perfect. 'There is nothing to worry about.'

As she reached the stone floor, Brampton could see the large timber star-shaped cross of St. Andrew embedded in the far wall, a metal manacle hanging from each arm. This wasn't about sex, Brampton thought, this was about power and control.

There was a sudden realisation in the girl's voice, an uncertainty. 'You are not Ayana?'

'No, I am a visitor. Do you speak English?'

The girl seemed to relax a little. 'Some, yes. I had Grade B plus at school.' Almost immediately, the anxiety in her voice returned. 'Is Mr Nazal with you?'

'No. I am alone.'

'*Allah akbur,*' the girl murmured.

As Brampton neared the bed, she reached for the blindfold. 'Let me help you.'

The teenager drew back. 'What are you doing?' she demanded.

'I was going to remove your blindfold.'

'It is not allowed. Not without permission.'

'From whom?'

'Princess Ayana.'

Brampton thought quickly. 'Ayana told me I could remove it,' she lied.

The girl breathed a sigh of relief. 'Then, thank you.' As Brampton untied the knot, the captive blinked against the sudden influx of light. Her eyes were a beautiful sable colour but sunken with exhaustion, and her mascara had run.

'And those handcuffs,' Brampton added, fishing in her shoulder bag. 'Here somewhere...' she muttered, before producing the red Swiss Army pen-knife. 'I was a Girl Guide in England, always prepared.'

Without hesitation, Brampton opened the main blade and sliced through the plastic ties.

The girl moved her arms painfully around to the front of her body and massaged her wrists. 'Who exactly are you?' she asked. 'Must I make sex with you?'

Brampton was taken aback. 'No, of course not. My name is Jo Brampton. I am a journalist from Britain. And what is your name?'

'I am Tabina. Tabina Salim. What do you want with me?'

'To talk. I will be writing an article.'

'No, I cannot talk with you. Ayana will not allow it.'

'It was her idea,' Brampton countered. She noticed the studded, red leather collar around the girl's neck.

'My parents…My family. They must know nothing about this.'

'You will not be named, I promise.'

'Can I trust you?'

'Of course, absolutely.' Brampton didn't want to give her time to change her mind. 'So tell me, how long have you been kept here like this?'

'A week now at this villa. I am being trained to pleasure Mr Nazal. When he thinks I am ready, I will be given to our Leader Guide.'

'How old are you, Tabina?'

'Nearly eighteen.'

'How did you come to be here?'

'I am studying medicine at the University of Tripoli. It is my first year. Our Leader Guide comes to give one of his many talks to students back in January. Quiet men with video cameras mingle with the audience.'

'For Gaddafi?'

Tabina nodded. 'I understand later that he studies the tapes and tells Mr Nazal which young women take his fancy. Sometimes it can be male students. He likes them with long hair and eye lashes. Nazal's teams from Special Affairs at the Department of Protocol then come looking.'

'You were one of the chosen ones?' Brampton guessed.

The girl lowered her head. 'Yes. I am with my new boyfriend at the time. We were eating lunch in the canteen when they come. Jalal protests, tries to protect me.'

'And you?'

The girl looked abashed. 'I am confused. I am flattered to be invited to meet our Leader Guide in person, but also nervous. I have heard rumours. Everyone has heard rumours.'

'About?' Brampton pushed.

Tabina searched for the right words. 'About bad things happening to people who do not co-operate.'

'What happened when Jalal challenged Gaddafi's men?'

'Nothing…at the time. The men from Protocol were friendly, polite. They laughed, told him not to be silly, that it was an honour for me to be invited by the country's revered leader. They invited Jalal to come too.'

'And later?'

Tears welled up in Tabina's eyes. 'We were taken to Bab al-Aziza. You know it?'

Brampton nodded. It was Gaddafi's vast fortified compound in the centre of Tripoli. 'There Jalal and I were separated,' Tabina continued, her voice low. 'We were assured we would be together again in a few minutes. I was taken to an underground dungeon. That is where Princess Ayana was waiting. She supervised as I was taken by other women to strip me, make me shower, be shaved and anointed in oils. Still naked, I was taken to an adjoining room. I was in for a most terrible shock.'

'What happened?'

'Jalal was there already. As I entered he was being held down over a table…' Her voice faded and she pressed a small fist to her mouth. She found it hard to speak the words. 'He was being raped by soldiers. Brutally. Our eyes met…'

Brampton reached out to her. 'I'm so sorry.'

But Tabina pulled away. It was as though she felt compelled to finish her story. 'Then it was my turn. Someone even had a video camera. Mr Nazal ordered the soldiers what to do, like some film director. Jalal was made to watch. I tried to fight them, I punched and scratched them, I even bite one of them badly. That was when they beat me. After it was finished, they all stood around and urinated on me.'

'My God,' Brampton breathed. 'Did anything like that happen again?'

Tabina shook her head. 'No, I was brought here then. As punishment for the injury I had caused the soldier, and for my disobedience. And to be taught…er…the word they like. Compliance, compliance to the Guide Leader, who I must address as Papa, it has been decided.'

Brampton could scarcely believe what she was hearing. 'Have you seen Jalal recently?'

That was when the dam burst. Tabina broke down, tears welling in her eyes, her shoulders heaving as she sobbed and tried to catch her breath. Brampton thrust a clean handkerchief into her hands and muttered words of consolation.

It was a full minute before the girl regained her composure enough to speak. 'I believe I will not see Jalal again. They showed me a video. I was told it was him, but he had a sack over his head. These were the torturers who would question the prisoners sent by America. The Terror War suspects.'

Brampton frowned. 'Extraordinary rendition?'

'Ah, yes, that is the expression, whatever that means.' She paused and swallowed hard. 'These were the men who killed my Jalal. His wrists and ankles were tied to two cars that drove off in opposite directions.'

Brampton felt sick, struggled not to vomit then and there. 'I am so sorry, Tabina, I should never have asked you.'

'Perhaps it wasn't him. Perhaps they were just trying to torment me.'

Something snapped in Brampton's head. 'Come with me. Come with me now.'

Tabina stared at her. 'What?'

'Come with me now,' she repeated. 'Escape. We have a car and an armed protector. Escape while you can.'

'I dare not.'

Brampton indicated the red satin gown. 'Do you have any other clothes you can wear?'

'Not here. They are taken away.'

'No matter,' Brampton replied, slipping off her jacket. 'Wear this over your top.'

The girl seemed in a daze as she obeyed. 'I am not sure this is good idea.'

'Of course, it is,' Brampton insisted, reaching under the bed for the girl's slippers. 'Put these on.' That's when she discovered the aluminium dog's bowl. 'What's this?'

'My food dish. How I am fed.'

Brampton said nothing, just shook her head in continuing disbelief.

She helped Tabina to her feet, the girl's calves aching at the sudden activity after days of captivity. 'Quickly, up the steps. Can you balance?'

Tabina reached for the handrail at the base to the stairwell. 'I am not steady on my feet.'

'I've got you,' Brampton assured, her arm around the girl's waist.

Together they shuffled upwards, one step at a time. Once they reached the top, Brampton eased open the door into the short passage that led to the entrance corridor. The hinges creaked. She could hear nearby voices. They were female, talking in Arabic.

'Is that Ayana?' Brampton asked, listening intently.

'No, it is a couple of other guards of Mr Nazal. I do not know their names.'

'Then let's move quickly,' Brampton said, urging Tabina forward into the corridor.

It was deserted. The voices they had heard came from the rear of the villa; there was no sign of Princess Ayana or Nazal Abu.

Brampton breathed a sigh of relief, and dragged Tabina towards the front reception room. Sinbad and his son were seated, thumbing through old magazines. Royce was standing, waiting impatiently.

'These are my friends, part of our media team.' Brampton said quickly. 'This is James. Sinbad and his son Tareg.'

Royce frowned. 'What's going on?'

Brampton knew she'd have trouble. 'This is Tabina. We're giving her a lift to the hotel.'

'What?' Royce was incredulous. 'Who is she?'

'A new friend,' Brampton answered vaguely. 'I'm helping her out.'

He nodded and smiled, acknowledging the girl. 'She's not even dressed.'

'Tabina speaks English,' Brampton warned. 'She'll be alright in the car.'

'Who is she?' Royce repeated.

Brampton became agitated. 'Can we please stop talking and kit-up? And just *go*.'

Royce slipped his flak vest over his head and indicated for Brampton to do the same. Alarmed by her obvious anxiety, he swiftly moved towards the door. 'Will you please tell me what we're dealing with?' he demanded as he glanced up and down the empty corridor. 'Exactly who is Tabina?'

Brampton relented. 'Tabina was being held captive in the cellar.' She added, hoping it would make a difference. 'Against her will.'

Royce froze. 'Good God, woman.' He couldn't believe it. 'You're trying to free a political prisoner?'

'Not exactly,' Brampton came back defensively.

'Are you mad?' he demanded.

The journalist was incensed. 'Probably. Can we just GO!'

At that moment the front door swung open. The petite and friendly bodyguard called Amal stood in the frame with her usual ready smile. 'Ah, you have finished your interview!' She patted the brooch radio mike on the front of her tunic. 'No one tells me…' The smile faded from her lips. 'Who is that you have with you?'

'You know Tabina, I think,' Brampton replied. 'She is coming with us.'

Amal's smooth brow fractured like broken porcelain. 'That would seem unlikely, Miss Brampton.'

'Really,' the journalist insisted, keeping her voice low and convincing. 'A reward for her good behaviour.'

Royce glanced at Brampton sideways, trying to make sense of the conversation.

'You understand,' Amal replied tersely, concern showing in her face, 'I will have to confirm with Princess Ayana.' She pressed the alarm button on her brooch mike.

Sinbad had been listening intently and now stepped forward. 'I am these peoples' guide from Ministry of Information. There is a curfew imposed. They must return to hotel now or be arrested.'

Another, sour-faced female soldier appeared behind Amal, carrying an AK47 short at the ready.

Royce tried to push forward. 'I'm sorry. We really do have to be going...'

Suddenly a voice crackled over Amal's two-way radio. *What is the problem?'* It was Princess Ayana.

'Your guests are trying to leave with Tabina? Is that correct, Ma'm?'

A pause. *'No it is not. Stop them.'*

Amal reached for the pistol strapped to her hip, but found that she was facing Royce's C8Z5 automatic. 'Leave it alone, Amal. Hands in the air and you won't get hurt.' He waved the 9mm pistol to the woman behind her. 'Put that AK47 down, slowly.'

The soldier looked confused. Sinbad translated the order in Arabic and she conformed, looking very nervous.

Royce reached forward and slipped the pistol from Amal's holster. He handed it to Brampton. 'D'you know how to use one of these?'

She looked at him curiously, as if suddenly remembering something. 'Yes,' she said, sounding oddly distant. With obvious reluctance she took it from him.

'Turn around, both of you,' Royce snapped. 'Stand with your hands up against the wall.'

The second soldier followed Amal's example, raising her arms and pressing her palms against the pink stucco.

Brampton was starting to panic. 'Let's get out of here -'

'STOP!' Princess Ayana's voice reverberated down the corridor.

Brampton turned, pointing the captured automatic.

Ayana stood at the far end of the corridor, her legs firmly apart and her arms raised to hold her pistol in a steady, double-handed grip. 'Drop your weapons, or at least one of you will die.'

Brampton didn't flinch. 'I'll take *you* down with me.'

'Then just let Tabina go,' Ayana said, changing tack. Brampton realised that with two of the opposition wearing flak vests, the odds weren't on her side. 'She is not yours to have.'

'No one's forcing her to come with us,' Brampton retorted.

Royce stepped in to defuse the situation. 'Let's keep calm and talk this through.'

Brampton glared at him.

'Let's all put the weapons away,' he suggested. 'Real slow and careful. All together…Yes. All lower our weapons on the count of three. Agreed?'

Ayana said nothing. Brampton glared at her.

Royce continued, 'One, two, three…'

Hesitantly, he dropped the snout of his CZ85 a fraction and waited until Ayana and then Brampton did the same. 'That's good,' he said. 'Now put them down and *slowly* put them away…'

It took a full and anxious forty-five seconds before the guns were fully lowered and holstered. Brampton pushed her newly-owned pistol into the waistband of her jeans.

'You took advantage, Miss Brampton,' Ayana accused. 'You betrayed my trust.'

Tabina looked petrified. 'It is my fault. I should never have agreed.'

'You were held captive,' Brampton reminded. 'Bound, a prisoner.'

Ayana put her hands on her hips in a defiant stance. 'And where will you go, Tabina? Back to your family? They will know what has been done to you, they will disown you. You will have nothing, you will be nothing. Come back here and Mr Nazal will take care of you.'

Tabina's voice barely rose above a whisper. 'He will punish me.'

'And you will thank him for that deserved punishment.' Ayana paused. 'Because you also know he will take care of you.'

'No, Tabina,' Brampton insisted. 'Don't go back to that obscene slavery. Come with us.'

It was Royce's time to intervene. 'Forget it, Bram. We're not here to get involved. You're here to write and report objectively and it's my job to protect you.'

She turned on him. 'Don't you patronise me, James! And don't try to lecture me on what my job is. I may be a journalist, but I'm a human being first. And I'm not even your client. I didn't want anything to do with you.'

Ayana chuckled. 'Well, well. We seem to have divisions amongst our ranks.' She raised her hand and beckoned to Tabina with her index finger.

Sullenly the girl slipped the leather jacket from her shoulders and handed it back to Brampton. 'Thank you,'

'You don't have to stay,' Brampton persisted.

'Leave it!' Royce hissed.

As Tabina walked back towards Ayana and the cellar, Brampton called after her. 'When this is over, I'll come back for you.' She added rashly, 'That's a promise.'

'Let's get out of here,' Royce snapped, 'while we can.'

He turned to the Libyan guard called Amal. 'Open the gates, please. I don't want to have to crash through them.'

She smiled meekly and pressed a button set in the wall beside the door. The electric gates slid open with a light hiss.

It was really dark now, the night air humid, cloying. On the way down the front steps, Royce took out his CZ85 again, in case of trouble. He ushered Brampton, Sinbad and Tareg ahead to the VW before he scrambled into the driver's seat. He suddenly remembered what had happened earlier. He had a premonition that it would happen again, could see it in his mind. The car would fail to start, he just knew it. He turned the key. The engine croaked, spluttered. Please God, he thought. It stopped, stubborn. Christ! Sweat gathered in the small of his back. He tried again. This time it fired. He breathed a sigh of relief.

Slamming it into gear, he accelerated down the short drive.

'God,' Brampton breathed. 'They're closing the gates!'

Royce pushed his foot to the floor and the little car seemed to leap forward.

'Careful, Mr James!' Sinbad squealed.

The gates were closing like steel jaws. 'We make it!' Tareg cried.

Ornate stucco gate pillars flashed past the driver's window. Then the steel teeth bit into the car's metalwork, somewhere around the rear wheel arch. Sparks burst into an energetic light display, the screech ear-piercing. The VW was stuck fast. Royce's foot pressed to the floor and he threw the steering wheel left and right. The front wheels span, kicking up a noisy hailstorm under the body-pan.

The VW seemed to wriggle with a life of its own, straining to be free.

Royce changed down a gear and hit the gas again. There came another scream of tortured metal. Something gave. The VW shot forward abruptly, suddenly released. Part of the rear bumper section was ripped off and clattered noisily into the verge.

The rear window cracked but held as a round hit the bullet-proof glass. An involuntary gasp came from Tareg.

Brampton turned in her seat. 'Incoming,' she gasped. 'Small arms fire. I think it's Ayana.'

Royce threw the wheel so that the VW zig-zagged across the street. Another couple of rounds hit the bodywork.

He swung the VW right around the first junction he came to, heading back in the direction of their hotel. As he accelerated hard to straighten it up, the vehicle fishtailed skittishly. Now hidden by buildings, they were out of the line-of-fire.

'Thank God for that!' Brampton gasped.

Sinbad chuckled. 'Your God is working with Allah today, I am thinking.'

'I can smell petrol,' Tareg said.

Royce said, 'Maybe a round hit the tank. Or a fuel line.'

Brampton was puzzled. 'I thought all that was protected on these cars?'

'Up to a point. No guarantees.'

The streets were eerily deserted. In the distance came the brittle sound of small arms fire, interspersed by the occasional muted thud of heavy weapons. Light pulsed randomly in the sky around them. It was impossible to tell if the explosions were from artillery, rockets or aircraft.

Royce was on the radio to Tremain. 'Iain, assignment over. We're on our way. Encountered hostile fire. Some damage, possible fuel leak. Returning along same route Red Five, passing Mike Eight.' Mike Eight was a particular mosque marked on their personal stylised map. 'Heading towards Sierra Six.'

'Roger that.' Tremain's voice offered calm and professional reassurance. *'For your info, others have returned from hospital. All OK, including Bud. He's being evacuated.'*

Brampton overheard as Royce switched off. 'I'm so happy he's alright. I thought he might not make it.'

'He still might not. Could still be a close call.'

She glared sideways at him. 'No need to be so cheerful.'

His mouth twitched. 'Realistic, that's all.' That reminded him. 'By the way, don't ever pull a stunt like that again. You could have got us all killed.'

'Again?' she echoed. 'There isn't going to be a next time. You're so full of yourself.'

'Just trying to keep you alive,' he replied stiffly.

His words irritated her, and made her remember something. 'Back at the villa...'

'Yes?'

'For a moment there, I thought I remembered you. Thought that we'd met before? Something seemed familiar.'

Royce leaned forward trying to see beyond the reach of the headlights. 'I don't think so,' he replied, not really paying attention to her.

She asked slowly, 'Were you ever an army examiner on close surveillance courses?'

That took him by surprise. 'I was Royal Marines, not army,' he corrected. 'But I was detailed a few times. To various Special Forces selection courses.'

'God I knew it. It *was* you.'

He threw her a sideways glance. 'Me, who what?'

'Failed my selection to the Recce Regiment.' She glared blindly ahead at the Tripoli street scene opening up in the headlights. 'I know it was you. You bastard.'

But Royce had stopped listening, concentrating on the scene ahead. All streetlamps were out so there was little illumination beyond the VW's headlight beam.

They were at the small square they had passed through on their way to the villa. Its yellowing grass was edged with fronded palms where previously the barricade had been manned by friendly rebels led by Dr Jaralla.

Now, as they entered, it was clear that things had changed. The barricade was no more. Caterpillar tracks had churned deeply into the sandy lawn and crushed burnt-out cars to a metallic pulp. Tyres and timber burned fitfully or smouldered, acrid smoke mingling with the choking residues of tear gas hanging in the still and humid air.

The surrounding buildings were riddled with the pock marks of a ferocious battle. The remains of dead rebels were scattered everywhere. A mangy dog trotted between them, looking for a free meal.

One of the charred bodies moved unexpectedly, a skeletal hand rising in one last and futile gesture, begging for mercy or for help. There was none, and no other sign of life.

And no sign of Dr Jaralla either, Royce realised. No doubt the man would have been one of those killed.

Royce forced aside his overwhelming feeling of sadness. War was so indiscriminate in who it rewarded or who it punished.

Ahead was a new barricade. The frontline had moved, had been turned around, turned on its head. Facing them now was a line of gleaming, newly-washed main battle tanks, armoured personnel carriers and scout cars. Fresh-looking troops of various nationalities stood around, loaded down with carbines and rocket launchers, braced for trouble.

Shit, he thought, this did not look good.

He saw the muzzle flash. Simultaneously he heard the shattering of glass as the left headlight went out.

8

RUNNING THE GAUNTLET

The lights of the armoured vehicles, spread out in a line in front of them, came on in a ragged sequence until the square was lit up like a film set.

Royce killed his own lights and threw the VW into a tight bootleg turn. Judging his speed to be around thirty-five, he jerked on the handbrake and held it. The car slewed over the sand-blown grass, its tyres bumping over a corpse, and continued until it had turned a full hundred and eighty degrees.

'Gaddafi's men blind,' Sinbad declared. 'Cannot they read word "TV" on our car?'

Gunning the accelerator, Royce straightened up and drove as fast as he could towards the street they had used to enter the square.

'They've been in a firefight with the rebels,' Royce pointed out. 'They'll be on edge, twitchy.'

He steered through smouldering remnants of the earlier barricade. Black smoke drifted over them.

'Oh, my God!' Brampton gasped. 'A tank.'

Royce saw it as the smoke cleared. It had come from nowhere, towering immediately before them in the middle of the street, blocking their exit. Half a dozen Libyan soldiers were running up behind it.

Royce assumed the unit was conducting mopping up operations after the confrontation, hunting down any rebel fighters who had survived the mêlée.

The old Soviet-era T55 was a rusting thirty-six ton monster with a huge 100mm rifled barrel. Of more immediate danger to Royce and his passengers was the heavy 12.7mm anti-aircraft machine gun. The commander was in the turret, swinging the deadly weapon towards them.

Royce veered hard to the right, seeking safety in a narrow side street. The tank commander let rip with the heavy machine-gun. It blew chunks of stucco and brick out of the house wall above them and the debris scattered noisily onto the roof of the VW. It was dark here, illuminated only by occasional window light from emergency candles. Royce continued as fast as he dare, avoiding bins and crates left outside shops and houses in the lane.

'It can't follow us down here,' Royce assured, now on the radio to update Tremain on their situation and position.

Turning in her seat, Brampton looked back through the bullet-scarred rear window. The tank had drawn level with the side street entrance behind them. She guessed the AA gun had jammed or was temporarily out of ammo because now the main 100mm barrel was taking aim.

'James! -' she yelled, her voice drowned out by the sudden explosion reverberating down the tight corridor of buildings and the distinct *whoosh* of displaced air as the round skimmed over the VW's roof, missing it by millimetres. They had almost reached a T-junction up ahead and the house in front of them disintegrated in an almighty flash of fire and smoke before their eyes. Debris flew towards them, snapping against the bonnet and cracking sharply against the windscreen.

'Fuck me!' she gulped in shock.

Royce cursed, steering through the carpet of rubble that had landed in front of them.

Seconds later the T-junction was reached. Royce turned sharply right into a wider, two-lane street that ran parallel with the square and would eventually take them back to the Golden Palms hotel. People were running out into the street in casual clothes, their children in pyjamas. There was screaming and shouting as the inhabitants tried to discover what was happening and rushed to help those trapped in the house that had been demolished by the tank.

'Keep going, Mr James,' Sinbad encouraged from the back seat. 'I will guide you to safety.'

Royce had serious doubts about exactly how familiar their fixer really was with the back streets of Tripoli, and it had already become obvious he couldn't read a map very well.

This wide, two-way street was now eerily deserted for mid-evening. There was nobody about. Everyone was indoors, keeping their heads down, peering out only at any signs of trouble.

Every few moments, the VW passed another narrow street on its right. Each time Royce glimpsed the Libyan tank at its far end, keeping pace with them. Its commander was clearly waiting for a street wide enough to continue his pursuit.

Suddenly the commander found it. The shopping arcade ran off the end of the square where the rebel barricade had been destroyed. Accelerating hard and noisily pumping out black smoke like a bronchial patient trying to sprint, the old T55 gathered pace as it raced past the shuttered shop-fronts and cafés.

Royce lost sight of it and when he looked in his rear-view mirror a couple of moments later, the tank had turned into their two-way street and had settled down in pursuit some hundred metres behind.

Driving without lights, so as not to offer an illuminated target, Royce restricted their speed to around thirty miles an hour in the good ambient light from a starry sky. He was satisfied that he could stay ahead of the tank. His main fear was that its commander would sort out the jam in his heavy machine gun or reload it.

That was when he felt the power fade. He pushed the accelerator to the floor, but the VW kept on slowing.

'What's happening?' Brampton asked, 'Why are you slowing down?'

Sinbad leaned forward from the back. He pointed to the dashboard. 'Look, we have no petrol.'

He was right. The gauge needle was on empty.

Handing his blue NATO-style helmet to Tareg, Royce said, 'Put this on, Bright Spark. And don't take it off.'

Brampton offered hers to Sinbad, but the man declined. 'No, pretty lady, it is yours to wear.'

Royce made his final decision. 'Grab the ammo and medical bags. Now, everyone out!' he glanced around him. 'To the left. That alley way over there!'

As the doors flew open, Royce leapt out and drew the CZ automatic from beneath the flap of his flak vest. Steadying himself against the side of the car, he fired two rounds at the commander of the tank. He missed. The man suddenly realised he was under attack and ducked down into the turret and out of sight. But the metal monster kept clanking on, slowly and remorselessly. Unstoppable. The gap was closing slowly but inexorably.

Royce glanced round to see Brampton, a small rucksack over her shoulder, taking the lead and holding Tareg's hand as she rushed across the street towards the dark alley. Sinbad, loaded down with a medical rucksack, hurried to keep up.

It was time to go, Royce decided. He sprinted across the street. As he did the cupola- mounted 7.62mm machine gun of the T55 opened up, triggered by the crew inside the tank. The rounds chased him across the dusty tarmac, snapping at his heels like a rabid dog.

When he made it to the mouth of the alley, he found the others waiting for him, all breathing heavily after the sudden exertion.

Brampton looked anxious. 'God, for a moment I thought you'd had it then,' she said.

But he wasn't really listening. Glancing down the alley, he realised he had misjudged. It was a little wider than he'd realised, probably just wide enough for a T55. He cursed silently. There was nothing he could do about it now. They were committed, could not go back into the main drag where they'd abandoned the car.

He could no longer see the tank, but he could hear it wheezing and coughing, and the noise of its tracks creeping towards them like the grinding bones of a metal Grim Reaper. Another volley of rounds stuttered from its cupola machine gun. Chunks of brickwork were chewed out of the corner of the building where they were sheltering. The stuff rained over them. There was no time to waste.

'Let's go,' Royce said, and led the way deeper into the alley.

Electric power to the neighbourhood was still out. Apart from the stars in an inky sky, only candlelight from a few windows illuminated the narrow passage. Washing was strung on lines above them like carnival bunting. A smell of cooking and spices lingered in the warm air. Muffled voices drifted from behind drawn curtains and blinds. Male and female, an old woman sobbing: families at supper. A couple argued fiercely. Somewhere a baby cried. In the distance a dog howled.

'I do not know this place,' Sinbad announced unexpectedly. He sounded concerned.

Brampton looked back. 'Oh, God. It's there.'

'What?' Royce asked irritably.

'The tank, it's stopped at the end of the alley.'

Royce jogged to a halt and glanced over his shoulder. There was enough light on the main drag to create a silhouette of the T55. It was like a dinosaur, getting its breath, deciding whether or not to pursue its quarry. The driver cranked it into gear and pressed on the gas, and the beast edged forward. Its headlights lit up the narrow lane like a tunnel as though someone had thrown a switch. Then the commander reappeared in the turret and turned on his spotlight. Illumination of the alley intensified until it was as bright as day.

Turning, Royce began to run again. But with the increased illumination from the tank, a terrible truth became obvious. Up ahead was a dead end. The lane culminated in a closed coffee-shop barring their way. Its scattering of rusted iron tables and chairs expectantly awaited the next morning's visitors for breakfast.

The machine-gun seized its moment and burst into action. Royce grabbed Brampton and dived to the left. Sinbad seized his son and leapt in the opposite direction. The rounds smashed up the metal tables and chairs and the front of the coffee-shop. Its window exploded, scattering shards of smashed glass all over the pavement. A fire started, curtains began burning. The front door fell in, hanging on by one obstinate hinge.

'Quick, inside!' Royce ordered. Brampton grabbed Tareg and bundled him into the building. Sindbad didn't have to be told twice.

The owner already had a large red fire-extinguisher in his hands and was hosing down the curtains, dousing the flames. His wife and daughter were crouched under a table, terrified. A couple of candles in saucers provided emergency lighting.

'The soldiers are after you?' the man asked in Arabic.

'I am afraid so,' Sinbad answered. 'I am so sorry for the inconvenience.'

The man noticed the word *PRESS* on Bram's flak jacket. 'But you are media. Gaddafi's men have no honour! I spit on them.'

Royce just managed to follow the rapid conversation. At least they seemed to be amongst friends. He peered back out down the alley. The T55 remained stationary, the commander in his turret, apparently fiddling with the heavy anti-aircraft gun, probably trying to unjam it. Perhaps he was undecided what to do next, Royce thought? The commander appeared to be in no hurry; after all, he held all the cards. Was he waiting for some infantry to catch up? In that case, Royce reasoned, they might have a few moments respite.

He went into the kitchen at the rear and looked out of the back window. The coffee-shop opened onto another alley. There were lights from a recce vehicle shining straight at him. Squinting, he could make out that it was a Russian-made armoured car. A number of troops hung around it, smoking and swigging from cans of drink. He counted at least a couple of dozen, heavily armed. They appeared pensive, restless, as though they could be awaiting orders.

Royce returned to the front window of the coffee-shop. The T55 still sat there, intimidating. Another crew member had emerged from the turret and was assisting the commander in the repair of the HMG. Royce forced himself to ignore them and peered up along each side of the alley.

The two-storey flat-roofed buildings were old, squeezed together, covered in stucco and many smothered in types of ivy or bougainvillea. Some had little wrought-iron or stone balconies to their second floor windows.

An idea began to form in Royce's mind. He turned to the coffee-shop owner. 'Can we get onto your roof?' he asked in broken Arabic.

Sinbad chuckled, and translated.

The man nodded and indicated a steep flight of narrow wooden stairs which disappeared sharply up to the next floor.

'We're going that way,' he told Sinbad. 'Please tell this man, I suggest he puts white table cloths or sheets out back and front. Let the soldiers know he's not fighting them.'

Sinbad gabbled his translation to the owner, who slowly nodded. Then their fixer extracted a crumpled magazine portrait of Gaddafi from an inside pocket and handed it to the man. 'Stick that on your wall. It may save your life. Allah akbah.'

There was no time to waste. 'Follow me,' Royce called. Then, remembering that Brampton was now armed, he added, 'Bram, you can come up the rear. We'll protect Tareg and his Dad in the middle.'

She nodded her understanding as he led the way up the steps. They were so narrow his shoulders brushed against the walls on both sides. He reached the first floor, which opened onto the family's quarters, a living room with a blank television and dining table, a couple of bedrooms, one scattered with fluffy toys. With the power lines down it was difficult to see, but Royce's eyes were quick to adjust to the gloom.

He found a door that he nearly mistook for a cupboard. It again led steeply upward, this time into total darkness. Attached to his key-ring was a Swiss Army knife and an LED mini-torch, which he twisted on. Its sharp beam showed the last few timber steps before a bolted tin door. Quickly he slid open the bolts and pushed.

The humid night air rushed in, although it felt relatively cooling to his skin. He gulped down a couple of deep breaths and stepped out onto the flat rooftop. A low parapet ran around its outside edge and there was a drop of some six feet to the adjoining flat roof. Peering down to the narrow lane below, Royce had a clear view of the tank. It still had not moved, but the commander was now alone in the turret. The heavy machine gun looked to be in working order again.

Royce slipped over the parapet and slowly lowered himself onto the adjoining roof. He was sweating heavily by the time his toes touched down on the concrete and he breathed a sigh of relief. Next Sinbad lowered down his son for Royce to catch, before following himself. Brampton came last, her calves and thighs slipping through his hands, until he found himself holding her waist. It struck him how muscular her body felt beneath his fingers, how slender her waist.

She turned in his arms, her face close to his. 'It's okay, James, I'm down. You can let go now.'

Relaxing his grip, he stared at her for a moment. Suddenly he remembered. He was back on that bleak Welsh hillside in January, when he was still in the Special Boat Service. Ten or eleven years ago? Annoyed that he'd been drafted in to help on the selection course for the army's 14 Int up-close recce unit, or whatever its latest incarnation had been called, he'd been in a mean mood. He could vaguely remember one particular girl, short curly black hair and mesmeric tawny eyes. She was crouched in the mud of an OP dugout, pale, exhausted and shivering in her sodden DPM fatigues. Despite the conditions and the driving rain, she'd managed the brightest of smiles when he arrived. For some reason he couldn't explain, that had irritated him.

Now, as he had then, he turned sharply and walked away. As he crossed the roof, he forced the unbidden thoughts from his mind and concentrated on their current plight. He was able to see sufficiently well by the ambient starlight peeking through high cloud. Distant explosions would suddenly pulse brightly against the indigo sky, followed by the sporadic grumble of striking artillery and mortar rounds. There were low dividing walls separating the rest of the roofs of the houses in the street, most bedecked with ubiquitous satellite dishes, many with washing swaying on lines and some with plastic chairs and tables for *al fresco* family evening meals.

He led the way across several house roofs until they found themselves behind the tank below and nearing the corner with the main street where they'd abandoned their car. There he stopped and looked back towards the coffee-shop. Its owner had heeded his advice and had hung a white linen tablecloth through the gaping hole of the front window. As he watched, the owner tentatively stepped out of the front door, both hands held high in a gesture of surrender. His wife and little girl were cowering behind him. It was obvious he wanted to establish clearly that he and his family were no threat to anyone.

The three of them stood there for several moments, a frozen tableau. Neither did the tank commander move in his turret.

Then the owner, sensing he'd made his point, slowly lowered his hands.

The tank commander said something into his throat mike. Without warning the cupola machine gun on the front glacis of the tank stuttered into life, ripping through the coffee-shop owner's body, tearing him apart, and into his wife and child. All three collapsed together into an untidy confusion of limbs, blood and innards.

Royce cursed beneath his breath.

Brampton blinked, not believing the evidence of her own eyes. 'Oh, God,' she breathed. 'It's our fault.'

Sinbad covered his son's eyes with one hand and turned his head away.

'No time to lose,' Royce said, and moved on swiftly to the next rooftop.

Once there he moved to the parapet and peered over. Guttering ran around the outer edge with a drain downpipe. He sat astride the low wall and tested the guttering with his left hand. It felt solid enough when he shook it.

'Follow me,' he ordered. 'One at a time.'

He swung his second leg over and lowered himself until he could grab the downpipe with both hands. Holding his breath, he edged down, inch by inch into the alley. Sweat gathered in the small of his back. Eventually he was able to rest one foot on the rail of a balcony. The downpipe fixings were holding.

With a sigh of relief, he continued down towards ground level. Suddenly the piping shifted a fraction under his fingers. A flurry of plaster cascaded down over his head and shoulders. His feet reached the ground. He looked up to see young Tareg fearlessly descending with all the speed of a monkey. Again the drainpipe shifted a little. Another small avalanche of dry powder fell from the fixings.

Tareg landed beside him, grinning triumphantly. Before the boy could speak, Royce put his forefinger to his lips and shook his head. He indicated the Libyan tank only twenty metres away, its commander with his back to them.

The drainpipe moved again, this time dramatically by half a metre. More plaster fell, and there was a distinctive metallic *ping* as several screws hit the ground. Sinbad landed beside him, pale and clearly unnerved by his experience.

Royce wondered if Brampton would hesitate. But as he looked up he witnessed her taking her chances, swinging in the air like a mad pole-dancer on the gyrating drainpipe. She slid down expertly, checking her speed with her feet to prevent burning her hands. It was a close-run thing, but she had gauged it perfectly. Her skill and light weight had allowed her to get away with it.

Within thirty seconds she'd successfully landed beside him. He allowed himself a smile. 'You could have been a commando.'

She barely spared him a glance. 'I would have been if you'd allowed me.'

At that moment the tank commander became aware of them. He twisted around in the turret and did a double take. He yelled into his throat mike for the driver to reverse back up the alley. Clouds of obnoxious exhaust pumped into the confined space as the engine revs deafened and reverberated between the houses. The caterpillar tracks began chewing up everything in their path. Chunks of scraped brickwork flew everywhere.

'Let's get out of here,' Royce snapped. He broke into a trot, leading them up to the main street. To the right was their abandoned car. It was now surrounded by Libyan troops. A number of them were black and Royce guessed they were some of the seasoned mercenaries Gaddafi had hired in because he couldn't trust his army members to fight their own people.

One of them spotted the group emerging from the alley. He yelled out. As he did Royce turned right and headed down the main street towards their hotel, the others hurrying to catch him up.

They'd barely covered fifty metres when the first shots rang out. Rounds kicked into the dust-covered tarmac around him as Royce slowed. He gestured towards a smouldering derelict building on his left that looked as though it had been the target of an earlier firefight. At least it might offer some cover from the fire of Gaddafi's soldiers.

'Over there!' he directed and threw himself to the ground, facing back up the street. The advancing mercenaries had been joined by the T55 tank that had been chasing them earlier, its commander having finally extradited it from the narrow alley.

He took a double-handed grip and loosed a couple of rounds into the tight gathering of soldiers with his CZ85. Two men dropped. The enemy quickly realised its mistake and the men spread out.

Royce was aware of someone by his side. Brampton had dropped down next to him. She lifted the automatic she'd taken from Ayana's bodyguard girl and pumped half a dozen steady rounds into the advancing enemy line. Two more stumbled and fell.

The barrel of the tank swung until it was pointing directly at them.

It lowered as far as it was able.

Oh, fuck, Royce thought aloud, he'd misjudged. He'd left it ten seconds too long.

A stream of alternate solid ball and tracer rounds stuttered from the tank's ranging machine-gun. It was so close above his head that he felt its slipstream part his hair. A recoiling boom followed, the heavy shell exploding out of its casing and whistling after the machine-gun rounds to skitter across the road surface and blast a great hole in the sidewalk behind him.

Royce breathed a sigh of relief and glanced sideways at Brampton. She stared back at him in near disbelief. The gunner had got it wrong. The tank was too close to them, the trajectory too low. Just a metre out, but it had saved their lives.

The commander tried to rectify their position, to pull back. The metal monster jerked into reverse gear and thick greasy diesel smoke belched into the night sky.

It was then that Royce saw it out of the corner of his eye. A short distance behind the tank, there was a small explosion and a sudden, bright burst of light from the window of a derelict building. The fireball streaked across the intervening distance towards the tank like a meteor.

9

ALL GUNSMOKE AND BROKEN MIRRORS

The shoulder-launched missile struck the rear of the T55 with awesome force. Its warhead smashed into the fuel tank and the vehicle became an instant volcano, spewing out shards of metal, a tongue of flame and a billowing coil of greasy black smoke.

Royce just glimpsed the commander being blasted from the hatch, his body simultaneously breaking into several parts as he disappeared into the billowing cloud of dust and oily fog. It was sickening. The turret became slightly detached from the main body of the tank, the barrel pointing down at a dejected angle.

Whoever had fired the missile knew exactly what they were doing. They had waited until the tank had passed and then fired at its rear, the most vulnerable part of the monster where its armour was lightest. Half a dozen of Gaddafi's mercenary fighters had been brought down by the flying shrapnel and the sheer force of the blast. A few lay dead, others helped injured comrades, and the rest had retreated back up the street.

'Over here!' a voice called.

Royce turned his head. Sinbad was waving from the derelict building where he and Tareg had taken refuge. Around them stood a dozen or so triumphant rebel fighters, dressed in miss-matched uniforms of camouflage cargo trousers, cutaway vests and the increasingly popular Rambo-style bandanas. Most were carrying either AK47s or rocket launchers. He realised the rebels had been moving from house to house by blowing holes in adjoining walls rather than exposing themselves to enemy fire on the streets. That was how their missile marksman had got himself into his excellent firing position against the T55.

Helping Brampton to her feet, Royce led her across to the waiting group. Only as they approached did he recognise the slight, neatly-bearded figure in simple open-necked white shirt and black trousers. The immaculate clothes of only a few hours' earlier were now covered in dust and smeared with blood. His short and tidy hair was now an unruly mess and his face drawn.

The man spoke gently. '*Salam* – again.'

'Dr Jaralla,' Royce greeted, remembering him as the leader on the rebel barricade on their outward journey earlier. He shook the offered hand and indicated the burning tank in the middle of the street. 'You've done well.'

'Not so well,' Jaralla countered. 'We were pushed back out of the square. And I have lost two good friends. Another doctor, we'd been friends since medical school, and a porter from the hospital.'

'I'm sorry,' Royce said.

Jaralla turned to Brampton. 'Did you get to your interview appointment?'

She nodded. 'Thanks to you.'

'Did it go well?'

'Sort of.' She hesitated. 'Tell me, could *you* spare a couple of minutes to talk to me?'

'Of course,' Jaralla replied, 'but I have wounded men to get to hospital. You can all travel with us in our ambulance. I will talk to you on the journey.'

As the doctor turned and walked towards two men laid out on

makeshift stretchers, Royce said to Brampton, 'You might have cleared that with me first.'

She glared at him, a sudden anger kicking in. 'Oh, fuck off, Royce. I've got a job to do. You don't own me. If you don't like what I'm doing you can piss off.'

He held her stare, but quickly realised she was in no mood to back down. Instead of challenging her further, he said, 'I'll bring Iain up to speed.'

With that he turned away and got onto the radio to give their Ops Base the latest update. At the other end, Iain Tremain promised to send their Land Cruiser to collect them from the hospital.

The ambulance was in fact an open-topped vegetable delivery truck. Brampton watched as the wounded and bloody-bandaged men were lifted into the back.

'Sometimes words just aren't enough,' Brampton thought aloud as she observed Dr Jaralla and his colleagues at work. The cries of pain and anguish were pitiful to hear. Some of these were lives that would be changed forever. She was taking some shots on her BlackBerry. 'I wish I had a decent camera for this. Or my chief could assign a photographer with me. This story's big enough to justify it.'

Royce said, 'I can take some shots for you, if you like.'

She looked at him. 'You?'

He pulled a small digital camera from the padded pouch on his belt. 'It's just a Powershot, but good enough.'

She laughed. 'You, a photographer?'

'Just a hobby.' Her expression of disbelief annoyed him. He added, 'I'm also a qualified pilot. Just a private licence, not with BA or Virgin.' With that he turned his back on her and began snapping away at the street scene with the burning tank, the band of rebels and the injured men in the makeshift ambulance as they began their journey to the hospital.

Dr Jaralla chatted to Brampton, answering her questions, as he changed dressings and gave morphine injections. Sinbad and Tareg gave the wounded men sips of water from flasks and tried to keep their spirits up.

The driver stuck to the back doubles. He was constantly on his radio and Royce deduced that he was being kept well-informed as to enemy government positions.

As they neared the hospital, Brampton handed Jaralla her business card. 'Keep in touch with me, doctor.'

He smiled gently. 'Mostly the phones are down.'

'Then email when you can. Tell me what's going on. I'll share your news with others, too.'

'Email can be dangerous. Gaddafi snoops and hacks.'

'Then try the dark net,' she advised.

Jaralla was puzzled. 'I'm sorry, what is that?'

'It's called TOR. The Onion Router – it has many layers,' she explained. 'You just download it for free and use it as your server. It uses multiple encryptions so that you and anyone you email or any site you visit remains anonymous. That's what I use. It's slower but untraceable. Email me on that.'

The doctor scribbled a note on the back of her card. 'I am most grateful. When I have a moment, I will write to you. Maybe I shall give you some exclusives, what you call some scoops.' He laughed.

When they arrived at the hospital, the A and E reception was congested with local, Red Crescent and converted ambulances, like their own, queuing up to offload the latest injured from both government and rebel forces. In a matter of moments more ambulances arrived, doors flew open, and more casualties were carried out. Women, children and old folk were among them. There were chest wounds, stomach wounds, and head wounds. Blood was everywhere. Living mourners mingled with the dead and dying, wailing in their grief. It was bedlam. The medical staff was totally overwhelmed.

Dr Jaralla turned to Brampton. 'Most of these people are not fighters. The majority were unarmed protesters on a march earlier today. Gaddafi had his snipers shoot to kill. There was no mercy.' Then the doctor followed his wounded men

Royce was relieved when, after five minutes, the Land Cruiser turned up. Stefan Seeff and Ollie Parsons could hardly disguise their joy at finding them.

'Thought we'd lost you for a time then,' Parsons admitted.

'I thought we'd lost us too,' Royce said.

Seeff didn't miss the chance of a wind-up. 'You *did* lose our VW, boss. That sort of carelessness won't look good on your CV.'

'It won't make it onto my CV,' Royce replied. 'Anyway, won't need a CV when I'm retired.'

'Let's hit the road,' Seeff said. 'I've got a new safe back-street route to our hotel.' He winked at Brampton. 'Jump aboard. Let's boogie!"

'So what happened exactly?' Ollie Parsons asked.

It was breakfast time the next day, a low-key debrief beside the hotel pool. The cleaning snake was dead in the water, due to another generator breakdown, and a thin film of algae was beginning to form on its surface.

The MI6 lead and the chilled-out Tasmanian Iain Tremain sat under the large umbrella canopy with Royce and Seeff around a table loaded with fruit juice, flatbreads, jams, dates and nuts.

Royce checked there were no hotel staff members or guests within earshot. 'Bram's appointment with Princess Ayana was at a very smart villa in the New City district.'

Parsons said, 'I understand Ayana's deeply involved with a very close colleague of Gaddafi?'

'Nazal Abu,' Royce confirmed. 'He owns the villa. We passed through the same government checkpoint where Bud was wounded, then a rebel barricade. They were friendly, especially their local leader, a Dr Jaralla.'

'A good man to know?' Parsons asked, scribbling in his notebook.

'I reckon. A neurology consultant working at the hospital.' Royce continued, 'When we got to the villa there were half a dozen female guards. I waited with Sinbad and Tareg while Bram interviewed Ayana. Nazal turned up unexpectedly while Bram was about to talk with some sort of female sex-slave, who was kept in the cellar.'

Seeff was straight onto that. 'Did you say sex-slave?' he asked eagerly.

'Not there of her own free will,' Royce pointed out. 'The next thing I knew, Bram was trying to leave, taking the girl with us.'

Parsons raised his eyes skyward. 'Nightmare,' he said.

'You can say that again, Ollie. There's no way you should have assigned me to going with her. The woman's a raving liability. She nearly got us all killed.' Royce was adamant. 'It's not what I signed up to.'

'That's not quite so, Rollo,' Parsons replied soothingly. 'Understandably, I realise you're a bit demob happy -'

Royce lowered his voice to a growl. 'Don't patronise me, Ollie,'

Parsons was taken aback, and raised his hands defensively. 'Okay, okay. But there are some things you need to know about the Brampton woman.'

'I think I know enough.'

'No, Rollo, not nearly enough.' Parsons realised he had Seeff's attention more than he'd realised. 'I'll explain later,'

Royce wasn't interested. 'If you insist.'

The usual smile returned quickly back onto Parson's face. 'So talk me through exactly what else happened *next* yesterday evening?'

'There was bit of a Mexican stand-off between Ayana and me, pistols drawn.' Royce continued, trying to recall the exact sequence of events. 'The girl Tabina decided to stay and we made our getaway. Shots were fired after us. One round must have hit the fuel tank.'

'That's not supposed to happen in a protected car,' Parsons observed.

'It didn't explode or ignite,' Royce replied. 'For some reason we got a slow leak. Later we were chased by a tank and some of Gaddafi's mercenaries and had to abandon the car. Sometime after that we met up with Dr Jaralla and his rebels again. They destroyed the tank and

Jaralla took us back to the hospital where you picked us up last night.'

Parsons sucked thoughtfully at the end of his pen. 'So Bram parted on bad terms with Princess Ayana?'

Royce said, 'It seemed so, but you'd have to ask Bram. Maybe the shots were fired at us for Nazal Abu's benefit. I don't think he knew Ayana was talking to journalists for money. She's as corrupt as they come, just looking out for herself – according to Bram.'

'And according to Chingford, Nazal Abu is just as bad,' Parsons added. 'So I'd like to speak with the both of them. I wonder if Bram will still be able to help?'

Royce shrugged. 'Here she is. You can ask her.'

The two women walked across the patio towards the pool. Brampton was tall and elegant, wearing a wide-brimmed straw hat and a kaftan-style gown open to reveal a blue floral one-piece costume. Her friend Rachel Starr was more petite, grabbing the men's attention with a skimpy white bikini that left little to the imagination.

'Just look at the lungs on that,' Seeff muttered admiringly. 'Now I know what Buzz saw in her.'

'Down, boy,' Royce growled. 'She'd eat you for breakfast.'

Seeff grinned. 'Can't think of a better way to die.'

The two women had stopped by the pool edge and were examining the surface.

'Wouldn't go in that water if I were you, ladies!' Seeff called out. 'Safer to join us for a coffee.'

Starr looked across to their table. ''Morning, gentlemen. You're BBC, aren't you?'

'World Service,' Seeff confirmed.

'Stefan, isn't it?' she asked, suddenly taking an interest in his tanned bare top. 'Thanks for taking Bud to the hospital last night.'

'Any news?' Royce asked.

'He's stable,' Starr answered as Brampton pulled up a couple of wicker-backed chairs for them. 'They're arranging to fly him out as soon as possible. Air ambulance.'

Seeff nodded. 'They'd soon be flying you out, too, if you swam in that stuff.'

'It looks a bit manky,' Brampton agreed, taking her seat beside Starr, and extracting a cigarette case from her shoulder bag.

Parsons didn't waste any time. 'How did your interview go with Princess Ayana yesterday?'

Brampton took out a Sobranie from the case. 'I can't believe James didn't tell you?'

'I wasn't at the actual interview,' Royce pointed out.

'No,' Brampton rejoined, 'but you know what happened after.'

'The shoot-out?' Seeff asked.

'What?' Starr asked. 'A shoot-out? You didn't tell me that.'

Brampton looked irritated and paused to light her cigarette. 'Hardly a shoot-out,' she said eventually, 'more a misunderstanding.'

Parsons said, 'You promised you'd put in a word for me. Are you and Ayana still on talking terms?'

'You'd have to ask *her*.'

At that exact moment the ringtone on Brampton's cell-phone started playing. She pulled it out of her bag and glanced at the screen. 'Talk of the devil. It's her.'

'Transmitters must have been repaired,' Tremain observed.

'Hallo, Jo Brampton speaking.' She clamped the phone to her ear, stood up and walked a few paces away. 'Back safe? Yes…No, no one hurt…Nazal Abu?…Oh, yes, I understand…The money?…Of course, I owe you. A deal's a deal…' Brampton began idling back towards the table. 'Yes, and by the way I've someone else who would love to interview you. A journalist from the BBC World Service…Pay you?' Brampton looked down at Parsons. 'Oh, I'm sure he would, he's a very generous sort of chap. Can I give him your number? Wonderful. We'll meet soon.'

Brampton flicked off her phone. 'You can call her.'

Royce said, 'I'm amazed, after last night.'

'It was a bit of a show,' Brampton replied, 'for Nazal Abu's benefit.

Ayana wanted to make her own story sound believable. She told the other girls to shoot at the car because I tried to get Tabina to run away with us.'

Parsons glanced at Royce. 'You guessed right about that.'

'I'm still surprised she phoned you,' Royce said.

Brampton laughed. 'It's because she still wants the money I promised her for talking to Tabina.'

'And she'll talk to me?' Parsons looked delighted.

Brampton smiled. 'Why not? More money.' She scribbled down the number on her notepad, tore off the sheet and handed it to Parsons.

He rose to his feet. 'Thanks. I'd better call her while the transmitters are still working.' For a moment he hesitated. 'And did your editor like your interview?'

Her smile was very wide. 'Front page this Sunday and the middle spread – as long as Prince Harry doesn't announce his engagement.'

It was to be another week before Ollie Parsons was able to find the right moment to tell Royce more about Jo Brampton. In the meantime the journalist herself had co-ordinated her diary with Rachel Starr and shared the services of bearded ex-legionnaire Yves, her French bodyguard.

Royce was at the wheel of the Land Cruiser, driving south out of Tripoli and away from the coast. Parsons was in the passenger seat, flicking through a copy of the *Sunday News*. 'The girl's done good. Jo Brampton's got the front page and spread, like she said. A bit lurid, mind. Gaddifi's secret life with drugs and sex slaves.'

'You're supposed to be reading the map,' Royce reminded.

'Sorry,' Parsons replied and picked up the route map that would lead them to a deserted ancient temple that was ruined enough to never make it to the tourist guide books. The rendezvous had been chosen by Princess Ayana herself. It was clear that she wanted no repeat of the fiasco with Brampton at the villa, no chance of anything going wrong like the unexpected arrival of her guardian and lover Nazal Abu.

Checking his rear-view mirror, Royce satisfied himself that Stefan Seeff was still close in their new back-up vehicle with Sinbad. The Libyan had helped them locate and buy a small Toyota Yaris. It wasn't armoured or protected in any way, but at least it was nippy and had a good mpg, which was useful as petrol shortages were an increasingly regular occurrence.

When Royce completed another regular radio update of their position to Tremain at their "Ops Centre" in the Golden Palms, Parsons said suddenly, 'Rollo, there are a few things I'd like you to know about Jo Brampton.'

Royce showed little interest. 'Other than the fact she's a menace to have around.'

The MI6 man's constant smile barely wavered. 'But a useful menace. Do you know the best way for spies to find out secrets?'

'Is that a trick question?'

Parsons chuckled. 'No, rhetorical. The answer is by reading newspapers.' He glanced out at the desert landscape flashing by. 'You can have all the spy networks and telephone bugs and computer hackers in the world, but often the best information you can get is just by reading a newspaper.'

'But not rags like hers. What is it, the *Sunday News*?'

'That's the *style*, Rollo,' Parsons explained, 'not the *substance*. Behind the tits and bums of the tabloids there are plenty of pro journos and reporters and seasoned stringers in different countries who know what's really going on. One or two broadsheet owners and editors are good friends with Lego House and Thameside.'

Royce knew most of the slang terms for the HQs of MI6 and MI5 that sat on opposite sides of the river in London. 'You mean mutual backscratching?'

'It can work well,' Parsons confirmed. 'It's not so widespread with the lower orders, the red tops. But the *Sunday News* has promise. I can't tell you exactly how it came about but co-operation with the intelligence services sort of saved it – or rather its editor – from extinction a few years' back. Russ Carver owes us. And it's a mutual relationship that is maturing rather well.'

Royce pulled out to avoid a donkey and cart. 'Is this where Jo Brampton fits in?'

'She's not aware of it yet, but it was at my suggestion that Carver sent her here.'

'And at MI6's expense?'

'Not exactly, but the *News* does struggle to make ends meet. We help where we can, when it suits us.'

'Why Bram?'

'She has a good pedigree. Do you know who her father is?'

Royce shook his head. 'Sorry, no idea.'

'Does the name Boris Bramberg ring any bells with you?'

'Bramberg,' Royce repeated thoughtfully. 'He's not some kind of journalist, is he? Did I read something by him recently? Maybe in the *Sunday Times*, that News Review section. An article about the secret ambitions of Vladimir Putin?'

'You are well read, old son.'

'I don't get much time to read nowadays,' Royce explained. 'I think I was waiting at a client's house and it was on his coffee table.'

'The Prime Minister of the Russian Federation is Bramberg's pet subject,' Parsons continued. 'Jo Brampton is Boris Bramberg's daughter. And I gather his scathing articles have been ruffling a few feathers in Moscow. Boris and Putin knew each other quite well back in the early days when it was the Communist Soviet Union.'

'Really?' Royce murmured, genuinely surprised at the link.

Parsons nodded. 'The two men met at Leningrad State University in the early 70s, became friendly rivals intellectually and in competition judo. In 1975 they both graduated and joined the KGB, the Soviet secret service. After a year's induction training at Okhta they went their separate ways. Putin worked briefly in counter-intelligence before being transferred to the First Chief Directorate – monitoring foreign officials in Leningrad.'

'Pretty low key stuff?' Royce guessed.

'Yes, Boris Bramberg was the early high-flyer of the two,' Parsons confirmed. 'He was from a lapsed Jewish background, but could speak Hebrew as well as having a gift for languages. His real love of literature and the arts was perfect cover for an early first posting abroad.'

'Where was that?' Royce asked.

'Teheran in 1977. He was a junior cultural attaché to the Soviet Embassy.'

Royce raised an eyebrow. 'That was before the fall of the Shah, wasn't it?'

Parsons nodded. 'Just before the Shah fled the Islamic Revolution in '79, which overthrew the monarchy. But, of course, all the signs were there before and Boris had predicted the sequence of events. He carefully used them, and the political turmoil, to plan his defection.'

'To America?'

'No, to Britain in 1978. With a beautiful Persian aristocrat called Farah Shirazi, whom he'd met on the Teheran arts circuit.'

'Let me guess,' Royce interjected. 'Bram's mother?'

'Well done,' Parsons said. 'Bram was born in Britain the following year. Farah sadly died of cancer a few years' later.'

'What happened to Boris?'

'Initially the couple were given a change of identity and a secret location in Cornwall,' Parsons explained. 'They changed their name to Brampton. Boris was milked for everything he knew by the intelligence community, and was given a post at GCHQ. He also got some work on the BBC World Service. That kick-started his journalistic career.'

'Boris reverted to his Russian name?'

'I think he felt safe after the Berlin Wall came down,' Parsons said. 'Like it was the end of an era. But it was after the surprise resignation of Yeltsin in 1999, when Putin became Acting President of the Russian Federation, that Boris really got his act into gear.'

'Was there some sort of grudge from the past?' Royce asked.

'That I don't know. All I can tell you is, from stuff I've read, Boris

Bramberg is developing an uncanny knack of guessing exactly what Putin plans to do next. I don't think the Kremlin's too happy about that.'

Royce considered for a moment. 'Is he at risk?'

Parsons shrugged. 'We hope not. He only writes under the name Bramberg. As far as we know he still keeps his new Brampton identity secret and separate. We've suggested he moves location, but he's too happy and settled in Cornwall.'

'And so Bram's following in Daddy's footsteps as a journalist,' Royce mused.

'She's already proving her potential worth to us.' Parsons indicated the road ahead. 'We're about to meet Princess Ayana.'

'So that's why you insisted I play babysitter the other week?'

'I couldn't explain in front of her.'

'That you're playing her like a violin?'

Parsons pulled a pained expression. 'That's a bit harsh, Rollo. More like helping her career.'

Royce grunted, unpersuaded. He nodded. 'We're approaching the temple. Up there on the left.' He sent a quick radio update to Tremain before slowing down.

All that was left of the ancient ruin was a couple of crumbling fluted columns atop a flight of decayed stone steps. In front of it was a stretch of bare sand, scrub and tumbleweed that was also home to a wrecked car without wheels, a door-less fridge and a rotten mattress. A smart black ministerial Mercedes with dark windows was parked in front of the monument. Beside the driver's door stood a slender woman wearing a smart camouflaged uniform and *hibab*.

As he drew close, Royce recognised her as the petite, friendly Amazon called Amal from Nazal's villa. She had an automatic strapped to her hip.

He halted the Land Cruiser some twenty paces from her, checking in his mirror to see that Seeff had now tucked the Yaris in at the roadside behind him.

Royce climbed out of the driver's seat. 'Move across and get behind the wheel, Ollie,' he said. 'Just in case.'

As his chief followed the instruction he strode across the intervening scrubland to the young soldier. She swung a sharp salute. 'Mr James, we meet again. I am glad last time I did not kill you.'

'You shot at our car.' It was more a statement than a question.

She smiled cheerily. 'I was following orders.' She lowered her voice. 'I aimed to miss. Alas my colleague didn't.'

'Princess Ayana is in the car?' Royce asked.

'Of course.' She indicated the Land Cruiser with its "TV" stickers emblazoned on it. 'And you have the World Service reporter with you? Mr Oliver?'

'Of course. I am his security adviser."

'And the car behind you? By the road?'

'Our back-up.'

Amal shook her head. 'No, it is too dangerous. They are too close. Tell them to drive away. And we will check that Mr Oliver is unarmed. You accept this?'

Royce nodded. 'It's a deal.'

Amal smiled tightly. 'Good. Princess Ayana and Mr Oliver will meet between the two cars. You will wait in your vehicle while they talk. I will wait in ours.'

Again Royce agreed. He returned to the Land Cruiser and instructed Seeff to drive the Yaris out of immediate view. The little car started and drove off.

Royce watched as Parsons got out the car at the same time Princess Ayana left the back seat of her Mercedes. She wore a mocha-coloured trouser suit that accentuated her long legs. As Amal frisked the MI6 man quickly and thoroughly, Royce was relieved that the wire wasn't discovered. He leaned forward and switched on the radio receiver and mini recorder.

He heard the conversation in his earpiece.

'I am pleased to meet you, Mr Oliver.'

'It is an honour to meet you, Princess, for you to agree to this interview. Can I use this mini tape recorder?'

'I'd rather you didn't. Somebody might recognise my voice. Can you just make notes to write-up later?'

'Er, of course. Although, actually I don't have a notebook with me.'

Royce cringed.

'A pen?'

'Er...I have a good memory.'

A pause. *'Did you remember the money?'*

'Five hundred US dollars. Do count it.'

'I trust you,' Ayana replied. *'Jo Brampton recommended you. And, after all, you are from the BBC World Service.'*

Royce continued listening as the couple slowly strolled away from the car, chatting, as Parsons clearly struggled to find questions to ask and Ayana gave increasingly irritated responses.

At last Ayana stopped walking. *'Mr Oliver, are you really a journalist? Is there something else on your mind?'*

'Ah,' Parsons took a deep breath. *'Possibly. You probably realise that the BBC is Britain's national broadcaster. We are independent by charter, but there are obvious links with the government of the day.'*

'Are you telling me, Mr Oliver, that you are a spy?'

Parsons looked affronted. *'Bless me, no. But as well as interviewing for the BBC I'm sort of looking out for anyone who is interested in helping to resolve this current conflict peacefully.'*

Ayana stared at him. *'I suspect you would like to know the whereabouts of our beloved Leader Guide?'*

Parsons was taken aback. After the briefest of hesitations he replied. *'Well, that certainly wouldn't go amiss. He might be persuaded to leave the country for a place of guaranteed sanctuary.'*

'Even if I knew where he was,' Ayana said, *'I can assure you Gaddafi would never do that.'*

'You are certain?'

'Absolutely. But there are others who might.'

'*Such as?*'

'*Me, if the price is right.*'

'*And Mr Nazal Abu, whom I believe you know?*'

She raised an eyebrow in surprise. '*That is a possibility.*'

'*So we can consider each other friends?*'

'*Assuredly.*' She extended a long and slender hand that glinted with exquisite gold rings. '*I am sure both Mr Nazal and I will do our best to assist you. But only with absolute discretion and nothing in writing,*'

Parsons nodded. '*Oh, by the way, Jo Brampton knows nothing of my other connections outside the BBC.*'

Ayana smiled. '*Dear Mr Oliver, don't be concerned. Your secret is safe with me.*'

10

OF ALL THE DEVILS ON EARTH

Timeline: May 2011

Ollie Parsons made his decision. 'I need to get to Misrata.'

'That will be easier said than done,' Royce replied.

The team was gathered around the poolside table that had become its favoured chill-out spot as the spring temperature gathered strength and the hotel air-conditioning more frequently failed. Weeks earlier, the stagnating water had been drained off to discourage the multiplying swarms of mosquitos.

Life had fallen into a routine. Outside the sanctuary of the Golden Palms, the glorious revolution of the so-called "Arab Spring" continued with fighting ongoing between Gaddafi's forces and his disenchanted people. The rebels were now assisted regularly by NATO airstrikes and supported with Qatari-funded weapons which were starting to make a difference.

That was just as well, because the two sides were still battling back and forth along the Libyan coast in a deadly comedy of errors like the Keystone Cops. As Seeff had pointed out, 'It would be funny if it wasn't so bloody tragic.'

Parsons had learned that London had finally rebuilt its bridges with rebel leaders of the National Transitional Council in Benghazi, after the unwanted global publicity of MI6's catastrophic arrival under the auspices of Hamish McDougall's E Squadron guardians. The NTC had smarted that the incident had given the illusion that their genuine people's revolt against Gaddafi was somehow a sinister plot in cahoots with colonialist Britain.

Apparently Parsons's MI6 chief, Mat Asquith, now had a temporary office in the city while 22 SAS Regiment and SBS regulars had mostly replaced the disgraced old guard of E Squadron. The two men were in routine radio and cell-phone contact in an effort to co-ordinate their plans. British Special Forces troops, mostly in semi-civilian dress, were teaching the civilian militias of the disparate rebel groups on basic soldiery and weapons use. Others were advising on local tactics and the NTC leadership in Benghazi on a winning strategy to beat Gaddafi's vast army.

Royce learned that Parson's had his own distinct plan. In his private life, the man was an avid war-gamer and armchair general with several historical and modern miniature armies in various scales. He had several landscaped tables in the cellar of his Peckham house where he would battle with percentage dice and rulers against fellow gamers while refighting famous old battles and imagined new ones. Parsons also read and studied military history at every opportunity.

'The battle here in Libya is going back and forth along the coast,' he told Royce and Seeff one evening after a few drinks. 'Between Gaddafi's Tripoli in the west and the rebels' Benghazi in the east. To break the impasse, we need secretly to build a new force in the south of Tripoli. Wrong-foot Gaddafi and take him by surprise.'

Neither Royce nor Seeff could fault him on that thinking. Persuading Mat Asquith to push that agenda successfully with the NTC in Benghazi was another matter.

Meanwhile Parsons had continued developing his network of Gaddafi insiders who might act as a conduit to negotiations with the man himself, give away his exact location for a precision strike or arrest, or be willing to work against the regime.

He had recently added Princess Ayana to his list, which already included Brigadier Cinti Hassan at Gaddafi's secret depot near the town of Zawiya, that had been a scene of much fighting. Parsons had forwarded co-ordinates of the compound to London for bombing consideration by the RAF, but nothing much had happened. Royce shared Parson's distinct feeling that the British government was waging a campaign of minimum effort and expense in support of the rebels.

Everyone in MI6's growing web of agents was given a satellite cell-phone so that they could be contacted regardless of the state of local mobile networks. Next on Parson's list of targets was Gaddafi's close friend and confidante, Nazal Abu. Each day they anticipated a call from Princess Ayana, confirming that he had agreed a meeting, and each day that call had failed to materialise.

This was yet another day, and still nothing. Parsons seriously wondered if Nazal could see any purpose in a meeting. It was nearly lunchtime.

'Why do you want to get to Misrata?' Royce asked.

Parsons thought for a moment, sucking noisily at his fruit juice cocktail through a straw. 'The rebel leadership there is cut off from the rest of the country.' He wiped his lips with the back of his hand. 'There are two strong elements in the city. One is loyal to the NCT in Benghazi, but another group has strong connections with the radical Muslim Brotherhood in Egypt. Mat Asquith is keen to make sure the NCT guys get the upper hand.'

'The city is surrounded on three sides by Gaddafi forces,' Seeff pointed out. 'The only way in and out is by sea.'

Tremain joined in. 'Mainly by ferry and other ships from Benghazi. That's how the rebels are bringing out their injured.'

'Then we also have to go in by sea,' Parsons decided.

'Getting back to Benghazi would be a nightmare,' Tremain said, shaking his head.

'Perhaps we could get a ship from here,' Royce suggested. 'I can't believe Sinbad wouldn't be able to get hold of a boat for us?'

Parsons gave a withering skyward glance. 'I would like to get to Misrata without sinking.'

'Oh ye of little faith,' Royce countered. 'I'll have a word.'

At that moment Parson's cell-phone began its irritating Arabic jingle. He snatched it up and looked at the screen, raising an eyebrow. 'Princess,' he acknowledged. 'Lovely to hear from you.'

All heads turned towards him. They all knew that Parsons had given Princess Ayana a new satellite cell-phone that bypassed local systems, allowing them unrestricted communications.

'He will?' Parsons asked. There was a lengthy silence as he listened intently. He pursed his lips. 'How much?'

He listened again, he puffed up his cheeks and blew. Finally he said, 'We have a deal. When and where?' After a few more moments he switched off his phone and snapped it shut. 'That was Ayana. Nazal Abu has taken the bait. We've got him.'

Of course it wasn't quite as straightforward as that. Gaddafi's close friend and confidant wanted a face-to-face meet. He suggested the rendezvous at a luxury villa on the corniche running east out of Tripoli. Chingford Charlie confirmed to Parsons that it was one of many of the Gaddafi family homes, with spectacular views over the shimmering Mediterranean.

Royce insisted that they park alongside the beach some ninety minutes before the agreed time in the late afternoon. It was as well that they did. All seemed quiet at the villa with its lemon-painted compound walls topped with coils of razor wire. There was no obvious sign of activity.

Meanwhile the faint but angry sound of mortars and artillery could be heard rumbling and thudding from beyond the eastern horizon. Smudgy pillars of smoke rose like black ethereal skyscrapers against a pristine sky. Occasionally the sun would catch the wings of a warplane high above as it hurtled on its mission of destruction.

But the street in front of them remained quiet. Then suddenly, after a thirty minute wait, an army staff car pulled up outside. It was followed by a green truck displaying the discreet motif of the notorious 32nd Brigade, a unit run by Gaddafi's seventh and youngest son, Khamis, and which chiefly devoted itself to protecting the personal interests of the extended family. An officer from the car joined eight men, dressed in battles fatigues, who jumped down from the tailgate of the lorry. They all wore balaclavas and three carried long sniper rifles. Occasional passing pedestrians scurried by, averting their eyes.

After a brief conversation, the officer pressed the security intercom on one of the concrete gate posts. A small side door was opened and Princess Ayana stepped out, accompanied by the petite bodyguard Royce recognised as Amal. The male officer chatted to Ayana for a short while as she pointed to a couple of nearby rooftops that overlooked the villa. He nodded his agreement and sent off his three snipers to deploy there. The rest of the men went inside, Royce guessed to bolster the resident troop of female Amazon guards.

'I don't like it,' Royce decided. 'Much too dangerous. We don't know what we're walking into.'

'That's rubbish, Rollo,' Parsons retorted. 'Nazal *wants* to meet us. Can't blame him for taking precautions.'

Royce shook his head. 'He might also fancy having an MI6 officer as a hostage to negotiate himself out of trouble with NATO.'

Parsons paled. He was so wrapped up in his mission, he hadn't thought of that. 'So what do you suggest?'

'Change the venue to an RV of *our* choice. It's common procedure.'

'To where?'

'Maybe that old temple where we met Princess Ayana. But don't give Nazal time to deploy any armed back-up before we get there.'

Parsons nodded and reluctantly picked up his cell-phone. When Ayana answered, he said, 'Ollie here, Princess, World Service. I need to change our plan.' He took a deep breath. 'I want to meet our mutual friend at another venue. Same time – in an hour – but perhaps at the temple where I met you.'

'He will not like that,' Ayana replied sharply.

'He does not have an option – if he wants the benefits I can offer.'

There was a brief pause. 'I am not sure that he does want them.'

'Oh, I think he does, Princess,' Parsons replied easily. 'And *I want* what he can offer me.'

She took an intake of breath before saying. 'Please wait a moment.' There was a rustling sound as she placed her palm over her phone. Seconds later she was back. 'He will not go to a place of your choosing. That is final. He is very aware that he himself could be a target of the terrorists from Benghazi or NATO. Even a drone attack.'

Parsons didn't want this opportunity to slip through his fingers. 'Okay – '

'No!' Royce grabbed his chief's wrist and pulled the phone away from his ear. 'Compromise. Send the reinforcements and the snipers away. Just the four of us.'

Parsons understood. 'Are you still there?' he asked, putting the phone back to his ear.

She was cool. 'Of course.'

'We'll still come to you. Me and my bodyguard. No one else.'

There was a mumble of voices at the other end. Then, 'Agreed.'

'But there are conditions. You've just deployed snipers and reinforced the villa with additional troops. Send everyone away. So it will just be the two of us and you and our mutual friend. Absolutely *no one* else.'

There was a tense pause, then an almost musical and genuine laugh. 'Oh, Mr Ollie,' she said, 'you really do play a hard game, don't you? You have already had us under surveillance. Congratulations. You can have a job working for me anytime.'

'I don't think so.' He hesitated. 'Call me back when you're ready. As soon as you like.'

He hung up and looked at Royce. 'Okay?'

'Not ideal, Ollie, but I guess we'll have to live with it.'

'You're a tough bugger to please, Rollo.'

Royce shrugged.

Over the next twenty minutes, they watched as the snipers returned to their army lorry and were joined by the reinforcements from the villa with their officer. Amal and another uniformed female bodyguard also left the building and joined them. Once loaded up, both staff car and lorry drove off. A tense silence fell over the stretch of road.

At the appointed time, Royce started the Land Cruiser and drove towards the villa gates. Before he had a chance to use the horn, they opened up before him. He drove into the sandy, palm-lined quadrangle and did a three-point turn so he was facing the gates for a quick getaway.

Royce and Parsons climbed warily out of the car. As the electric gates glided shut, the two men turned towards the magnificent villa with its ornamental turrets and domes that could have been a Disney-inspired Arabian palace. An extravagant flight of terracotta steps swept up to the double-door entrance. There stood Princess Ayana, dressed in her immaculately-pressed sage and black camouflage fatigues. Beside he was the man that both Royce and Parsons recognised from their intelligence file mug-shots. Nazal Abu.

Royce glanced sideways at part of the garden laid to grass in the shade of palm trees. Water tinkled in an ornate fountain and pond.

'Let's talk here,' he hissed at Parsons.

The MI6 man nodded, and looked up the steps to the villa doors. 'Princes Ayana, Mr Nazal…May we talk down here in the garden. No hidden microphones, no secret cameras.'

Nazal was elegance personified, master of all he surveyed from the top of the palatial stairs. His pale grey suit was offset by a black shirt and ivory tie. The tie matched his lush white hair and no man of his age had eyebrows and a beard the deep colour of his shirt without help from a bottle. He plucked at the left cuff with his right hand, freeing it from the Rolex Oyster on his wrist.

His English was perfect with just a hint of an Italian accent. 'You are just a little paranoid, my good friends?'

Only Royce answered. 'Just a little,' he said. There was no humour in his tone.

'You are welcome anyway.' Nazal began his near regal descent of the steps, Ayana obediently just behind him. 'The great BBC World Service is always welcome.'

As he reached the level of the garden, there was a distinct waft of sandalwood cologne in the air.

'What a fun game you do play. What is it – Mr Oliver?' His eyes narrowed as he met Parsons's gaze. For a moment neither man spoke. Then he glanced at Royce. 'And you?'

'Doesn't matter,' Royce answered.

Nazal grunted. 'Hmm. Mr Nobody, eh?'

Parsons kept cheerful. 'James is my bodyguard, you understand that.'

Nazal raised an eyebrow. 'Babysitter?'

'As Ayana is yours.'

An insipid smile lingered within Nazal's neatly-manicured facial hair. 'And if my men were to emerge from the bushes here and take you hostage..? What could he do?'

Royce said quietly. 'NATO has the co-ordinates of this villa. And certain instructions, including very tight time limits.'

The smile stayed on Nazal's face, but became a little more fixed. 'Are you trying to frighten me, James? Because I was only joking with you.'

'I wasn't,' Royce replied flatly.

Parsons intervened. 'I'll lay my cards on the table, Mr Nazal. You have things that I want and I have things I suspect that you would like.'

'So?' Nazal's smile melted. 'You would like me to pass on a personal message to our beloved Leader Guide? Perhaps make him an offer to leave quickly for another country, perhaps staying with his friend President Mugabe in Zimbabwe? To be allowed to retain much of his personal wealth and immunity from any illegal prosecution?'

'That is a possibility.'

Nazal chuckled quietly. 'No, it isn't. Because Gaddafi will never give in to the rebel terrorists and he will never leave his beloved country. He would rather die.'

'Then he will lose and he *will* die,' Parson asserted.

'We shall see.'

'You do not have to die with him.'

The Libyan's eyes narrowed. 'I do not intend to,'

'We can make a similar offer to you as we would to Gaddafi.'

'In return for what?'

'Gaddafi's whereabouts. The target co-ordinates of anywhere he stays at any given time.'

Nazal shook his head. 'He is always on the move, never sleeps in the same house twice. Even I have not seen him in days. Mostly he is with his family and immediate trusted body-guards. And he has the Khamis Brigade to protect him to the last man.'

'And does he still trust you?'

'I like to think so.'

'Why don't you find out?'

'Why should I?'

'Because there will come a time when you will want a new identity, a new life and immunity from prosecution.' Parsons's snapped the trap shut. 'For the men and women you have persecuted, tortured and executed. For the sexual terror you have inflicted on women – no, not just women – to blackmail influential families and maintain power for Gaddafi and his sons. We know all about the underground sex chambers. And the mutilation of young women, the secret gynaecology clinics to repair their genitals after drug- and drink-fuelled abuse in the cellars of Bab al-Azizia.'

The colour drained from Nazal's face, beads of perspiration breaking out on his skin. 'That is all filthy lies.'

'That is all filthy truth, Mr Nazal.' Parsons produced a copy of the *Sunday News* from inside his jacket with a magician's flourish. 'It's been exposed in the press. It has been noted. We know that you were largely responsible. You will be investigated and held to account.'

Nazal's expression changed to one of anger. He slapped aside the tabloid with his open palm. 'Gutter press!'

Ayana looked flustered. 'He is named in the article?'

'No, but *we* know who you are. So will the NTC in Benghazi – even if we don't tell them – you can be sure of that. There will be no hiding place.

'It is why you will need our help.' For once there was no smile on Parsons' face. 'We may not know Gaddafi's location, but we do know yours. Without our help you will be put on trial here in Tripoli or in The Hague.'

Royce added, 'If your own people don't lynch you first.'

Parsons scowled sideways at him, Nazal glared. In the brief silence that followed, the Libyan looked more thoughtful than concerned. It hadn't taken long for him to regain his composure. 'I'll think about it. I would assume that apart from your attempt at intimidation and blackmail, there might be some other more enticing inducement?'

It was all Royce could do to maintain his quiet and calm façade.

'We'd arrange to spirit you out of the country,' Parsons said, forcing a smile back onto his face. 'A new identity, a new life. A fresh start.'

'And my wife and children?'

'Of course, with excellent housing and the best private education for your sons and daughter.' Parsons paused for effect. 'And not forgetting a new offshore bank account for the bounty you will get – which will be dependent on the information you've provided.'

'Such as?'

'Anything on Gaddafi,' Parsons persisted. 'And anything to help NATO degrade the power of the Khamis Brigade and Libyan Army units that are laying siege to Misrata. Strategically, that siege needs to be broken.'

Nazal scratched his goatee beard for a moment. 'That may be something I can help you with.'

Parsons dug into a cargo pocket in his travel vest and pulled out a large packet. 'Call me on this. A satellite cell-phone and charger, operates almost anywhere.'

Nazal accepted it with some reluctance. 'Let me think about it. It will depend.'

'On what?'

'The size of the bounty you offer.'

'Abu Nazal is a slimy creep,' Royce said.

The team were breakfasting at their poolside table when Ollie Parsons had unexpectedly received a call on his cell-phone from Nazal. Their chief had wandered off for some privacy into the shade of the towering palms as he continued his conversation.

Stefan Seeff laughed. 'I'm sure Nazal speaks highly of you.'

'I don't think so,' Royce retorted. 'It's a shame we have to do business with bastards like him.'

Parson's colleague, Iain Tremain, chuckled and said in his lazy Tasmanian drawl, 'It's as they say, Hell is empty now. All the devils are on earth.'

'Too bloody right,' Royce agreed.

Seeff nodded towards the hotel 'At least there are some angels too.'

Jo Brampton and Rachel Starr were sauntering out into the sunlit gardens from the hotel, respectively wearing a swimming costume and a bikini.

Seeff raised his sunglasses to view Brampton as she bent over to pluck off a flower head from a path-side shrub. He grinned. 'Smacka that sweet ass!'

'Behave,' Royce reprimanded.

As the two women approached, Seeff leaned sideways towards his friend. 'Bram fancies you.'

Royce allowed himself a wolfish grin. 'Nice thought, but highly unlikely. I ruined her army career apparently.'

'It's true, she does,' Seeff repeated. 'Rach told me.'

'And told you not to tell me?'

'Something like that.'

'Well you can keep your pillow talk to yourself, because I don't fancy her.'

It was Seeff's turn to grin. 'Yeah, right, of course not. You know, Rollo, you're starting to get decidedly boring in your old age.'

Starr waved at the South African. 'Hi, Stefan, hi guys. We heard you're going to Misrata, is that right?'

'Just Chinese whispers,' Royce replied dismissively.

'Any chance we could come along, too?' Brampton pushed. 'Misrata's where it's all happening. But there's hardly any reliable news coming out of there. We could share the costs with you.'

Parsons returned to the table with a broad smile on his face. 'Abu's agreed to do an interview with me.'

'Well done,' Royce congratulated.

Brampton was quick off the mark. 'Is that Nazal?'

Parsons shrugged evasively, but his smile remained. 'Could be?'

'You outflanked me then,' she said. 'I was hoping to get that.'

'I'll put in a word.'

'Then you owe me a favour.' Brampton decided to try again. 'Rachel and I need to get to Misrata. Any chance we can come with you?'

'Is nothing secret?' Parsons asked.

'Sinbad told me he's found a boat for you.'

Royce said, 'I'll swing for that man.'

Parsons sat on one of the chairs, clearly in a buoyant mood. 'Can't see why you can't come with us. World Service, TV Global and the *Sunday News* together – quite a media circus that'll be.'

'Right now,' Royce said, 'Misrata's probably the most dangerous place on earth and you want to expose more people to risk.'

'It's our job,' Brampton cut in. 'Sometimes you soldier boys don't realise other people have dangerous jobs to do, too.'

Seeff laughed. 'That's told you, Rollo.'

Royce realised that the attraction to Parsons of going with a party of genuine journalists was that it improved his cover. But numerically, it still increased the overall exposure to risk.

'We'll take my man, too,' Starr added. 'Yves is good. Ex-Foreign Legion.'

'That's agreed then,' Parsons decided. 'Our fishing boat will set sail at sunset. We can travel to the harbour together.'

11

MISSION TO MISRATA

Brampton was in a rare bad mood as she packed. Ever since she'd been a child she'd been told how her mere presence, her ready smile and easy laugh, brightened up people's lives. But James Royce had annoyed her, and really got under her skin.

Despite the BBC World Service producer Ollie Parsons inviting her and Starr to join them on a visit to Misrata, his security adviser had made it quite clear that he did not want them to be included. Luckily Parsons had pulled rank and overruled him.

Then she'd gone to take a shower and found there was no water, hot or cold. Shit.

She pushed her thoughts of both Royce and the hotel plumbing from her mind. Returning naked to her bedroom, she pulled on a pink Damart long-sleeved vest and a pair of thermal leggings. Even in the Mediterranean, at sea at night in a small fishing boat it would be treacherously cold – or at least Royce had kindly reminded her, as if she were still a child.

Ever since her few years spent in the British Army, Brampton had been almost obsessive about choosing the right kit for any assignment and travelling as light as possible.

She'd abandoned her favoured jeans for quick-drying windproof cargo pants and a short sage canvas over-jacket. Once dressed, she put a spare pair of trousers into her khaki daysack, together with a selection of deep-collared plain shirts that were simple but smart and a few vest tops that took up little space. Similarly, a tangled ball of thongs in either black or white cotton, and matching soft lace bras, and a silk kimono dressing-gown completed her wardrobe. Her only cosmetics were a tub of moisturiser, mascara, and shampoo that also doubled for soap.

Then more bad news arrived. Just as she zipped up the daysack, an e-mail came through on her laptop. It was from Russ Carver, her boss in London and editor of the *Sunday News*. He was coming out to assess the Libyan situation for himself as soon as he could get a flight. Meanwhile he ordered that she keep safe and acted within the company's terms of employee insurance, especially as she was currently without a personal security adviser. That, Brampton assumed, certainly wouldn't allow her to travel to Misrata, currently considered probably to be the most dangerous city on the planet.

She allowed the auto Out-Of-Office reply e-mail to kick in, closed the laptop, and left her room to join Parsons and the others in the hotel lobby.

The *Sea Orchid* was an old but lively thirty-footer, her timbers coloured in faded white and blue paint with orange trim. She bucked gamely beside the wooden jetty, as though eager to get going.

Viewed in the dim light after sunset, she offered a practical rather than elegant silhouette, with a short foredeck and tall, jutting wheel house which gave a slightly top-heavy appearance. The working area was the extended aft end with its davits to handle the fishing nets she usually carried. Tonight those nets were absent.

Sinbad and Tareg led the extended party down onto the jetty with Royce beside them, showing the way using the beam of his flashlight. Parsons followed with Brampton and Rachel Starr. Seeff and Yves came up the rear, checking that no one had followed them through the streets to Tripoli harbour. All the Westerners wore flak jackets and everyone carried their personal daysacks. The load of medical kits, satellite phones and recording equipment was equally shared.

As they approached the boat, a figure rose from the array of sacks and crates in the aft well. The skipper was heavily bearded and wore a scruffy turban and a green body-warmer over a long white shirt. Despite having a hunched back and bare feet, he moved with the speed and agility of a man half his years as he hopped onto the jetty to meet them.

It was then Royce realised that the boat was sitting exceptionally low in the water, and that was before she had taken on her passengers.

'*Salam aleykum,*' Sinbad greeted.

'*Aleykum salam,*' the skipper rejoined without enthusiasm, inspecting the new arrivals warily.

Without smiling, the man invited them to board with a gesture of his hand. Tareg stepped forward to help the two women and Parsons step over the rise and fall of the gunwale. That was when the skipper took Sinbad to one side and whispered urgently in his ear. The team's fixer nodded and followed the rest of the team aboard.

'I am afraid the quoted price has doubled,' Sinbad addressed Parsons solemnly. 'It is a regret.'

Parsons was incandescent. 'We have a deal.'

Sinbad smiled and tilted his head sympathetically. 'We *had* a deal, says Captain Ajeeb. Sadly there is diesel shortage. Its price goes up and dinar value goes down. He says you are most welcome to make alternative arrangements. There will be no hard feelings.'

'Are you on a percentage of all this, Sinbad?' Parsons demanded.

Sinbad shrugged and smiled. 'Of course, Mr Ollie.'

Royce gave a wry grin. 'Move the goalposts at the last minute. Can't blame them for trying.'

Parsons glowered.

Royce prodded one of the sacks. 'What's in these?'

Sinbad asked Ajeeb, who looked crestfallen at having been

discovered. 'He says it is coffee, flour and cigarettes for the people of Misrata.'

Then Royce nudged one of the wooden crates with his foot. He realised that they were the reason the boat was sitting so low in the water. 'And these?' he asked.

'Car parts,' Sinbad replied, smiling too much.

'Arms,' Royce replied tersely. 'It's stamped. Czech.'

Parsons looked horrified. 'God, we're smuggling arms.'

Royce smiled and shrugged. 'That's life up the sharp end, Ollie. Hope we get away with it.'

A dark mood had already settled over the team. Just before they'd sneaked out of the Golden Palms to the taxi rank, there'd been a breaking news story on the radio of yet another reporter shot in the siege of Misrata. It was rumoured that Gaddafi's snipers were deliberately targeting anyone from the media.

Yet it came as a relief actually to get under way. While Captain Ajeeb started up the ageing, heavy-duty outboard, Royce helped Sinbad and his son cast off. It went against all his Royal Navy and boyhood Sea Cadet training to see the tyre fenders – or "washing" – not taken in, but left out, creating additional spray to drench the passengers. They huddled for shelter in the wheelhouse where a single hurricane-lamp swung, offering a modicum of light.

The engine was noisy and dyspeptic, belching on dirty fuel at irregular intervals. Along with the chugging sound came the solemn slap of the black sea against the hull as the fishing boat made its way out into the open water beyond the harbour.

It was cold and unwelcoming, no longer any hint of desert warmth. Yet Royce felt a sudden relief, finding himself at home again. The stiff breeze, the sting of ozone in his nostrils, the taste of salt on his lips from the spray – these were probably the first sensations that he'd ever felt and remembered from his earliest childhood days in Plymouth. He was the son of a Royal Marines Commando, a son of the sea. He'd grown up messing around on boats, swimming, fishing or shrimping in the rock pools. His mother, before her unfair early death from cancer, had more than once described him as "half boy-half fish".

He'd graduated from Sea Cadets to the Royal Marines at the first opportunity, encouraged by his father to have him follow in his footsteps, as well as tales of derring-do from the Falklands War. He served in the First Gulf War before passing selection to the Special Boat Service or SBS. The Royal Navy's equivalent to the Special Air Service, the unit's remit was seagoing operations and land-based missions up to approximately three miles inshore.

There followed a period of assignments around the world, many conducted from ships of the Royal Navy. It was the best ever period of Royce's life and he'd loved it. While enjoying the proverbial girl in every port, true and lasting romance eluded him.

The one time he thought he'd found it, he hadn't. She thought she was pregnant, she wasn't. He thought he'd love married life, he didn't. They thought they could make it work, they couldn't. After three years, they both decided to go their separate ways.

Then in 2001 came the devastating 9/11 attack on New York by a terrorist cell affiliated with al-Qaeda.

After the Alliance invaded Iraq, Royce was subsequently assigned to joint US-UK missions in the south of the country, although it had no links with the terror group. Later he was also sent to Afghanistan, where the Taliban government *had* actually given sanctuary to al-Qaeda.

Following regime change in Kabul, Royce and his fellow SBS colleagues returned to their world-wide deployment, including the Royal Navy's disruption of narcotics traffic in the Caribbean.

After the Allies' hasty withdrawal and broken promises to the fragile new Afghanistan democracy, the radical Taliban movement was already making a comeback by 2006. Because of SAS overstretch in Iraq, it fell to the SBS to provide the special forces lead in Afghanistan.

With the British contingent undermanned, under-equipped and underfunded, Royce was totally disgusted and disillusioned at the bedlam and chaos, and lack of tactics or strategy that he found. In the quick succession of two incidents, he lost three good friends, two dead and another horribly maimed. To his mind, both incidents were totally avoidable. It seemed to him that the British military itself had forgotten the lessons on insurgency it had once learned and used to great effect until recently.

At the end of 2006 Royce did not renew his extended contract. He left the SBS for good and joined a British private contract company called IAP, International Asset Protection. As a civilian working with several former comrades, he trained and became a Close Protection expert on "The Circuit". It was dangerous but highly lucrative work in Iraq, Afghanistan and other trouble spots around the world. That was when his and Stefan Seeff's paths had crossed again and they had become firm friends.

Looking up at the breath-taking expanse of indigo cosmos, dusted with distant stars and galaxies, the realisation came to him that he was reaching the end of an era. Although he was only forty-two, retirement now beckoned – or, at least, retirement from the sort of work where someone, somewhere was always trying to kill him.

This was probably his last mission, the remaining few days of his contract. There was always the temptation to drop one's guard, become demob happy. Get careless. He didn't want to end up dead in Misrata.

He glanced down at the Breitling on his right wrist. They were making around seven knots. Allowing for the outward and inward legs of the journey, the *Sea Orchid* had around a hundred and seven miles to cover. According to Sinbad, they should reach Qasar Ahmad dock in about twenty-four hours, arriving safely under cover of the next nightfall. Neat.

Royce pushed any concerns about the visit to Misrata to the back of his mind, and joined the others in the cramped rear of the wheelhouse. Everyone was seated cross-legged around an up-turned plastic crate that served as a table. Brampton and Starr were playing hostess, dividing out the packed meals that had been provided by the hotel kitchen. It was turning into a veritable feast, with flasks providing hot soup and beverages. Arabic music drifted from the skipper's portable radio, adding to the festive mood and infectious laughter. Cans of cola snapped and fizzed. Yves and Starr produced bottles labelled cough syrup which Allah would most certainly not have approved. It smelled distinctly of dark rum. Royce and Seeff declined the offering. The ebbing of tension in the air was almost palpable.

The party mood continued as they played Cheat with Seeff's dog-eared pack of cards. As soon as young Tareg learned the rules – or lack of them – he became the star player.

Brampton noticed Royce's expression soften. Tareg's crafty playing clearly amused him. She thought sometimes how Royce could often have a look of murderous intensity about him, as though having dark and demonic thoughts. It was as though he didn't like to think too much about people's feelings or emotions as he concentrated obsessively on the job at hand.

She smiled. 'I think that's the first time I've seen you laugh.'

Royce glanced across at her. 'Yes?'

Seeff said, 'Should have known him in the old days.'

'The old days?'

'Before Baghdad. He was the life and soul of any party.'

Royce said, 'Don't talk about me as if I'm not here.'

'What happened in Baghdad?' Brampton asked.

Seeff looked awkward, sensed Royce wanted him to shut up. He just said, 'Some bad shit.'

She looked across the makeshift card table, thought she could see the hurt in his eyes. 'I wish I had,' she said suddenly.

'Had what?' Seeff asked.

'Had known him then,' she said and immediately wished that she hadn't asked.

Parsons sensed the emotive atmosphere building in the confined space. He coughed lightly. 'It's getting late and we've a long day tomorrow. Best we all get some shut eye.'

It was after midnight before everyone was settled down in their sleeping bags, packed tightly together like frozen fish. While the civilians struggled to doze off, those with military backgrounds had little problem, having learned the hard way to snatch catnaps wherever and whenever there was the slightest opportunity.

Sinbad's high-pitched and volatile argument with skipper Ajeeb broke into Royce's subconscious. As he stirred, he found himself already checking for the CZ85 on his hip. He opened his eyes to the blinding beam of sun-bright light. Even before he was out of his Gortex bivvy-bag he realised they'd been spotted by a ship. The question was, whose ship?

Parsons had told him that Gaddafi corvettes from the nearby naval base at Al Khums were trying to mine the approaches to Misrata in an attempt to stop reinforcements and supplies for the rebels reaching the city. It was the job of Royal Navy and other NATO frigates to prevent them.

'Keep down everyone,' Royce ordered as he joined Sinbad and Ajeeb at the helm.

The skipper shielded his eyes with his forearm. 'It is the vengeance of Allah!'

'Shut up, my friend,' Sinbad said in Arabic. 'Allah is fast asleep.'

The searchlight beam swung away, seeking new targets. Once out of the glare, a sleek, inky outline could be determined.

'A British destroyer,' Royce decided, 'HMS Liverpool, if I'm not mistaken.'

Parsons said, 'Must have realised we're either fishing for real or taking in supplies for the good guys.'

Royce glanced at his watch. In another half an hour it would be sunrise. He extracted a small pair of 8 x 21 binoculars from his travel vest and settled in the bows as self-appointed look out.

It proved to be an eventful day, all played out to the background of jangling Arab music that reverberated from Ajeeb's portable radio. In the last minutes of darkness, explosions pulsed in the dark southern horizon beyond the coast. They were followed moments later by the earthy boom of heavy shells landing. Whether the barrage came from Gaddafi forces on land or from the guns of NATO warships at sea, it was difficult to determine. But as daylight crept across the sluggish seascape, pillars of black smoke rose until they looked as though they were propping up the sky.

As the hours passed, more and more shipping was seen. At one point Royce thought he identified a Libyan corvette slipping like a phantom in the mist where the sea and sky merged. Every now and again a fighter aircraft would pass by high overhead, trailing a sonic boom in its wake, on a mission to somewhere. Again, it was impossible to know which side the aeroplane was on.

Other fishing boats were also at sea, although none looked as though they were trawling nets. Like the *Sea Orchid* itself, most were low in the water and looked to be heavily loaded with supplies, all moving towards the Misrata docks. At one time Royec glimpsed a ferry headed out towards Benghazi, transformed into a hospital ship to carry out the injured from the deadly fighting in Misrata. Seagulls gathered, circling in huge flocks, screeching and squawking and dive-bombing the trawlers. As the sun began to sink in the west, the noise of war from the land grew in intensity as though someone had turned up the volume on a television set. The heavy thud of landing shells was interspersed with the percussion of small arms fire that sounded like distant rattles at a football match.

Suddenly it caught his eye. Light glinted on metal. 'MINE!'

Sinbad jumped forward, scrambling onto the short foredeck to join Royce. The man waved frantically and jabbed his finger to the right. 'STEER STEER!' he yelled in Arabic.

Royce held his breath. Ajeeb spun the wheel, and grudgingly the boat obeyed and changed its course. The steel ball of explosive drifted past, just inches away.

Night settled over the docks like a black velvet cloak. Somehow, despite having any obvious means of communication, friends of Ajeeb were ready to meet them and unload as the boat slowly chugged into the port. A cacophony of explosions and gunfire became a constant and unnerving backdrop to the city of over three hundred thousand souls enduring hell on earth.

'We leave again tomorrow evening.' Royce impressed. 'Be sure. No confusion.'

'Yes, yes,' Sinbad agreed and embarked in a long and furious debate with Ajeeb. Hearing only snippets of their heated conversation, Royce just sensed that the cost of the team's return trip had just doubled.

He and Seeff had studied street-maps and knew which way to go. Parsons had arranged an appointment with a Misrata militia known as The Brotherhood, given the name by Nazal Abu.

'Their leader is a man called Wasam Hatem,' Nazal had solemnly informed over the phone. 'He is from Qatar. He can be trusted.'

When Parsons had asked Chingford Charlie about the man, the long-term MI6 "alongsider" had shaken his head. "No, can't say I know him. Perhaps he *can* be trusted. The bigger question is, can Nazal Abu? As slippery as a bunch of snakes in Vaseline.'

Brampton and Starr had their own agenda, to meet another rebel militia group known simply as the "Misrata Freedom Battalion". Apparently they were at the forefront of the fighting in the south of the city on Tripoli Street which had seen the brunt of the fighting against Gaddafi's heavy armour and artillery. Houses on both sides of the thoroughfare had been reduced to rubble and had been infiltrated by both army and mercenary snipers.

One of the Battalion's representatives, a polite accountancy student who was barely out of his teens, met them on the quay. He was neatly dressed in jeans and a plain blue shirt, but he carried an AK47 and wore a bandana around his head that made him look more childish than rakish, which Brampton assumed had been the intention.

'Like Rambo.' Brampton said with a nod of her head.

'Just like him, madam.' He grinned widely. 'Come, I will look after you ladies.'

The big Frenchman Yves followed watchfully towards the waiting pick-up. Young Tareg went with them as an interpreter.

'You take care,' Royce called after them, 'Good luck.'

Royce then led his team through the feverish quayside activity, the loading and unloading of small boats, towards their own destination.

The temporary headquarters of the so-called Islamic Brotherhood Alliance was in a seaman's hostel, a dilapidated building that hung a limp green Islamic flag from the pole above its rotted wooden door. A large, heavily-bearded man, in scruffy robes and a black turban, stood outside brandishing a Czech-made machine pistol.

Royce fronted them, but Sinbad did the talking in Arabic. 'BBC World Service. We are expected. To talk with Sheikh Hatem Wasam.'

There was little interest in the guard's eyes. He grunted, turned and knocked on the door behind him. A rusted cover over the small observation grille slid open and the doorman passed on the message.

The heavy door swung open and they were shown inside. Its shabby reception lobby and narrow wooden staircase was full of hard-eyed and armed militiamen sitting around smoking, playing dice or cards or just talking to each other. Many wore black turbans or bandanas with white Arabic script on them. The fighters fell silent as the strangers entered. One of them deliberately spat at Sinbad's feet. Sinbad smiled at the man, held up his open palm and blew him back a kiss. Some of the men laughed.

They were shown to a small room with lime-washed walls, one of which was decorated by a moth-eaten Persian carpet that might have seen happier times a hundred years earlier. Most of the space was taken up by a worn, bare timber dining table that was surrounded by chairs.

The doorman indicated for them to sit down. They were left alone.

When the door shut, Royce said, 'These guys are hardliners.'

Sinbad said, 'They are *jihadis*. Most I see here not from Libya. Not good peoples.'

Parsons grunted. 'War makes strange bedfellows.'

'I suppose,' Sinbad concluded, 'We need all help we can get.'

Without warning the door was flung open. Two men burst into the room. They wore jeans and black shirts. Balaclavas covered their faces and they pointed heavy duty automatics.

A tall, well-built man stepped in behind them. He wore a distinctive, long camel leather waistcoat over a long white shirt and baggy trousers. The letters of his name were branded into the waistcoat on each side in Arabic script. No ego, there then, Royce thought. The man's dusky hair and beard were an untamed riot, a primitive statement of superiority. His hooked nose was like a beak between the watchful eyes of a desert eagle.

'Sheikh Hatem,' Parsons began.

Hatem raised his hand. 'Please. Security first. No guns, no recorders.'

Seeff glanced at Royce, who shook his head. Both men understood. They placed their respective automatics on the table in front of them. Parsons put his tape-recorder beside them.

Hatem seated himself at the head of the table, his two bodyguards closing in on both sides of him. 'Gentlemen, Brother Nazal Abu has told me who you are. You are not journalists from the BBC World Service. You are spies sent here by the British Government to help us. Us? The rebels to overthrow Colonel Gaddafi.'

'You are not Libyans,' Sinbad blurted.

Hatem spared him a withering glance. 'No, quite right. I am a Qatari. Qatar is spending much resources to assist the Libyans. Arms and some Special Forces. I represent my government. It is my duty to ensure that those resources are deployed wisely. We also fund your local Taureg tribesmen, who support the Brotherhood.'

Royce noticed that Sinbad looked decidedly unhappy.

Parsons got on with it. 'Our mutual friend, Nazal Abu?' he reminded.

Hatem relaxed. 'Quite so.' He raised his hand and immediately veiled women carried in copper trays of jugs and glasses. Mint tea was served.

When the women had disappeared, Hatem produced a sheath of paper in a plastic cover from a leather attaché case. 'Mr Nazal knows that the rebel alliance cannot move west to Tripoli to overthrow Gaddafi until Misrata falls to them. The city is in ruins, the siege could break at any moment. The rebellion is at a tipping point – either way. Mr Nazal asked me to produce a list of targets for NATO strikes. Both naval bombardment and airstrikes. I now have these from my area commanders. Tank and artillery positions, troop concentrations. Co-ordinates. Targets that are vital to defeat the siege.'

Parsons took the paper and glanced down at it. 'It's a long list.'

Sheikh Hatem interlaced his fingers. 'It is a big and important battle. If we lose this battle for Misrata, Gaddafi will win the civil war. The consequences of that are unthinkable.'

'I'll take steps now,' Parsons replied, and took out his mobile phone. By way of explanation, he added, 'Satellite.'

He went outside into the open courtyard and seconds later was through to Tremain in their Ops Room back at the Golden Palms. Laboriously he began reading down the long list of co-ordinates and double-checking them.

Finally done, Parsons returned inside to re-join the others. 'The list will be sent by encrypted radio to London and then NATO. Of course, I can offer no guarantee of when and how attacks will be made or co-ordinated. We'll ask for them as soon as possible, of course. The attacks could come by air or sea.'

Sheikh Hatem nodded graciously. 'I understand. It is out of your hands. We are happy for any help that the Allies can give us. Now you must be tired. I have a spare room upstairs. It is bare without furniture, but is dry and clean. You are free to use it during your stay. We have stocks of army blankets. Our kitchen is open twenty-four seven for fresh water, broth and bread. Make yourself at home. You may take your weapons now.'

'Thank you, Sheikh,' Parsons replied and handed him a small package. 'A satellite-phone like mine. My number is already on it. Any time you want to reach me, use it. I think we can be friends.'

The big man rose from the table. 'Of that I am sure, Mr Ollie.'

Sheikh Hatem and his bodyguards made a hasty exit and the team followed the doorman up the stairs, which were crowded with fighters trying to find a few spare feet of space to curl up and sleep. They were shown the privileged single room, where a Tilley lamp illuminated its bare floorboards and whitewashed walls. A pile of brown army blankets had been stored in one corner; one of them had been strung up to form a curtain for the solitary window.

As everyone settled in, Royce and Seeff sat down beside their kit and, using torches, began checking the list of co-ordinates given to Parsons by Sheikh Hatem with a large scale map of Misrata.

Finally Parsons was set up for the night. 'God, I'm famished. Anyone for some grub?'

Neither Royce nor Seeff seemed to hear him. The two men glanced up from the map and looked at each other for a moment.

'Are you thinking what I'm thinking?' Seeff asked.

'I've got a horrible feeling,' Royce said.

Parsons frowned. 'What's up?'

Royce said, 'I think we may have a problem.'

12

WAR WILL BE OVER BY RAMADAN

It had been a long, dark road from the docks to the city of Misrata.

Tareg had to sit on Yves's lap so that Brampton and Starr could also fit into the cabin of the pick-up. They were squeezed violently together – first left and then right alternatively – as their driver swung the wheel to miss bricks and chunks of masonry in the middle of the ruptured tarmac. Only one headlight worked, which made it more difficult for him to spot the obstacles and avoid them.

Tremulous explosions rent the night sky all around, throwing the wrecked buildings into bold relief against the scorching flashes of light. The acrid stench of smoke, burning oil and spent gunpowder was everywhere.

'What is your name?' Brampton asked the young driver.

'Abdul Rizik.'

Rachel Starr laughed. 'Then definitely Rambo Rizik to us.'

Brampton shared her humour as she felt the adrenalin kick in. 'Always the eye for a headline.'

'Caption,' Starr corrected. 'I'm TV, remember.'

'While I'm just a humble press hack, yeah?'

'Something like that.'

'You are famous Madam Brampton,' Rizik said. 'My commander

has the article you wrote recently pinned on his noticeboard.'

Brampton felt an unexpected flush of pride. 'Oh really?'

Rizik nodded enthusiastically. 'He says it boosts our morale when many think we will all die.'

'I'm Rachel,' Starr said. 'TV-Global.'

'I am sorry, Madam Rachel,' Rizik apologised, 'I do not know of your programme.'

Brampton laughed aloud. Starr pulled a face, while Yves kept silent but grinned broadly.

'Your other journalist friends?' the young accountancy student-turned-freedom fighter asked. 'Where are they going?'

'To interview your allies, the Brigade of Brothers,' Starr replied.

Rizik gave a snort of derision. 'We are both fighting Gaddafi, but we are hardly allied. My people are the Misrata Freedom Battalion, we were born in this city. We are part of the Tripoli Street Brigade. They are outsiders, the Muslim Brotherhood by any other name, radical jihadists that will have this country sent back to medieval times. They are meddling here and in Egypt. Sheikh Hatem is from Qatar.' The conversation was distracting Rizik and he just missed a jagged piece of metal railing in their path. 'That is also the country where most of our weapons are coming from. So you see, we have obligation to co-operate with the Brotherhood.'

Brampton nodded her understanding. 'No co-operation, no weapons?'

'Exactly that, Madam Brampton.'

An artillery shell suddenly landed and blew up in the adjoining block of wrecked housing. The flash was blinding and the noise so loud that it hurt her ears. A demonic force of displaced air actually pushed the pick-up sideways as the ground itself trembled as if in fear. Broken bricks and rubble rattled down on the cab roof and bounced off the bonnet.

'Bloody hell,' Starr muttered. 'That was close.'

'We are nearly there,' Rizik said in attempt to reassure them.

'And how is the battle going?' Brampton asked. 'If that's not a silly question.'

The young man looked distinctly downhearted. 'Not so bad. The siege is two months now. Gaddafi has tanks and artillery surrounding us and he has snipers in the ruins. They shoot even the wounded and doctors who try to help them. But we have taken back the airport, recently, as well as some key high buildings from them. The centre of the city will soon be ours. We *must* win here in Misrata. It is holding up the whole rebel advance along the coast to Tripoli. If we lose Misrata, we lose the people's war.'

'But you are not alone,' Brampton said, trying to cheer him up. 'You are getting weapons and reinforcements. And the world knows about your brave fight.'

He nodded. 'That is true. Miss Colvin, the reporter with the eye patch comes here. And Miss Alex Crawfie of Sky television. Now you…But mostly they are freelance journalists and bloggers trying to make a name.' Suddenly he grinned widely. 'Here we are now. This is the head office of our battalion.'

A sangar, made of sandbags and corrugated iron, guarded each side of the steel compound gates, heavy machine guns defying any Gaddafi forces to come too close. An array of Heath Robinson converted pick-up trucks was parked outside, carrying everything from rocket launchers and mortars to HMGs and anti-aircraft cannons. Their crews were hard at work maintaining the weapons systems or making mechanical repairs under the cover of darkness, using carefully shaded torches.

Guards wearing jeans, T-shirts and bandanas swung open the gates to let their vehicle into the compound of what was clearly once a school. There were dozens more converted vehicles in the yard. Armed rebel fighters were everywhere, chilling out, talking and joking excitedly as they smoked and drank soft drinks from cans.

Rizik pulled on the handbrake and killed the engine. 'There is a basement. You will be safe there. I will arrange for our commander to come and talk with you.'

He was as good as his word. They were shown to the basement to where most of the schools desks and other unwanted items had been stored. Yves wasn't too happy about the shelter it offered. Although there was a concrete floor above them, a direct hit would almost certainly cause a collapse. However they were out of options, and it was probably safer there than upstairs. Yves presented Tareg with his own blue helmet and insisted that he wore it at all times, even when asleep.

When they checked, there was no cell-phone reception. Gaddafi's forces had been targeting all telephone transmission towers, water and electricity supplies to strangle the life out of the city. All its lighting was by candle or battery unless, like this school, there was an emergency generator and fuel could be found for it.

The group had barely time to sort out the sleeping arrangements and lay down their kip mats and sleeping bags when the battalion commander, a former architect called Saad Musa arrived with Rizik behind him.

Musa was a very thin, tall man in his forties who looked as though he'd be more comfortable in a smart suit than the green T-shirt and camo trousers that he wore. His appearance was very unmilitary with heavily-framed black spectacles and a thick beard but, according to Charlie Chingford, he was a natural tactician and commander. He also had charm and a very friendly demeanour.

However, his English was limited and Rizik had to interpret the numerous questions and answers between Brampton and Starr. Yves had a back-up role as cameraman. He set up one video camera on a tri-pod, permanently facing the commander, and a second smaller hand-held model to film Starr as she asked her questions.

It was a fairly successful and frank session. But Brampton didn't envy Starr the later job of editing the interview and splicing it all together with b-roll footage of the fighting. Brampton completed her own work in a notebook with a simple snap of the commander on her

35mm digital.

The commander had barely left the basement when somebody else clattered down the steps. 'Ah, yes, I think that it maybe you! I think I recognise your voice.'

Brampton turned and frowned at the new arrival. The unkempt black hair and wild beard threw her for a moment. 'Dr Jaralla? I hardly recognised you.'

The man she'd first met on the car journey to interview Princess Ayana, and who had later come to their rescue, looked so different now. He had aged unbelievably in such a short time. His face appeared etched with lines and skin the around his eyes was grey with fatigue.

He shook her hand. 'I no longer feel like a young man. My group was driven out of Tripoli. So we came here to Misrata to make a difference.'

'And have you?'

Jaralla smiled modestly. 'Only Allah knows that. But I think the tide has started to turn. Gaddafi's forces are being driven to the outskirts of town.'

At that moment they all heard it. It was the terrifying banshee wail of incoming rockets. Fear struck into Brampton's heart like a physical thing, her heart missing a beat. A rapid drumming of explosions followed some little distance away.

'Wow,' Starr gasped, unaware that she'd been holding her breath.

But Jaralla was unmoved. 'The hounds of the night, that is what we call them. Russian-made Grad multiple rocket-launchers. A fearsome bark, but they will not strike here. This HQ is a new location, not known to Gaddafi's scouts.'

'I hope you're right.'

'You should be safe enough here. It is good to see you again. Can I help you in any way?'

Starr grabbed her opportunity. 'Hallo, doctor, I'm Rachel Starr, TV-Global. We're only here until tomorrow evening. I'd love to get some frontline footage in Misrata.'

He said, 'It is still very dangerous here, you should be warned.'

Considering for a moment, he continued, 'My men are fighting along Tripoli Street, trying to drive out the Gaddafi snipers. I will take you there. We will leave early tomorrow morning. Our fighters move from house to house through holes in the wall. You should be safe enough if you take no risks.'

'Thank you so much,' Starr said, delighted at the prospect of some "hot shots", as she liked to call them.

'If the tide is turning as you say, Doctor, what do you think will happen?' Brampton asked. 'After Gaddafi is defeated?'

'It'll be good, yes?' Starr prompted.

'Maybe, maybe not.' Jaralla didn't look exactly joyous. 'Gaddafi is not a good man, but he created a fairly good health service free to the people. Under sanctions from the West that disintegrated. And now in the fighting it has almost ceased. And when his regime is finished, there will be a vacuum. It is inevitable.'

Yves made a rare intervention. 'That is true. I see it all before,' he said in his deeply-accented French. 'All over the world. A dictator falls and all the alpha males they rush in, seek their opportunity. The warlords and the power brokers. Libya will be no different.'

'You think?' Jaralla asked.

'It is the way of humans and animals. The strongest always lead the pack.'

Jaralla nodded. 'And I think here the strongest will be the Brotherhood. I feel it. In Egypt, too, and maybe in Syria. The poor and ignorant will support them because they want Allah on their side.'

Yves grunted. 'God is usually on the side of the biggest army.'

Brampton smiled. 'Or the smartest one.'

'We shall find out soon enough,' Jaralla replied. 'With any luck this war of ours will be over by Ramadan.'

'Let's hope so,' Brampton said.

'Meanwhile,' Jaralla concluded, 'they are serving food upstairs. Goat and rice. You are most welcome to eat with our fighters.'

They spent the next couple of hours in the smoke-filled main hall of the school, sitting around on cushions, eating and chatting and laughing with the young fighters of Misrata. Although there were older men, including some deserters from Gaddafi's army, they were overwhelmingly students. In the background conflicting music came from different radios and portable CD players. Traditional Arab music clashed with Western pop. Many of the fighters were flattered at being asked for their opinions and being invited to tell their stories to the two journalists, although others were not so keen to be caught on video for TV. It became clear that many half suspected that Gaddafi might yet survive the rebellion and that they and their families would have to pay the price.

After eating, exhaustion caught up quickly with the young fighters and they were soon preparing for what they were aware might be their last night's sleep in this world. The journalist team returned to the basement and got its heads down in anticipation of an early start the next day.

'Seems like there's no reverse gear on this,' Parsons said. He was deeply unhappy as he sat on his sleeping bag in their makeshift accommodation at the seamen's hostel. He switched off his satellite mobile after talking to Tremain, who was running their Ops Room back at the Golden Palms in Tripoli.

'He got through to the MOD?' Royce pressed.

'Ministry of Defence were a bit sniffy. Said they passed all co-ordinates we gave them to NATO,' Parsons drawled wearily. 'But no one knows what priority those targets will be given. Like will they slot in with existing planned missions, or be included in missions planned for next week in the same area?'

'So an abort is impossible?' Royce asked.

Parsons grimaced. 'Well, out of ninety odd target co-ordinates we gave them, you're querying five. And that's on a hunch. We're trying to stop a few pebbles in a huge avalanche.'

'I can see NATO's problem,' Seeff said. 'And we're half-guessing about some of those site co-ordinates that Sheikh Hatem has given us. We're certain most *are* Gaddafi positions.'

'I'm still trying the mobile numbers we've got for Bram, Rachel and Yves,' Royce added. 'They're all dead. Our team's mostly okay on a satellite system, but all *their* local networks in Misrata are down.'

'We should have given Brampton one of our own cell-phones,' Parsons admitted to himself.

'A bit late now,' Royce muttered. 'Our best hope is to reach them and advise them to pull out. We don't even *know* for certain where they are tonight.'

'On a hunch,' Seeff pointed out. 'We don't even know that the schoolhouse *is* the new Freedom Battalion HQ.'

Parsons grunted. 'Fog of war. No one has a clue what the fuck is going on until it's all over.'

Royce said, 'We haven't even got our own transport here. The sane thing is to sort something out with Rizik at first light, drive out, try and locate them, persuade them to come back. Terminate this whole mission in Misrata.'

'What a bag of worms,' Parson said, shaking his head in despair.

In fact Dr Jaralla called the group of journalists even before first light. With gluey eyes and no water to wash, they gathered with a small group of fighters in the front yard. Small cups of strong coffee were thrust into their hands to kick start them for the journey.

Yves was adamant that young Tareg should be left behind in the safety of the battalion's HQ rather than join the journalists on their risky frontline assignment, much to the youngster's disappointment. Meanwhile they donned their bullet-proof vests and helmets, feeling slightly embarrassed that neither Sinbad nor the Libyan fighters enjoyed any such protection.

Daylight was feeling its way across the sky, melting the shadows. It promised to be another warm and humid day.

A Nissan pick-up stopped outside the yard gates, and Jaralla invited them to climb into the open back cargo area. Yves helped the two women up.

Tareq stood on the ground beside the pick-up next to Abdul Rizik. '*Please*, Miss Jo,' Tareg asked, 'let me come with you.'

'I'm sorry, Bright Spark,' Brampton said, 'it's just *too* dangerous.'

For once there was no smile on Tareg's face, just a petulant grimace.

Rizik gave the boy a hug. 'Hey, how about we have a game of football? We can play it in the yard. I'll get some of my friends. Our team will be Man U.'

'Thanks, Abdul,' Brampton said. 'You're a star.'

'No problem. I have a break until this afternoon. Then I will take you back to the docks.'

The pick-up engine started with a jolt as Rizik and Tareg turned back into the yard.

'Bye, sweetpea!' Brampton called out to him. 'See you soon,'

Gears crunched and the pickup gathered speed, moving towards the nearby cross-roads. It was uncannily quiet. Only fighters ventured out of doors and petrol was scarce. Jaralla sat with them in the back of the vehicle, his AK47 at the ready in case they came under fire from Gaddafi snipers.

A taxi appeared at the crossroads, coming from the direction of the docks. Someone was waving furiously from the rear passenger window. Jaralla lowered and pointed his weapon cautiously.

Starr said, 'I do believe it's Royce. What's he doing here?'

'Looking for us?' Brampton guessed. She turned to Jaralla. 'The man in the taxi is a friend. Can we stop a minute?'

The doctor nodded and thumped three times on the roof of the pick-up's cab. Instantly the driver stamped on the brakes and the wheels locked into a dramatic skid on the coating of loose rubble and debris on the ground.

A second later the taxi drew alongside and Royce scrambled out from the back seat, closely followed by Sinbad. Royce ran over to the open rear of the pick-up. 'Thank goodness, you're all here,' he gasped.

Brampton looked down. 'What's the matter, James? Why are you looking for us?'

'It may be something or nothing,' Royce replied. Suddenly his and Seeff's concerns seemed paranoid. He nodded towards the compound that the pick-up had just left on the far side of the cross-roads. 'Is that the schoolhouse?'

Brampton frowned. 'Yes. Why?'

'Is it the new Freedom Battalion HQ?'

Jaralla interjected. 'Hallo, Mr James. It is good to see you again. Yes, we moved in a couple of days ago.'

Royce was surprised. 'Doctor, I hardly recognised you…Listen, it's just possible that the schoolhouse will be targeted by NATO.'

Brampton was incredulous. 'Why on earth would NATO want to do – ?'

Her words were drowned out by the scream of a jet fighter rocketing across the sky high overhead, the light from the newly-risen sun glinting on its wings.

Far away to the south, bright lights pulsed along the perimeter of the city where Gaddafi's army tanks and heavy artillery were positioned. The huge flashes were followed split seconds later by the earthy thud of explosions. Oily black smoke spiralled skywards from the hit targets.

Jaralla sprang to his feet in a spontaneous response. '*Allah akbur!* Death to Gaddafi!' he shouted, waving his AK47 in the air.

That was the moment that the fire-and-forget air-to-surface missile hit the schoolhouse. The tremulous burst of light from the compound seared the retina with its blinding intensity and instantly deafened with its almighty percussion. Bricks and chunks of mortar exploded in all directions. Within the maelstrom of smoke and dust further secondary detonations went off as stored ammunition ignited.

'Oh, my God, Tareg!' Brampton cried.

Sinbad stared in shocked disbelief. He took in the demolished, smouldering wreck of the schoolhouse, the tangled remains of vehicles and bodies strewn everywhere. His gaze moved to Brampton. 'He is not with you?'

Brampton tried, but she could not speak. She pressed her clenched fist to her lips and shook her head.

He looked back at the schoolhouse. Tears welled in his eyes as the realisation struck home. His mouth moved around the words, 'My son…Allah, forgive me.'

13

THE END WILL ONLY BE
THE BEGINNING

Timeline: Late May 2011

'The bastards,' Brampton said with feeling. Starr nodded her agreement.

Three days' on, Ollie Parsons' team and the two journalists were seated together on the zebra-skin settees in reception at the Golden Palms.

Charlie Chingford had joined them for lunch. 'Don't say I didn't warn you,' he said, sipping at his Gaddafi Sunrise. 'Nazal can't be trusted. I think he's banking on the jihadists coming out on top when all this is over.'

Brampton wiped a tear from her eye with the back of her hand. 'And poor little Tareg paid the price'.

'And Rizik,' Rachel Starr added. 'He was so sweet, so innocent.'

Royce leaned forward in earnest, his forearms on his knees and his fingers interlaced. 'Nazal doesn't strike me as anything like a typical *jihadi*.'

Chingford gave a snort of derision. 'No, you're right. He's a typical opportunist. Nazal *is* backing the Muslim Brotherhood. Because he knows – and they know – that *when* Gaddafi is finished, they are most likely to be in control of the vacuum that's left.'

'Their main rival in Misrata is the democratic Freedom Battalion,' Parsons pointed out. 'That's why the Brotherhood sneaked in those co-ordinates to NATO amongst the Gaddafi targets. To wipe out their rival's leadership in the city. The radicals are determined to win there, and in Benghazi and Tripoli too.'

'I can see a pattern emerging in this so-called Arab Spring,' Chingford agreed. 'Next door in Egypt, President Mubarak has resigned. If there's an election it's reckoned the radical Muslim Brotherhood will win by a country mile.'

'Even Syria is kicking off,' Tremain pointed out in his lazy Tasmanian drawl. 'Who'd have thought that, the people actually standing up against President Assad?'

Brampton was intrigued. 'Maybe Britain will help to get rid of Assad – like they have here with Gaddafi.'

Parsons shook his head. 'There'll be no winners in Syria,' he said decidedly. 'Roughly fifty per cent of the population are Assad's tribal supporters, fifty per cent aren't. Half of those opponents are likely to be peasants who are comfortable with extreme Islam. And Assad is backed by the Russians.'

Tremain agreed. 'At best twenty-five per cent of Syria's population would ever support the West. Do the numbers.'

Brampton looked puzzled. 'You two guys certainly know your Middle East politics for just a couple of hacks.'

Royce raised an eyebrow. Had the two MI6 men rather given themselves away?

But Parsons seemed happy enough to brazen it out. 'BBC World Service hacks, Jo, there's a difference.' He laughed heartily. 'Sad to say, unlike our Foreign Office, I'm not at all sure I believe this so-called "Arab Spring" will be in Britain's or the West's interests.'

'How do you mean?' Rachel Starr asked.

He shrugged. 'Put simply, most Arab states are run by absolute monarchs and dictators which are supported by either the West or, like Syria, the Russian camp. If all or any actually get a democratically-elected government that our woolly-headed pinkos think they should have, it's ten to a penny that the working masses will have voted for what we in London would consider to be radical Islam. After all, the people want Allah on their side, obviously.'

Brampton's frown deepened. 'Are you saying we would lose most of our Middle East allies?'

Parsons considered for a moment. 'Possibly or probably. Any adviser to our government would have to say we should try and stick with the status quo. Better the devils we know.'

Chingford noisily finished off his cocktail though a straw. 'I can tell you one thing, the end here in Libya will only be the beginning. I can see extreme Islam on the rise all across the Middle East, the re-establishment of an international *jihad* – a holy war against the West – and the establishment of a caliphate.'

Starr touched his forearm. 'Charlie, that sounds really scary. What is a caliphate *exactly*?'

Chingford placed his hand over hers, pressing his fingertips down suggestively. 'Sweet, Rachel, it is an Islamic state that could possibly sweep all the way from Iran and Iraq across North Africa to the Atlantic coast.'

Brampton shivered. 'But that's not likely, is it?'

There was a dry chuckle from Chingford. 'No more than a Muslim President of America or a Muslim Prime Minister of Britain.'

Brampton and Starr glanced at each other.

Starr said, 'It's like we're replaying the crusades all over again – a thousand years later.'

Parsons' phone began its Arabic jingle. He snatched it up. He listened and acknowledged what was said. Then he turned to Brampton. 'Jo, that was your editor. He's cleared Customs at the airport and he's on his way, in a taxi now.'

She looked flustered. 'Oh, God, I'd almost forgotten Russ was due today.' She hesitated. 'But why'd he phone you? *I'm* his feature journalist. You're BBC.'

Parsons shrugged. 'We go back a bit, Russ and I.' He then added, 'And my mobile nearly always works.'

Brampton frowned. 'I've got one bar today,' she replied, clearly puzzled and a little put out that her editor hadn't chosen to call her personally. 'It's still a bit weird.'

Seeff said, 'Talking of which, Rollo, have you got your departure date confirmed?'

Royce nodded. 'Friday.'

'Two days?'

'My replacement should be arriving on the same flight as Russ Carver.' Royce grinned widely. 'Time for a handover and then I'm off – to a new life in Civvie Street with no one trying to kill me.'

'You'll miss that,' Seeff predicted. 'And *my* company.'

Royce grinned. 'No, I won't. Just because you saved my life once, doesn't mean I have to like you.'

Brampton watched him banter with his South African friend. She'd been aware how much more relaxed he'd seemed over the past couple of days since their return from Misrata. She hadn't realised his "close protection" contract with the BBC was coming to an end, and that was probably the reason for his icy personality thawing suddenly in the way that it had. It occurred to her now just how much she would actually miss him.

It was then that one of the waiters from the restaurant approached them. 'Mr Parsons, your table is available now.'

'Is there hot food today?' the MI6 man asked.

The waiter looked pained. 'I regret not, sir. We are out of fuel for the generator. But we have a nice new salad with pomegranate on the menu.'

Parsons grimaced as he rose to his feet with the rest of his team. 'Can't wait.'

While everyone else went to the restaurant, Starr stayed with Brampton. Still without her own close protection operator, Brampton was now working closely with the television journalist so that she could share the services of Yves, the former legionnaire. The arrangement seemed to be working reasonably well although it meant she was unlikely to land herself a totally exclusive story.

'Do you ever wonder about Parsons?' Starr asked. 'And Tremain for that matter?'

Brampton was taken aback. 'Ollie and Iain? How d'you mean?'

Starr forced a smile. 'Do you think they really do work for the BBC? That they *really* are journalists?'

'I've seen their letters of accreditation,' Brampton replied defensively. 'Nothing's made me think otherwise..?' She fished a pack of Sobranie from her bag.

'It's just that...' Starr began. 'They don't act like any journalists I know. It's the way they talk. Rather than ask questions, it's as though they think they know all the answers.'

Brampton nodded. 'I sort of know what you mean.'

'And Royce...' Starr shook her head. 'He may be a bit hunky, but doesn't he *ever* drop his guard for a minute? It's almost like he's still in the army.'

'Marines,' Brampton found herself correcting.

Starr laughed. 'Well, he's certainly got you well trained, lady.'

The two women went on to discuss their plans for interviews and coverage over the next couple of days until Brampton caught sight of her editor entering the hotel foyer.

Russ Carver's lanky frame was dressed in an expensive suit of pale blue linen. He moved with the nervous, exaggerated way of a man who habitually overdosed on strong coffee and nicotine. Tossing the long hair from his eyes, he scanned the foyer, quickly spotted Brampton and waved. He made straight for the reception desk to check in, towing a small, wheeled pilot-bag behind him.

'That's Russ Carver?' Starr asked. 'Quite delish – for a man of certain years.'

'Down girl,' Brampton replied. 'He's got an open marriage with his earth mother wife, and he's been shagging my best friend for the last year.'

'Anoushka? From what you tell me he's met his match with her. He'll be in need of a change.'

'I thought you fancied Stefan?'

'Yeah, but he's a boy.'

'Hardly.'

'Thinks like one.'

Another man entered the lobby, walking with a slight bounce to his step. He was thin and youthful, maybe in his mid-twenties, and wore cargo trousers and a short-sleeved casual shirt. Fierce grey eyes glared from a mean, pinched face that was crowned with a fashionably short haircut of gelled porcupine quills. A compact designer rucksack hung from his shoulders. He joined Carver at the desk and the two men appeared to share a joke between them.

'Is he with Russ?' Brampton asked herself aloud. ''Haven't seen him on the staff before.'

'You won't have,' Starr said. 'He's just joined the *Sunday News*.'

'What?'

Starr raised an eyebrow. 'Chesney Sykes.Know the name?'

'No.' Brampton shook her head.

'The latest bad boy of the redtops.'

'Really?'

'Don't you keep up to date with what's happening on the scene back home? On Twitter or Facebook?'

'No, there's too much going on here.'

Starr smiled with just a hint of pity. 'Chesney was too much for the *Sport*. A bit too inventive, would you believe? Upset the Royals. No one would touch him. Then they announced the *News* had hired him.'

'You knew this? You didn't tell me.'

'I never thought. Besides, I assumed you'd know.'

'So what's he doing here?'

'Guess you'll know soon enough.' Starr inclined her head. 'They're coming over.'

The plastic wheels of Carver's pilot-bag rattled noisily over the tiled floor. 'Jo, sweetheart, there you are! Good to see you.'

Brampton rose to meet him and offered a cheek for the perfunctory kiss. 'Hi, Russ. D'you have a good trip?'

'Apart from the mayhem and chaos at the airport,' Carver replied as he flopped heavily on to the settee. 'Seemed like the entire population was trying to leave at the same time. Then some dork from immigration was questioning Chesney's visa…' The aspiring journalist had remained standing, glancing down worriedly at the mobile phone in his hand. 'Oh, sorry, didn't introduce the newest member of our team, Chesney Sykes.'

Sykes didn't look up, too engrossed.

'You probably won't get a signal,' Brampton explained helpfully. 'Either power cuts or else the phone masts are down.'

'This is Jo Brampton,' Carver offered.

Sykes finally dragged his eyes away from the phone screen. 'Hiya, doll.' His voice was sharp and its tone an odd mix, like a public school boy trying to affect an estuary accent. He either didn't see or ignored her offered hand. 'Heard all about you.'

'Likewise,' Brampton lied, and introduced the two men to Rachel Starr. 'Can I get you both a drink? No alcohol, of course, though the Gaddafi Sunrise packs quite a punch.'

'Just fizzy water for me,' Carver replied. 'Ice and a slice.'

'A coke, doll, if they've got it,' Sykes replied, finally unshouldering his rucksack and sitting down.

Brampton beckoned a waiter and placed the order. 'Nice to meet Chesney,' she said. 'But it's a bit unexpected. Is he on assignment or assisting you?'

Carver's cheeks flushed slightly. 'Not exactly. I'm giving you a break.'

She was shocked 'What?'

'That piece from Misrata…' Carver began, clearly struggling to find the right words. 'Cracking stuff, but you obviously placed yourself in considerable danger. I thought it was time to give you a break. Let young Chesney here have a go for a while.'

'I've just cultivated a solid network of contacts,' she retorted. 'Developed trust and understanding.'

'Great, Jo. You can hand them on to Chesney. It'll make his life easier.'

Starr felt compelled to intervene. 'It's not that simple, Mr Carver, not in conflict situations like this. It's a long and difficult process to build contacts who can be persuaded to talk to you, knowing you will be discreet and not get them in trouble – with either the government or even rebel authorities. Everyone is paranoid about spies and spying.'

'I know that,' Carver replied sharply. 'I've been around the block. Chesney will be a model of understanding and sensitivity, trust me.'

Starr grunted. 'Like he was over Prince Harry and the showgirl.'

'That was a misunderstanding,' Carver snapped.

'That cost him his job,' Starr reminded.

The waiter returned with a drinks tray and distributed the glasses.

Carver took his water and gave a lazy smile. 'One newspaper's loss is another's gain.' He smiled reassuringly at Brampton and raised his glass. 'Listen, Jo, it's only a temporary measure. Your stories on the sex-slave and the bombing of the rebel headquarters in Misrata…terrific stuff.'

Sykes nodded. 'It just needed sexing up a bit.'

Carver turned on him. 'Leave this to me please, Chesney.'

The young journalist shrugged. 'It's true. We're the *News*. Our readers aren't the same stuffed-shirts who get the *Times* or the *Telegraph*. We need to be the *Stunday News*.'

'God help us,' Starr murmured.

Brampton was becoming seriously angry and fought to keep the lid on it. She found herself mesmerised by Syke's pronounced Adam's apple and was almost overcome by her desire to punch it. Forcing herself to look away, she said to Carver, 'It's why I became a journalist, Russ. To report truthfully and honestly. I love my work.'

Carver smiled, unaware how patronising it looked. 'Of course you do. I know that, Jo. But I have to put the paper first. And I need you back home for a while.'

'For how long?'

'Maybe six or eight weeks,' He replied. 'Seems the fighting's reached a bit of a stale-mate just now.'

She still wasn't happy. 'Can we talk this over, Russ?' Glancing sideways at Sykes, she added, 'In private.'

Carver downed the last of his water and held up his room key. 'Sure. Let's do it. We can chat while I unpack.' He glanced at Starr and Sykes. 'We'll catch up later.'

As the lift wasn't working, Brampton showed him the stairs and led him up to his room on the second floor. It was small and shabby and he clearly wasn't impressed.

'I'll talk to management,' she promised. 'We get on well. See if I can get you an upgrade.'

Dumping his pilot-bag on the bed, he said, 'Shouldn't be difficult to find an improvement on this.'

She nodded. 'Look, Russ, I hope you don't mind. I didn't want an argument in front of boy wonder.'

'Sykes?' Carver laughed. 'He might seem a bit arsy, but he comes from a good pedigree. His father was once assistant editor of the *Star*.'

'I've got a good pedigree, too.' Brampton retorted. 'My dad's a prize-winning journalist of international renown. And I've done my apprenticeship in magazines.'

Carver sat on the edge of the bed and looked up. 'Fashion and food.'

'From what I hear, all Sykes has done is upset the Royals. Upset people around here and he'll soon lose more than his credibility...'

'It's also your *first* assignment,' he pointed out. 'You have a lot to learn.'

'At least I know about international politics from both my parents, I grew up on it. And about war. I was actually a serving soldier, for fuck's sake. What's Chesney ever done? How old is he? Christ, Russ, I've got knickers that are older than him.'

He raised an eyebrow. 'Really?'

It dawned on her how desperate she sounded, and smiled. 'Not quite. Sorry, I'm a bit upset.'

'I can see.'

'Downstairs you said it would only be for a short period back in London.'

He nodded. 'I need to see what Chesney can do. He's brimming with ideas. I can also see you need a break back home. You can return here if it ever gets near to an end game – if Gaddafi ever looks like losing.'

'He'll lose,' Brampton assured. 'And I want to be here when he does.'

'I promise you, Jo.'

'Downstairs, you said you needed me back in London,' she reminded. 'Why?'

'We're revamping the fashion and home pages. I've pensioned Iris off.'

Brampton groaned. 'Oh, I've left all that stuff behind, Russ. Besides, Iris was great.'

'She was older than Mrs Beeton.'

'She was still mustard at what she did.'

'You'll be better!' Carver enthused. 'Miles better. I need a fresh modern look, sexy fashions, the bra-less 20s look from TV's "Downton Abbey" making a comeback, latest foraging food fads from Denmark, and a look at the seamy side of ballet after that "Black Swan" movie.'

Brampton smiled. 'You know, Russ, it sounds like you could make a better job of it than me.'

He frowned. 'You *are* a ballet fan, aren't you?'

'I'm a failed ballerina, if that's what you mean? Like, I'm also a failed soldier.' She sighed. 'Now it looks as though I can add failed foreign correspondent to the list.'

He patted her knee. 'Rubbish. Like I told you, you'll be back here before you know it.'

'Sure.'

'I mean it.' He smiled a secretive smile. 'Because there's something else I haven't mentioned. I'm trying to set up a *Sunday News Channel* – digital TV on the Internet.'

That caught her off guard. 'No, really?'

'When you come back to Libya, it won't just be as a reporter, you'll also be our first ever TV journalist.'

''Looks like we're catching the same flight on Friday,' Royce said.

Brampton had just joined him in the umbrella shade of a poolside table that had become the favourite meeting place for the group of media friends. Starr was discussing her next assignment plan with Yves.

'Who managed that?' Brampton asked.

Parsons laughed. 'BBC influence, don't you know?' A look of concern flashed in his eyes. 'Side-by-side seats, I hope that's alright? I know you two haven't always seen eye-to-eye…'

'That's fine,' Brampton replied quickly, touching Royce on the arm. 'That'll be lovely – as long as he doesn't try to look after me.'

Royce gave a wolfish grin. ''Wouldn't dream of it. My contract's at an end. Just got to meet my financial adviser, add up my investments and decide where and how to retire.'

Seeff said, 'South Africa's the place, I keep telling you.'

'You do. And I'm thinking about it.'

'Eighty thousand pounds for a four-bedroom villa near Durban,' Seeff enthused, 'a pool and staff quarters. Petrol a fraction of UK prices and whisky at three pounds a bottle. You could even afford to start smoking again. I'll come and be your live-in handyman and chef.'

'You can't cook.'

'I'll go to cook school. I'm a quick learner.'

Royce's eyes narrowed. By force of habit, he was seated with his back to the bougainvillea-covered wall of the hotel, facing out so that he could see everyone as they entered the poolside area. 'We've got company, Ollie. You expecting anyone?'

Parson shifted in his seat, turned his head. 'Oh, that's all we need. Captain Mainwaring and Black Adder.' He scrambled to his feet. 'Let's keep this private.'

He was already striding across to meet the group who had just emerged from the hotel. Behind the two familiar figures in front, who had organised their disastrous arrival in the country, were half-a-dozen men, unshaven, wild-haired and wearing a mix of military and civilian tropical clothing. Although not obviously armed, they appeared distinctly unsavoury and menacing, like characters out of an Armageddon movie. It took a moment for Royce to recognise some of the members from their original E Squadron arrival party.

Seeff gasped. 'It's Asquith – and fucking McHaggis. I thought we'd seen the last of them. What are they doing here?'

Royce was already on his feet, following Parsons as Seeff hurried to catch up with them both.

'Ah, there you are, Ollie!' Mat Asquith greeted.

Parsons shook his MI6 chief's hand with his right and steered him away with his left to the shade of a secluded pergola. 'Can we be a bit discreet here, Mat?' Parsons said. 'Remember I'm with the BBC World Service.'

The tall Scottish SAS major, whom earlier no one could recall ever having met before, overheard. 'We're not worrying about all that cloak-and-dagger stuff now, Parsons.'

Seeff shook his head. 'So the Transitional Council rebels have finally let you back into Benghazi?' he asked. 'They must be a very forgiving bunch.'

'A bloody desperate bunch,' McDougall replied, seemingly missing the South African's sarcasm.

'It took a lot of diplomatic bridge-building,' Asquith admitted.

McDougall sniffed airily. 'But now our boys are all over the place like a rash. Virtually running the show.'

'So what exactly are you doing here?' Parsons asked.

Asquith was surprised. 'Didn't you get the message from London?'

'From the FO or Lego House?' Parsons asked, referring to the Foreign Office and the oddly art deco edifice of the MI6's riverside headquarters.

'Vauxhall Cross,' Asquith replied, using the proper name. 'Maybe it hasn't arrived yet.'

Parsons didn't hide his irritation. 'And when it does arrive, what will it say?'

'That you're being recalled. They need you back at base.'

'What?' Asquith tried to look sympathetic, but it didn't really work. 'You've done a splendid job, Ollie, set up a good network of contacts for us to work with. However, things have moved on.'

'We're closing in on Gaddafi,' McDougall chipped in. 'He hasn't got long.'

'That's true enough,' Asquith confirmed. 'At the moment we're playing a bit of a waiting game. Along the coast, everything is bogged down around Misrata. I don't foresee much in the way of advances or retreats on either side along the coast the next couple of months or so.

'That'll give us time to train the rebels and secretly build-up a new force inland, to the south of Tripoli. When that's ready, we'll surprise them with that and break the deadlock.'

Parsons stared at him. 'You mean the original strategy I suggested?'

'Was it?' Asquith blinked his innocence. 'I don't recall. There were a lot of wild ideas flying around in MI6 at the start.'

'So it's all-change,' Royce suggested.

Parsons shook his head in despair. 'Are you going to base yourself in this hotel?'

Asquith nodded. 'If there are enough spare bedrooms here. You've got an ops centre established?'

'Tremain's up there now, talking to London. You might as well just take our rooms over.' Parsons didn't attempt to hide his disappointment. 'I'll see when I can get a departure flight, call in a few favours.'

Royce had heard enough. He certainly didn't want to listen to McDougall's pompous preaching or Asquith claiming credit for Ollie Parsons's original strategy, which he himself had first heard back in London before they'd left. He walked away and back to their table.

'Who are those guys, James?' Brampton asked.

Starr said, 'They don't look like journalists to me.'

'Mercenaries,' Yves opined with a glower. 'You can tell some are carrying, and not trying to hide it.'

'Ollie seems to know them,' Brampton observed.

Starr peered at the group over the rim of her glass. 'Ollie seems to know everyone. I'm sure he's a spook.'

'Spook or not,' Royce said, 'Apparently he's leaving too. The BBC has recalled him to London.'

'All my friends are going,' Starr realised. 'Yves and I will be all alone.'

'I'll be back as soon as I can,' Brampton promised.

Her friend smiled. 'I'll keep your seat warm for you.'

14

'RUSSIA – A NATION DAMNED BY ITSELF'

Timeline: Moscow, early June 2011

Almost two thousand miles north from Tripoli, Ivor Kromlikov sat at his desk in the antechamber of the office which was occupied by the Chairman of the Government of the Russian Federation.

From his position he could see that the great man himself, whom he counted as a dear friend, was now standing at the window of the Moscow White House and staring out over the slow-flowing river.

Vladimir was angry, Kromlikov could tell that. He knew the Chairman well, ever since they had first become companions as young graduates to the KGB over thirty years' earlier. The attraction of the man to him had been immediate if, to his endless chagrin, never reciprocated in any physical way. But then that was part of Vladimir's allure, his insular disregard of others, an arrogant aloofness. It showed in the way he carried himself, with a ramrod spine and slight swagger to his walk. The firm set of his jaw, and those cold, cold eyes that were the colour of ball bearings, eyes that could look straight through you.

It had become Kromlikov's duty and pleasure over the years to serve his master with unrecognised devotion and unrequited feelings.

His position was not official, he was not Vladimir's permanent secretary who was summoned as required. Kromlikov was listed in the Kremlin directory simply as an "aide-de-camp", belying his true power and influence and ability to call on the Chairman whenever he felt it appropriate.

Seeing the man so clearly rattled, now was such a time.

Kromlikov made his decision, rose to his feet and moved towards the Chairman's office, rapping briskly on the door.

Vladimir turned sharply away from the window, casting his face in an austere half shadow. 'Ivor?'

'Prime Minister?' Kromlikov used the Chairman's informal title. 'May I come in?'

A bleak smile passed over Vladimir's face like a glimpse of sun on a cloudy day. 'Of course, Leninsky. You are the one person who never has to ask, how many times do I have to tell you that? What do you want?'

Kromlikov smiled at Vladimir's tease, his playful use of the pet name, referring to his passing resemblance to the great Soviet founder leader, Lenin. He shared the same balding pate, the same trim moustache and beard, but Kromlikov himself believed he had a more kindly facial expression. Although anyone who caused his displeasure would soon notice the absence of any warmth behind those steel blue eyes.

'I believe that you are troubled, sir,' Kromlikov replied, and looked around the half-timbered, pale blue office with its art deco motif floor tiles. This was a relatively modernistic 1960s building, but it had been modelled on the famous Aeroflot headquarters of thirty years' earlier still. He scanned the vast L-shaped desk, with its bank of telephones and computer-conferencing monitor, for a clue.

There was no missing it. A copy of the *Washington Post* was spread open on the green leather top.

'Ah, the article,' Kromlikov said apologetically. He peered over his silver-rimmed half-moon spectacles. 'I see you've read it.'

'Did you try and hide it from me, Ivor?' Accusing.

'No, sir. I just didn't particularly want to draw it to your attention.'

Vladimir crooked an eyebrow. 'Because you thought it would anger me? You are too kind. Happily my permanent secretary has no such concern for my sensibilities.'

'I am sorry.'

'I am not a girl, Ivor. I need to know these things, not be shielded from them. It is important that I know everything about everyone.' He paused. 'Especially my enemies.'

Kromlikov indicated the newspaper. 'People like our friend Boris Bramberg'.

Vladimir dropped heavily into his leather swivel chair. 'It is strange to think that once we really were all friends. Before he defected, and then became a journalist.'

'And changed his name to Brampton,' Kromlikov added.

'How can a man change so much?' The Chairman read the headline of the feature again, this time aloud, 'Russia – A Nation That Has Damned Itself.'

Kromlikov looked over his master's shoulder at the newspaper. 'Russia has done this – according to Bramberg – by having voted for you as President and now Prime Minister.' The aide-de-camp hesitated and smiled. 'And, hopefully, voting you in as President for your second term in next year's election. I can think of nothing better for our country.'

'That fucking Jew,' Vladimir almost spat his description, 'could hardly disagree more with you.'

'But he is writing in America or Europe, sir. You are here.'

'But his influence is spreading, his vitriol increasing.' Vladimir glanced up at the man stooped at his side. 'You must have noticed, Ivor. The article in *Vanity Fair* last month, the British *Telegraph* before that, also *Le Figaro*, *Der Spiegel*. He is in increasing demand.'

'That is true, I suppose.'

'And what I find particularly disturbing, Ivor, is that he seems to be able to see into my head. To know what I am thinking before I think it myself.'

At that moment they both noticed it, heard the aggressive meow. The scrawny, one-eyed black cat was poised in the doorway, its back arched and hissing for attention.

'Ah,' Vladimir observed. 'Crimea wants his lunch.'

'Quite so,' Kromlikov sighed, 'even the office cat knows his place in the order of things.'

Vladimir chuckled dryly. 'You sound jealous, Ivor. This cat was here long before I arrived. He is due respect.'

'And why, sir, did you think to call him Crimea?'

'D'you know, Ivor, you know me well enough. But that is not a question that Boris Bramberg would need to ask -'

Kromlikov rolled his eyes. '*Him* again, sir?'

'Yes, him again,' Vladimir snapped back. 'It is as if that man has a torch shining in my brain. He knows that when I am re-established as President of Russia again, I intend to put right the wrongs that have befallen our once great nation.'

'I know...we discussed Crimea in our early KGB days,' Kromlikov recalled. 'You and Bramberg, and me in the drinking club. Talking politics and military strategy. How Crimea should have never have been given to Ukraine in the 50s. We all know how it had been illegal at the time.'

Vladimir shook his head. 'That fucking imbecile Nikita Khrushchev and his love affair with Ukraine, his favourite socialist state.'

Kromlikov shrugged. 'Like many of his era, he considered Kiev to be at the heart of modern Russia.'

'That was no reason to give away Sebastapol and our naval access to the Mediterranean to another state,' Vladimir retorted. 'The short-sighted actions of an unstrategic mind. Look how Khrushchev played Cuba. Now Brussels is wooing Kiev, luring it into its clutches with soft words and an endless supply of Euros.'

'It isn't enough for them,' Kromlikov said, 'that they have Poland and the others. Ukraine and Crimea would be a step too far.'

Vladimir spun in his chair and glared up at his friend. 'Can you remember that is what I said back then? When you and I drank and talked to the early hours with Bramberg?'

'In all truth, sir, no. Not really.'

'That fucking Jew can,' Vladimir swore. 'He remembers every bloody word, my thoughts on Crimea, Ukraine and the Russian-speaking Baltic states. Everything. In these articles he writes his predictions of how I will want to get back our nation's pride and its honour. He foretells how I will act to achieve that aim, to restore Russia's place on the world stage. And, dammit, he is pretty much right on almost all of it.'

'Not surprising, sir,' Kromlikov said,' when you consider that he is a traitor, after all.'

The cat had closed in on them, was rubbing its flank seductively against the Chairman's calf, mewing softly.

Vladimir reached down, scooped it up and cradled it in his arms. 'A traitor,' he echoed. 'Of course. Defection is treason. What do we know about him?'

'Appreciating your concern of late, sir, I called up research papers from the FSB.' Clearly he had no need to explain that the federal FSB was the successor of the infamous KGB, for whom all three men had once worked.

'The three of us were all members in the intake of 1976,' Vladimir confirmed. His smile was bleak. 'Baby spooks – what, twenty-four years' old – learning our craft. We are student friends, drink together. Too much, have sex with the lady spies.' He paused. 'But not you, I recall, Leninsky.'

Kromlikov's cheeks coloured. 'I am shy, saving myself.' He smiled tightly and pushed on. 'We are posted as office juniors in research. Bramberg is an immediate high-flyer. He claims to be an agnostic Jew and talks a little Arabic, so some idiot in the KGB thinks that makes him suitable to be posted to Iran, where they speak Farsi.'

'What appointment?'

'He can write and paints watercolours, so he becomes a junior

Cultural Attaché.'

Vladimir stretched his memory back. 'This is the last days of the pro-West monarch in Iran, the Shah, yes?'

'Tumultuous times,' Kromlikov agreed, 'with the rise of the people and the Islamic Revolution.'

'This is when he met that woman?'

There was a nod from Kromlikov. 'Farah Shirazi, a Persian aristocrat. Very beautiful, I understand.'

'And smart, if I recall?'

'Bramberg met her at the launch of an art gallery,' Kromlikov explained, 'when he is on short secondment to London. Her family had strong connections with the Shah and Iran was close to ordering British-made tanks, the forerunner to the Challenger.'

Vladimir nodded. 'Well ahead of its time.'

'And excuse enough to follow up with Farah when he was back in Iran.' Kromlikov grunted. 'At some point cupid fired his arrow and the two of them fell in love. The next year Farah used family connections with MI6 to help Bramberg defect when he next returned to London. After the fall of the Shah, there was no future for her or her family in revolutionary Iran.'

'So what happened to the happy couple?' Vladimir asked, stroking the cat's head. It gave a little shiver and sighed contentedly.

'They vanished off the face of the earth. MI6 spirited them into the ether.'

'New identities, new countries perhaps?' Vladimir suggested. 'Usual routine.'

'Bramberg was considered of minor value at the time,' Kromlikov replied. 'The KGB was happy he'd at least delivered some stuff on the Challenger tank before he disappeared and the trail went cold. Only years later, they discovered he'd spent a year in Canada under the new name of Brampton, before returning to Britain with his wife where she gave birth to their only daughter. A girl called Josephine Farah.'

'Did Bramberg have a job?'

'When last the KGB knew, he was working for GCHQ in England as a translator and doing some freelance journalism -' Kromlikov folded his arm across his chest. 'And that was in 1988 and that was that. Our great nation crumbled, the Soviet Union died…and with it any interest in Boris Bramberg or Boris Brampton.'

'Until now,' Vladimir pointed out icily.

Kromlikov nodded vigorously. 'Of course, sir. A few years ago, it would have been a walk in the park. But since the Sasha Litvinenko polonium incident in London, British security has been reviewed and tightened. He could be living anywhere in the world.'

'So what is the best the FSB can come up with now?' Vladimir asked, the irritation clear in his voice.

'That Boris Brampton is published mostly in English-speaking media,' Kromlikov replied. 'So he most probably lives in an English-speaking country.'

That didn't impress Vladimir. 'Or Israel, or Ukraine or another Russian-speaking state?'

'Possibly.' A shrug. 'He has literary agents in New York, London and Geneva. Gentle inquiries have met with a very solid security wall in all three.'

'It hardly needs dynamite to breach the security of a literary agent.' The Chairman laughed harshly and the cat meowed. 'A good lunch and the ruse of a big advance should get an address out of them, I'd have thought.'

'After Litvinenko, we don't want to leave any large or obvious footprints,' Kromlikov cautioned.

Vladimir gave a dismissive snort.

'Bramberg's daughter,' Kromlikov said simply.

'What about her?'

'Known as Jo Brampton or "Bram",' Kromlikov replied. 'Now aged thirty-two. Also a journalist. She lives in London and is currently reporting from Libya.'

'Libya,' Vladimir echoed.

Kromlikov said, 'She may be a more promising route in.'

The cat suddenly propelled itself from the Chairman's lap and scurried towards the door. There it paused, looked back at the two men and gave a short shriek of annoyance.

'I'm coming, Crimea, I'm coming.'

'And Bramberg, sir?' Kromlikov asked cautiously. 'Would you like me to take a *special* interest in him.'

The Chairman nodded and replied softly, 'Thank you, Ivor, if you would be so kind.'

Ivor Kromlikov decided to walk from the Prime Minister's White House office to his home at Patriaski Ponds. It was a beautifully crisp, late spring day under a cloudless sky and he felt he needed the fresh air to clear his head and concentrate his thoughts.

On the way he stopped for lunch at a pavement café under the fresh leaf canopy of a cherry tree. He had a light appetite and ordered only chicken with buckwheat porridge, washed down with strong black coffee.

His thoughts concentrated on the traitor Bramberg and how best he could obey his master's desire to have the journalist brought to heel. Whom should he choose? Certainly not another psycho like Lugovoy, who had been charged in his absence with Litvinenko's murder in London by the British police.

Kromlikov needed someone more circumspect, sharper and wiser who would not create even more enemies of the new Russian state. The outside world was picking up on the fact that unfriendly journalists, hostile politicians and businessmen, who dared to challenge the might of Moscow, were dropping like flies. And not just within Russia's own borders. Dozens abroad had also met with an early end to their lives.

That was why Kromlikov had suggested the creation and development of Department 3. It was listed – without any description – in the structures of the FSB's 9th Directorate and the Federal Protection Service. Actually manned and managed by seconded or former officers from military intelligence and Spetsnaz Special Forces, it was under direct orders from the Kremlin. It was also totally, utterly secret.

This would be where Kromlikov would find his man for the job. As he drank his coffee half a dozen faces flashed up in his mind, possible candidates. One was a woman. He dismissed her from the line-up, along with two of the men. He had narrowed it down to three.

Then he was distracted by a team of road repair men, working out of a municipal van towing a generator. Not before time, Kromlikov thought, given the pitiful state of Moscow's roads since the unexpected explosion of car sales in the capital. The heart of Russia was dying with the clogged arteries of its streets and – as Boris Bramberg had written in his *Washington Post* article – the cancer that was Putin.

Sweating heavily, the men with their axes, sledges and a pneumatic drill, were stripping off their shirts, enjoying the watery sunshine. Kromlikov took in the ripped torsos and flexing biceps, their skin alabaster white after the Russian winter, and dragged his eyes away. He had work to do and no spare time to be diverted. His decision made, he drained his coffee and paid the waiter.

Five minutes' later, he arrived at his home in one of Moscow's old districts. His apartment was in an *art deco* mansion block overlooking Patriarshi Ponds, a park with a lake bounded by an embankment of trees and walkways, studded with wooden benches. His had been a fairly lonely life and he liked nothing more than to sit on those seats and watch the world go by. Couples, women with prams and, occasionally, single men. It wasn't a renowned cruising area like Kita-Gorod or Nikitsky Gates, but he had occasionally got lucky.

The last time had been back in January, when the frozen lake became a snowy wonderland and magnet for skaters from all over the city. That was when he had met the young political graduate, a bright, beautiful and intelligent boy called Leonid who was studying international affairs at the Lomonosov Faculty of Political Science. For Kromlikov, their relationship had become the dream of his life that he had thought would never become reality.

Since then, life had become worth living. More importantly it had released him from his obsession with his master, allowing him to think and care about someone else. Someone who also cared about him.

He climbed the steps and pushed open one of the double doors to the mansion block. The wealthy residents still enjoyed the mixed blessing of a babushka's services. She wore a colourful headscarf and sat at her own little desk on the other side of the echoing, tiled lobby.

He gave a small wave in her direction as he moved towards the old-fashioned lift-cage.

She showed him a toothless smile. 'The boy's gone out.'

'Oh, when?' He couldn't keep the disappointment from his voice.

'Five minutes' ago.'

'Did he leave a message?'

'He won't be back until later this evening, a re-scheduled tutorial. Unexpected.' There seemed to be a knowing glint in the old crone's eyes, or did he imagine it?

He nodded his thanks and dragged open the lift gate. As the cage clanked its way upward in complaint of metal fatigue, he cursed his decision to grab some lunch. On the top floor he crossed to the heavy, veneered door and inserted the key. He wasn't surprised that the alarm didn't go off as it opened. As usual Leonid had forgotten to set the keypad code, or couldn't be bothered. Either was equally likely.

Kromlikov sniffed the air. It was fusty and smelled of furniture polish and emptiness, like it had always used to. And yet Leonid had been barely gone ten minutes. Of late, it seemed to Kromlikov, the place now always smelled of youthful perspiration, hormones and hair gel.

He stepped inside and walked down the central passage. Through the open doors on either side, he noticed cereal plates and mugs in the kitchen sink, unwashed. His bedroom was neat, the sheets smartly folded as he had left them. Leonid's a mess, the unmade bed scattered with text books, DVDs and rap and punk music CDs. A large poster had been stuck to the wall of some emerging anarchic female band wearing coloured balaclavas.

He was sure Leonid used to enjoy deliberately teasing him, shocking him even, testing his old conservative views. Only now Kromlikov was learning not to rise to the bait, to stay his tongue before chastising the youngster.

Reaching his study, he punched in the code number to the specially fitted electronic security lock before entering. Like the rest of his apartment, it was filled with heavy dark Russian antique furniture. There were three telephones on his desk. The white one was for private calls, the black to the Kremlin switchboard and the red one was a direct line to the Chairman. He lifted the black handset and waited for the operator. 'Kromlikov here. A car to my apartment.'

'ETA ten minutes, sir?'

'Fine.'

He replaced the handset and moved to the tall cupboard behind his desk, swinging it open. There was a collection of press cuttings pinned to the inside of the door. They all featured photographs of the Chairman, bare-chested. Bare-chested riding horses, bare-chested firing rifles, bare-chested river fishing and wild-water swimming. It had been Kromlikov's suggestion for a series of macho public relations images that would resonate around the world. He had been surprised when Vladimir eventually agreed and even enjoyed the global media coverage it attracted. He was rather less amused that it led to him unintentionally becoming a gay icon back home.

Smiling to himself, Kromlikov removed from the middle shelf a black cardboard folder.

He pushed it into the neat crocodile skin document case he kept on his desk and zipped it up, before leaving the apartment, careful to lock up properly and set the alarm as he went.

It was only a five minute wait before the black armoured Audi saloon with its smoked bullet proof windows pulled up outside.

A twenty minute drive took them to the dacha on the far western outskirts of the city, where a twelve-foot high security fence, topped with coils of razor wire and covered by CCTV surveillance, guarded its vast acreage of birch and pine woods, river frontage and an airstrip. There was no name on the pillars each side of the electronic security gates because no mail was ever sent. All communication was either electronic or in person by pre-agreed right of admission.

The camera on a steel post beyond the steel gates twitched. Kromlikov knew its operator was reading the car's official number plate, and matching it to the file of expected visitors before opening up and lowering the steel dragon's teeth ramp to allow it access.

After half-a-mile the track opened up into a large forecourt before a magnificent three-storey timber-clad dacha which had a history that went back to the time of the last Tsar. Whilst the faded building was clearly in need of some cosmetic care and attention, it was structurally sound and operationally functional as the de facto headquarters of Department 3.

Its highly-secret formation and purpose had been Kromlikov's own brainchild. The idea came to him after the highly-publicised murder by polonium of former KGB man Litvinenko in London. Kromlikov had once joked that it would become Moscow's dedicated University of Death. Here the subject studied would be assassination: how to do it and get away with it anywhere in the world – inside Russia's own frontiers and beyond – without creating unwanted attention.

The country's experts would be drawn from all intelligence and martial specialities. It would be an eclectic mix of former KGB and current FSB officers, GRU and Spetsnaz officers. All would come together under one roof to discuss methods and technologies in the dark arts, drawing on their own experiences and those of the American CIA, Israel's Mossad and others. Coursework was planned, handbooks written and examinations drafted.

Its secret structure was such that it was the perfect personal tool for the top echelons of the Kremlin. Some wag had dubbed it K3. The Kremlin's Kommando Killers.

But things had not stopped there. Its syllabus had rapidly expanded to cover other topics, especially irregular warfare, the training and use of insurgency forces and political manoeuvring in foreign states. Moscow had created a blueprint with Georgia in 2008, now establishing enclaves in Abkhazia and South Ossetia to ensure that the compromised nation could never join Moscow. It had done the same earlier with Transnistria, a breakaway territory of Moldova where Russians had been stationed.

Kromlikov was aware that lately the Chairman had also been thinking long and hard about Ukraine. In fact, he also knew perfectly well why his old friend had named the one-eyed office cat Crimea.

The Audi drew smoothly to a halt and the bodyguard, seated next to the chauffeur, exited swiftly to open the rear door for his passenger.

Colonel Zlotnik, who had been sitting on the verandah of the dacha enjoying a glass of tea, rose to his feet. He was a tall, lean man with a shaven head and sharp features. His rimless spectacles went almost unnoticed against his weather-tanned face.

'Boris,' he greeted, throwing a lazy salute, 'what a nice surprise.'

'Colonel,' Kromlikov acknowledged, shaking the other man's hand.

'Can I get you a drink?'

'No, thank you. I've come to see Volkov.'

'The wolf?'

Kromlikov nodded. 'I have an assignment for him.'

'I believe he's in the gallery just now. Let's find him.' He stooped to pick up his peaked pancake hat and led the way into the lobby and down some steep wooden steps.

Only when the sound-proofed door at the bottom was pushed open was Kromlikov able to hear the whip-crack of pistol rounds. There were five lanes in the shooting gallery, with pictorial targets at the far end. Two were standard silhouette military figures, but the three others were blown-up photographs of world leaders. One was President Obama of the USA, another was former British PM Tony Blair, and the third was current Russian Prime Minister, the Chairman himself.

'I'll pretend I haven't seen that,' Kromlikov murmured.

Zlotnik was unfazed. 'Just someone's black sense of humour,' he said.

Yours, Kromlikov thought silently, but didn't comment.

Only one man was shooting. Hyper alert, he had immediately noticed them entering the gallery, even though they were behind him as he fired and he was wearing heavily-padded ear-guards. Satisfied they were no threat, he resumed his double-handed grip on the 9mm GSh and emptied the rest of the eighteen round magazine at the target.

A perfect grouping, Kromlikov noted, each hole made by the last six bullets within half a centimetre of each other.

The man defty applied the safety, ejected the empty mag and ripped the ear-defenders from his head. As he did so, Kromlikov glimpsed the double-headed Russian eagle tattooed on the back of the man's left hand.

'Wolfie,' Zlotnik called. 'There is someone to see you. Mr Kromlikov.'

Volkov stood a shade over six feet and a heavily-muscled torso strained at the seams of the tight green military T-shirt and black jeans that he wore. Ice blue eyes glinted in the square hewn face with its head of fine-cropped hair. The thin lips curled into a smile, quickly and unexpectedly transforming his expression. 'I remember. We met once. Aide to the Prime Minister, I believe?'

Kromlikov was flattered, more sure than ever that he had made the right choice. Viktor Volkov was sharp, intelligent and vastly experienced in the black ops of the Spetsnaz in Chechnya. Moreover, unusually, Volkov spoke English with an English accent rather than an American one.

'Indeed, Viktor, we met some six months ago when you began here. How is it going?'

'Well, sir, thank you. To what do I owe the pleasure? Anything in particular?'

'In fact, there is, Viktor. An assignment for you. I'd like you to take a special interest in someone.'

'Yes?'

Kromlikov unzipped his crocodile document case and handed over the plain black folder.

Viktor Volkov looked down at the typed label on the front. *For Kremlin eyes only: BRAMBERG.*

15

FOOL'S GOLD

James Royce had left his Jaguar coupé in the central London stack before beginning his first shopping expedition in ages. He had a sensation of almost floating over the sun-warm pavements of the city. As each day had passed since leaving Tripoli, it had felt that another weight had been lifted from his shoulders.

His departure with Jo Brampton had been a nightmare in itself. Such was the exodus from Libya that catching a flight had proved impossible. Even pre-booked airline seats were mysteriously commandeered by high-ranking members of the Gaddafi regime and others. In the end Sinbad had magically arranged a cabin for them on a ferry packed with evacuating foreign workers who were desperate to flee the fighting. It dropped them back in Benghazi from where they had to negotiate a long taxi ride over the Egyptian border and an eventual flight home from Cairo.

For two weeks now he hadn't had to watch his back, worry about road-blocks or ambushes or incoming fire of any description. It was amazing how long it took to adjust, to wind down. Any sudden noise – from a television or a plate being dropped – could trigger a reflex reaction.

So far he had spent his time chilling out in his small Parsons Green flat in north London, going to war on the dust and cobwebs that had accumulated during his long absence, catching up on reading and re-establishing contact with his family and friends. At the top of that list was Royce's financial adviser and old friend Toby Harbin.

Harbin was a dapper former Royal Marines officer whom Royce had known for many years. As ever, Harbin was a busy boy, always with a full diary and in a rush to make one meeting or another. But his hard work appeared to pay off. He always wore stylish Henry Herbert suits, a Rolex watch and drove a top of-the-range car. More often as not, he had a top-of-the-range woman to go with it, usually an aspiring actress or fashion model. It had taken Royce daily phone-calls and left messages, emails and texts before he eventually caught the elusive Harbin. That was the one time he'd selected to hide his number before calling once again on his mobile.

He recalled the effusive reception he'd received. 'Hi, Rollo, it's you! Great to hear your voice. Thought you were in Libya.'

'I've been back a couple of weeks. Fully retired now, and getting bored already. I need to meet and work out my plans. How are you?'

'Frantic, old son.'

'But time for lunch, I expect? Soon.'

'My diary's full to bursting, of course. But for you…Let me see.'

Royce stamped down hard. 'Tomorrow? On me.'

'I'm not sure…'

'I am. This is important to me, Tobes. I don't want to have to come looking for you.'

Harbin's voice sounded hesitant. 'No, of course, I understand.'

'You can choose where.' That was the final worm on the hook, Royce decided.

'I can squeeze that in,' Harbin said grudgingly. 'It'll have to be a quick one though. Le Gavroche?'

Royce had winced at the name of the top end restaurant, but he reasoned later it was worth pushing the boat out to celebrate the fruit of his investments in some style.

He took the opportunity to do some essential clothes shopping in Oxford Street before strolling down past the glitzy hotels on Park Lane to Upper Brook Street and the chic French eatery. As he paused beside its elegant façade with its floral railing boxes, an opened-topped Mercedes sports car swept alongside him and pulled up.

'Rollo!' the driver called and leapt from the vehicle.

Royce turned, taking in the tanned, clean-shaven face and expensive silk-thread suit in pale blue. The open-necked navy shirt looked like it could be an Armani and the shoes were old-fashioned crocodile.

'Tobes! Good to see you again.' As Royce shook his friend's hand, the cool blonde in the Mercedes passenger seat deftly slipped over the gearstick to settle behind the wheel. There was a brief flash of white-knickered crotch. She waved her goodbye and swung out into the stream of traffic with barely a second glance. Car horns tooted as she forced her way in.

'I hope that's her car, not yours,' Royce observed.

'Neither. I've got it for a test-drive.'

Royce frowned. 'You're thinking of buying it?'

Harbin laughed. 'No, no. I'm thinking of starting this magazine for an up-market hotel chain. Got a dummy first issue and everything. It allows me to test drive top-end cars, review posh restaurants and West End shows.'

The penny dropped. 'Do you actually intend to publish this magazine?' Royce asked.

'Sure.' Harbin smiled. 'Eventually. Let's go inside.'

They climbed the steps under the portico and entered the restaurant, where Harbin was immediately recognised by the maitre'd. 'Hello, Mr Harbin. Michel was asking when your – *Consul* magazine, isn't it? – was coming out, he can't wait to see your review.'

'Very soon,' came the quick reply. 'Just hit a couple of last minute glitches.'

'Of course you are paying this time.' It was a statement not a question.

Royce intervened. 'I am.'

The maitre'd smiled thinly and led them to a secluded table before bringing the menus and taking their drinks order.

Royce sipped his Campari and soda after ordering. 'So, Tobes, this new magazine wheeze gets you free cars, restaurant meals and shows?'

Harbin looked affronted. 'It's not a wheeze, Rollo. Everything has to be written up for publication.'

'But it doesn't exist, does it?'

'It will. Very soon.'

Royce pursed his lips. 'A bit labour intensive, I'd have thought. And all that writing. I'd have thought you've got enough on your plate with all your financial advising stuff.' He smiled. 'Surely that's making more than enough.'

It was like a dark cloud passing behind Harbin's eyes. Royce noticed it and suddenly felt uneasy. His friend laughed lightly. 'Things have been a bit tough since the bank crash.'

Royce nodded. 'But you're still doing okay? Still got the Rolex and the smart suits.'

Harbin pulled a tight smile. 'A lesson in salesmanship, Rollo. Everyone loves a winner, who's going to invest with a loser? I've only got two designer suits I wear for client meets and the Rolex is a fake. Look at the second hand, the movement *should* be faultlessly smooth. It isn't.'

The waiter delivered their meals. Royce had the salmon with lemon and vodka jelly and Harbin the beef fillet in red wine. 'About your investments, Rollo,' the man said casually.

'Yes?' Royce looked up. 'They are okay, aren't they? You assured me last time we met. By now you said they should be worth around 750K.'

'Did I really?' Harbin cut another slice from his steak. 'This really is delicious.'

Royce's appetite disappeared. 'Was that over optimistic?' he asked.

'As I'm always saying, Rollo, in finance past indicators don't always predict future returns. Shares go down as well as up. It's been pretty rough in the financial markets since we last met. Especially that gold mine investment I told you about…'

Royce nodded. 'Fool-proof, you said.'

'So it was with the jittery stock market back then. But suddenly some things improved and the bottom fell out of gold overnight.' He wiped his mouth with his napkin. 'Then there was that strike at the mine. Totally unexpected '

'What are you trying to tell me, Tobes?'

'I lost money too, you know.'

'What is my investment worth today?'

'I looked it up just before I came out, double-checked the latest figures.' He raised his eyebrows. 'At least 150K.'

For a moment Royce thought it was a wind-up. 'That's less than I gave you in the first place.'

Harbin smiled blandly and nodded. 'You gave me 250K. Don't worry. A couple of good years and you'll get it all back. The good times will return. They always do, trust me.'e HH

Royce left the restaurant over half-a-million pounds poorer than he should have done. His friend Toby Harbin left it ten minutes later with a front tooth missing, just before the police arrived.

Although he had a cheque from the investment adviser, Royce was already expecting it would bounce like a trampoline. He couldn't believe his own stupidity, his own trust that a former oppo, a fellow Royal Marine could do this to him, ruin him. And seemingly not even care.

He crossed to Hyde Park and strode along the path, trying to focus his thoughts and to quell his rising anger, unusually blind to the number of pretty office girls lunching on the benches and camped out on the grass. But by the time he reached the glittering water of the Serpentine, his rage had subsided.

In truth Royce wasn't one to do anger, at least not for long. By natural instinct and by his Royal Marines training, his first reaction when faced with adversity was to seek a solution. In this situation there wasn't really an answer. He was back to square one financially, some five years' of dangerously-earned savings lost forever. To look on the bright side, he still had his fitness and a peerless "skills set" to allow him to continue earning that sort of money. And each day the sun still rose. While work for the British government in Iraq was dwindling, close protection assignments in Afghanistan were still available. Only a few weeks earlier he'd turned down the opportunity to join the Ambassador's bodyguard team in Kabul.

Just as he stopped to stare out across the water, his cell-phone rang.

It was Ollie Parsons. 'Hi, Rollo, how you doing? Busy?'

'Not just now.'

'I wonder if you could do me a favour?'

God, Royce thought, don't tell me he already knows I'm on my uppers again. Of course he did. The latest Developed Vetting – or "DV" – meant Parsons would know everything about his bank accounts, investments, emails, Internet porn sites visited, the state of health of his pet goldfish and how often he changed his underpants. He took a deep breath. 'Depends what that favour is, Ollie?'

'Nothing too onerous, mate. Can you drop over if you're not doing anything?'

'Now?'

'As good a time as any.'

In fact it suited Royce. Being in central London, he was already halfway to Parsons's home in Peckham, which was south of the river Thames. And he could do with any mental diversion from the sudden dire state of his financial affairs. He returned to his parked car, which was loaded with shopping bags, and headed south. In the slow traffic, he idly studied the passers-by on the pavements as he drove towards the vibrant and multicultural neighbourhood that Peckham had become in more recent years. Although it still had several run-down social housing estates, it was thriving as the newcomers fought each other to snap up cheap terraced properties to renovate and make a killing. Bistros, artisan bakers and coffee shops were springing up everywhere despite the recession.

Royce parked his Jag outside a very tall and elegant end-of-terrace Edwardian house. He rang the bell beside a timber door that had a genuine stained-glass window at its centre. Parsons's boisterous laughter preceded him down the passageway, before the door was flung open in an exuberant gesture of welcome. The familiar bald, eggshell head and bespectacled face was beaming as usual. Parson's generous belly was covered by a red-and-white striped chef's apron that was covered in flour. So were his hands, which he frantically tried to rub clean as he offered one for Royce to shake.

'Bloody stuff gets everywhere,' he complained. 'Thought you might fancy a scone.'

Royce grinned. 'You must be clairvoyant, Ollie.'

Parson shut the door behind them and led the way to the kitchen, where his petite Filopina wife Myla was ironing. He introduced her as he hung up his apron and led the way down some steep steps to the basement. 'We'll have the scones with tea after our chat.'

It was not the first time that Royce had been allowed into Parsons's "War Room" as he liked to call it. Fluorescent bars flickered hesitantly to illuminate the large underground space that was home to four full-sized table tennis tables. Each one was beautifully landscaped for battles with military miniature figures in different periods and scales. Today one was covered in British battle squares facing up to Napoleonic ranks in brightly coloured uniforms, marching over flock grass, and the other a 1/76 scale re-enactment of a World War Two skirmish in Normandy with plastic tanks and Bren-gun carriers.

But what immediately caught Royce's eye were the remaining two tables, joined together to represent the entire coast of Libya. Rival forces were represented by 1/300 scale armoured vehicles, artillery pieces and soldier groups. Parsons was playing out the entire conflict at home in his basement. Immediately Royce spotted the gathering of vehicles clustered to the south of Tripoli.

'That's what you've recommended all along,' he observed.

Parsons nodded. 'No one wanted to know because I'm an armchair general playing with toy soldiers. But now they've finally realised it's the only sensible way to break the impasse.'

'When will it happen?'

The other man shrugged. 'Hard to tell. But I don't think before August at the earliest.' He turned his attention away from the model desert landscape. 'But this isn't why I rang you.'

'No?'

'It's about Bram. Jo Brampton?'

Royce was surprised at his own sudden concern. 'Is she okay?'

'Oh, yes, yes.' Parsons was dismissive. 'I don't think there's any real problem. It's just something I've been copied from the Russian Desk. You know about Bram's father?'

'Only that's he's a journalist,' Royce replied. 'He defected from the old Soviet Union when he was a diplomat serving in Teheran. That was before Bram was born.'

Parsons nodded. 'A lapsed Russian Jew. His name was Boris Bramberg, which he changed when he arrived here and married her mother, who was Persian. He was given a new identity and lived in Canada for a while before returning here. He'd served in the KGB, joining at the same time as Vladimir Putin. The two knew each other quite well.'

'Friends?' Royce asked.

Parsons shrugged. 'More work colleagues, I'd say. Boris worked for GCHQ for a while and later became a journalist. More recently he's been writing a lot of stuff about Russia and in particular about Putin himself. MI6 has heard that Moscow has become increasingly irritated at some of the articles he's been writing, predictions he's been making.'

Royce frowned. 'How do you know about this?'

'I honestly don't know,' Parsons replied. 'Some asset we have in Moscow. The Russian Desk isn't going to share that much with me. There's a whisper that the Russians might have taken out a contract on him.'

Royce was taken aback. 'On Bram's dad? That's a bit harsh.'

'It *is* harsh, Rollo. You'd be surprised how many anti-Moscow reporters, politicians and businessmen have met with a sticky end in recent years.'

'Like Litvinenko?'

'Exactly. Now Bramberg should be safe enough, but his new identity was set up thirty years ago. We can't guarantee it's still watertight.' Parsons took a deep breath. 'It occurred to me they might try to find him through Jo. She's a valuable new asset of ours and I don't want her coming to any harm.'

'Asset? An asset of yours?'

'Yes.' He chuckled, 'although she doesn't know it yet.'

'You're reeling her in?'

'Playing a long game.'

Royce was puzzled. 'What d'you want me to do about it?'

'Are you very busy just now?'

There was a hesitation before he replied grudgingly. 'Not very.'

'Then keep an eye on her for me,' Parsons said. Royce noticed he seemed anxious as he added. 'But discreetly, make her more aware – security-wise. You know.'

'I'm not signing up again,' Royce warned.

'No, no. I understand. It'll be off the books, but you'll be paid top dollar.'

'I'm not sure she'd be pleased to see me.'

'I'm sure she will.' Parsons smiled expansively. 'We'll contrive a meet by accident.'

The thought of meeting Jo Brampton again had a sudden appeal, Royce had to admit. 'Okay, just let me know.'

'Now, let's go back upstairs for a scone and a nice cup of tea.'

*

It was Chechnya again. It was always fucking Chechnya.

And it was always winter. Bleak and damp and grey, even the snow there was always muddy and dirty. Again it was in that cellar, or one like it. There were three Muslim *shahidkas*, or female suicide bombers, one pretty but gormless kid of only about fourteen, her older sister and an aunt in her thirties. They were drugged up on something, their eyes glazed as they tried to focus, smiling at Volkov's unit of Spetnaz boys, taking the piss. In the nightmare the women still wouldn't speak, just as they hadn't in reality. They refused point blank to answer the questions from his Alpha anti-terrorist team. All they did was smile back stupidly.

The boys had lost three mates of their own in a booby trap only the day before. Another had lost an arm and a leg in the explosion, another had been blinded with half his brain blown out. They were in no mood to compromise in the treatment of the witless females who sat there taunting and mocking them. There wasn't even any desire to rape. The women were blindfolded, taken next door, stripped naked and subjected to a bucket of ice water and an electric cattle prod. Still they refused to speak.

Viktor Volkov had had enough then. He snapped. The women were lined up in a row, on their knees with their hands tied behind their backs. Their heads were bowed, their wet hair hanging like small curtains and water glistening on the bare skin of their backs as he walked behind them. He pulled the automatic pistol from its leather holster and fed the first round into the chamber.

The child was killed first, a single round into the back of her neck. She pitched forward without a word, as he moved swiftly to stand behind the next and fired again. Only the older woman had a chance to utter some brief obscenity. Or was it a final prayer?

As he had so many times before, he told his men to, 'Take them outside. Prepare the bodies.'

While they followed his orders, he smoked a cigarette and poured himself a "sharpener" from the bottle on the table. Four parts local beer, one part anti-freeze and one part pickles. The devil's brew, both disgusting and invigorating in equal measure.

He went outside onto the veranda to find it was sleeting again, the sky iron grey and the air damp and acrid with occasional wafts of black smoke. His boys had finished preparing the three naked corpses, stuffing an explosive charge and detonator up between each one's legs and pushing another down each gaping throat, before wrapping every one completely in rolls of industrial cling film.

Leaving the bodies in the mud in the shadow of a wrecked apartment tower block, his boys retraced their footsteps. They joined him, unshaven and unkempt, laughing and joking with grim humour. One of them was young Yuri, barely eighteen with crew-cut hair and a missing front tooth, but always with a smile on his face. Difficult that, as Yuri had been dead for at least two years. He held the electrical radio charger, glanced up at his master.

'Abracadabra,' Volkov said softly.

Four muffled explosions ignited simultaneously. That was how to "disappear" bodies, no identity left, just a mush of flesh, bone and innards in a cellophane wrapper. A body and a war crime vanished by magic, victim and murderer never to be known.

But two of the charges had failed, the mummified corpse of the older woman remaining intact.

Volkov cursed beneath his breath, made his way across the mud to the cellophane-wrapped body and looked down. The face stared back up at him, eyes wide. Despite the explosive charge in her mouth the dead woman suddenly sat bolt upright and screamed at him.

His startled voice echoed around the bare walls of the bedroom as he was blasted out of his nightmare.

He sat up with a start and swung his legs off the bed. His boxers and singlet were drenched in cold sweat. Blood pulsed in his temples. Chechnya again, he hissed beneath his breath, always fucking Chechnya – a place where the devil stole your soul. Black ops against the Muslim separatists that you would never want to remember, but in truth could never forget, unspeakable acts committed on both sides. No quarter asked for, none given.

The bland walls of the Premier Inn started back at him, almost mocking in their calm normality. What's the problem? It's quiet, it's peaceful, and you have everything you need to hand. What's the problem?

He held his fists level in front of him, stretched out his fingers, examining the double-headed eagle tattooed on the back of his left hand. Both hands were still trembling slightly.

My fucking head, Volkov muttered, that's the fucking problem. The things I've seen, the things I've done. That's the problem.

He stood up, stripped off and took a shower. It helped to clear his thinking and bring his mind back to the matter in hand. Snatching a towel, he rubbed himself down briskly before pulling on fresh underclothes, a pair of worn jeans and a white, short-sleeved shirt. He made a coffee without milk or sugar and sat on the edge of the bed to study the Bramberg folder. It had been reconfigured and placed in the middle of a long print-out of company minutes so that it would pass unnoticed by anyone going through his luggage. Any specific names and places had been changed; he was quite able to memorise the originals.

Flying into Britain from Riga on a Latvian EU passport, he had completely bypassed the Russian embassy in Kensington Palace Gardens. It was currently home to some hundred case officers running a network of over a thousand spies and informants that riddled all strata of British life. Under Vladimir Putin the Russian Federation's intelligence networks had ballooned to cover all interests in military and foreign affairs, business and technology.

Volkov was well aware that Britain's Security Service, MI5, was struggling to cope with an explosion of Muslim extremists and the resurgent New IRA, as well as keeping track of the increasing activities of his fellow countrymen. However Volkov wasn't going to make life any easier for them. That was why he had booked into the modest budget hotel in King's Cross. It had been well known for years in the intelligence community that all big, expensive hotels in all major capitals in the world were a hotbed of espionage activity. At each was a concierge or manager who was in the pay of that nation's security apparatus. That was why Volkov was here, unnoticed and unassuming in a budget hotel.

Attempts to breach the defences of Boris Bramberg's agents in America, London and Switzerland had so far been thwarted because they had been highly defensive and exceptionally well briefed. No one giving a clue to in which country he now lived. He was not accepting media interviews or commissions for work. He would only submit articles and features of his choice through his agents. And that was non-negotiable.

Volkov stood up and pulled on his denim jacket. His first stop of the day would be the East End of London. And then..?

Replacing the folder in his suitcase, he relocked it.

One name from the last page of the report was alight in his mind. DOE – a female deer.

Codename for: Josephine Brampton.

16

DANCING IN THE DARK

'I'm not exactly into ballet,' Royce had said when Ollie Parsons told him of his plan. 'Men in tights aren't my thing.'

Parsons had laughed. 'You won't be disappointed, I promise.'

And he'd been right. God knows how, but Parsons had learned that Jo Brampton was visiting the Sadler's Wells Theatre in east London to watch her long-time friend, Anoushka Routkov, perform on stage.

From the moment the curtain went up and the music began, Royce was blown away by the sound, the stunning visual effects and the exuberant choreography. The flowing and skimpy silk costumes left very little to the imagination with either sex.

Nowhere much to hide a Browning automatic, he mused to himself. He focused the opera glasses Parsons had given him on the lead female. Anoushka might as well have been naked as she danced, spinning on tip-toe across the stage in a defiant and proud series of high-speed *fouettés*, culminating in a high *grand jeté*.

As she landed at the feet of the imposing black male lead, the audience burst into applause and the curtain fell on the first half.

'Let's get to the bar,' Parsons enthused, standing quickly.

Royce followed. 'Last ballet I saw was my sister aged eight. Giselle. Under sufferance, on orders from our mother.'

'These girls are a bit taller and sexier,' Parsons laughed, pushing his way into the moving crowd.

The bill of four avant-garde, half -hour works by this contemporary troupe were a far cry from the tutus and feathers of traditional ballet. Called "Fables of the Forest", it was apparently an allegory of Russia in modern times since the reign of the Tsar. So it came as little surprise to Royce to learn that the Petchkin Ballet Company was owned by a ballet-loving oligarch from St Petersburgh.

Maxim Petchkin was big in the field of alternative energy and had fallen foul of President Putin a few years' earlier. 'Now he's struggling to survive,' Parsons had explained in the taxi on their way to the theatre.

However his new production was proving popular. The theatre bar, which had the sweeping panoramic window of a star-ship bridge, was already packed full with ballet lovers, east European accents and languages quite noticeable in the excitable hubbub of voices. Their pre-ordered drinks were named and waiting for them on the bar.

Royce spotted Brampton first, dressed in skinny cropped jeans and a plain cream blouse. 'There she is.'

Parsons turned. She had a small video camera perched on one of the tables as she spoke to a small man with thinning dark hair and pebble-lensed tortoiseshell spectacles. From the ballet's souvenir programme, Royce recognised him to be Maxim Petchkin himself.

As Royce approached, Brampton shook hands with the Russian and gathered up her camera.

'Fancy meeting you here,' he said.

She turned, startled. 'Oh, my goodness, James! What a surprise?'

'My lucky day, Jo.' He leaned forward and kissed her cheek. 'I'm with Ollie. I was visiting him, but his wife wasn't well. He didn't want to waste the ticket and persuaded me to come.'

Brampton pulled a face. 'I'm surprised he likes ballet.' She had now located him and waved. He lifted his glass in response.

Royce said, 'His wife's the real fan.'

'And you?'

'I'm enjoying it more than I expected. Maybe it's those costumes.'

She laughed. 'They are very risqué in this one. But if it gets bums on seats…'

'And you're *filming*?' He indicated the video camera she was clutching.

'I'm doing a technical course at the moment, ready for *Sunday News TV*. It'll be a digital channel. Russ is very excited about it. Well, to be honest, so am I. I thought I'd do some feature work on the Petchkin Company for when we go live. Some interviews and B-footage.'

'You're sounding very professional. B-footage?'

'Background stuff and scene-setting between me-to-camera shots and the talking heads.'

'But ballet? Some culture for the masses?'

Brampton laughed drily. 'Russ said it's an excuse to get girls' nipples and male budgie smugglers on the screen before the watershed, so I suppose you're half right. It's still the *Sunday News*, don't forget.'

The intermission warning bell sounded over the PA system to the usual intake of breath from the ballet-lovers, who all wanted more time to drink and talk, as much as to return to the second half of the performance.

Royce struck. 'I suppose you wouldn't like to join Ollie and me for something to eat after the show?'

She hesitated. 'That would be so nice, but…I'm meeting up with friends, some of the cast.'

He smiled easily. 'Why don't they join us too, then? My treat.'

A smile broke on her face, lightening up her eyes. 'Oh, I'm sure they'd all love to.'

'How about The Brasserie on St John Street?'

'Magic. See you both there.'

As the melee of drinkers dispersed back towards the auditorium, one man remained near the window with a young trainee ballerina who was nursing a bandaged foot. She had taken a shine to his hard good looks and was trying ineptly to chat him up, but she became aware that he was actually paying little attention to her.

One last go, she thought, and commented on the double-headed eagle tattoo on the back of his left hand. 'Gosh, that's pretty.'

This time he looked at her, as though for the first time. It was as though a cold shadow passed over her, and she shivered slightly. He did not appear pleased.

In a low voice, he said, 'Pretend that you have never seen it.'

He placed his empty glass on the nearest table, and was gone.

Royce rejoined Parsons with a small sense of triumph as they returned to the auditorium for the second half. After the curtain rose, it quickly became clear that "Fables of the Forest" had moved into a darker place.

The distinguished male lead dancer, named Adrian Okilo, represented the dark soul of modern Russia in the form of Vladimir Putin, flirting and enticing the beguiled people of the motherland into his web of intrigue and danger.

The whole thing was really quite effective and left Royce surprisingly deep in thought as he and Parsons took a cab to The Brasserie. His former MI6 boss had pre-booked a table on the raised floor overlooking the floodlit garden. It was bright and airy and serene, the polished wood floors and simple modern tables reflecting in the numerous mirrors to enhance the feeling of space and light.

They took their seats and Parsons ordered a bottle of champagne to be put on ice. He turned to Royce. 'No wonder Petchkin has upset Prime Minister Putin with ballets like that.'

'Pretty powerful stuff,' Royce agreed.

'But I gather the two of them fell out before Petchkin set up his dance company,' Parsons replied. 'That's according to our Russian Desk. A lot of big businessmen were fighting over oil and gas rights. Then they noticed Petchkin stealing a march behind their backs on alternative energy. I don't know the details, but Putin's mates tried to muscle their way in. Petchkin flat refused to let them have a share of the action. It's been total war between them ever since.'

The bubble of tranquillity amongst the after-theatre diners was shattered with the arrival Jo Brampton and the two members of the Petchkin ballet troupe.

'Dah-lings!' Anoushka Routkov declared as she entered the room. 'How kind of you to invite us!'

The prima ballerina may have been no more than five seven, but she had a towering presence and personality that filled the room and caused heads to turn. Black leather jeggings accentuated her long legs and the nipped, tobacco-coloured jacket hugged her tiny waist. Her honey hair had been spun and pinned into a soft, muddled beehive, leaving a curl to fall across her forehead.

In an instinctive response, both Royce and Parsons sprang to their feet, shaking Anoushka's ring-bedecked hand and withstanding the onslaught of exuberant faux kisses. It took a moment for them to recover and notice Brampton and male lead dancer Adrian Okilo waiting patiently behind her.

The black dancer stepped forward. He was very tall with his broad shoulders constrained beneath a blue tweed hacking jacket and grandpa shirt. His shaven head glistened, emphasising his strong facial features and shadow beard. His eyes were intelligent and alert.

'Hardly recognised you both with your clothes on,' Parsons began heartily.

'Thanks for that, Ollie,' Brampton cut in. 'Let's set the tone before we start. ..This is Ollie Parsons, allegedly someone at the BBC World Service."

Anoushka ignored that and fixed Parson's with a seductive stare that had him frozen like a rabbit in a car's headlights. 'I like an honest man, Mr Pah-sons.' Her wide, violet eyes seemed to bore into his brain and made him feel that she understood exactly what he was thinking. 'I like a man who knows what he wants and how to get it.'

'And this is James,' Brampton interrupted. 'James Royce.'

'Ah, the famous Rollo,' Anoushka gushed. 'Half man, half lion, I understand from Bram.'

He felt his cheeks flush along with an involuntary grin. 'Really?

That is just a slight exaggeration.'

Anoushka focused her gaze. 'I like modesty in a man.'

'And your leading man?' Royce asked quickly.

'Addy?' Anoushka smiled. 'Indeed my leading man and the love of my life.'

'For this week, at least,' Okilo interjected in a deep, quiet voice. He took Royce's hand in a steely grip. 'Please call me Adrian.'

As they took their places around the table and the waiter handed out menus, Parsons asked, 'So Bram, how long have you and Anoushka known each other?'

'Since we were both eighteen. We joined a dance academy on the same day.'

'Nice,' Parsons remarked.

'I failed my exams,' Brampton said, 'Anoushka didn't.'

Anoushka peered at her friend over the rim of her champagne glass. 'I slept with the examiner.'

Brampton raised her eyes heavenward in exasperation, then added, 'I was also a shade over ideal height and had two left feet.'

'So that was before you joined the army?' Royce asked.

'Yes, and before you failed me at Selection.'

'It was for your own protection.'

'Of course.' She tilted her head to one side and smiled a little too sweetly. 'You haven't changed a bit.'

The waitresses arrived to take their orders before Parsons asked Anoushka, 'You've enjoyed a successful career then, since you were at the academy with Bram?'

With her elbows on the table, the ballerina clutched her glass in both hands, concentrating Parsons with her mesmeric gaze. 'I will never be another Osipova, but I do not complain.'

'You are the primanova at the Petchkin Company,' Royce observed.

'Perhaps, because I sleep with the ballet master.'

Parsons frowned and plucked the show's programme from his inside pocket. 'According to this, the ballet master is Olga Sedova. A woman.'

'So?' Anoushka replied with a shrug. 'A small, disciplined woman of steel. She knows how to bend the most unruly pupil to her will.'

Parsons grinned. 'Even you?'

'Especially me. There is a very fine line between pain and pleasure. Between exquisite pain and exquisite pleasure.'

Okilo leaned forward in earnest. 'Do not make the mistake of thinking Anoushka is a lesbian. She just takes her pleasure from wherever it is available.'

Anoushka's laugh was deep throated and richly plummy. 'Life is too short and miserable to be any other way. All foetuses is female in the beginning and only later males will develop from half of them. So sex between man and woman is just different sides of same coin.' She looked directly and deliberately at Royce, toying with him. 'I like to think of it like the double-headed Russian eagle of our flag.' She added. 'I like to drink from many cups.'

'Anoushka also loves to shock,' Brampton added. 'You'll get used to it.'

Parsons persisted, 'However you got the job, Anoushka, your career is going well. You've had some great reviews. I'm guessing you can't have slept with *all* those reviewers.'

Her mesmeric violet eyes levelled with his and began to draw him in. 'You cannot eat or pay your rent with reviews. Maxim Petchkin has made enemies with Prime Minister Putin and his clique, and is paying the price. He struggles with bank, there are foreclosures. After we close at Sadler's Wells this week our future is uncertain.'

'A few provincial theatres,' Okilo agreed. 'Even some pop-up performances in shopping malls. That is our immediate future.'

'That bad?' Parsons asked.

'Tomorrow I go for audition as showgirl,' Anoushka said. 'A French follies revue for the summer on the South Bank. So demeaning.'

'But I'm sure you'll be good at it,' Royce interjected rashly.

Her gaze froze. 'You are so kind, James, so kind.'

He was saved by the timely arrival of their meal.

Once everyone was settled and eating, Parsons made his move. Sitting next to Brampton, he asked her, 'Is your father a friend of Petchkin?'

She seemed taken aback by his question. 'Why should he be?'

Parsons shrugged. 'I don't know, similar age and similar views.'

'You mean anti-Putin?'

'I suppose.'

Brampton considered for a moment. 'I've never heard my father mention Petchkin. But then we don't get a chance to talk much nowadays.'

Parsons said, 'Petchkin has made enemies with the Kremlin over new energy development. I hear that it is thought his life could even be in danger. He has made a lot of enemies in high places. As indeed your father has.'

Brampton regarded him closely. 'You have heard this at your offices in the BBC World Service?' she asked suspiciously.

He smiled that disarming smile of his. 'We are very well-connected.'

'With the Secret Service?'

'Amongst others,' he admitted. 'We do get briefings sometimes from the – quotes – Foreign Office. Usually about security issues if we're travelling.'

'Then you'll be aware that my father changed his identity,' she replied, adding pointedly, '- a long time ago. He's never had any problems, certainly not since the end of the Cold War.'

Parsons nodded. 'As you pointed out yourself, that was a long time ago. Times are changing. Your father has become increasingly active of late. He's become a major influence in the international media, I've noticed.' He hesitated for effect. 'It's not impossible that the Kremlin could be taking a serious interest in him.'

Brampton looked alarmed. 'Have you heard something?'

Parsons looked uncomfortable. 'I couldn't possibly confirm. But, yes, let's say I've heard something, a whisper. He's rattled some cages, shall we say? Quite seriously.'

'I'll warn him to be extra careful,' Brampton replied, concern in her voice. 'I was planning to take the train down to see him tomorrow. Maybe stay for a couple of days.'

Royce decided to intervene. 'If Russian agents are having trouble locating your father, it's quite reasonable to suspect they could be taking an interest in you. Hoping you might lead them to him.'

She paled visibly. 'Really? I haven't noticed anything…' Her voice trailed off as she realised what she was saying. 'But then I suppose I wouldn't, would I..?'

Royce nodded and smiled kindly. 'That's the point.'

'That sounds a bit scary,' Okilo observed. 'Especially when you think what happened to Litvinenko…'

'Stop it, dah-ling,' Anoushka chided. 'You will scare the poor girl.'

'I could run a security check over things for you,' Royce offered swiftly. 'And I'd be happy to drive you to his place, if you'd allow me.'

Brampton frowned, suddenly suspicious. 'I thought you'd retired, James?' she challenged.

'Almost, not quite.' His smile was disarming. 'I'd be happy to do it as a friend. Basic, simple stuff. Just to make sure you're not compromised or accidentally compromise yourself.'

'Stuff like what?'

He put down his knife and fork. 'That you're not already being followed or your home bugged. Check you vary your regular routes of travel. Basic field-craft.'

Something flashed in her head. 'I trained in that stuff,' she said. 'Remember?'

'And I failed you,' he reminded with a wolfish grin. 'You really can't be too careful.'

Anoushka was listening intently. 'What they say makes sense. I had a journalist friend who writes against Kremlin. He dies in a mysterious road accident at night. Someone puts a large mirror on road after a bend. He sees his own headlights coming towards him and drives off into ravine.'

Brampton winced. 'How awful.'

'Why don't you come back with us tonight?' Anoushka decided . 'We have a sofa bed at the flat for you to sleep.'

'*My* sofa bed,' Okilo protested.

She fluttered her eyelids at him. 'Tonight, you may share my bed.'

'I'll be found dead in the morning.'

'Possibly.'

Brampton looked uncomfortable. 'I'm sure James has other plans…'

He winked. 'Actually, I don't. I've nothing planned for the next few days, but after that I will be pretty busy. So it would actually suit me.'

'Won't you need a change of clothes?'

He shook his head. 'I always have an overnight bag in my car. Old habits.'

Before Brampton could say another word, Anoushka closed the deal. 'That is decided then. We have spare blankets and towels. And I have an unopened new toothbrush.'

'You must have been terrified in Libya, dah-ling!' Anoushka gushed.

They were back at the flat that the two women shared. It was on the top floor of a converted three-storey Regency terrace, which had once served as the accommodation for the household staff of a modestly wealthy family. It comprised two bedrooms, a bathroom and combined lounge-diner with a kitchenette.

Parsons had departed alone for his home while the remaining four left the restaurant and took a taxi to the exclusive Westminster district of Pimlico. After tip-toeing up the main staircase to avoid disturbing residents in the apartments on each floor, a clearly inebriated Anoushka had thrown open their front door onto the shambolic mess of their living room, strewn with coffee mugs, dance and ballet magazines and one large, overflowing ashtray.

Ignoring Brampton's embarrassment at her untidiness, Anoushka proceeded to liberate a bottle of Pinot Grigio from the fridge and pour glasses for everyone. Pastoral classical music was soon wafting from the CD player.

As the four settled down, Anoushka had quickly persuaded Brampton to expand on her adventures in Libya. 'We have hardly a chance to talk since you are back. Tell me all.'

'Well, yes it was terrifying at times,' Brampton agreed. 'But I had my CP men – one was Royce, here – to look after me.'

'CP?' Anoushka raised an eyebrow. 'Is that corporal punishment? Now that sounds intriguing.'

'It stands for close protection,' Brampton chided, chuckling, 'and you know it.'

Brampton went on to recount some of the events, including their trip to Misrata and her encounter with exotic Gaddafi bodyguard, Princess Ayana.

'She held the key to many secrets about Gaddafi, but it was difficult to get her to talk openly.'

'Ayana?' Anoushka echoed. 'She sounds gorgeous.'

'She was. And very statuesque.'

'Did you kiss her?'

Blood rushed to Brampton's cheeks as she glanced sideways at Royce. 'Of course not.'

'You might have got more from her if you had.'

'I'm not into that sort of thing.'

Anoushka held her gaze, teasing. 'You kissed me once.'

Brampton clearly wished the room would swallow her up. 'I was drunk, confused. I got carried away.'

'And with me you had one of your best ever orgasms.'

'Oh, please!' Brampton protested.

'That's what you told me.'

Royce intervened. 'If you've got an audition tomorrow, Anoushka, perhaps we ought to call it a night?'

The relief showed in Brampton's face. 'A good idea, James.' Immediately she made a move. 'This is a sofa bed. I'll get some clean sheets and spare pillow.

Royce was instantly awake, the vivid Arab characters in his dream melting into darkness, taking their guns and their angry, shouting faces with them. Bram had been in trouble but there was nothing he could do about it. It was pitch black and he didn't know where she was.

It took several seconds for him to orientate himself, to remember what day it was and where he was. The flat was unusually dark for London. Heavy felt curtains at the windows helped extinguish all ambient street light and any traffic noise that dared to permeate the triple-glazed windows. It was close to being dead in a coffin. Utter darkness.

He just lay there, trying to recall the position of the sofa bed he was on within the layout of the room. That was when he heard the faint sound. A rustling? This was an old building, so could it possibly be a mouse? Or a cat? No one had mentioned a cat, not Bram, not Anoushka. God, it was so quiet it was barely distinguishable above his own breathing.

The idea suddenly came to him. He remembered he had a tiny twist torch on his key-ring. Turning on the bed, he managed to get a hand into his trouser pocket and find it, dragging it free as it caught on the lining material. His fingertips found the ring, turning it on. Nothing. He hadn't used it since before he'd gone to Libya. Unsurprisingly the battery had expired.

He sighed. For two pins he'd have just gone back to sleep, but now awake he began to feel a mounting urge to use the toilet and was also gripped by a raging thirst. Too much alcohol and no water. At home he'd have poured a bedside glass to drink. Could he find his way to the kitchenette?

Another sound. Like a cupboard catch clicking or a drawer opening? A sigh?

Was it his imagination? It must be.

He decided he had to find the light switch, make his way to the bathroom and then the kitchenette. Swinging himself off the sofa bed, he planted his feet firmly on the floor and stood. He was wearing only navy-coloured trunks, so he hoped he wouldn't crash into anything and disturb either of the women.

Now he was confident he knew which direction to move, his hands out in front of him feeling for the door like a blind man, feeling for the light switch that he knew was beside it.

He didn't hear the footfall behind him, just someone's sudden grunt as the pain seared through his skull and the tide of nothingness swelled over him, carrying him into complete oblivion and unconsciousness.

17

DADDY'S GIRL

Royce came round as though he was emerging from a dream, amidst a dark swirling mist. Bright sunlight from a window was throwing the people crouched around him into bold relief, their voices echoing strangely as though from another planet.

'I think he's coming to.'

He knew that voice, recognised it, but couldn't name it. Female. Knew the face – dark, pretty – but couldn't name her. Couldn't damn well remember.

'Don't crowd him. Let him breathe.'

Stroke he thought, I've had a stroke. This must be what it feels like.

No pain in my left arm, no pain in my heart.

Oh, shit but what a pain in my head, he thought. He could feel the back of his brain thumping like someone was hitting it with a mallet wrapped in a towel.

'Can you hear me?'

Was she talking to him?

'Can you hear me?' she repeated.

He nodded and the bolt of pain shot through his skull.

That distant voice again, from outer space. 'What's your name? Tell me your name?'

Name? he thought. I know my name, just can't think of it right now.

'Can you remember your name?'

What's that to do with anything? Where am I? On the street, on a pavement? No, carpet under my hands.

Then another voice. 'Dah-ling, shall I call an ambulance?'

'Just a minute, he's coming round.'

'James,' he answered suddenly. It all came flooding back in a rush. The ballet, the restaurant, the flat, sleep and darkness…the noises.

'Your surname?' the woman pressed.

He knew, he knew, almost there. It began with an R. Like a car… 'Royce.' Got it.

'What's *my* name?'

He squinted at the face just inches in front of his. 'Jo. Jo Brampton. What happened?'

'You must have passed out,' she replied. 'Banged your head.'

He struggled into a sitting position, his head still swimming.

'You alright, mate?' Okilo asked. 'I got up for a whizz and found you in a heap by the front door.'

Anoushka peered over the man's shoulder. 'I get brandy.'

Brampton said, 'A cup of tea might be better.'

Okilo stepped in to help Royce to his feet and to inch his way towards the sofa bed.

'Nice body,' Anoushka observed, on her way to the kitchenette. 'Almost as good as Addy's.'

Royce sat on the bed and pulled on his shirt. Moments later a mug of hot sweet tea was thrust into his hands and the long, slow drumbeat in his head began to fade.

Brampton sat beside him. 'Concussion. We must get you checked out at A&E.'

'I'll be okay.'

'I remember my training. Concussion is brain damage, even if it's minor.' She touched his forearm. 'There's no great hurry to visit my Dad.'

As he drank the hot sweet tea, the events of earlier started to come back to him. He turned to Okilo. 'What position did you find me in?'

'Flat on your face, mate?'

'So I'd pitched forward?'

'Flat out.'

'So how did I bang the back of my head?'

Okilo shrugged. 'Er, good point.'

'If I fell forward onto a carpet, how have I got damage to the back of my head?'

'What are you saying?' Brampton asked.

'I thought I heard something in the room,' Royce explained, 'but it was pitch black. I was feeling my way to the front door, where I knew there was a light switch. That was the last thing I remember.'

Okilo got there first. 'You think someone struck you? It wasn't me, guv, promise!"

Royce was finding it hard to think straight. 'Is it possible I disturbed someone who'd broken in? They wouldn't necessarily have been expecting anyone to have been sleeping on the sofa.'

Brampton checked the front door. 'We didn't bolt it last night, but there's no sign of a break in, no damage.'

'Is that your desk?' Royce asked, indicating the glass-topped work station tucked in an alcove beyond the sofa.

She turned. 'Yes, and my laptop and printer.'

'Has anything been disturbed?' he asked.

'Not that I can tell.'

'Do you have your father's address or contact details written down anywhere?'

Brampton shook her head. 'No, I was brought up very strictly on that. I memorise all that stuff.'

Royce decided not to pursue it. Of course, if the job had been professional there would have been no signs left. Entry to the flat would have been silent, probably with a key copied at an earlier time. Any intruder would have probably worn a night vision device of some sort. Brampton's desk would have been photographed and everything put back exactly as it was found.

He didn't want to alarm them. 'I guess it's one of life's little mysteries,' he concluded.

'*Another* mystery,' Anoushka declared, 'is how I am going to get to audition if I don't get a move on. I am commandeering bathroom for next thirty minute!'

On Brampton's insistence, Royce let her drive him in his Jaguar to the A&E Department of the local hospital.

While they waited, Royce took himself to the men's toilets and used the opportunity to put a call through to Parsons, explaining the weird nocturnal event.

If he was anticipating a sceptical reception from the MI6 man, he was wrong. Immediately Parsons said, 'Let me speak to my oppos at Thames House. We'll get the tech boys to give the flat a sweep.'

'Really?' he was surprised. Parsons was getting the Security Service – MI5 – to take a look at Brampton's apartment.

'Is anyone in during the day?'

'Not this morning. Anoushka will be at an audition. You'll want a key.'

Parsons chuckled. 'That's okay. Not necessary. I'll call back later.'

After a three-hour wait he was eventually seen and examined by a doctor, who confirmed he had mild concussion and should not drive for a few days.

After a pub lunch, with Brampton again at the wheel, they set off on the long journey to Cornwall, the remote county in the mild and wet far west of England. Its people were devoted to farming and fishing and summer tourism.

Brampton was amazed to find Royce so quickly asleep beside her as she began the two hundred and fifty mile drive. It seemed so unusual for him not to be at the top of his game, alert and on edge. She could only imagine how exhausted he must have been after the mysterious incident back at her flat. There was no way she wanted to believe that an intruder could have manipulated his way into her home so easily, yet she didn't feel comfortable with any other explanation. With some effort, she pushed her worries to the back of her mind and did her best to enjoy the journey.

It was a pleasant route but not fast, offering some dual carriageways but no motorway. She knew from experience it would probably take around six hours before they arrived at the harbour town of Porthleven on the south coast, just short of Land's End where the Atlantic Ocean began.

Royce surfaced again when they had just passed South Petherton on the upgraded 303 in Somerset.

'Hallo, sleepy boy,' Brampton greeted. She was wearing a pair of Ray-Ban Aviators.

'God, I must have dropped off.'

'You went out like a light.'

'What's the time?'

'Coming up to five. You've been out cold for a couple of hours.' She glanced sideways at him and smiled. 'How are you feeling?'

'A lot better than I was.' He looked around at the undulating summer landscape. 'Where are we?'

She knew the road well, having made the trip many times. 'Approaching Ilminster, about halfway to Dad's.'

'Are we being followed?'

'I'm pretty sure not. I've been keeping a watchful eye in the mirror. I've slowed right down a couple of times, and then given a burst of speed.'

'Good girl. '

She frowned disapprovingly in response. 'But if they were Russians running a box formation, I wouldn't spot it?'

'Probably not. Would you mind if we tried once more? There's a left turn coming up...' He reached out and adjusted his side mirror. In the lane behind – some distance back – appeared to be a red Volvo.

She glanced up as the road-sign flashed past and nodded. 'There's nothing immediately behind. I'll wait until we're nearly there…'

Brampton braked hard. The car slithered momentarily as the ABS kicked in. She threw the wheel and tucked tightly into the country lane at the last minute. Royce studied his wing mirror until they reached the first bend in the lane. Nothing showed.

'Pull in at the first opportunity,' he instructed.

She recalled her training. 'Immediately after a bend…' she murmured.

Two more bends followed before the opportunity presented itself. It was the muddy entrance to a farm warehouse. The Jaguar squelched to a halt. Brampton killed the engine and they both listened intently, studying their rear view mirrors. Royce was anticipating a red Volvo, or possibly a motorcycle.

Fifteen seconds passed on Royce's Breitling. Thirty. Nothing.

'Something's coming,' Brampton whispered.

Something red flashed by.

A Volvo?

'A Mondeo,' Royce breathed.

They allowed another few minutes to pass, but no other vehicles materialised. Brampton restarted the engine, reversed onto the lane and they headed back to the main road to the West Country, satisfied that no one was following.

By the time they'd journeyed into Devon and through Dartmoor to the final leg into Cornwall it was gone eight o'clock. Shadows were lengthening as they entered the harbour village of Porthleven.

On Royce's instruction, they parked a couple of streets away from her father's cottage. As he had explained, 'I know no one appears to have followed us, but let's not drop our guard.'

'You really are getting paranoid, James. It's almost like we're back in Libya.'

He grinned. ''Doesn't mean they're not out to get us.'

Just as they removed their overnight bags from the car, Royce's mobile rang. It was Parsons. 'I've just had Five on the blower. The sweep found a bug in the desk phone – I think that was on Bram's laptop work station – and another in a lamp fitting in the living room. No sign of the front door being forced.'

Although he'd raised the suspicion himself, Royce now found it hard to believe. 'So I was right?'

'Someone's taking an interest in Bram,' Parsons said. 'Don't alarm her, Rollo, but she needs to take care. We don't want her or anyone else leading the Moscow thugs to her father.'

'Of course,' Royce said, and terminated the call.

'Who was that?' Brampton asked.

'Parsons.'

'You and he are still very cosy,' she observed.

'He's pestering me to come out of retirement.'

'Already?'

'I might have to. I'm not as rich as I thought I was.' He grinned at her. 'Let's go.'

He checked the deserted pavements before following Brampton down the slope to a parallel narrow street with a view of the harbour. A huddle of quaint terraced cottages clung to the hillside.

One had a particularly untended small garden and rickety front fence. 'This is Dad's. Not the greatest gardener or DIYer, I'm afraid.'

The window frames and door had clearly been waiting in hope for years for a rub-down and a coat of paint. 'So I see,' he said.

She trudged up the short steep path. 'Dad's life is all writing and fishing.'

Royce smiled. 'Guess that doesn't make him a bad person.'

Brampton put her key in the door and pushed.

It opened onto a narrow, dark passageway. There was a faint smell of must and cooked seafood lingering in the stale air. The whole place had the casual untidiness of a bachelor home, not dirty but undusted and unloved by someone with more important things to do.

'Dad!' Brampton called out. There was no answer.

She indicated the open door to the front room.

'This is where Dad works.' A desk strewn with papers and files faced the window, overlooking the sea. There was no sign of a computer or laptop. Columns of books and magazines, many in Russian, stood to attention at intervals around the skirting board. A single, ageing photograph was framed on the wall: a woman with most alluring dark eyes stared out into the small room from beneath a Persian headscarf,

'Your mother?' Royce guessed. 'There's a strong likeness.'

'That's what Dad says,' Brampton replied. 'And not just in looks. He reckons I'm even more stubborn than she was.'

Royce followed her past the living-room to the kitchen. Like the rest of the house it was clean but untidy, unwashed dishes and pots on the draining board, awaiting attention. A lot of fishing kit was stored in the far corner, various rods, nets and tackle boxes.

She spotted the hand-written note on the small pine table. 'Ah, down the pub. I might have known.'

Royce grinned. 'Excellent, I could murder a pint.'

'Me too,' she agreed.

The Ship was down on the harbour wall, filled to bursting with locals and early-season holiday makers. Smokers were clustered outside next to its lime-washed walls. Brampton led the way into the throng, negotiating a route to the seat at the bar where she knew her father would be holding court.

Boris Bramberg was a large man, in both physique and personality. Perched on a bar stool he looked even taller than his six feet four, his broad chest and shoulders filling out the fisherman's cable sweater. His broad unshaven face was deeply lined and smiling beneath an unkempt tangle of greying ringlets as he chatted expansively with a group of friends.

He spotted her through the heavy horn-rimmed spectacles. 'Josephine! Here at last!' Dropping deftly off the stool, he stepped towards her. 'I am thinking maybe you might not make it tonight. '

'I'm sorry. We got held up.' She kissed him on both cheeks in the

Russian manner.

Her father was as sharp as always. 'We?'

She turned. 'This is James, a friend of mine.'

Bramberg raised a bushy eyebrow. 'James, pleased to meet you.' His handshake was a bone-breaker. 'I have not seen one of my daughter's boyfriends in a long time. She tends to keep them away from me in case I don't approve. Which usually, of course, I do not.'

'James isn't a boyfriend, Dad,' she corrected, her cheeks colouring. 'We worked a bit together in Libya when he was my close protection.'

'Ah, *that* James!' Her father grinned mischievously. 'I know *all* about you.'

'Dad, stop it,' Brampton protested.

Bramberg chuckled heartily. 'I only joke with you both. You have a long journey. You must be thirsty. Let me get you a drink.'

'Sparkling water, please, Dad,' Brampton said. 'Loads of ice and a slice.'

'To think you are the daughter of Russian loins.' Her father shook his head in disapproval. 'A teetotaller.!'

'What's the local bitter?'Royce asked.

'Doom Bar is good.'

'A pint of that, please.'

With their drinks collected they made their way to a spare table in a quiet corner of the bar. Brampton was keen to get to the point before her father got on a roll of beer and vodka chasers as the evening wore on.

'Dad, there's something important that I have to tell you…'

Momentarily Bramberg looked crestfallen. 'You are not – ?'

She shook her head vehemently. 'No, no, nothing like that.'

'Or getting married?'

'No, not that either.' She took a deep breath. 'Apparently the BBC World Service has been tipped off by the Foreign Office that Moscow is very unhappy with your recent articles and features.'

Bramberg pulled a face. 'That, I am not surprised. But why did

Fuck Office tell the BBC, of all people? Radio station of the EUSSR!'

'Perhaps, Dad, because they know you won't listen to them.'

Royce said, 'I've become friends with a senior producer at the BBC World Service. A man called Parsons. I minded him in Libya when we both met your daughter. So when your name and hers cropped up in a conversation about you at a Foreign Office security briefing, he felt concerned.'

'And wanted you to warn me of a danger?'

'A possible danger,' Royce confirmed. 'And Jo, because they may think she could lead them to you.'

'They?'

'People in the Kremlin you've upset with your newspaper articles and features,' Royce said, repeating what Parsons had told him. 'Especially your predictions of how Vladimir Putin will behave if he gets a second term as President.'

'Ah, now I see it!' He picked up his jar of Doom Bar with both hands and took a big swallow. Then he wiped his mouth with the back of his hand. 'My forecast that he will grab back Crimea from Ukraine. That it had ever been given to Kiev in the first place always upset Vlad when we were interns together in KGB. We discussed it many times over beers in cafés. He believed secure Russian access to the Black Sea was always paramount to Russian security and freedom.'

Parsons had shown Royce a copy of an article by Bramberg that had appeared in *Esquire*. 'And how he will do it?'

Bramberg shrugged. 'But sure. He was fond of an expression. Not by strength, by stealth. I remember him discussing over a coffee, more than once. If ever the Soviet Union would collapse, how he would never invade. No tanks and divisions of troops to alert the world. No invasion, just confusing political unrest. By the time the world realised what had been done, it would be too late. He would use ethnic unrest and fund Russian-speaking partisans to do his bidding, backed by Spetsnaz.'

'You think that's what he might do?' Brampton asked.

'I am as certain as I can be, it is what he *will* do.'

'Would he dare?' his daughter asked.

Bramberg took another gulp from his jug. 'America and NATO are withdrawing from Europe and have no stomach for a fight, so why wouldn't he? Then he will look at Russian-speaking east Ukraine. He may even be tempted to try getting back the Baltic states if he's allowed to get away with things.' He stared into the middle distance. 'And then there is the Arctic.'

'Arctic?' Royce echoed.

'It was always a big thing of his, that at least half of the Arctic oil, gas and mineral wealth should belong to Russia. There will be conflict, mark my words.'

'You really dislike him, Dad, don't you?'

The journalist nodded. 'I always found him disagreeable. Small man syndrome. He was an unfeeling KGB man when I knew him and his mind-set hasn't changed. He wants Russia to be great again – I don't really blame him for that. But he pisses away the opportunity of its people to be free and prosperous like the West. Such extreme politics is as bad as extreme religion – and you know what I feel about that.'

Brampton turned to Royce. 'Dad is a very lapsed Jew.'

Her father chuckled. 'My advice is have nothing to do with any religion that tells you what to eat or what to wear.' He lifted his jug, finished the beer and belched lightly.

Royce said, 'I just ask that you take special care for a while. Our people at the Foreign Office suggest maybe you visit friends, take a holiday for a few weeks. You will be funded. Do not allow yourself to be a sitting target.'

Bramberg leaned forward across the table and lowered his voice. 'I have to ask then, were you followed here today, followed to Porthleven?'

'Not to our knowledge,' Royce replied.

'You are nice man, James -' the irascible smile was back ' – even if you are courting my daughter. But I left Motherland a long, long time ago and even if I do irritate Comrade Putin, I do think he has bigger concerns than me right now. And I will certainly not allow him to dictate how I live my life. You understand?'

Royce nodded slowly and smiled his understanding. 'Of course,' he replied. 'My round.'

The rest of the evening descended into a joyous swirl of conversation, laughs and jokes with Bramberg's seemingly many friends, male and female, fishermen, artists and boat-builders, and lifetime escapees from urban life. A local folk trio kicked off mid-evening with hilarious sea shanties sung to the sound of accordion and fiddle. When the landlord finally shut up for the night, Bramberg led the way, swaying slightly, back to his house.

Aware that his cutting edge was somewhat blunted by too much good beer, Royce managed to keep a look out for anyone attempting to follow them. Once away from the pub, the streets were clear of people, glistening slightly with the sheen of sea spray carried in on the breeze. The smell of salt and seaweed lingered in the air. While Bramberg went to bed, leaving his daughter in the second guest's room, Royce camped on the living room sofa for the night. He fell asleep quickly, realising he hadn't enjoyed himself so much for years.

The next day Bramberg took them out for a day's fishing on his beloved 13 foot, Canadian-built lugger, which he'd named the *FaJo* after his daughter and late wife. It was warm for the time of year and the sea was kind, Royce at home on the water and recapturing some of his boyhood memories, aware of Brampton watching him with obvious amusement as he succeeded in landing half a dozen mackerel. She, too, did well, clearly schooled by her father from a young age. But Bramberg was the real star with another tally of nine mackerel all to himself, plus the contents of his own lobster pot providing a prize specimen.

It was home to a lobster supper, cooked by the old man, while Royce helped Brampton gut the fish for the freezer. Then it was a return to the pub for another rousing night of chat and music.

In a lull in the noise while the two folk bands changed over, Bramberg leaned towards Royce and his daughter in a conspiratorial fashion. 'I think a lot about what you say. I sleep not too much last night. I have always kept copies of notes and files about what I write and think. It is an old habit from when I am a hot potato, newly defected from Mother Russia.'

'A back-up file?' Brampton asked.

He nodded. 'Exactly that.' He grinned broadly at her and reached his big paw of a hand across the table to ruffle her hair. 'I am so proud of you. Maybe I should let you have my file…just in case, just in case my dear friend Vlad is really more upset with me than I realise… For safe-keeping, you understand?'

'Of course, Dad. That would be sensible.'

A hoarse Cornish baritone tapped and tested the mike and the next band struck up.

On the morning of their departure, Royce awoke on the sofa with a start. He'd had a bad dream. He was back in Baghdad, driving down a street lined with parked cars, each one exploding as he passed. The windscreen shattered in front of him as he came to.

'Are you okay, James?'

Brampton was at the door, peering in. Her long legs whipped at his senses; she was wearing one of her father's cable sweaters as a dressing-gown, which kept her decent by half-an-inch.

He dragged his eyes away from her. 'I'm fine, thanks.'

'I thought you cried out.'

'A bad dream,' he realised. 'I get them sometimes.'

'I'll make a pot of tea.'

'Good idea.'

As she left, he climbed from his sleeping bag and quickly pulled on his clothes. The dream had left him with a sudden worrying thought.

With the door on the latch, he left the cottage and set off up the hill to his parked car. When he arrived there was a taxi parked next to it, belching diesel as it waited for its passenger to emerge from the adjacent house.

Royce lowered himself down and quickly scanned under the Jaguar as best he could. He could see nothing untoward, so he checked again, including each of the wheel arches. The two front ones, nothing. The right rear, nothing.

On the last wheel arch he saw it. Cautiously he felt it, a smooth moulded metal casing. He forced it with his fingertips, but it held tight like a limpet. At last he prised away its magnetic grip. He stared down at it in his palm. A radio tracking-beacon.

The shock hit him like a physical thing. He felt sick. What a fool, he'd been!

Suddenly the door of the house opened and an old lady emerged. The taxi driver got out to help her into his cab. 'Hospital, love, is it?'

Royce bent swiftly down and put his hand under the rear wheel arch of the taxi. The tracking-beacon was snapped from his grasp, attaching itself to the metal underside.

He stood back and watched as the taxi drew away and disappeared up the street.

18

END GAME

Timeline: Tunisia, mid-August 2011

The pilot of the twin-engine Airbus 319 thoughtfully tilted the airliner first to port, and then to starboard to allow his passengers a view of the shimmering swathe of turquoise Mediterranean waters.

However Brampton could not drag her eyes away from the tabloid newspaper spread on her lap. For the umpteenth time on the flight she'd pored over the garish centre spread with its fuzzy photograph of Princess Ayana – clearly taken surreptitiously on a mobile phone – and artists' impressions of Gaddafi's harem, full of leather-clad Amazons and naked slave girls being spread-eagled and whipped. Once more she glared at the by-line and thumbnail image of a bespectacled face that increasingly reminded her of Harry Potter. *Chesney Sykes.*

'Little shite,' she again murmured under her breath before folding the paper roughly and stuffing it into her shoulder bag. Sykes, she knew, had had one meeting with Ayana and it had lasted barely minutes before the Colonel's bodyguard had kicked him out of the room. She knew because Ayana had actually emailed her over the Dark Web at the London office to complain about him.

Brampton had actually found herself in the ridiculous position of having to apologise to one of Gaddafi's torturers and slave mistresses for the rude, adolescent behaviour of her fellow journalist. Moreover, Chesney had resorted to plagiarising her own previous article, "sexing it up", as he liked to call it, with additional pages of lurid speculation and illustrations. Needless to say, the paper's sales had rocketed.

It certainly didn't help with Brampton's persistent personal campaign for Ayana to release the slave-girl Tabina back to her family.

Even more upsetting was to hear in similar fashion from the friendly rebel leader Dr Jaralla, who had been offended by some of Sykes's throwaway comments.

With bell-chimes and a Tannoy announcement, the Tunisair liner began its descent towards Carthage International Airport. Brampton's frustration and anger with both the arrogant Sykes and her boss Russ Carver began to subside along with the aircraft's drop in altitude. By the time the wheels of the undercarriage hissed on the sizzling hot tarmac of the runway, those emotions had been replaced with a heightened sense of excitement and anticipation of what was to come.

She was back in the saddle, on the job as a journalist for the paper and its new digital news outlet. The whole media world sensed that the Libyan conflict was nearing its climax, the evil dictator was in hiding and facing the ultimate end game. It was just a question of exactly where and exactly when.

God, she thought, I'm dying for a cigarette, as she stepped out of the aircraft and into the oven-blast heat of desert air, sweet with a musky hint of cinnamon. Just the exertion of carrying her shoulder bag and new lightweight video camera, drew sweat in the small of her back during the short walk across the baking concrete apron to the air-conditioned sanctuary of the terminal. As she waited at the carousel for her single wheeled suitcase, she stripped down from her light cotton travel waistcoat to just a white T-shirt and khaki cargo trousers. Feeling cooler and calmer she made her way across the vast and shiny floor towards customs and immigration. It was filled with media types of all nationalities from around the world, many laden with both luggage and equipment. There was a distinct buzz in the air, an excitement that was almost tangible. She recognised several journalists from her previous assignment, a broadcaster from Japan and another team from al-Jazeera, all mingling with clusters of British holiday makers who were headed for the Tunisian beach complexes.

Distracted by the formalities, she forgot her earlier speculation on the flight out from Britain as to who would be meeting her. Russ Carver had been vague, unable to handle trivia like security when he had a pair of breasts to select for his readers' pleasure.

As she cleared arrivals and scanned the sea of hand-held signs, she read *Jo Brampton* first – before she saw the face of the man holding it.

'James!'

'Hi, Curly.'

'Still not retired?'

A grunt. 'Still working on it.'

'What did you call me?'

'Curly. Sorry, it's what Stefan always calls you. It sort of stuck.'

'Behind my back?'

'Just between ourselves.'

Her cheeks coloured and her brow furrowed. 'Do you think that's appropriate between a professional and a client? We only drove down to Cornwall together. That hardly makes us best mates.'

'It seems not,' Royce replied defensively, raising his palms in a gesture of surrender.

'I don't call you Rollo,' she thundered on, 'do I? I leave that for your military chums.'

'Got out on the wrong side this morning, did we?'

She looked at his wolfish grin, and relented, relaxing her shoulders. 'Sorry, yes. I am a bit wound up.' The single dimple deepened as she smiled. 'But I'm still not calling you Rollo.'

'Then I won't call you Curly, Curly.'

She punched him playfully on the arm. 'Where to?' she asked, lighting a cigarette.

Two armoured Range Rovers were waiting in the airport carpark.

By the time they reached them, Bram was perspiring heavily again in the high humidity, her T-shirt clinging like a second skin.

'The vehicles were supplied for the BBC via our embassy here,' Royce explained. 'The British government is keen to be seen as keeping at arm's length from developments in Libya, but wants full BBC coverage.'

'Especially as the Foreign Office is up to its neck in it?'

'That's international politics for you.' He indicated the people clustered around the two vehicles. 'A few familiar faces.'

'And is Parsons *really* BBC World Service?'

'That's who I'm assigned to.'

'That's not an answer, James.'

'It's the only one you're getting.' He added, 'Stefan and I are on private contracts now, not MOD.'

'Which outfit?'

'IAP. International Asset Protection. Run by an ex-SAS guy called D'Arcy.'

'I've heard of it. Offices in Canary Wharf.'

Seeff spotted the journalist first. 'Hey, Bram, how are you, chick?'

'Not Curly?'

He didn't miss the opportunity to kiss her full on the mouth. 'What did you say?' he asked as she pushed him away.

'Oh, nothing,' she replied, turning to take the formal handshake of Parsons and Tremain.

'Like old times,' he commented, 'except maybe this time there'll be an end to it.'

'I sure hope so,' she replied, patting her camera. 'I've got to get it all on this for posterity.'

Sinbad came scurrying up to her. 'Miss Jo, it is my pleasure to meet you again. I hear you are coming.' He pointed to the mountain of provisions loaded in the back cargo area and on the roof rack. At a glance she calculated there must had been some twenty jerry cans of fuel, a couple of hundred litres of water, plus dozens of linen bags tagged with magic marker for loo rolls, pasta, dried nuts, canned fish, coffee and tea. 'So I get your favourite fig jam. We will not run out.'

'I don't think we'll be running out of anything, Sinbad,' she observed.

'No, not before it is all over and the Fat Lady she sing!'

'What?' Brampton asked, bemused.

'Nassr al-Mabrouk, he goes! Flees to Egypt with family.'

'Er, who? The Interior Minister?'

'That's him,' Royce confirmed.

'Yes, yes! If he go, they all go!' Sinbad added.

Royce said, 'And Gaddafi's made his first radio appeal in a long time, calling for the people to rise up against NATO. It all sounded pretty desperate.'

'I wonder where he's hiding out?' Brampton thought aloud.

'There are plenty of rumours,' Royce replied. 'Not least that he's in the Rixos or Corinthia media hotels, possibly hiding in the basement on the basis they will not be bombed.'

'That would be quite a smart move,' Seeff said. 'And, by the way, I think we're ready to rock 'n' roll.'

'Let's go,' Royce decided.

It was a relief to get underway and have the chill draft from the air-cons running through both vehicles. Royce drove the first with Brampton and Sinbad; Seeff manned the second with Parsons and Tremain. The sense of anticipation and elation was short-lived. As soon as they reached the main highway to Libya, they hit gridlock. It was a two hour grind to the border. In the lead Range Rover, the engine overheated and the air-con expired.

At last they cleared the border crossing into Libya at Dahiba. The transformation from their last time in the country was marked, with shops and markets open for business and women out on the busy streets with children in tow. Life had virtually returned to normal, and the rebels were clearly in control. There were occasional smoking wrecks of government vehicles, unloved and ignored at the roadside.

The traffic had begun to dissipate and the two-car convoy speeded up. That was a relief for the passengers in the lead vehicle as the slipstream helped cool the baking interior. They passed through Nalut, where other journalists and media teams were in a chaotic roadside circus as they switched drivers and taxis, negotiating hard for a good deal on their forward journey. The re-united Team B drove somewhat smugly on, through village after village clearly in rebel hands. No Gaddafi green flags in evidence anywhere. More and more blackened tanks and armoured vehicles lay expired on the desert roadsides.

Night was closing in as they entered the town of Zintan. It had been totally overwhelmed by the influx of foreign journalists and TV news crews, all scrambling for a place to sleep for the night and something to eat. Local cafés and coffee shops were making an unexpected killing. Patches of light sprang up on waste ground as correspondents began recording pieces to camera or used satellite phones in preparation to catch the nine o'clock news schedules around Europe.

The lead Range Rover bumped into the unmade parking lot of a tyre repair shop. It was closed, there were no lights and the steel shutters were down. Bullet holes pockmarked its front wall. The headlight beams picked out an open topped vehicle that was familiar to Royce. It was a British Special Forces long-based Land Rover in the latest desert camouflage colours.

The driver waited with obvious impatience, tapping his forefinger on the steering wheel, with his head wrapped in an Arabic red-and-white *shamag* scarf. His passenger leaned laconically against the front wing, waiting for the new arrivals to stop. He wore a mixture of civilian and military clothes, topped with a Nike baseball cap.

'Fucking McHaggis,' Seeff breathed as he left the second Range Rover to join Royce.

'Evening,' Royce greeted McDougall stiffly.

'Gentlemen,' the E Squadron major greeted without enthusiasm.

'You're an hour late.'

'Heavy traffic,' Royce returned.

Seeff added, 'And a kamikaze camel on the road outside Nalut. Had to wait for the local butcher to bless and bleed him, chop him up and take him away.'

McDougall ignored that. 'Follow us. Got you a safe house with a friendly farmer who's on board.'

Royce and Seeff had barely returned to their respective vehicles before the Land Rover driver gunned up and flew off the parking lot, onto the dusty main drag and out into the all-enveloping blackness of the night.

The primitive breeze-block farm building had the benefit of an independent generator that provided power for both lighting and to drive the well pump. Its owner was a shy, middle-aged farmer and his buxom wife, who was jolly and thoroughly enjoyed cooking up a tagine of goat stew with an aroma that immediately had everyone salivating.

Royce observed Bram as she set up her video camera in the farmyard. She set it on a tripod on automatic and filmed a short piece to camera. Speaking in hushed, secretive tones she made it sound as though she was on a journalistic mission into dangerous territory. Obligingly the horizon suddenly lit up with an array of rumbling explosions.

'That'll be Zawiya,' Royce explained. 'According to McDougall, Gaddafi's forces have made a last gasp attempt to seize back the key town of Zawiya and its surrounding oilfields.'

'Really? That's great, thanks. I'll do an add-on. I also got some good B-footage on the journey here. It'll edit together nicely.'

Ten minutes later, she'd finished and went back inside the farmhouse with Royce. 'Is McDougall something to do with the British Army?'

'More likely Foreign Office,' Royce answered vaguely.

'He's too old to be in the SAS,' she decided as they entered.

Everyone was seated around the rough-hewn timber table in the kitchen as the farmer's wife ladled out the thick goat stew into bowls full of rice.

McDougall was saying, 'We won't be able to get you back to Tripoli until Zawiya falls. It's in turmoil because of Gaddafi's counter-attack. There's been fierce street-fighting in the town all day and no remotely safe way through or around it.'

Parsons asked, 'What about my contact Brigadier Cinti?'

'Who?'

'Cinti Hassan,' Parsons replied, clearly impatient. 'Mat Asquith must have mentioned him to you, one of my most valuable assets. He runs that special depot on the other side of Zawiya. It adjoins – or is technically part of – 32nd Khamis Brigade Headquarters.'

'Oh, him,' McDougall replied dismissively as he spooned some stew into his mouth. 'Not a key player, I think.'

Royce picked up on Parsons' growing irritation. 'I think Brigadier Cinti will be very much a key player if Gaddafi or any of his family do a runner. The Khamis Brigade is dedicated to the personal protection of the Gaddafi family and Cinti's armoury has enough equipment and fuel to create a fully-fledged fighting brigade.'

'*You* think,' McDougall said, wiping his toothbrush moustache with the back of his hand. 'Your boss, Mr Asquith, clearly doesn't think so. Opinions – as we like to say in the army – are like arseholes. Full of shit and everyone's got one.' He glanced at Brampton. 'Apologies.'

She scowled back at him. 'Don't. Women have them too.'

McDougall did a slight double-take at that and smiled awkwardly as the meal continued in a strained silence.

When it was finished, the farmer's wife invited Brampton to use a room that belonged to her student son, who was away fighting with the rebels. After Royce organised a stag rota for the night, the rest of the team settled with kip mats and sleeping bags around the living room, dining area and kitchen.

The humidity and the spasmodic muted noise of explosions from Zawiya conspired to make sleep uncomfortable and disturbed.

Finally, with the sunrise, came the strangulated call of the farm's cockerel. Slowly everyone came to life as though participating in a low-budget zombie movie. While the farmer's wife prepared breakfast, Parsons made his way outside to the courtyard where he found Royce leaning against a corral fence, nursing a coffee.

'Sticky night,' Parsons complained. 'No air-con.'

'Cool now,' Royce returned. 'For an hour or so.'

'I'm not happy,' Parsons announced, unburdening himself.

'Brigadier Cinti?'

'Absolutely. I don't know what Asquith is playing at.'

'Asquith isn't you,' Royce replied evenly.

'What's that supposed to mean?'

'From what little I know of the man, he doesn't think like you. He doesn't think outside the box.'

Parsons said, 'All the time I was in London, I kept out of it. I didn't interfere. I never even used to phone the man. I kept out of it, didn't want to queer Asquith's pitch – especially after that rocky start he had with the rebel leadership.'

'And now you wish you had?' Royce suggested.

Parsons extracted the sat-coms cell-phone from his pocket. 'Clearly it was a bad decision of mine.'

He scrolled down the list of contacts and thumbed the button. There was a brief pause before Royce was able to hear the faint squawk of Arabic on the other end. 'Brigadier! How are you? It's me, Mr Oliver. I'm back in the country.'

Parsons indicated for Royce to move closer as he switched on the phone's amplifier. *'Mr Oliver? I do not believe it! For the love of Allah, I think you have forsaken me. I hear nothing from you. There is a man who says he replace you, Mr Mat. And a Scottish man called Mac…So rude.'*

'I'm sorry,' Parsons said. 'But as I say, I am back in country.'

'Where?'

'Just outside Zawiya.'

'Ah, not far.' He sounded relieved. *'But there is heavy fighting. If Zawiya falls, I think they will come here. I fear for my life, and the lives of my wife and family.'*

'They? Who will come to your depot?'

'Maybe even Gaddafi himself. Or his sons and family. Only they know what is secretly stored here.'

'If they come, you will let me know? Immediately?'

'Of course, it is what we agreed.' Both men could hear the fear in his voice. *'But I will not be able to stop them.'*

'You have armed guards.' It was a statement, not a question.

'I have detail of twelve men. Three have already run away, frightened they will be caught by rebels. There have been many killings of army deserters.'

'I know it is difficult,' Parsons said sympathetically, 'but if anyone from the Gaddafi regime comes to take stuff, you must resist and let me know immediately. Britain has assets on the ground that may be able to intervene and assist you. I will be there with you just as soon as I can,'

'It will not be a moment too soon.'

The brigadier's last words left both men feeling uneasy.

As they made their way back inside the farmhouse, Royce said, 'Maybe we can bypass Zawiya to the south. Avoid the worst of the fighting.'

There was a delicious smell of freshly baked flatbread in the kitchen, where everyone was again gathered around the table. McDougall was standing to one side, talking on his radio in staccato army-speak. Seeing Royce and Parsons enter, he abruptly finished his conversation. 'Gentlemen,' he said, putting away the radio, 'I'm getting reports that the battle for Zawiya is virtually finished. Our boys have been helping out, guiding in a few airstrikes. Apart from a couple of snipers holding out, it's all over.'

An hour later, they'd finished breakfast and stowed everything aboard the over-laden Range Rovers which were clearly marked "TV" on both bonnets and sides. At Royce's insistence, everyone was wearing body armour and helmets. It was oddly quiet. For once there was no distant crump of artillery rounds, boom of a bomb finding its target or machine-gun fire sounding like a rattle at a football match. It was eerie and even a little unsettling, because everyone was waiting for it to start again, to catch them by surprise. Already the morning air was beginning to simmer and shimmer with heat. After thanking the farmer and his wife, the three-vehicle convoy set off down the track towards the town, with McDougall's Land Rover leading the way.

When they arrived in the decimated wreck of newly-liberated Zawiya town, it was unnaturally quiet. Royce was surprised to see so few people on the rubble-strewn streets of damaged houses.

'It is middle of Ramadan,' Sinbad explained, waving his arms expressively. 'Last night everyone have great feast and celebrate the victory and sleep in.'

'Don't drop your guard,' Royce warned, as he swung the wheel to follow the Land Rover around another corner. 'There could still be snipers or isolated Gaddafi fighters.'

'We're heading towards the East Gate,' Brampton observed, poking her video camera out of the passenger door window.

'And the road to Tripoli,' Sinbad added happily.

Royce was nervous, his mouth suddenly dry. The last time he had been here, back in the spring, the area had been full of government tanks, APCs and artillery laying siege. There had been government troops everywhere. Until only last night, Gaddafi's forces had held the town in its iron grip.

Now it was totally void of military vehicles, apart from the scorched remains of half a dozen main battle tanks. They lay like dead dinosaurs on empty tracts of sandy grass. Acrid smoke hung in the still air. Abandoned uniforms were everywhere on the ground like little piles of green excrement from an army that had run away.

Small groups of rebel 4x4s, beaten-up trucks full of young fighters, and pick-ups converted into heavy support weapon "technicals" were gathering.

Royce could sense it in the air. An excitement, an electricity that was almost tangible.

He glanced at Brampton. She recognised it, too, he knew, as she nervously lit a Sobranie and exhaled rapidly. 'It's happening, James, isn't it? This is the big one.'

They were appearing from all directions, coming as if from nowhere. One by one the rebel vehicles were edging off the wide verges, onto the road to Tripoli to form a vast, moving column. Royce followed McDougall's Land Rover into the gathering stream of traffic.

'I think this is it, Jo,' he agreed.

As they speeded up, the slipstream blew her hair from her face. Brampton felt exhilarated; as though all her earlier hard work on this mission had been leading up to this climactic point. She looked at Royce and grinned. 'The big push?'

He nodded. 'I think so. Tripoli here we come.'

19

BREAKOUT

As they cleared Zawiya, a couple of government trucks could be seen burning on the desert scrub beside the main road to Tripoli.

The huge column of cars, trucks, tractors and converted pick-up "technicals", mounted with anti-aircraft guns or heavy mortars, formed the endless procession. Its fastest speed was dictated by the slowest vehicle. Many fighters were on foot, their numbers simply too great for all to be able to hitch a lift. The red, black and green colours of the rebellion were fluttering everywhere.

Overhead two NATO jets screamed across a sky of eggshell blue, tearing white trails of vapour behind them. One of the aircraft did a spectacular victory roll, the sun catching on its wing like a shooting star. A cheer of appreciation went up from the excited young rebels riding the convoy.

More vehicles, many trucks loaded high with crates of ammunition, were feeding into the column from the left and right all the time. The onward movement seemed inexorable and unstoppable, the air of excitement near intoxicating.

Soon they were on the outskirts of the next town of Judaim. Here there were even more vehicles and rebel fighters milling in their thousands, ready to join the advance.

'These must be the reinforcements McDougall was talking about,' Brampton observed. 'The men they've been training and preparing in the south.'

Royce nodded. 'This is it, no mistake.'

'Rats is what our Brother Leader called us,' Sinbad said gleefully. 'Now these rats are turning on him.'

Fighters were chanting and singing and dancing, green Gaddafi flags had been torn down and now burned fitfully on the ground. The excited crowds were pressing in, adding to the heat and humidity.

'I really must make another transmission to London,' Brampton said. 'Any chance we can pull over for a few minutes?'

'Of course,' Royce replied.

He'd spotted two tall buildings up ahead and stopped beside the dusty alleyway that ran between them. It offered shade and cover from sniper fire. He picked up the radio and called over his intention on the net.

'Roger, I'm with you, boss,' Seeff shot back immediately. 'I'll cover your ass. Out.'

'What the hell, Rollo?' McDougall demanded. 'We're not here to nursemaid the media.'

'If we did' Royce retorted, 'they might show more respect for us.'

With few exceptions he had never had problems with journalists. If things got screwed up, it was usually once the original copy had been filed in faraway newsrooms where sales suddenly took priority over facts and truth.

As McDougall grudgingly pulled over to the side of the road in front of Royce's Range Rover, Bram scrambled out into the alley. She quickly set up the compact Hughes B-gan satellite dish on top of the vehicle for line-of-sight connection with one of the three satellites that gave continual global coverage between them. After connecting her laptop, which contained copies of her filmed reports, she was able to transmit them at 492 kbps to the *Sunday News* office in London. For once it didn't cut out, and there were no other baffling technical or atmospheric glitches. The operation was smoothly over in ten minutes.

Nevertheless, McDougall still showed his impatience to be going. His driver wasted no time in pulling away into the slow and steady current of traffic passing by.

Out of nowhere a CNN news team pulled over, recognising that the alleyway offered a good position for both security and a satellite transmission. Irrationally, Brampton became annoyed and urged Royce to drive off.

'Let's get away, I can't stand that reporter.'

Royce chuckled. "A bit like inter-Service rivalry.'

'No,' Brampton replied. 'We really do hate each other.'

'So do we.'

After only minutes back in the queue of traffic, they came under sniper fire. Gaddafi's men were firing from rooftops or ruined buildings on both sides of the road.

Groups of young rebel fighters peeled away from the convoy, to the left and to the right. They smashed down doors and broke through windows to enter buildings. The fighting was going to be devilish, close-quarters, and to the death. Winners would take all, and that was unlikely to include prisoners. Rockets suddenly landed close by. Blast from the nearest shockwave rocked the lead Range Rover, shrapnel spitting at the bodywork.

'Stop filming!' Royce ordered. 'Keep your window closed!'

Brampton obeyed, straining to see what was happening through the drifting black smoke of the explosions. For the next couple of hours the inexorable slow surge of vehicles ground on, ever under fire from sporadic rounds pinging on metal, the almost musical sound betraying the lethal rain of lead. Gradually, metre by metre, the vehicles edged forward and the fighting ebbed away with it.

'Who's that?' Royce asked unexpectedly. 'Isn't it Doc Jaralla? From Misrata?'

Brampton glanced sideways at a stream of fresh vehicles that was pushing itself into the flow from where it had been lined up at the roadside.

'No, surely not,' she said, squinting. 'It can't be.'

'It bloody well is,' Royce confirmed.

The man was standing in the open back of a truck. He was staring ahead, over its cab, looking for all the world like a tank commander preparing for the fray. The men travelling with him looked different from most young fighters they had observed that day. These were the veterans of the Misrata Freedom Battalion, and it showed. Their courage and endurance had been forged and tested in the hell of Tripoli Road. You could see it in their sunken eyes, in the exhausted expressions. No elation at the prospect of victory, just quiet recognition that they had been through hell and still had a job to finish.

Royce hit the horn to catch Jaralla's attention. The man turned his head abruptly, taking in the huge "TV" logo before he clocked Brampton grinning at him.

'Doctor! Doctor! How lovely to see you!'

'Miss Brampton!' The serious face broke into a smile of recognition.

Immediately he hopped over the side of the crawling truck and jumped to the ground.

'Quick, let the doctor in,' Brampton ordered and Sinbad dutifully threw the rear door open so that Jaralla could clamber in.

'How are you, doctor?' Brampton asked breathlessly. 'I'm *so* surprised to see you here.'

'We came by ferry from Misrata,' he explained. 'Landed at Zawiya last night. It is all over back in Misrata now. Gaddafi is defeated, his men have run away. We are here now for the finish.'

'You came with the Islamic Brotherhood fighters?' Royce asked.

Jaralla shook his head. 'Sheikh Hatem's jihadists came here ahead of us, on orders from Nazal Abu.'

'But Nazal is one of Gaddafi's closest allies,' Brampton reminded.

The doctor gave a contemptuous grunt. 'Nazal is Nazal's closest ally. He knows Gaddafi is finished, so he will be looking after himself. I understand Nazal has ordered Sheikh Hatem's jihadist fighters to seize a secret depot at the HQ of the Khamis Brigade.'

'Secret depot,' Royce echoed 'That's Brigadier Cinti's depot.'

'Cinti?' Brampton asked. 'Ollie Parsons' contact?'

Royce nodded. 'That's where we're headed now.'

'Then we have the same mission,' Jaralla said. 'If that equipment falls into the hands of the Sheikh Hatem's jihadists, then Libya's future will be in jeopardy.' He glanced at his wristwatch and at the impenetrable jam of traffic all around them. 'Forgive me, I must get back.' He opened the rear passenger door. 'I just hope we are not both too late.'

The slow rolling tide of vehicles was now passing the small village of Maia. It had just been recaptured by the rebels with the support of NATO airstrikes. Evidence of the aerial bombardment were everywhere, bomb craters and smouldering army vehicles at the roadside, and buildings with collapsed roofs on either side. Everything had been brutally smashed to give no hiding place to any of Gaddafi's remaining forces. Those forces had simply vanished into thin air, evaporated. Discarded green uniforms were everywhere as soldiers swapped sides and joined the people's army.

Dazed villagers, mostly veiled women with their children, stood and watched as the rebel fighters and their vehicles streamed past. The tide was gathering momentum. Shots were fired in the air excitedly and the sky rained with hot lead as the sun lowered into the burning western sunset and the shadows lengthened. Dying amber light set aglow the sulphurous clouds of trailing dust from the traffic.

McDougall's leading Land Rover was passing a small bottling factory when Parsons' voice cut in over the radio. *'X-ray Papa to Team Silver, we are fast approaching Yarmouk and Khamis Brigade headquarters. Proceed with caution. I must speak to our asset there at all costs.'*

McDougall didn't like that at all. He was straight on the net. *'X-ray Papa, this is your safe escort. Abort any idea of visiting Khamis HQ. It's not going to happen.'*

Parsons answered smoothly and firmly, *'Sorry, escort, you're overruled.'*

'X-ray Papa, I repeat, my orders are to escort you safely to Tripoli. End of. Please comply, over.'

'Then your mission is at an end, Escort,' Parsons retorted evenly. *'Thanks for your company. Out.'*

Royce and Brampton looked at each other and grinned. 'That's true love for you,' Royce assured.

And, when the dominating grey walls of the army base emerged out of the dusty twilight, McDougall was still lurking in his Land Rover.

Team B's second vehicle pulled up alongside Royce, Seeff at the wheel.

Royce observed the monumental entrance, topped with its huge stone eagle, of the compound that had been built as a fortress to guard the western approach to the capital. It was known colloquially as "Gate 2" because it was just that many miles from Tripoli.

Hundreds of fighters were streaming in and out of its main entrance, ransacking and pillaging anything that wasn't nailed down. Office equipment, furniture, televisions, computers had become the unexpected spoils of war. Instant entrepreneurs were loading their pick-ups with stolen wares.

Parked across the street from the entrance was an orderly row of trucks and armed "technicals", flying the flag of Dr Jaralla's Misrata Freedom Battalion. Their uniformed men were entering the headquarters compound in disciplined groups, each looking as though they were on a specific mission.

'Let's take a look,' Parsons suggested.

Royce shoved the gear into first and drove them slowly and steadily towards the open gates. There was no one to stop them.

'I expect you know all this,' Brampton said, glancing down at a small notebook, 'but, according to Chingford Charlie, 32 Brigade is in fact a militia run by Gaddafi's youngest son, Khamis. A right little shit and favoured heir apparent. A couple of years ago it received some eleven billion Euros worth of Belgian arms.'

'That's some shipment,' Royce murmured beneath his breath.

'The brigade is the most well-trained and best-equipped in the Libyan military,' she continued. 'As we know, its primary function is to protect the leader and his family. Gaddafi's Pretorian guard, if you like. It comprises some three thousand troops, many or even most mercenaries from across sub-Saharan Africa.'

'Who sell their own mothers for gold,' Sinbad interjected bitterly. 'Will always fight and die for money.'

'The only people Gaddafi can trust are not his own,' Royce murmured.

He drove slowly on through the milling crowds of rebel fighters. In the mirror, he noted that McDougall was still bringing up the rear. Despite the spat between the E Squadron officer and Parsons, Royce still felt thankful for the SAS officer's presence. It became clear just how vast the base was as they passed barrack blocks, huge sheds and warehouses, now being looted.

'Look,' Brampton pointed out, jabbing a finger as she focussed her video camera. 'That must be Khamis' palace, or what's left of it.'

From the architectural wreck, it had clearly been a neo-classical construction with white columns and apricot walls that had been reduced to a heap of rubble by well-placed NATO strikes.

Sinbad explained, 'His son is – how you English say – chip off old block. He is his father's son. He tries to mimic his father's compound at Bab al-Aziziya. If anyone succeeds our Brother Leader, it will be this man, Khamis, not his brother Said.'

'Khamis has been reported to have been killed,' Royce replied. 'Several times.'

'Not enough,' Sinbad growled.

They had reached another perimeter metal fence of another compound within a compound. It was topped with coils of razor wire and extended for a good few hundred metres in both directions, whatever lay beyond obscured by sheets of hessian screening material. The two main wire gates had been smashed aside like two broken butterfly wings by a powerful vehicle – most probably a tank – and the sand-bagged emplacements on either side were riddled with bullets.

Royce picked up his radio. 'Silver One to X-ray Papa, I'm going in, okay? Over.'

'Roger that,' Parsons confirmed. *'Proceed with maximum caution. We're right behind you. Be prepared for a fast abort if things look bad. Over.'*

'Confirm. Out,' Royce snapped back and switched off.

The Range Rover edged through the gap between the broken gates and into a sandy lane that ran between piles and piles of loaded pallets that rose like mini-skyscrapers on either side. Vast quantities were clearly missing. They passed several vast warehouses with the gates left open, each revealing rows and rows of empty racking.

'My God,' Brampton said, 'If this was all full of weapons and ammunition, I can't imagine how much has been taken. Enough to start World War Three, I should think.'

'Fuel, too,' Royce added, indicating a couple of damaged bowsers remaining where clearly many dozens had stood in a row.

'Where would you expect to find the Brigadier?' Brampton asked. 'What's his name?'

'Cinti,' Royce replied. 'There must be some kind of admin office, I should think.'

'Could that be it?' Brampton said, pointing a finger.

Darkness was rapidly settling over the landscape, visibility fading away. A long stretch of track led to a wide stucco building with an Italian style terracotta roof.

'Could be,' Royce replied and swung the wheel.

There were half a dozen military pick-ups parked outside the single story villa. A cluster of men was gathered beside them, smoking and talking excitedly with much waving of hands.

'Rebels,' Royce decided.

'I think they Misrata Battalion,' Sinbad said.

'He's right,' Brampton agreed. 'I do believe that's our friend, Dr Jaralla.'

As they approached the villa, they could see an adjoining bungalow structure that obviously served as the administration office block for the depot. Brigadier Cinti literally lived next to the job.

Royce stopped and Seeff pulled alongside with the second Range Rover, both leaving their engines running. Meanwhile, McDougall pulled over some distance away to keep an eye on them. He was clearly keen not to get involved.

Dr Jaralla waved as he recognised the new arrivals, but he didn't look very happy.

As everyone exited their vehicles, the warm humidity of the night air smothered them, the silence filled with the sound of cicadas. Royce and Seeff automatically fell into their "close protection" rôles, maintaining a short distance behind their clients and between the group of rebels, looking out for any signs of approaching danger.

'It is not good, Miss Brampton,' Jaralla said immediately.

'In what way?' Parsons asked anxiously. 'The brigadier hasn't been answering my calls.'

The rebel leader frowned. 'I'm sorry, do I know you, sir?'

Parsons smiled his famous melting smile. 'Ollie from the BBC World Service. We met briefly once in Misrata when NATO bombs hit your HQ.'

The doctor smiled apologetically. 'Ah, yes. I thought you look familiar.'

'What has happened?' Brampton urged.

'Sheikh Hatem and the Islamic Brotherhood arrived here this morning.' Jaralla replied with a flat voice. 'They have taken everything.'

Parsons swivelled on his feet, scanning the panorama of warehouses, vehicle parks and storage facilities. 'Surely not.'

'Enough for what they need,' Jaralla replied. 'That is what I mean. Vehicles and fuel, light and heavy arms, and anti-tank and anti-aircraft missiles. And manpower.'

'Manpower?' Brampton echoed.

'The Brotherhood in Misrata was made up of many foreign fighters,'

Jaralla explained wearily as if to a child. 'Sheikh Hatem himself is a Qatari – like Nazal Abu – and a jihadist. Many, if not most of the soldiers of the 32nd are also foreign mercenaries. They can see that Gaddafi is finished, his regime is over. They know there is no future for them here. It seems that a good number may have joined the Brotherhood for a new future.'

'Where have they gone?' Parsons asked.

'That we do not know,' Jaralla said.

'Brigadier Cinti should have stopped them going anywhere,' Tremain pointed out.

The doctor looked at the Tasmanian strangely. 'He did as much as he could, believe me. He only had a handful of guards. Something began here today and I do not like it.'

Brampton picked up that the doctor was nervous, unsettled. 'What's wrong?'

Parsons said, 'I spoke to Cinti by phone only yesterday. Is he still here, can I speak to him?'

'This is his home, isn't it?' Brampton pushed.

'Yes, yes,' Jaralla said quickly. 'This was his home. Home to him, to his wife and family.'

Royce noticed the tense. 'Was?'

Parsons pushed forward. 'We're wasting time. I need to talk to Cinti. Find out what happened? Where the Brotherhood column went, to Tripoli, Misrata...?'

Jaralla said, 'It was more than a column, more like a battle group. Even as we are speaking now, jihadists are still loading up individual trucks to join the convoy. There is chaos here. Nobody knows what is happening.'

'That's ridiculous,' Parsons said. 'Cinti should be stopping them.'

'I'm sure he would if he could,' Jaralla replied.

'What do you mean?'

'Follow me,' the doctor said.

He turned and led the way up the concrete path between two

scrubby, sun-parched lawns to the front entrance of the villa. The door had been smashed off its hinges. The scene of simple domesticity had been turned into one of complete vandalism, furniture overturned and deliberately broken, pictures torn from walls.

A mound of blood-stained rugs covered something in the corner.

'What's that?' Brampton asked stepping forward.

Jaralla restrained her. 'I suggest not. I think it is Brigadier Cinti's wife and daughter. The woman has been horrendously raped before she was murdered. And the youngster was bayonetted to death.'

'What?' Parsons was aghast.

'I am sorry,' Jaralla said. 'I cannot know for certain, but I think it was done in front of Cinti to make him confess.'

'Confess to what?' Royce asked.

Jaralla extracted a couple of sheets of crumpled paper from his pocket . 'We found these on the floor. Notes in Cinti's own hand. A list of payments, apparently in sterling. And a name. Mr Oliver of the BBC. It looks like Cinti confessed to accepting money, perhaps even spying for the British. A confession to save the lives of his wife and child.'

'That didn't work,' Tremain muttered in his flat Tasmanian drawl.

'Is Cinti still alive?' Brampton asked.

Jaralla shook his head. 'No, I am afraid not.'

'Where is his body?' Brampton pressed.

'In the back garden.'

As Brampton moved forward, Jaralla restrained her again. 'No, please.'

She shook herself free, and moved down the passageway, Royce close behind her. They both heard the doctor's scurrying movements behind them, trying to catch up.

Reaching the double doors, she threw them open and stepped out into the fragrant night air and onto an ornate patio with a stone balustrade. The stars were not yet fully out and thankfully only the light from the villa illuminated the garden.

It was just enough to show the green-uniformed torso and thick, sun-dried sludge of blood that had spread from it to form a congealed pool on the paving.

Brampton gasped and pulled back.

Someone had stuck Cinti's severed head on a stake in the lawn. His face bore the expression of sheer, wide-eyed terror at his very last moment of life.

20

VICTORY PARADE

'I don't know if Russ would dare run it,' Brampton said. 'Too gruesome.'

They were back in the Range Rover, driving towards Tripoli. She had her video camera on her lap and was running back the grotesque footage of the dead army brigadier and of his detached head on a stake.

'He'll run it,' Royce said flatly. 'Anything to grab attention and get higher ratings.'

'Regardless of good taste?' she asked.

'You've answered your own question.' He considered for a moment, 'Of course, you could just *not* send it.'

She shook her head. 'I couldn't do that. The public have a right to know.'

'Do they care?'

'Some do,' she retorted sharply. 'They're the ones I write for. That's what my father always says. He's not writing for the ones who don't want to know. He's writing for the ones who do.'

Royce allowed himself a smile as he concentrated on the congestion of traffic all around them. 'I think I'm a bit cynical.'

'So do I.'

The movement of the traffic was again sluggish. There were no street lamps operating and the only illumination came from the vast dome of stars above and the lights of the vehicles themselves. The ever-growing mass of cars, pick-ups and trucks seemed to be feeling its way along the route like a blind man. It was hot and oppressive, the air filled with dust and fumes as the humidity soared. The Range Rover's air-con had expired and everyone was sweating. Winding down the windows made no difference, it just allowed more warm air in as there was no slipstream. But there was something else, an excitement in the air. They could all sense it, feel it. The rebels had won, this was the last march on Tripoli, a momentous event, a victory parade. The atmosphere was intoxicating.

Brampton opened her shoulder bag, fished out her cigarettes and went to light a Sobranie. 'Sorry, Jo, no smoking,' Royce snapped. 'It's just what a sniper wants.'

She was hot, sticky and irritable. 'Oh, fuck you, James.'

Sinbad intervened. 'He is right, Miss Jo. I see it happen, to my cousin in Benghazi. They shoot him right between eyes. Not good.'

She relented and gave a half laugh. 'Stop ganging up on me.'

The tide of traffic towards Tripoli slowed again.

'We're on the outskirts,' Royce intoned.

Like the hot and humid air, the noises of the desert also closed in on them. The ubiquitous sound of cicadas was drowned out by the blast of Arabic pop hits from car radios, chanting and singing from the civilians who were now lining the streets.

'GADDAFI GO!'

'FREE LIBYA!'

Bystanders were cheering, crying and women tongue-trilling in the way that they celebrated at weddings and births. Car horns blasted all around and fighters began firing in the air. Dead rounds bounced off the roof and bonnet of their Range Rover.

'There's Crawfie!' Brampton shouted suddenly.

'Who?' Royce asked.

'Alex Crawford.'

'Who's he?' Royce asked.

'She,' Brampton corrected. 'From Sky TV. She's doing a report to camera. It'll be a scoop. Stop! I've got to cover this too.'

'It's much too dangerous,' Royce warned.

She turned on him. 'I have a job to do, James, like it or not. Stop the fucking car or I'll get out anyway. Help me or not, it's up to you.'

He braked. 'Stay in the car,' he snapped, 'I'll film you.' Then he was gone.

A couple of seconds later, he appeared beside her at the open front passenger door. 'What are you doing?' she asked.

'Give me the camera,' he ordered. 'Just talk to me.'

She grinned, switching on the Paglight attached to the top of the camera that would illuminate her face as she spoke. Without further word, she handed it to him.

'I'm here on the outskirts of Tripoli,' she began earnestly, 'riding with the rebels on their victory march on Tripoli, home of the defeated dictator, tyrant and sexual predator Colonel Gaddafi…'

When she'd finished, she asked, 'Second take?'

'I've got it. It's good. Nothing that can't be edited out.'

'You're an expert?'

That grin again, that had so fascinated her of late. 'I watch, listen and learn.'

'Smug fuck.'

Royce returned swiftly to the driver's seat, and they rejoined the triumphant cavalcade. Within the hour they were entering Green Square in the centre of the capital. The scene was surreal with thousands of people milling around, many of them fighters brandishing AK47s and firing rounds into the air. Fireworks joined the sound of celebratory gunshots, rockets spraying skyward and illuminating the happy, perspiring faces. Some were singing, some praying and yet others intent on ripping down the green flags that festooned the square.

The small convoy pressed on until, just past midnight, a familiar voice burst onto the car radio, distorted with static. 'It Gaddafi!' Sinbad declared. 'He cannot be dead.'

'What's he saying?' Brampton asked.

'He say criminals are coming to destroy Tripoli,' Sinbad translated. 'They are here to steal our oil. Come out of your homes, people, and fight these betrayers.'

Colonel Gaddafi's final, desperate plea had barely finished when the Golden Palms Hotel came into view.

'I never thought I'd be so pleased to see this place again,' Brampton said with feeling.

As the two Range Rovers stopped together in the car park, McDougall pulled up alongside. 'Mission accomplished, Royce. Got you back safe and sound.'

'For which I'm deeply grateful,' Royce replied.

'Don't go getting yourselves into any trouble,' the E Squadron commander continued. 'Got enough on our plate without having to play nursemaid to you lot.' With an arrogant twitch of his moustache, he nodded to his driver and the Land Rover roared off into the night.

Royce found the carpark night watchmen and paid them extra to look after the Range Rovers, with the promise of a bonus if they were still undamaged and had nothing stolen by the next morning.

It was good to see the beaming figure of Farouk still there to recognise and welcome them at the door in his matching red waistcoat and fez. Despite the late hour, the hotel lobby was still wide awake, full of people and alive with excited chatter. All manner of nationalities, mostly media teams from all around the world, were milling in groups.

Royce noticed that many were clutching tumblers of bright red cocktail cordials.

'Bram, honey!' Rachel Starr of *TV Global* spotted them the moment they entered through the front doors. She rushed over, throwing her arms around her friend and kissing her on both cheeks. 'Oh, I've missed you so much.'

'Me too,' Brampton said, 'I couldn't wait to get back.'

Starr then noticed Seeff. 'And you, Stefan. My, how you've grown!'

Seeff looked baffled before she kissed him full on the mouth. She stepped back, 'Have you heard the latest?'

'What?' Parsons asked.

'Apparently two of Gaddafi's sons have been caught,' Starr said. 'Word is the rebels have got Saif and Saadi. I don't know if I believe it.'

Brampton said, 'From what we've seen out there, on our way from Tunisia, it's virtually over.'

Starr nodded. 'What *am* I thinking of! You must be famished – and thirsty?'

'I could murder a drink,' Brampton agreed. 'Everyone's got a red cocktail, I see. What's that all about?'

'The latest. It's replaced the famous Gaddafi Sunrise. A Gaddafi Sunset – with tomato juice and angostura bitters. The anti-freeze remains the same.' Starr grinned widely. 'Not half bad actually.' She beckoned a waiter.

Brampton extracted her cigarette case and lit a Sobranie. 'God , I needed this,' she said, inhaling deeply. 'James was up to his old tricks, bossing everyone about. I thought he'd mellowed but I was wrong.'

'I'm sure he had your best interests at heart,' Starr joked.

'I did,' Royce said, then added, 'We'll get ourselves all booked in.' With the rest of the team, he headed for the reception desk to organise and negotiate the best available rooms with Parsons.

In the meantime Brampton's cocktail made its welcome debut. 'Where's the *enfante terrible*?' she asked Starr. 'I suppose he hasn't installed himself in the penthouse suite?'

Starr laughed. 'Chesney? He probably would if they had one. What a little knob head, thinks he knows it all. God's gift to journalism, it seems.'

'Then may God himself help us,' Brampton added. 'I was just reading some of his articles on the flight out. I swear he's made most of it up. I am damn sure Princess Ayana would not have told him half the stuff he's quoted.'

'You can ask him yourself,' Starr said. 'Here's Mr Fleet Street himself.'

Brampton turned. Sykes approached them without quite the bravado she remembered. Wearing cargo shorts and a baggy T-shirt with the slogan *I REALLY JUST DON'T CARE* emblazoned across his chest, he sauntered up to them and flopped onto the sofa. As she recalled from their first meeting, his glaring grey eyes continued to avoid making direct contact with hers. His modern pert hair cut was also more limp than before, no doubt due to the high humidity and his excessive sweating. Once again the hotel's air-conditioning system had run out of generator power.

'Hi, doll. How was London?' Sykes asked, as though he had no interest in any answer she might offer.

'Not as exciting as here, I'm sure,' she replied. 'What happened to your nose?'

It was clearly swollen and badly bruised. He looked embarrassed. 'I broke it. It was reset at the hospital.'

'They were brilliant,' Starr interjected. 'We took him to the Emergency Department and they were incredible. Despite serious injuries coming in, terrible wounds, they managed to sort Chesney out.'

'I had to wait six hours,' Sykes said. 'It fucking hurt when the bloke reset it. No bloody anaesthetic or anything.'

'But how did you break it?' Brampton persisted.

'I walked into a door.'

Starr laughed. 'You little liar. If your nose starts growing, Pinocchio, it'll get broken again.'

'Just drop it,' Sykes said, irritably.

'It was after that last article in the *Sunday News*,' Starr explained. 'The one about Princess Ayana. She was furious with some of the stuff Chesney wrote, some of his accusations.'

'Huh!' Sykes protested. 'We all know it was bloody true, whether Ayana actually admitted it or not.'

Starr ignored him. 'She'd granted him an interview. All in confidence, no names, no pack drill, usual stuff. The meeting lasted all of five minutes, according to Chesney himself. He managed to upset her over something. Can't think how! Then the story is published, naming her and quoting all sorts.'

'I know that bit, read it myself back home,' Brampton said. 'And then what?'

'Hardly surprising, Jo.' Starr patted Sykes on the knee. 'Chesney got a visit from a couple of Ayana's Amazon bodyguards from the Protocol Department . Three days ago.'

'Two girls?'

Starr nodded. 'They had a quiet word with him. I reckon they were black belts in origami, or one of those martial arts,' she joked. 'It was more than his nose they broke. He also had cracked ribs and bruised kidneys. Luckily my CP guy interrupted them.'

'Your French minder?'

'Yves.'

'I remember him.'

'Yves saved Chesney. He gave them a seeing-to and sent them packing. Possibly saved Chesney's life.'

'Don't over-egg the pudding,' Sykes protested. 'It wasn't that dramatic.'

'It was from where I was sitting. They'd have half killed you.'

'You prat, Chesney,' Brampton said.

'No sympathy then?' Chesney asked.

Brampton shook her head in disbelief. 'Ayana was one of my prize contacts.'

'Not any more, I think,' Starr said.

Digging into her shoulder bag, Brampton pulled out her satellite cell-phone and pressed Ayana's number. For a few moments it rang unanswered. Was the woman not able to answer or had she seen who was calling and decided to blank her? Her heart sank.

'Hallo, Jo.' The sudden sound of Ayana's voice startled her.

'Oh, God, sorry! You surprised me!'

'Really? That's odd as you are actually telephoning me.'

Why was it Ayana always managed to make her tongue-tied, put her on the back foot? 'You know what I mean. I didn't think you were going to pick up.'

'Well, I have. Where are you?'

'That's why I'm phoning you. I'm back in the country, back in Tripoli.'

'Are you now?' A heartbeat of a pause. *'And why should that interest me?'*

Brampton scrambled for the right words. 'I want us to be friends.'

'Do you? Have you been thinking of me?'

'Too much,' Brampton replied quickly, and then corrected herself. 'No, I didn't mean like that. I've been thinking about what we discussed, wondering how you were getting on with my successor.'

The silence at the other end was deafening. Brampton felt the blood flooding to her cheeks. What was it about Ayana, it was as if she knew? Knew that on more than one occasion, relaxing in her bath back in London…With candlelight and radio music playing, she had dreamily thought back to that Italian villa, of Ayana's gleaming ebony torso and the basement dungeon…Her own fingers had stroked the scenes as if they were on a keyboard in her mind, had allowed her idly swimming thoughts off the leash like those dogs in the villa garden…

She shook her head. Just sodding sexual fantasies, everyone had them for Christsakes! She was angry with herself. Ayana was no fucking clairvoyant.

Brampton took a deep breath and came back strongly with, 'Look, I've heard about what happened, Princess.' She threw in Ayana's title in a panic to try and smooth the waters. 'I am appalled at what he wrote and published.'

'He broke every pledge you made to me,' Ayana retorted coldly. *'Everything we had agreed. Someone should be punished for that. You made the promises, so that person should be you.'*

'I know, I'm phoning to say sorry, to apologise.' Brampton could hardly believe she was apologising to this evil woman, pleading, metaphorically on her knees. Was that exactly where Ayana wanted her? An involuntary tremor went through her, her mind again filled for a fleeting second with the vision of the honed, muscled black torso in the shower, recalling the unmistakeable tension between them.

'Well, now you have.'

'Sorry?'

'You have apologised.'

'I wondered if we could meet?'

'Why?'

'To talk some more.'

The laugh at the other end was harsh. *'After what your colleague wrote about me?'*

'There could be more fees.' Brampton added, 'Higher than before. Considerably higher.'

'I am not a whore, Jo. Whatever you might think of me, I am not a whore. I would like to see you again, there is something…' She hesitated. *'…something between us. But to meet you after what has been written would be a death sentence for me. Literally. Abu was furious with me when he was told about that article in your paper. He had me flogged. Naked in front of his men and my own girls. And then he made me come while they were flogging me.'*

Brampton didn't quiet catch the whispered words. 'I'm sorry?'

Ayana cleared her throat. *'He made me orgasm.'* She hesitated. *'I can't believe I'm telling you this. Do you know how humiliating that is? In front of his staff and mine, so that they can always laugh and snigger behind your back. There is no way to recover your authority after that. It's always been one of our dear Brother Leader's favourite party tricks. Mixing pain with pleasure confuses the mind, plays tricks in your head.'*

'I'm so sorry.'

'Abu made it clear what will happen to me if I talk to you or anyone else in the press again. Besides -'

'Besides what?'

'I'm going away.'

'Leaving? When?'

'Now. The car is waiting.'

'Where are you going?'

'I cannot tell you.'

'With Abu Nazal?'

'Our Brother Leader is finished,' Ayana said, dropping her voice to a whisper, as though the words she spoke were a heresy in themselves. *'I cannot survive without Abu. He is my only future, maybe the only future for Libya.'*

A thought occurred to Brampton. 'If you must go, can you release Tabina? I could pick her up. Arrange to take her to a place of safety.'

Ayana's laugh sounded almost like a snarl. *'What did you say?'*

'I promised Tabina I'd come back for her,' Brampton said. 'If you're going, it's the least you can do. I don't think Gaddafi is going to have need of his harem any more, d'you?'

'Tabina has become one of Abu's favourites.' Ayana quickly corrected herself. *'His actual favourite. She pleases him in whichever way he wants. And I can tell you that he has some very bizarre pleasures."*

'Trained by you.'

'Naturally.'

Brampton changed tack. 'I'm sure Abu could find another willing slave. She's barely more than a child. Have some pity. I promised I'd come back for her.'

'Then you were a fool to make a promise to a child that you could never keep.' Ayana hesitated. *'I have to go now, Abu is calling for me. I wish you well for the rest of your life. Maybe fortune has it that our paths may cross again. Until such time -'*

The cell-phone went dead in her hand.

'She's hung up on you?' Starr asked.

Brampton still felt stunned, oddly rejected. 'She had to go.'

'The Ice Queen?' Sykes asked. 'Good riddance then. I *bet* she had to go. Running for her life now Gaddafi's finished.'

'Put a sock in it, Chesney,' Brampton retorted.

'Or your foot,' Starr added. 'That's what you're best at.'

Brampton glanced over to the reception desk as she finished her cocktail. 'Looks like the lads have got the rooms sorted out. I'd better see what they've arranged.'

'Is it true you're sleeping with soldier-boy Rollo?' Sykes asked casually.

The journalist turned on him. 'What did you say?'

'You heard.'

'No, I am not.' She felt the blood rush to her face. 'And he's not a soldier, he's a Royal Marine.'

Sykes shrugged. 'A cabbage hat then. Same difference.'

'Who's been saying that?'

'Lots of people.' He indicated Starr. 'Including your mate here.'

'I did not!' Starr protested. 'I just said I thought you fancied him. You just hadn't realised it yet.'

Brampton turned on her. 'Just because you fancy anything with balls.'

Sykes laughed. 'Methinks thou doth protest too much.'

Brampton swivelled round, back to face him. 'That obviously doesn't include you, Chesney,' she added.

As she walked away, Sykes called out after her, 'Princess Ayana had the hots for you, you know? It was obvious. Virtually admitted it to me.'

'Shut up, Chesney,' Starr admonished wearily.

Brampton had stopped listening. Any more of Sykes's inane prattling and she felt she was increasingly liable to deck him. She'd done some very basic unarmed combat training during her time in the army, and had not forgotten all of it. In fact, recently, she'd often run through some basic routines in her mind. It made her feel safer, sort of.

Royce was steering their group towards the emergency staircase. The lift wasn't even an option, despite his own strict rules, because hotel management had forbidden its use to save generator fuel.

'Hi, Jo,' Parsons greeted. 'We've got a couple of rooms on the third floor. Hope you don't mind sharing. It's all we could get.'

She frowned. 'As long as we're not sharing beds.'

'I wish,' Parsons laughed, then stopped abruptly as he saw her expression. 'Sorry, shouldn't have said that. You, me and Rollo in one room. You have one of the twin beds. Iain, Stefan and Sinbad will be in the other room.'

They paused at the Fire Exit doors that led to the staircase. That was when it happened.

Royce picked up on it first. He heard the voice of the genial doorman Farouk, unusually bellowing in anger above the noisy chatter of the guests. Across the lobby floor he glimpsed the red colour of the man's waistcoat and matching fez, saw the gathering of green uniforms clustered around the glass doors of the entrance.

Seeff picked up on it, too, and turned around.

AK47s were being waved in the air. A single shot was fired. It hit the central chandelier that released a shower of glass crystals raining down on horrified bystanders. The chatter stopped abruptly as though someone had thrown a switch.

'GET OUT!' Farouk demanded loudly. 'YOU CAN'T COME IN!'

There was another single loud whip-crack of a sound. The larger-than-life character was blown off his feet, dead.

'God!' Brampton gasped.

'Gaddafi's men,' Royce decided, throwing open the door to the stairwell. 'Up to our floor, quick!'

21

HUMAN SHIELD

Royce ushered everyone through the swing door and into the concrete stairwell. 'Stefan, get up to their rooms as fast as you can. 305 and 307.'

'Do you think Farouk was killed?' Brampton asked.

'He didn't look too healthy,' Royce answered.

'What the hell are those soldiers doing here?' Parsons asked. 'This hotel is only occupied by journalists…'

'That *is* why,' Seeff answered. 'My guess is they want hostages, a human shield to protect them from rebel lynch mobs.'

'Looked to me like they were African mercenaries,' Royce said. 'They don't so easily merge into a Libyan crowd.'

'They'll be in fear of their lives,' Tremain added. 'Wouldn't want to be in their shoes.'

'Just now, I'm not sure I want to be in ours,' Stefan quipped.

Royce said, 'I'll stay here, and see what happens.' He lowered himself right down to the floor, and pushed the door open a fraction. No one looking in that direction would likely spot a face peering out at ground level.

'Don't take any chances, mate,' Parsons warned as he grabbed the iron railing and began to climb the steps.

'I won't,' Royce assured. 'I'll join you as soon as I can.'

He unsheathed his CZ85 automatic, just in case. The lobby full of guests had frozen into a tableau, terrified to move as the uniformed gunmen walked amongst them. They were shouting and giving orders, trying to divide the people into manageable groups. There appeared to be seven soldiers, five with the deep coal black skin colour that suggested west or central African origins. The other two looked either Arabic or Asian. That indicated they may be some of Gaddafi's favoured local mercenaries, who would have no family or tribal qualms or allegiances when fighting Libyan rebels. Their evident leader was an exceptionally tall man with a shaven head, a giant with an oddly high-pitched voice.

'MOVE, MOVE!' he screeched. 'STAFF TO LEFT! WOMEN IN MIDDLE! MEN TO RIGHT!' He waved his Kalashnikov to indicate what he wanted them to do.

In their anxiety, the staff and guests got it all wrong, bumping into each other and going in opposite directions. If the bizarre choreography hadn't been going on under a still-smoking gun muzzle it might have seemed amusing.

In the chaos, one of the restaurant waiters seized his opportunity to escape. Royce saw him slip away, at first unnoticed. The man ducked behind the zebra skin sofas; then he made a dash for the kitchen door. That was when he caught the eye of one of the soldiers. Swiftly the mercenary had the AK lifted to his eye and unhurriedly fired a single shot. Its impact carried the waiter forward with no further need to move his legs. He smashed into the kitchen door. With hands outstretched to try and stop himself, he slid down to the floor, leaving a smear of blood across the panel in front of him. The hinges creaked as the door swung slowly to and fro under the momentum.

The silence in the lobby of so many people was stunning. For the first time ever the overhead fans could be heard squeaking, along with the distinctive tick of the large clock above reception .

'I AM NINKA,' the giant of a leader declared. 'DO AS I TELL YOU AND NO ONE GETS HURT. NOW, ALL SIT!' As everyone fumbled around indecisively, he added impatiently. 'QUICK, QUICK! SLOWEST WILL BE SHOT!'

You couldn't fault him for style, Royce mused bitterly to himself. The man had his audience terrified.

Then a thought occurred to him. If the city's neighbourhood supply power was back on, what about the mobile phone masts? He decided to try Rachel Starr's cell-phone, recalling that she usually kept her profile on Discreet.

To his surprise he got a breathless response, *'Rollo, thank God.'*

'Be careful,' he warned. 'Can you use your Bluetooth device without them seeing?'

'Yeah, my hair is covering it.'

'Keep the channel open. Listen for any instructions.'

'NOW, HANDS ON HEADS!' Ninka added loudly. In unison, the entire gathering obeyed.

One leader and six followers, Royce calculated. They were weighed down with ammunition vests stuffed with spare mags for their AKs, but none appeared to be carrying personal small arms, such as semi-automatics or revolvers. Importantly, neither did anyone have a grenade clipped to his rig.

Ninka turned to his men. 'Two of you stay here with me. Two of you go and get any waiters and kitchen staff, bring here. Other two go upstairs and bring down guests. Any trouble, kill them, no question. Let no one go or use phone.'

His men discussed who would do what, then divided into three couples. One stayed with Ninka, one team headed to the restaurant and the third team began marching towards the stairwell where Royce was watching.

Rapidly he withdrew, scrambled to his feet and started up the stairs, taking three steps at a time.

On the first landing he met a Canadian TV news team coming down, a woman and three men.

'Hi, Rollo! Long time, no see -' the woman began.

He waved her to silence. 'Hi, Jenna. Stop right there. Turn round and go back!'

The reporter looked aghast. 'Gosh, what's happening?'

'Armed soldiers,' he warned. 'Gaddafi's men are in the lobby, taking hostages. They've started searching all the rooms. Go back to yours, lock yourselves in and barricade the door.'

The sound of the two mercenaries on the steps below spurred the Canadians to turn swiftly and retreat back up the steps as fast as they could. Royce was close behind them, leaving on the third floor landing for the corridor that led to his team's two rooms. They were facing each other on opposite sides of the corridor.

Everyone in the team had gathered in the room facing the front of the hotel. Seeff was armed with his automatic when he opened the door to let Royce in.

Someone had laid out all the combined weaponry that the team possessed on the bed.

'What's happening downstairs?' Parsons demanded.

'They're holding everyone in the lobby,' Royce replied, speaking rapidly. 'Appear to be seven hostiles in total. Four black and two Arab or Asian. Their leader is the tallest and calls himself Ninka. He and two others are guarding the hostages. Two other hostiles are dragging waiters and cooking staff to the holding area. Another two hostiles are heading this way, clearing each floor of guests, taking them back downstairs.'

'What's our strength, Rollo?' Seeff asked. 'You and me with MP5s and handguns.'

'I've got the same,' Tremain added.

Parsons raised both his hands in protest. 'Count me out. I've got an automatic but I'd be more of a liability. You're more than welcome to have it.'

'You're a dark horse, Ollie?' Brampton challenged. 'Since when has the BBC issued side arms to its producers?'

Royce cut in. 'Does anyone know where Yves is?'

'I didn't see him downstairs,' Brampton said.

Making an instant decision, Royce called Starr on his mobile. 'Rachel, where's Yves?'

Her voice was tremulous, almost inaudible. *Taking a shower. Room 309.'*

'Room 309,' Royce repeated. 'Thanks, Rach.'

'I'll grab him,' Seeff decided, and left the room.

'Count me in,' Brampton said. 'I can use Ollie's pistol.'

Royce did a double take. 'You?'

'Yes, me,' she snapped and reached for the .38 Sig Sauer lying on the bed. 'I was in the army, James, I just didn't make the Det – thanks to you.' The single dimple deepened in her cheek. 'If I have to use this, I promise I'll keep both eyes wide open.'

He ignored that. 'Just remember the Sig's only got seven rounds. Make them count.'

'Do we have a plan?' Tremain asked.

'Safety of the hostages is our top priority,' Royce said. 'Agreed?'

Everyone nodded. 'We have two hostiles advancing on us now. So we know where they are. They're coming to us.'

'So give them a warm welcome?' Tremain guessed.

'Good idea,' Parsons decided.

'Then we can deal with the rest,' Royce confirmed.

He became aware of sporadic muffled gunfire, sounding as though it could be coming from the floor immediately below. He envisaged the hostiles clearing each bedroom, and marshalling any stray guests that they found.

At that moment the door opened and Seeff returned with Yves. The Frenchman looked unusually well-scrubbed and shaven. Tremain sniffed pointedly. 'Lavender?'

Yves shrugged. 'I borrowed the boss's. We're short on stuff.'

'The hostiles will be approaching from our left,' Royce pointed out, 'from the stair well. We lock the door of this room, giving them something to get excited about. Meanwhile we wait for them on the right. That will give us a clear field-of-fire.'

'Use my room,' Yves offered. '309.'

'Let's go,' Royce decided. 'They'll be on this floor at any moment. Rest of you remain here. Use the door jambs and keep your heads down in the bathroom. Can't guarantee no stray rounds.' He turned to Seeff. 'You and me – with Iain as back-up.'

Seeff grinned widely, as always fired up by any thought of action. 'Sure thing, bro!'

'I'm not your bloody bro',' Royce retorted.

Tremain's Tasmanian humour kicked in, 'Hell, Rollo, we're a Band of Bros, are we not!'

Royce ignored him and ran up the corridor to where the door to Yves's room had been left ajar. Just as the three of them stepped inside, Royce was aware of the stairwell door opening at the far end of the long corridor. Again dropping to the floor, he peered around the bottom edge of the door frame.

The two soldiers in their green uniforms moved swiftly and noisily, blasting away the lock on each secured room door.

Thankfully no guests emerged from the first three bedrooms. At the fourth, a Caucasian emerged just wearing his pyjama bottoms. He was ordered at gunpoint to stand at the edge of the stairwell with his hands on his head. The two soldiers continued their advance, blasting away doors and searching.

A terrified Japanese news woman appeared in her bra and pants from another room. She was unceremoniously grabbed by one of the soldiers and pushed towards the stairwell. Her three-man camera crew followed, all in various states of undress. They too were ushered to join the other guests, cowering by the stairwell.

Royce whispered hoarsely, 'Hostages positioned behind hostiles.'

'Roger that,' Seeff acknowledged, and gestured to Tremain to ensure he understood the situation.

Now the two Gaddafi mercenaries had reached Room 305. One of the soldiers tried the handle. He shook it hard, angry at the delay.

His colleague raised his automatic pistol and shot into the lock, metal pinging musically around the corridor. He threw his shoulder against the door. It gave an inch before the wooden jamb did its job. Both men cursed.

'NOW!' Royce shouted, stepping into the corridor with his CZ85 raised. He let off the first of two rapid double-taps at the left hand target. Beside him, Seeff similarly dealt with the second mercenary. Both men went down before they knew what had hit them, their weapons falling from their grasp.

Tremain stepped into the corridor behind them, providing cover as Royce and Seeff advanced to the bodies and checked for any sign of life. Any doubt and he'd have delivered a final killer round to the nape of the neck. You can never risk even a wounded man coming back from the edge of death to kill you unexpectedly. But it was not a good thing to do for the soul, the deliberate extinction of a human life. It came back to haunt many a soldier, particularly those engaged on close combat in black ops.

That these two fuckers were dead, left Royce feeling no remorse whatsoever. He beckoned the surprised and relieved-looking hostages from the end of the corridor. As Yves opened the door to their room he indicated for them to join Brampton and Sinbad for safety.

Meanwhile he checked the corpses for spare mags and handed them over to Brampton with two AK47s for their arsenal.

Once everybody was in, the door was closed again and the jamb replaced. Brampton thought the jamb a brilliant but simple piece of kit! She would make a note to take one with her on any future travels, she decided, as she found a spare dressing-gown in a wardrobe for the Japanese journalist. The diminutive woman bowed in polite and gracious thanks.

'That leaves five hostiles left downstairs,' Royce said.

'Let's get everyone here out and down the back fire-escape,' Seeff suggested. 'Before the bad boys in the lobby wonder what's happened to their mates.'

'Excellent,' Royce agreed.

'I cannot leave Rachel in danger downstairs,' Yves intervened. 'I have to do something.'

Tremain said, 'I'll escort everyone out, if you like. Also find out what's happening outside. The last thing we want are rebels trying to rush the place.'

'Too right,' Parsons agreed.

'Take Sinbad with you,' Royce added. 'He might explain more clearly the dangers of the situation in here.'

'Right,' Tremain said. 'Follow me, everyone. We're going down the corridor and out through the back fire escape.'

Royce turned to Brampton. 'Can you go with Iain, please?'

She lifted the Browning pistol. 'And this?'

'Back-up Iain. And if you have to…'

The dimple deepened in her cheek. 'Shoot to kill?'

'With both eyes open.'

He watched Brampton follow the column of escapees retreating down the corridor towards the outdoor fire escape. A flicker of pride pulsed in him as he observed her deftly cover their rear as they moved forward. She clearly remembered more of her training than she'd forgotten.

Royce turned back to Seeff and Yves. 'Let's take a look downstairs. Stefan and I go first, and you back us up? That okay with you, Yves?' The Frenchman nodded. 'Remember we could meet more hostiles coming up to find where their mates are.'

He led the way down the stairwell with Seeff close behind and Yves farther back. Voices reached him as he arrived on the ground floor by the door to the large reception lobby. It sounded like an American journalist having a heated exchange with the soldiers holding them hostage.

At that moment the adjoining door to the kitchens flew open, catching Royce by surprise. The two soldiers were halfway into the stairwell before they realised that they were confronting armed civilians.

Royce recovered from the shock first, grabbing and twisting the wrist of the first man, wresting the rifle from the other man's grip. As he did so, Seeff pumped two rounds from his Browning automatic into the soldier's stomach at point blank range. The body collapsed instantly and heavily to the ground, beginning to convulse. Seeff reached down and calmly put two more rounds into the back of the man's neck.

It was all too much for the second mercenary who managed to pull back into the kitchen, turn and run. Yves was on him.

Stepping over the body in the doorway, Yves calmly raised his automatic and fired two shots into the centre of the man's back as he ran between the shiny rows of kitchen work surfaces. The force of the double impact propelled him forward faster, as his legs appeared to try to keep up with the top half of him. But it didn't happen and the mercenary ended up in a headlong dive for the far door. He didn't make that either. Instead he slid along the floor until he came to rest in a spreading pool of his own blood.

Royce clapped the Frenchman on the shoulder. 'Good shot.'

Yves replied, 'I've wanted to do that to one of the bastards ever since we have been here.'

Royce peered through the small window in the door into the lobby.

'Then there were three,' Seeff said.

'Yep,' Royce confirmed. 'Just standing there, looking nervous.'

He was aware they couldn't just open fire on the soldiers, who were guarding their hostages with automatic weapons. Taking out all three in one go wasn't necessarily impossible, but sod's law promised that even a dead man's finger on a fully automatic trigger could kill or maim several innocents. It wasn't a risk that anyone could take, let alone someone charged with the hostages' protection.

Seeff said, 'They must be wondering why their mates haven't returned with more guests.'

'We need a diversion,' Royce agreed. 'What I wouldn't give for a flash-bang right now.'

Seeff was familiar with the British Army slang for a stun-grenade.

It gave him an idea. 'I've got it, boss.'

'What?'

'A fire, a diversion. I need to get to the reception desk behind them.'

Royce was on it. 'You need a diversion for the diversion.' He turned to the Frenchman. 'I need your okay for this. We ring Rachel's phone. The hostiles will make her hand it over. During that distraction, Stefan can get to the reception desk.'

Yves thought for a moment. 'Rachel always keep her phone on "Discreet."'

'Then we need to tell her to switch it.' Royce hesitated. 'Do you think it's too much of a risk? Sorry, my friend, she's your client. It has to be your call.'

'We are running out of options,' Yves replied. 'It is the lesser of other risks, I think. I will call her.' He picked up his mobile and rang Starr's phone.

Royce studied the audience through the small aperture of glass. He noticed the distant figure of Starr suddenly stiffen as her Blue Tooth earpiece came alive.

'Madame, it's Yves,' the Frenchman said quickly. 'We are about to rescue you. Put your phone on "Loud" as a diversion. When it rings, co-operate with the soldiers, but let it ring.'

Yves listened to her response before switching off his phone. 'She is agreed. But she is terrified, too, her voice shakes. But she is also brave. A tough one.'

'She is,' Royce agreed and turned to Seeff. 'If you're ready, I'll cover you.'

The South African dropped down to his knees by the door. Royce nodded to Yves who punched his redial button. Immediately a loud musical jingle filled the tense silence in the lobby. Heads of the herded hostages turned in surprise and unison towards Rachel Starr.

She looked startled and lifted the offending cell phone in the air. 'I'm sorry. What shall I do?' she pleaded loudly to the angry-looking mercenary leader called Ninka.

His two comrades stepped forward with him and the squatting hostages stirred uneasily.

'Should I answer it?' Starr asked.

'NO!' shouted Ninka.

By now Seeff was halfway across the gap between the stairwell door and the reception desk. He was moving in a fast, low leopard crawl, passing behind the zebra-skin sofas and on towards the bamboo desk.

'I can't turn it off,' Starr complained as the ringtone seemed to swell to fill the room. 'It's sticking.'

'Don't panic!' Ninka commanded. 'Come here with it.'

Royce observed Seeff completing the last part of his crawl to the reception desk. Once hidden behind it, he drew himself up onto his knees, scooped up an overflowing wastepaper basket and flicked his Zippo lighter.

Meanwhile Starr made her way to the front of the gathering, proffering her mobile phone to the leader like a naughty child. Ninka snatched it from her with one hand and swiped the barrel of his AK47 across her face with the other. She staggered back, tripped and fell to the floor.

'Infidel bitch! Ninka spat.

'FIRE!' a voice cried from the seated guests. Royce saw that it was Sykes.

Flames were leaping skyward, catching on the bamboo desk, black smoke issuing from some plastic printer cartridges in the basket. Seeff had vanished, presumably through the cotton drapes that hung immediately behind the desk.

Ninka turned away from the guests, distracted as his two henchmen rushed to put out the sudden raging fire.

22

VANISHING ACT

Royce made his move, bursting into the lobby alongside Yves.

In a pre-arranged choreography of fire, Royce double-tapped the mercenary leader with rounds from his 9mm CZ85. As Ninka skidded on the polished tiles and crashed to the ground, Yves took out the man's number two, blowing him backwards with the force of another double-tap.

There was nothing more for them to do, as Seeff reappeared as if by magic in front of the third mercenary. The man had been struggling with a soda syphon in an attempt to extinguish the waste-paper basket that had now set the drapes on fire.

Glass shattered on the tiles as he dropped the syphon in panic and raised both his hands to surrender.

With a gun in one hand, Seeff used the other to rip the drapes from the ceiling and smother them. Smelly black smoke wafted across the lobby. That was when the emergency sprinkler system kicked in, water spraying like a welcome summer downpour across the entire lobby.

Seeff grinned widely. 'Kapow! Never thought I'd get fucking lead rôle in Singing In The Rain.'

Royce and Yves checked over the two fallen bodies for any sign of life. There was none.

'Bloody hell,' Starr complained as she became steadily drenched in the rancid sprinkler water. She grabbed Seeff as he walked past, 'Look what you've done, ruined my hair.'

He looked bemused. 'I just saved your life.'

'I know, I saw you.' She smiled with exaggerated gratitude. 'Thank you. But couldn't you have done it without ruining my hair?'

'I was going to rough it up later anyway.'

'Promises, promises.'

The seated gathering of terrified guests had suddenly become animated and started to move. Staff members rushed to turn off the sprinkler system and to help extinguish the still-smoking drapes. Others dutifully removed the body of the doorman Farouk, putting his famed fez and red waistcoat to one side; remarkably the only damage to it was one small scorched hole.

As the indoor rain ceased, Sinbad entered the hotel in company with Brampton and Dr Jaralla of the Misrata rebels.

Royce beckoned him. 'Dr Jaralla. We have a prisoner for you. I trust he'll be dealt with fairly in your hands.'

Jaralla gave a rueful smile. 'I would not be so trusting. I cannot guarantee anybody's safety. Now that victory is theirs, some are seeking revenge and the spoils of war.'

'I would cut off ears and hang bastards from lamp post,' Sinbad confirmed with feeling.

Royce nodded. 'Nevertheless...'

Jaralla indicated for one of his rebel minions to take the surrendered mercenary away.

Brampton said, 'The doctor has been telling me that they've been getting mixed reports of various government convoys on the move. I've just been talking to Ollie and Iain about it.'

'From Brigadier Cinti's depot?' Royce asked.

'That's the general picture,' she replied, 'but it's far from conclusive. Some reports say vehicles and government troops or mercenaries are from 32HQ. Others talk about jihadists from Misrata. All very confused. The general feeling is that they could be gathering for one last stand.'

'Gaddafi's final concerted effort to take back Tripoli from the rebels,' Royce guessed. 'The very last thing we need.'

'The equivalent of Hitler's Battle of the Bulge,' Seeff pointed out.

Brampton nodded. 'That's exactly what Ollie said.'

A new voice joined in. 'What did Ollie say?' Parsons appeared through the glass doors. 'All over, James?'

Royce nodded. 'A clean sweep. Four hostiles slotted and one in custody with the rebels.'

'Thanks for that.'

'It was a team effort with Yves and Stefan.'

Brampton turned to Parsons. 'Ollie, can I borrow one of your cars?'

'One of the Range Rovers?' He frowned. 'Whatever for?'

'To pop over to Nazal Abu's villa.'

'Why?'

'Before these mercenary guys broke in to the hotel, I was on the phone to Princess Ayana,' she explained. 'She said she was leaving, but I tried to persuade her to leave that slave girl Tabina behind .'

'The one you foolishly promised to rescue?'

'She's a child, Ollie. She's being horribly abused.'

Parsons sighed. 'Did Ayana say the girl has been left there, at the villa?'

'Not exactly, but I think she was hesitating, thinking about it. We got cut off. '

'It's not a good idea,' Royce said.

Brampton turned on him. 'I don't remember asking you, James? You never want to do anything.'

'Nothing that puts lives unnecessarily at risk,' he agreed.

'Things have quietened down now,' Brampton persisted. 'I want to go to the villa before any fighting starts up again.'

'This is precisely the time people drop their guard,' Royce warned,

'There are still snipers around and a lot of people with itchy trigger fingers. Not to mention the sky raining bullets from celebration shooting.'

'I have a duty of care,' Brampton retorted, 'to get that child to a place of safety if I possibly can.'

'You have no such thing,' Royce replied evenly. 'You made a kindly humane gesture on the spur of the moment. I'm sure Tabina's not expecting you.'

She turned on him. 'Don't you know the meaning of the word honour? I gave her my word.'

Jarella had heard enough and stepped in to defuse the argument. 'I will be happy for some of my men to escort Miss Jo to wherever she may want to go.'

Royce certainly didn't want to risk that. 'Thanks, Doctor,' he intervened, 'but the young lady's persuaded me. I'll go with her.' He turned to Brampton. 'But vests and tin hats, right?'

She grinned widely, triumphant. 'Whatever you say, boss.'

He decided to take Sinbad with them in the Range Rover and accepted the offered escort of two armed student rebels in a Nissan pick-up. Although it was the early hours of the morning, there were still plenty of people roaming the streets. Mostly they were rebel fighters but also civilians who were coming out of hiding for the first time in months. Several cafés and coffee shops were staying open late to cash in on the unexpected celebrations.

By the time Royce had found his way back across the streets of Tripoli to Nazal Abu's Italian-style villa, the distant eastern sky was just beginning to lighten. The building may have been abandoned, but it remained locked up. There was no response from the intercom or bell.

'Let's just forget it,' Royce suggested.

'After coming all this way?' Brampton retorted. 'You're joking. Tabina could still be inside. Anyway, you never know what else we could find.'

There was razor wire coiled atop the walls, but not on the double electric gates because it would have prevented them operating properly. It was a useful omission. Grabbing the bars, Royce heaved himself up and over the same metal gates that had once threatened to crush their vehicle as they escaped had under fire. He glanced at the control panel and unlocked them, allowing Brampton and Sinbad to enter. Jaralla's two fighters were more than happy to wait outside with the two vehicles, smoking and chatting and sharing war stories.

The imposing solid wood front door wasn't giving way to anything apart from a skilled locksmith or half a kilo of explosive.

'Let's try downstairs,' Brampton suggested.

Stone steps led down to another solid single door. A fancy multi lock said no entry.

'Stand well back,' Royce warned and let off three angled rounds at each hinge. He threw his shoulder against the door and it gradually surrendered, gaping open at an odd angle. Brampton pushed her way through.

For her it felt weird, stepping back in time into a familiar scene but from a different perspective. The concoction of human smells, stale perspiration and urine were concentrated in the mustiness of the stale air. She was hardly surprised when Royce produced an ultra-bright mini-torch; the bastard would no doubt magic up a Tardis spacecraft if it were unexpectedly required. The orbs of light showed up the brick walls, the sacrificial St Andrew's Cross and the cot where Brampton had first interviewed Tabina.

'Look, more rooms,' Sinbad said. Sure enough another door led onto a small surgical theatre with a bed and gynaecological stirrups. Professional surgical instruments lay on shelves in the glass cabinets beside a stainless steel sterilising machine.

'Christ knows what this room was used for,' Brampton said, picking up her video camera and scanning the room in slow motion.

Royce looked around. 'Some serious body repair work, I'd say.'

Brampton winced.

The next room was lined with bookcases filled with rows of floppy discs and DVDs.

Royce glanced at the labels on the videos and graphic blow-up prints that had been pinned to cork boards on the wall. They left nothing to the imagination.

'Jesus, James, how can they?'

'Stuff with those dogs.'

'Jesus,' she repeated. 'Those poor girls.'

Royce said, 'Parsons needs to know about this.'

Brampton turned on him. 'Ollie? Why? He's bloody World Service.'

Realising his error, Royce said, 'He's also connected, Bram. You realise that?'

She glared at him. 'Fuck me, what, James? He's a fucking spy? All this time and you haven't told me?'

'He's not a spy.' he replied. 'Damn me, woman, he's *just* connected. It's not the same thing.' Royce was on his cell-phone, making the call. 'Hi, Ollie, you need to get someone over here to the villa for evidence of war crimes and a lot more…'

On the floor was a small red bra. Brampton stooped and picked it up, looked at the tag. Size 32A, probably anorexic.

God, she thought, possibly smaller than me. The teenager had been held down by men as she was humped by a salivating two hundred pound Tosa Inu and videoed for the amusement of Nazal and his regime cronies. From an out-take print on the wall, she saw that they put woollen socks on the animal's front paws so that it did no unintentional damage in its mating frenzy.

Brampton had seen enough, looked away abruptly and retraced her footsteps across the basement to the foot of the wooden staircase. Aware that Royce was close behind, she climbed the steps and pushed at the door into the front passage of the villa. It was not locked.

The ground floor was empty, abandoned. Between them, she, Royce and Sinbad opened and briefly examined each room for anything of interest. Everything they saw showed indications of departure in a hurry. There would be clues left aplenty for any lawyers to put before the international courts of justice.

As Brampton reached the landing on the staircase to the first floor, they heard the sound. All three of them stopped in their tracks.

'Someone hurt,' Sinbad said, 'in pain.'

He made a move forward, but Royce restrained him. 'A wounded man is like a wounded animal. Dangerous.'

Sinbad blinked, uncomprehending. Royce smiled at him, reassuring.

Brampton realised then that Royce had had his CZ85 pistol in his hand the whole time. She shrugged and smiled; the man was nothing if not consistent. An image of Anoushka flashed across her mind. Her lips moved around the word. 'Reliable,' she was saying, but before she'd clearly heard them they had faded away.

Royce overtook her on the ornate, marble staircase, bounding up two steps at a time.

He reached the next floor and paused, listening. That sound again. A faint rasping breath, someone trying to suck in air.

It came from the nearest bedroom door that was just ajar, a sword of light cast across the dark surface of the floor. Royce edged closer, careful to make no noise on the tiles. With the toecap of his suede desert boot, he pressured the door ever so gently open. The hinges gave the mildest squeak of protest, but it was enough to alert the man inside.

Royce peered around the door jamb. The gun was pointed straight at him.

'Can't see,' the old man said. 'Who the fuck are you?'

Chingford Charlie was propped up on the single bed, his white linen suit sodden with blood.

'It's me, Royce.'

Chingford peered in his direction. 'My vision's going. Can't see you properly.'

Brampton moved up to the door and peered in, shocked. 'It's Royce,' she said. 'And Jo.'

'Ah,' Chingford said, clearly dazed. 'Ollie phoned me, said you were coming back. Huh, I was about to take you out.'

'Bad idea, Charlie,' Royce replied. 'You're in a spot of trouble.' He turned to Sinbad. 'Go and grab our medical bag from the car.'

'Sure thing, boss,' the Libyan replied, now familiar with British Army lingo, and rushed away.

Royce took the automatic from Chingford and handed it to Brampton to deal with. 'Let's take a look, Charlie,' he said as he began to inspect the wound. 'Who did this?'

'Abu fucking Nazal, of course.' Chingford breathed. 'He never did really like me. Too close to Muammar for his liking. He only ever put up with me because I'm so friendly with Gaddafi. And Ayana. It's a jealousy thing. Nazal never fully trusted me. Quite right in that, as you know.'

Royce stepped back. There appeared to be no exit wound, so the slug must still be in Chingford somewhere. 'You've lost a lot of blood,' he said.

'I can see that. Oddly, I'm not in much pain, just weak.'

'The round might have missed your vital organs, Charlie,' Royce said. 'God knows how. But it makes you the luckiest man in Tripoli today.'

He quickly dug out an army-issue dressing pad from his cargo trouser pocket to temporarily staunch the flow.

'An ambulance should be on its way,' Chingford said casually.

Brampton did a double-take. 'What?'

'Ayana phoned the hospital. She's got a contact there.'

'What exactly happened, Charlie?' Brampton asked.

'Knowing that Ollie was coming back to Tripoli, I thought I'd drop in on Princess Ayana,' the man explained. It was a long sentence and he had to pause to catch his breath. 'See if I could get an update for him. Ayana and I go back a long way, since she first came to Libya. I've done her a lot of favours, believe me.'

'Why,' Brampton asked, 'do you like her so much?'

'We just get on. At my age it's not easy to find a woman who is willing and seemingly happy to suck your cock.'

Brampton's jaw dropped.

'Sorry,' Chingford said quickly, coughing. 'Probably shouldn't have said, but you did ask. And she let me play with some of the girls. It was done with Muammer's approval, of course. It amused him to see young girls playing with old men.'

'Tabina? Her as well?'

'Who?'

'Tabina,' Bram repeated. 'The girl who was held downstairs.'

The penny dropped and Chingford chuckled. 'Oh, Buttons, her pet name. Yes, she was a shy, sweet thing. Very compliant.'

Brampton glared at him. 'You are one sick fuck,' she snapped.

'Cool it,' Royce warned, very aware that Chingford's life hung in the balance.

'Happy enough for the information though, eh?' The Englishman coughed again. 'Ways and means didn't worry anyone then.'

Royce was relieved as Sinbad entered the bedroom with the medical bag from the car. He went to work immediately, cleaning the entry wound and adding QuikClot granules before bandaging it up and sealing it with tape. However disapproving of the man, Brampton didn't hesitate to assist Royce in his work.

Feeling bored, Sinbad wandered off to explore the building that seemed to him like a sultan's palace in all its over-the-top opulence.

'Can I have some water?' Chingford asked. 'Parched as the bloody desert.'

Royce found a jug and tumbler on the bedside table. 'Just a small sip, just moisten your mouth.'

Chingford resisted the temptation to gulp some down. He said, 'I think I'm feeling a bit better.'

'Good,' Royce said, and asked, 'So where are Nazal and Ayana now, Charlie?'

'That I don't know,' the old man replied, inspecting his bandaged torso. 'I hadn't long arrived and was talking to Ayana when Nazal turned up unexpectedly. He was with that bloody Nubian bodyguard of his, Azziz, the one who looks after the dogs. Nazal was furious to see me here. Ordered Ayana to throw some things in a suitcase because they had to go immediately. Something about 32 Brigade that I didn't quite catch.'

'And you've no idea where?' Royce asked.

'He mentioned heading south.'

'To re-group?' Royce guessed aloud.

Chingford shook his head. 'Nah, not Nazal. He knows they're finished here, even though Muammar won't until the rebels have actually got his head on a pole. Gaddafi used to drive Nazal nuts with his mission for women's rights in the Arab world.'

'Gaddafi?' Brampton echoed. 'With *what* we know about him?'

Chingford inclined his head. 'I know, I know. Double standards. But inside his mad, drug-addled head he saw himself as the champion of women in the Arab world. In education, in the hospital service, in the military...unlike elsewhere across Arabia.'

His speech had gradually slowed. The man took a deep breath and winced in pain. He carried on between gasps of discomfort. 'Nazal is Gaddafi's polar opposite in that respect. Just as ambitious and just as ruthless, but Nazal sees the future as an Islamic Caliphate – across the whole of the Middle East – with him at its head. It's all about money and power with him. He's tried to persuade Muammar to go that route but has got nowhere.'

'Caliphate?' Brampton repeated. 'A Muslim super-state under strict Sharia law?'

Chingford nodded. 'All this political upheaval, what they're all calling the "Arab Spring". I've heard Nazal tell Gaddafi it's an opportunity. Here, in Tunisia and next door in Egypt and in Syria...all the old regimes are buckling. When they go, there will be a power vacuum. Nazal believes that will be the time of the Caliphate. Al-Qaeda and all its brother offspring will take over.'

'Scary stuff,' Brampton said.

'Nazal is good friends with Abu Bakr al-Baghdadi.'

Royce felt like he'd just been struck by a bolt of lightning. He could have sworn that his heart missed a beat. Hearing that name again in the confines of the room, brought him out in a sweat.

'Baghdadi?' Royce repeated. 'The same one? That self-claimed leader of some extremist Islamic group…western Iraq, isn't it?'

'I've read about him, too,' Brampton confirmed. 'He's head of some emerging terror group they're calling ISIS. Can't remember what it stands for.'

Royce fell silent. Al-Baghdadi. The man believed to have ordered the assassination of his client in Iraq, the man behind the murder of Maynard Price. Blurred images of her face and her naked, bullet-ridden body swilled unbidden around his mind, clogging his brain, choking his thoughts.

'The Islamic State,' Chingford told her dramatically, 'of Iraq and Syria. Mind you. They'll have to overcome President Assad in Damascus first, and he'll be no pushover.'

Brampton said, 'I've heard the Americans are thinking of putting a price on Baghdadi's head. Something like ten million dollars.'

'Nazal saw Gaddafi as being its figurehead,' Chingford said, 'but Muammar was still wedded to his old Marxist demi-god dreams.'

At that point, Sinbad re-entered the room. Royce tried to focus his thoughts and immediately noticed that the Libyan seemed agitated about something. 'What is it?' he asked.

'Something you should see, Mr James. In a room across the corridor.'

'I think he means Nazal's war room,' Chingford said. 'That's what he likes to call it. I've never been allowed in, but Ayana has told me about it. You take a peek.'

Royce turned to Sinbad. 'Keep an eye on Charlie, will you?'

'Sure thing, boss.'

'And if that ambulance doesn't arrive in five minutes,' Royce added, 'we'll take you in ourselves.'

Chingford waved them aside. 'I'm fine now. Much better. Peaceful.'

Brampton was already on her way across the corridor to the ornate and expansive office filled with a large antique desk and chair. On one wall was a giant custom-made map of North Africa and the Middle East, studded with flag markers and attached notes about each, hand-written in English. All were colour-coded, clearly indicating the depth of following for extreme Islam.

Seeing it like that, the affect was quite shocking. It began in the western Mediterranean with Algeria. A jihadist group called *Jund al-Khilafah*, or Soldiers of the Caliphate, was present, as well as al-Qaeda, in a vast desert territory that stretched down into northern West Africa. Nazal had marked it as the "Lands of the Islamic Maghreb".

Al-Qaeda was also marked as an established presence in adjacent Tunisia, which had been the birthplace of the so-called "Arab Spring." It had moved towards a secular democracy but what about its discontent and unemployed youth, Royce wondered?

In Libya itself, Nazal had marked Sheikh Hatem and his Qatari-backed jihadi friends in Misrata.

To the east in Egypt the Muslim Brotherhood was on the rise. In the Horn of Africa there were the terrorists of al-Shabaab and the al-Qaeda stronghold of Yemen. Marked in fainter colours were the southern Russian Islamic states, then Afghanistan and Pakistan. In Europe, Turkey and the Balkan states were marked as targets of the Caliphate of which Nazal dreamed to lead with al-Baghdadi.

Minutes earlier, Royce would have dismissed this as the ranting dreams of a psychopath. Now, so carefully mapped out, it seemed more like a calculated plan, a possible political achievement – given time, and the recent turn of events.

Brampton shivered. 'God, James, it makes you think.'

'South,' Royce murmured.

'Pardon me?' Brampton asked.

'Sorry,' Royce said. 'I'm just thinking. Those vehicles that vanished from Brigadier Cinti's compound. Reports of several convoys on the move…But not to regroup, not now.'

'In the future?' Brampton asked.

Royce stared at the map, trying to make sense of it. 'When Gaddafi's gone…ready to return to Libya to fill the power vacuum.'

'Planning ahead,' Brampton murmured thoughtfully. 'That's what Charlie said.'

'I think Nazal Abu has gone south with those convoys,' Royce said. 'To disappear into the Sahara – until the time is right.'

'Easy enough,' Brampton replied. 'Its land mass is larger than the United States. It's where al-Qaeda was incubated before moving to Afghanistan, wasn't it?'

Royce nodded. 'Sudan, I think.'

'But what allies would Nazal find there now?'

Royce moved closer to the map, ran his finger down the road link into Niger, into the middle of nowhere, to a small flag. 'Boko Haram,' he read.

'Who are they?'

He shook his head. 'I'm not sure.'

At that moment Sinbad entered the room. 'Mr Boss, there are peoples downstairs. I think it is the ambulance. Shall I unlock the front door for them?'

'Thanks,' Royce said. 'Charlie's one lucky bastard. And a tough one.'

Brampton grunted. 'Well, you got the bastard bit right. He was always groping me or Rachel given half a chance.'

Royce nearly joked that he couldn't blame the old man for trying, but thought better of it.

As they headed back into the corridor towards Chingford's bedroom, Brampton said, 'If we're right and that's what Nazal and Ayana are doing, I want to find out for sure.'

'By doing what?'

'Follow them. They can't be that far ahead of us, just a few hours.'

'We don't even know if that's what they're doing. Or what route they'd take.'

'How many routes are there?'

Royce shrugged. 'Not many, that's true enough.'

'I suppose you're going to try and ban me.'

'I can't recommend it, Jo, now can I?'

'I'm sure Jaralla's men will take me. It'll make a fantastic story for the *News* if it's what Nazal is up to.'

There was a sudden commotion below as Sinbad threw open the front doors and let in the two medics and their folded manual stretcher. 'Upstairs, upstairs!' he cried excitedly in Arabic.

The two young medics, who looked as though they were probably students, took the staircase several steps at a time. 'He's just in here,' Brampton said, stepping back and indicating the open door.

Then everything went silent as the two ambulance responders bent over their patient. Royce and Brampton exchanged glances. One of the medics straightened his back and looked at them. In perfect English he said, 'I am afraid, sir, we are too late. This gentleman is dead.'

23

THE DEVIL RIDES IN

'We should have taken Charlie to hospital ourselves,' Royce said as they watched the ambulance pull away from Nazal Abu's villa.

'You can't blame yourself,' Brampton said. 'Besides, I'm not sure there'd be much left in Libya for him with Gaddafi gone.'

'True enough,' Royce admitted.

'So are you going to come with me?' Brampton persisted. 'Try and pick up the trail of Nazal and Ayana?'

Royce frowned. 'You know damn well I'm not going to let you run off on your own.'

Her eyes narrowed. 'Do I take that as a yes?'

'I'm on Ollie's payroll now,' he replied, switching on his radio, 'so I need to clear it with him. But I don't foresee a problem. He'll be as anxious to know the whereabouts of any missing forces as you are.'

Royce's prediction of his boss's response was spot on target. If anything he had underestimated the man's enthusiasm. *Whatever Nazal is up to, James, we need to know… as soon as! He's got enough equipment to field a small army. Whether he's planning a counter-attack on Tripoli or Misrata, or going into hiding, we need to know about it. Once he's out in that frigging desert, it'll be like trying to find a needle in the proverbial haystack.'* Parsons paused for breath. *'No heroics, mind.'*

'None intended,' Royce answered. 'I plan to keep our distance and work out his position and intentions if we can.'

'Iain's setting up his control room in the hotel like before.' Parsons said. *'Once we hear from you, Stefan and I will come over in the second Range Rover. So let me know as soon as you have anything concrete.'*

'Roger that, boss,' Royce concluded. 'Out.'

'Thank God for that,' Brampton said, 'I was afraid he'd pull you off.'

Royce indicated the two rebel fighters, who were standing beside their Nissan pick-up, smoking and drinking from cans of fizzy lemonade. 'Let's see if we can persuade our friends here to join us.'

He sauntered over to the two young Libyans and introduced himself and Brampton properly and formerly for the first time since they had been allocated their escorts by Dr Jaralla.

'I am Leon,' said the tall, thin one, showing a set of slightly rabbit teeth. 'I am trainee dentist.'

'I am Ramzi,' the shorter, plumper man said. 'Like the famous English chef, but spell different. I study engineering.'

Neither man had seen a barber in months, nor a razor in weeks. Their green T-shirts and worn camo trousers could probably have stood up by themselves, judging by the heavy odour of congealed sweat.

Royce made an attempt to explain the situation. 'We have reason to believe that elements of the Colonel's Khamis Brigade have headed south into the desert. With them is a man called Nazal Abu -'

Leon gulped in surprise. 'Him! I have heard of him. He is high-ranker, friend of Gaddafi.'

Brampton indicated the villa. 'This is his house.'

'You are journalist?' Ramzi asked.

'Yes. The *Sunday News* in England and also a new digital TV channel.'

'We can watch in Libya?'

'When you get the Internet back.'

Both men looked overjoyed at that prospect. 'What weapons do you have with you?' Royce asked.

'We have heavy machine-gun to fix up and we have rifle grenades,' Leon said. 'Not too many. And, of course, our personal AK47s.'

'Water and food?'

'We are low on water now. And no rations as we eat at camp with our brother fighters.'

Royce made a decision. 'It's 0200 now. The two of us are pretty shattered; I imagine you are, too. I suggest we bed down here for the night. Plan to leave early, fill up water containers and grab any non-perishable foodstuff we can find from the kitchen.'

Exhausted by the high drama as the day had unfolded, no one put up any protest at the plan. The Libyans used one of the bedrooms while Royce, Brampton and Sinbad were equipped to camp out in one of the downstairs reception rooms. Although Leon volunteered to take the first two-hour watch, in case of trouble, Royce found him fast asleep at the window when he took over from him at four in the morning. He went easy on the youngster, not wanting to alienate him while he was trying to create a team that could work effectively together.

Royce woke everyone at six for a seven o'clock departure. After the Libyans' jerry cans of water were filled, the kitchen was raided for any additional tinned or dried food supplies.

The two rebel fighters listened intently as he handed them a spare short-range radio each and a mobile satellite phone to share. He explained briefly how he wanted their two-car convoy to travel and operate together in different circumstances. Such a crash course could be confusing but the young men were both intelligent and enthusiastic, so Royce had fairly high hopes they wouldn't cock up in a crisis.

Slightly later than planned, Royce drove out of the villa compound in the Range Rover with the Libyan Nissan pick-up close behind. Almost immediately they passed the second Range Rover arriving with Seeff and Parsons to check out the intelligence treasures in Nazal Abu's war-room.

After an exchange of waves, Royce settled in for the long haul.

Heading due south it was some 600 plus miles to the nearest border. That might be the country of Chad to the east, or Niger to the west. As yet he had no way of knowing which Nazal had chosen. Either could swallow up the British Isles seven times. The areas were vast and inhospitable.

Parsons had talked about geo-satellite surveillance, but Royce detected that the man wasn't hopeful. Whether unhopeful of co-operation with NATO, the Americans or whoever operated the damn things, or just in the technology, he wasn't sure. What Royce did know was that in real life technology was rarely quite like the pumped up magic of Hollywood movie thrillers that irritated him so much.

Nazal had split up his force into several smaller convoys to avoid detection. So clearly the man was aware that at some point NATO aircraft would come looking for him. Increasingly Royce was coming round to the opinion that Nazal Abu was playing a long game. He and his formidable force would melt away, vanish into the vast deserts of north Africa...until the time was right. But right for what?

Joining the Muslim Brotherhood in Egypt against the political establishment in Cairo? Retaking Libya from the liberal rebels at some future point? From what Chingford Charlie had told him that seemed the most likely scenario. But that didn't help them knowing where the hell the convoys were going now.

There were few roads into the desert wilderness but countless tracks, some always passable, some only seasonal. Mostly locals knew which were which. Royce's best guess was that Nazal would plan to give any shared borders a wide berth and take a more central route towards the northern border of the nation of Niger. It was about as vast, remote and uninhabited a place that you could hope to find on the continent of Africa and could swallow up an entire division of troops and armour. Nazal's column would have no difficulty disappearing there by using just a few elementary precautions.

On Royce's behalf, Parsons had put in a request to the Royal Air Force to use one of its twin-engine long-range Sentinel R1 surveillance aircraft to help track Nazal's armoured columns. He was apparently given short shrift by Northwood. They were concentrating on the Libyan coast and just ever so slightly busy monitoring the collapse of Gaddafi's forces. If they could spare the time and energy on such a distraction, the aircraft's effective hundred mile surveillance range would be of little benefit to Nazal Abu's pursuers.

The RAF was right. Four hours' drive south-east and over two hundred miles away from Tripoli, they were already well out of the effective range of a Sentinel R1.

Ash Shuwayrif shimmered ahead of them in the high noon heat haze. Veering to the right, the road skirted the perimeter of the small town with its mostly lime-washed bungalows and scattering of two-storey buildings. Royce spotted the bright restaurant sign and pulled in alongside a low picket fence in the shade of two large palms. Only two cars were parked outside and there was no one else to be seen out in the scorching midday heat.

Royce was pleased to see that their two Libyan companions had obeyed his radioed instructions to the letter, parking some thirty metres back with a clear view of the restaurant in case of any trouble, their rifles discreetly at the ready.

He picked out three men seated around a table in the shade of the trees. He turned to Brampton. 'Best you wait here,' he said. 'I'll go with Sinbad.'

'Stuff you, James,' she replied, 'this isn't a war-zone. And you're not my minder.'

He shrugged as she flipped up her Italian silk scarf from her shoulders to cover her head and began opening the door. 'Please yourself ,' he replied resignedly as she left.

After the chill air of the Range Rover, the heat of the desert hit the three of them like a physical force. Brampton looked up at the blistering white sky as she was cocooned in the intense warmth. Immediately sweat gathered in the small of her back, around her groin and inside the desert boots she wore.

'This heat,' she murmured. 'Like being in an oven. You wouldn't last any time at all if the car broke down.'

Royce nodded. 'That's why you should never travel with less than two vehicles. But people do – and pay the price.'

They approached the seated men and smiled broadly.

'*Kayf halik?*' Sinbad greeted.

Royce could see them more clearly now. One looked like the owner, judging by his grubby white apron, a man with a balding pate, who was sitting with two customers. Their shabby *dishdashas* and ragged turbans suggested that they were local farmers or field workers. The men were sharing a simple plate of rice and dates and puffing at a hookah pipe on the centre of the table. There appeared to be no other customers in the dark interior of the building beyond them. An aroma of cooked lamb hung in the air.

The owner rose to his feet. '*Ahlan wa sahlan,*' he said. Then continued in Arabic, 'What can I get for you?'

Sinbad translated, although Royce understood.

'I wonder if he's got some *sharba* cooking?' Brampton thought aloud.

The owner understood and nodded. 'For everyone?'

'Please,' she confirmed in English and held up one hand. 'For five persons.'

'And tamarind to drink for everyone,' Royce added in Arabic. 'We do not have much time.'

Nodding his understanding, the owner shuffled off into the gloomy interior. His two customers regarded the newcomers suspiciously.

Aware of this, Sinbad tried to engage them. 'You live around here?' he asked in Arabic.

Only the man wearing a brown turban and matching shawl over his *dishdasha* responded. 'I have a date farm down the road.' He indicated the Range Rover with its makeshift livery of black tape. 'You are television crew? Sky?'

Not one to miss a trick, Sinbad replied, 'Sure thing. We look for military convoy, going south.'

'You miss it.' He corrected himself. 'Not it. Them. Several. All through the night. Heavy vehicles. They wake me and my wife. The road passes near my farm and the whole house shakes. Last one was soon after dawn.'

Royce managed to follow most of the conversation. 'Did you see them?' he asked in strangulated Arabic.

The farmer struggled to understand. 'Last one, yes. I want to see how many more. They had emblems on vehicle of Khamis Brigade. And blue men.'

'Blue men?' Royce queried.

Sinbad knew what the date farmer meant. 'Tuaregs.'

Then Royce understood. Tuaregs, the roaming nomads, famous for their blue *tagilmus* veils that would leave their skin dyed indigo in the heat and sweat of the desert. The tough breed of desert gypsies had been a favourite of Gaddafi, who recruited them into the ranks of his ruthless mercenaries. Their name literally translated as "Abandoned by God", their atheistic and marginalised race had been attracted to *al-Qaeda* and other Islamic radicals in recent times. Parsons had told Royce once that Tuaregs and *al-Qaeda* were not natural bedfellows, but he wondered if the nomads thought if they found Allah and his more radical followers, they would be smiled upon more kindly for once in their history.

'There were many, many lorries,' the farmer added in response to more of Sinbad's questions. 'Many blue men and many stores. Some big tanks on low-loaders, and wheeled armoured cars driving themselves. Also pick-ups carrying anti-aircraft guns and mortars.'

The owner reappeared carrying a tray of flatbreads and bowls filled with spicy lamb and vegetable soup. A young lad followed behind him with a tray of tumblers and a jug of iced tamarind juice. At Brampton's request he took some soup and drink over to the Libyans waiting in their Nissan pick-up.

After making short work of the meal, Royce glanced at his Breitling watch. 'It seems they have a good four or five hours march on us,' he calculated. 'But we'll be gaining on them all the time, closing the gap. Those tank-transporters can't move fast on these roads.'

Brampton stood up. 'Then let's get going. We really don't want to lose them.'

Minutes later the two vehicle convoy was on its way south again, eating up mile after weary mile. Dust billowed in their wake across the parched landscape. The high ground on their right was matched by desiccated mountain slopes rising to their left, squeezing the road between them.

Birak beckoned, another four hours' mind-numbing drive deeper into the desert. The town sat on the fertile south eastern edge of a vast stony plateau. Date plantations and fields of barley sprang up around them in an area that boasted over fifty artesian wells and a string of oases. After passing over a succession of *wadi* beds, they finally drove through the open modern settlement. It was situated in the middle of a palm grove, which boasted a dominating Italian fort and an Old Quarter of dark and narrow alleyways at its centre.

His watch told him it was five o'clock but Royce decided to press on. They had ample provisions on board and he wanted to travel through the night, driving and sleeping in shifts in order to gain on their quarry. Driving on for another hour, with vast waves of sand now on both sides of the road, the much larger, modern town of Sabha loomed.

Again the sea of the desert was replaced by a more fertile landscape that supported a much larger population.

'This Gaddafi city,' Sinbad warned. 'It pro-government.'

Brampton read from her notes. 'It's the capital of the region – and southern Libya – with around a hundred and thirty plus thousand inhabitants. There's a small domestic airport and a military airbase. '

'Gateway to Africa,' Royce murmured. 'And almost certainly there'll be pro-Gaddafi roadblocks.'

'Nazal Abu will be amongst friends,' Brampton said.

Royce made a decision. 'Let's stop and eat. Then, at last light, we'll go off road and see if we can't go round the outer edge of the city.'

After radioing his plan to Leon and Ramzi, he pulled over into the edge of a date plantation, sheltering under the palms and out of sight of the road. Using portable stoves and army rations they rustled up boil-in-the-bag meals, coffee and tea. It was a welcome opportunity to relax, stretch their legs and discuss Royce's plan.

Forty minutes later, they were packed up and on the move again, this time going off-road to by-pass the city limits and avoid confrontation with any soldiers who continued to support the Gaddafi regime. By now the landscape was fading into a sulphurous yellow haze of dust and dying sunlight.

Royce picked a careful path across country, slowly, minimising any dust trail. To their left, the outline of the city was fading away into dusk, its dominating Italian castle rising above the modern low-rise blocks and occasional mosque minaret. The air was dense with the smell of spices, and reverberated with the alluring and melodic call to prayer. Disturbed dogs snapped and barked angrily at their own shadows.

It was a long and sometimes tricky bypass of the city, but eventually they were on the road again, pressing on south. As darkness enveloped them, they alternatively switched from visible tarmac to wind-hardened tracks – and back again.

Driving on ill-defined roads by only headlight beam was eye-straining and mesmeric. Even taking turns and doing only one-hour shifts was exhausting. They passed through occasional ghost villages with no lights and no signs of life. There were one or two tense moments when vehicles approached from the opposite direction. Each time they were trucks or pick-ups, their drivers going about their business with no interest in the two vehicle convoy.

Taking turns to drive the lead vehicle, both Royce and Brampton separately nearly drove into a ditch as the sand-smeared road took an unexpected turn which they didn't. Leon and Ramzi became highly-amused and not a little cocky at the prospect of having to winch the Westerners back onto the track. Speed was reduced to a thirty or forty mile an hour crawl. It was nearly eight in the morning before they finally approached Tajarhi.

The sun was already cranking up the blistering heat as the village came into view, shimmering through the desert haze. Mud and reed buildings were surrounded by groves of date palms and a lush oasis that attracted a host of wild ducks.

Being the southern-most settlement in the Fezzan region, it formed a crossroads astride the ancient desert trading routes to the Niger River, Lake Chad and the Sudan. There was also a landing strip for aircraft on its southern outskirts.

Although this was the last opportunity to refuel in Libya, Royce didn't want to draw attention to themselves and he reasoned they had ample on-board fuel supplies for the foreseeable future. Although the place was isolated and almost deserted, there were enough people seated in the shadowed porches for the chance of at least one to be a spy for Gaddafi or Nazal Abu.

There were two routes out of the village. One was a road that stretched south-east into the country of Chad and another rough overland track, which ran more directly south into Niger. This was what all the indications suggested would be the ultimate destination for Nazal's convoys.

Once clear of the suburbs, Royce pulled over into the shade of some wild olive trees, the Nissan pick-up pulling over behind him. He had decided on a thirty minute break to rustle up some coffee and breakfast. While the three Libyans took care of that, he tried phoning Parsons at the Control Room back in Tripoli. Although it was a satellite service, the local atmospherics conspired to deny him a signal. It was not the first time it had happened.

'No luck?' Brampton asked.

Royce shook his head. 'Perhaps we're too far south, getting to the outer limits of satellite coverage.'

She had been trying to send a report to the *Sunday News* in London. 'I'm having similar problems, dammit.'

He pushed the problem from his mind and settled down to enjoy a few minutes of relaxation, eating British Army porridge and apple flakes washed down with black coffee.

Soon they were on the move again, climbing slowly into the ragged mountains that skirted the Manguént Plateau. As they were approaching the thousand metre peak and the border with Niger, the sky darkened unexpectedly and rapidly as though threatening the end of the world. The landscape dimmed dramatically and the sandstorm struck.

Sinbad shivered as the temperature suddenly plummeted. 'It is said that when desert wind blows, the devil rides in.'

'I don't like it,' Parsons said. 'An area of nothingness about the size of the United States.'

He was standing beside Stefan Seeff in front of the giant wall map in the office that Nazal Abu referred to as his "War Room". Major Hamish McDougall had his SAS E Squadron team going through the desk and filing cabinet for papers and documents. Others had already photographed the wall map and sent electronic copies to both Hereford and MI6 HQ at Vauxhall Cross.

'You could lose an entire army in that desert,' Parsons added.

'I think we already have,' Tremain added with a straight face.

He was seated at the desk with their large Inmarsat M satellite phone case for secure digital communications with London.

'Isn't Rollo due to call in?' Parsons asked.

'Fifteen minutes ago.'

'That's not like him. Any signal problems?'

'Not this end,' Tremain drawled.

Seeff said, 'I've just tried calling him and I'm getting nothing. That means they're out of the satellite coverage area, there's local atmospheric interference, or the phones have been lost, damaged or confiscated by someone.'

Parsons raised an eyebrow. 'Are you worried?'

'I don't think you should have let him off alone with Jo and Sinbad,'

Seeff replied darkly.

'Don't mince your words, son, will you?'

'No, I won't.'

'He was very keen,' Parsons answered defensively.

'He always is,' Seeff replied.

'And he had those rebel fighters as back up.'

'As much use as a couple of chocolate soldiers in a scrap,' Seeff retorted. 'You let them go trailing into the desert alone, chasing an entire army.'

'Following, not engaging,' Parsons pointed out.

'If they have a choice.'

Parsons became irritated. 'Nazal Abu is a peripheral concern. The war's up here in Tripoli and the coast…At least until Gaddafi is caught.'

'By then it could be too late,' Seeff replied. 'At least let's get them some back-up. Maybe Major McDougall can spare some crew to follow after them.'

The major heard that. 'When did you last hear from Royce?'

'At last light yesterday. From around Tajari.'

'That's nearly on the border. I can't commit anyone that far out. I need all my men here.'

Seeff snapped. 'Then I'll make my own arrangements. I'm sure Yves will be up for giving me a hand, and Rachel. Hopefully I can use their transport.'

'You're under my command,' Parsons reminded sternly.

'I resign. If you don't like it, shoot me.'

24

BAD PLACE

'I'm not sure this is a good idea,' Parsons moaned. He was already regretting his change of mind.

The two vehicle convoy was speeding fast south towards the town of Ash Shuwayrif, following in the tracks of Royce and Brampton.

'Sure,' Seeff rejoined, a dazzling boyish grin beneath the wraparound Raybans as he slipped up a gear, 'you know it makes sense.'

Using the team's second Range Rover, both Parsons and Iain Tremain were nervous passengers as the younger South African tried to close the gap between themselves and Royce's team.

The second vehicle was a BMW belonging to Rachel Starr of *TV-Global* and driven by her French bodyguard Yves. The television reporter had taken little persuasion to join them as a buddy-buddy safety team when Seeff invited them. Parsons wasn't too happy about their inclusion, but as McDougall had point blank refused to involve any of his E Squadron members, the SIS man felt he was in no position to object. Moreover, waiting for them to prepare had cost vital time and it was eleven in the morning before they finally set off in earnest.

'Sandstorms down south,' Tremain informed in his soft Tasmanian drawl. 'That'll slow everything down. Give us a chance to play catch up.'

Parsons winced as Seeff swerved to avoid a pair of wild camels wandering in the middle of the road.

It was three hours before the wind abated, stopping even more abruptly than it had begun. The darkness faded as the trillions of sand particles floated back to the baked earth and the blazing sun forced its rays through holes in the floating fabric of the storm canopy.

Although the vehicles had remained stationary and closed up during the maelstrom, the passengers in Royce's team had spent too many vital moments outside as it began.

'I can't tell you where that sand's got,' Brampton complained. 'Unbelievable.'

'You'll be digging it out of your ears and nose for days,' Royce promised.

Sinbad said, 'Do you drive through Madama, Mr James?'

Royce had been studying the map under torchlight while the storm raged outside. Some seventy five miles over the border, Madama was the Niger frontier station, a ramshackle settlement and old fortress. He shook his head. 'I want to avoid any government troops. This is pretty much like the Wild West and we'd be a prime target for bribery demands or hostage-taking – from bandits or officials.' He jabbed his finger at the map. 'To the west there's a huge and pretty spectacular escarpment – or shelf – from the plateau we're now on. It extends for some hundred and fifty miles. If we can pick up a *wadi* running down, we may be able to work our way around Madama and bypass it altogether.'

'A *wadi*?' Brampton queried. 'A dried up river bed, right?'

He nodded. 'At this time of year.'

'Sounds like a plan,' she agreed.

By now most of the floating sand had settled and the heat was cranking up under a white hot sky. Royce was anxious to get away and quickly explained his idea to the two young Libyans. They grinned enthusiastically, obviously considering it to be a great adventure. Their humour soon changed to suppressed fury when the Nissan's engine refused to start. Half-an-hour later, with all the plugs cleaned, it finally fired up, although unhappily.

Royce led the way towards the head of the *wadi*, its channel marked by the occasional patch of sparvo grass and stunted thorn trees on either side. It was a precarious descent over a riverbed of small pebbles that had been eroded by millennia of flowing water. Especially in the steeper sections, it began to resemble a cataract or waterfall more than a river. Once or twice the unpredictable grip of the tyres on the loose bed of stones allowed the rear of Royce's vehicle to slew and threaten to overturn.

It was midday before the heart-stopping, fifty mile crawl down the escarpment *wadi* was completed. In the last steep section, Royce pulled over.

Unexpectedly, they had come across a vehicle wreck. It was an overturned truck that had been abandoned. The green paint did not look especially old or faded. Leon leapt from the Nissan to inspect it.

After a moment he called back gleefully, having examined its insignia. 'It is from Khamis Brigade! Thirty two! We find them!'

'Brilliant!' Brampton enthused.

'If we're closing on them,' Royce warned, 'we must be seriously cautious. Establish their location and report back to Ollie.'

As the land flattened out, Royce drove them out of the *wadi* and across the aching emptiness of the stony plain, running parallel with the main road into Niger. Where possible, he kept to the cover offered by depressions and defiles in the landscape. At all times he avoided offering a silhouette or "hard target" that would make it easy for an enemy to identify them outlined against the sky. They were headed across country on a series of compass-bearings that would keep them close but parallel, rather than directly behind, the apparent route of their quarry.

Royce was no tracker, having only attended a couple of specialist lectures during his entire career. Picking out anything in this harsh, encrusted table-top, eroded by constant eddies of sand, was near impossible for him. However, at one point, it seemed that they had stumbled across evidence of Nazal's convoy having passed through the area.

For a few miles there was a profusion of discarded fruit drink cartons and food wrappers, countless cigarette butts, even a few torn items of army uniform. At one place there was a trail and pool of fuel that had been dried by the sun, suggesting that a lorry had ruptured its fuel lines on a rock and spewed diesel into the sand. The baked earth itself was hardly disturbed, although in places impressions of large tyre tracks were clearly visible. Royce guessed that they were no more than a few hours old, since the morning sandstorm would have covered everything.

Then, as suddenly as the swathe of clues had been found, it disappeared. The convoy they were tracking had clearly veered off in a new direction.

'Where are we?' Royce asked.

'Middle of nowhere,' Brampton answered. 'About five miles west of the main north-south road, running parallel.'

Sinbad, who had been snoozing in one of the back seats, was suddenly awake and shouting. 'Hey, boss, look, look! Up there.'

Royce and Brampton followed the line of his pointing finger.

The figure in black robes and turban seemed like just another shadow in the rocks of the cliff face, until it moved a fraction. Royce picked out the shape of the AK47 against the bleached stones.

'Where?' Brampton asked.

'Eleven o' clock,' Royce said.

'He gone,' Sinbad said. 'Like ghost.'

By the time Royce had blinked, the figure had seemingly evaporated.

'I can hear an engine kick-starting,' Brampton said. 'Motorcycle?'

'Or quadbike,' Royce wondered aloud. The noise reverberated across the flat plain, sounding much closer than it really was, hidden by the jagged outcrop. 'We've been well and truly clocked.'

There was nothing to be done. As they proceeded they could see a small trail of dust from the lookout disappearing into the distance on his machine. It made them all the more aware of the enormous tell-tale dust storm they themselves were creating.

Several hours on, it was only the circling vultures that indicated the presence of the remote settlement. It wasn't even marked on the map.

Half a dozen of the giant birds glided high on the desert thermals, kept aloft by their massive wingspan as they searched the landscape for an opportunistic meal. The leftovers from previous feasts were becoming more common, the ribbed carcasses of cattle that had died in the frequent droughts.

'There's an oasis,' Brampton said, examining the map. 'But no named village.'

The ragged palms came into view first, followed by the confusion of mostly flat-roofed, mud brick dwellings, others made of dried reeds or alternatively with corrugated iron and plastic sheeting.

Half a dozen goats were tethered, munching forlornly on the sparse patches of grass and thorn shrubs on the outskirts. They looked up, curious, at the approaching vehicles.

It was like a prospectors' town in the days of the Gold Rush in America: basically a main street with a T-junction at the top, formed by the most important building in the settlement. In this case it was not a town hall and local government office, but a flop house hotel.

Built of dried mud bricks, it had a raised sidewalk with a wooden hitching rail to which a couple of haughty camels were tied, standing beside a couple of beaten-up trucks. Several scruffy locals in turbans sat at tables on the shady veranda, smoking and drinking coffee. They watched with idle curiosity as Royce reversed his Range Rover into the parking space, ready for a fast getaway if necessary. Leon followed his example and backed up the Nissan.

'Get in the driver's seat,' Royce told Brampton. 'If anything goes wrong, just get the hell out of here. Don't hang about for anything.'

'Yes, boss,' she replied, not bothering to hide the sarcasm in her voice. 'Anything you say.'

Royce indicated to Sinbad to join him outside on the steps to the hotel. A fat bearded man in blue Tuareg turban and robes rose from the first table. He extended his hand and introduced himself to Sinbad, virtually ignoring the Englishman.

'He is Abdul,' Sinbad translated. 'Owner of this establishment and welcomes us.'

'What's the name of this village?' Royce asked, looking back down the near-deserted main drag.

'Abdul says Makan Darar.'

Royce frowned. 'Devil's..?'

'Called Bad Place,' Sinbad helped. 'Built recent to house new workers. For uranium mines north of here. Buses leave in morning, return at night.'

'Does he have rooms available?' Royce asked.

'He asks how many? Only premium rates available.'

'I bet,' Royce murmured. 'Three?'

'Only has two.'

'That will have to do.' Royce said, then returned to the car.

'Is everything okay?' Brampton asked.

He nodded. 'The natives seem friendly enough. They have a couple of rooms. You can have one to yourself – or share with me, for safety.'

'That's the oldest war zone chat-up line in the world,' she joked.

'It works,' he replied with a straight face. 'I won't jump you, I think you know that.'

'Shame.' She stared at him for a moment. 'Sorry, you're back in work mode. I was forgetting…Anyway, whatever you think.'

'Let's get unpacked,' he said. 'Then something to eat and get a decent night's sleep.'

'And tomorrow?'

'It's too dangerous to follow Nazal any farther,' he decided. 'We have to get back into contact with Ollie. At least, now we can confirm the convoys have come this way and this far. He'll have to decide what

he wants to do about it. Or what the British authorities or NATO want
to do about it.'

She shrugged her disappointment. 'I guess it's still quite a story for
me. Not all whistles and bells, but Gaddafi's mysterious vanishing army
is quite good.'

'No other newspaper will have it.'

'True,' she agreed, slipping her Italian scarf over her head before
she climbed out into the burning afternoon sunshine.

As they unloaded their personal equipment, both became aware of
the noisy approach of an aged, canvas-topped Peugeot P4 four-by-four.
Two gendarmes in moth-eaten desert DPMs and khaki forage caps
emerged, SIG 550 assault rifles slung carelessly over their shoulders.

It was then that Royce noticed the sun-faded sign on the neighbouring
adobe hut; it was the local police outpost.

The policemen swaggered slowly over to the Range Rover with a
studied arrogance. Taller and clearly more senior, one of them took an
unseemly interest in the whale's tail of Bram's thong riding above her
linen hipsters as she leaned into the back of the vehicle.

Sensing trouble, Sinbad scampered out of the hotel to intervene.
'*Mesa al-kher!*' He greeted, continuing in Arabic, 'I translate for you.
These my friends from media, world news. Very important.'

The officer viewed him with disdain. In English, he replied, 'I need
no translator. Please go back inside hotel while I conduct interview.'

Royce stepped forward. 'English?' the gendarme asked directly.
'From Libya?'

'Yes, officer. Press and TV.'

'Why here in Niger? War in Libya, not here.'

Brampton turned around. 'We're following a news story.'

'What sort of story?'

She tried to play it down. 'Just a rumour. Mercenaries returning
south. Maybe a convoy.'

The officer had a very thin moustache like a line of mascara.
Brampton found herself fixated by the exceptional whiteness of his

teeth. 'There are no soldiers here,' he said, 'no caravan.'

She smiled at him. 'I understand, thank you.'

'Passports,' the gendarme said coldly. 'I see passports.'

Brampton searched in her shoulder bag, while Royce extracted his from a pocket in his cargo trousers. The officers flicked through them both. 'There are no entry visa stamps.' Royce had anticipated this and had his answer ready. 'We got lost in that sandstorm earlier, came off the road. We're on our way to Madama now, to get our passports stamped.'

The gendarme's teeth flashed briefly but it scarcely constituted a smile. 'Then you are lucky. I give you visa here.'

Brampton realised he was blatantly studying her nipples through the perspiration-damp material of her shirt. She glared back at him defiantly, facing him down, until he finally averted his eyes.

Meanwhile Royce said, 'Thank you, officer.'

No longer distracted, the gendarme added. 'But it cost.'

I bet, Royce thought.

'Fifty dollar. Each of you.' The man waved his arm indicating that he included the two Libyan fighters and Sinbad in his catch. 'And then there fine for illegal entry – another fifty dollar.' Now he really was smiling. 'Each.'

After Royce had discreetly removed the money from the steel cash-box in the car and handed it over, the senior officer did not actually stamp the passports. He merely squiggled a biro signature in Arabic and dated it. Then, without further comment, the two policemen did not return to the police hut, but instead went back to their battered Peugeot and drove off. Royce watched the dust trail disappear slowly into the distance.

'Hope that last we see them,' Sinbad said and spat in the sand.

The team carried their overnight bags inside the hotel, following the owner Abdul. There was a communal reception area with a low table and hookah pipe, surrounded by a sea of plump, ornate cushions. To Royce's surprise three heavily-veiled women were seated in the darkness of a far corner. Their brightly made-up eyes watched, following the new arrivals as they passed through to the rear rooms. In fact most were hardly rooms, but cubicles with flimsy partition walls of woven rattan. Each contained no more than a cot with a garish red satin sheet and a side table and tin wash basin. It was strikingly obvious that this place doubled as a love hotel, a brothel for the mine workers. The actual accommodation, such as it was, comprised more cubicles at the back of the compound, slightly larger, with two sets of bunk-beds in each.

Royce indicated the stained sheet and straw mattress. 'Don't sleep on that. Use your own kip mat and bag.'

'Don't worry,' she replied, tugging at the holed mosquito netting. 'I'll zip it right over my head. God knows what's crawling around in here.'

He grinned and dumped his bergen on the floor. 'We'll use the bottom bunks. I wouldn't trust the top ones to hold much weight. I'll take the one by the door.'

Brampton sniffed the air. 'I smell cooking. Spices.'

'Let's see if we can get something to eat,' Royce said. As they left the room, he dragged the rattan door closed behind them. There was no lock or bolt.

On their way back to the reception room they found some older women cooking over embers in the compound yard, the air filled with wood smoke, and hints of cinnamon and nutmeg.

Abdul became more welcoming, his heart no doubt warmed by the sudden influx of visitors and unexpected profits. On Royce's advice, Brampton tucked herself away in the dark corner with the camp hookers. The women were shy, but polite and smiling in her presence. She engaged them with her pidgin Arabic, which they found amusing but clearly appreciated, slowly warming to her open manner.

Abdul joined the visitors from Libya around the table, together with his farmer friends from the terrace. A meal of goat kebabs and rice was served, washed down with fruit juices, cans of Pepsi and strong coffee.

Sinbad changed up a gear, his usual charismatic and amusing self inevitably winning the hearts of the dour local tribesmen. Later buses arrived, bringing workers back from the mines. The room quickly filled with chattering noise, cigarette smoke and a claustrophobic humidity.

Later Royce joined Brampton on the outside veranda for some fresh air. They sat at a table where Royce poured some juice into two tumblers. But the atmosphere was hardly cooler, the desert warmth cocooning them like a warm, moist blanket. Above them, the dome of indigo sky stretched forever, dusted with the silver wash of a trillion sugar crystals.

'Hermes the Thrice Great,' Royce said quietly.

Brampton looked at him and smiled. 'What?'

'Who?' he corrected. 'The great Egyptian philosopher and sage from 3000BC. Described the universe as "the mind of God".'

She looked up to see a shower of asteroids shooting across the heavens like molten arrows. 'That's a beautiful thought,' she murmured. 'I wonder if it's true.'

He smiled. 'Why not? I'm a mine of useless information like that.' He indicated the front entrance. Discordant Arab music from a transistor radio now joined the hubbub of conversation. 'How was it for you in there?' he asked.

'Quite fun,' she replied. 'The girls were sweet. Very sheepish with me at first, but friendly. Asked lots of questions. I don't think they begin to comprehend the freedom women enjoy in Europe. I just wish my Arabic was a bit better.'

'Did you learn anything?'

'A bit. I didn't want to probe too hard. According to the girls, a lot of Gaddafi's mercenaries and vehicles have passed through here in the past couple of days. Some senior Libyan officials visited this hotel last night. I think one may have been Nazal Abu.'

'What makes you think that?'

'His description,' she replied. 'The things he did to one of the girls who he particularly liked. They wouldn't tell me exactly, but I got the gist. His usual turn-on. Flogging them, combining pain and enforced pleasure against their will, humiliating them in front of others. Then he just bought this one particular girl. Outright. Paid a couple of hundred US dollars to her father. And there's another reason I think it was Nazal...'

'What?'

'Princess Ayana. She made the arrangements. A tall, beautiful black woman in green DPM fatigues.' Brampton stared back up at the vast sky. 'It just had to be her, I know it. They took the girl away with them when the convoy left.'

Royce shook his head. 'It's like the ancient Tuareg slave trade never actually stopped.'

Brampton nodded. 'That's certainly the impression I got from the girls. They weren't particularly surprised.'

Royce nodded. 'Sinbad is also on top form. Winning the Tuaregs over, even got them laughing a bit.'

He opened one of his chest pockets and extracted a small leather pack.

'Cigars?' she asked. 'You smoke? I didn't realise.'

He grinned at her. 'Rarely nowadays. This just feels like the time. We can head back to Libya, job done.'

'I'll join you,' she said, fishing in her bag for a Sobranie. 'And give up tomorrow.'

At that moment the front door swung open behind them and Sinbad swayed onto the veranda, unsteady on his feet. Smoke from the rollup in his right hand drifted in the still air, the distinct smell of marijuana.

'Ah, boss, there you are.' He pulled up a chair and collapsed into it. 'I tell you stuff before I sleep.'

Royce offered Brampton the flame of his lighter before starting his own cigar. 'What stuff is that, Sinbad?'

'What these desert gypsies tell me, these Tuaregs,' he said disparagingly. 'In recent times, this territory home to a Zarawa family.'

Brampton exhaled. 'Family? You mean tribe or clan?'

Sinbad nodded irritably at the interruption to his concentration. 'Yes, big family. Parents, grandparents, cousins…distant cousins. Its history from border territories with the big river.'

'The northern frontier with Nigeria,' Brampton added helpfully. 'The clan is noticeably dark-skinned, Afro-Arabic in their features.'

Royce nodded. 'I noticed that.'

'Tuareg clans tend to be matrilineal, unlike more conventional Muslims,' she explained. ''A bit of a cultural mishmash.'

Sinbad's eyes were glazing over as he lost track of what the journalist was saying. He clearly wanted to deliver his message before he fell asleep and blurted his words, 'There is new chief. Amir Gerard Mbobo al-Zarawa.'

'What?' Royce asked.

With increasing difficulty, Sinbad repeated the name. 'He is young prince, just sixteen years of age. He is chief just two weeks – after his father dies in fighting in Sirte with Gaddafi's soldiers. The clan also in brotherhood with Islamic Maghreb.'

Brampton frowned. 'That doesn't sound too good.'

Royce exhaled a stream of smoke. 'The Maghreb? That's virtually *al-Qaeda* of the eastern states. Covering what? Algeria, Mauritania, Mali…'

She finished it for him. 'And here, Niger.'

'So we've landed right in the middle of the lion's den,' Royce observed.

'Prince Mbobo,' Sinbad said,' is a bad boy-man. That is what the men inside say.' He corrected himself. 'Sorry, boy is now Chief Mbobo. He is guided by his mother, widow Basira. She is…I think, in English, a witch. She is born underground, in desert cave at a full moon.'

Brampton stifled a laugh. 'Then we are well and truly stuffed.'

Sinbad shook his head vehemently. 'Do not joke at such things.'

Royce raised his hand. 'I'm sorry, Sinbad, you're right, we shouldn't joke. In fact our plan is to be away from here first thing in the morning.'

He nodded. 'That is good. I will be happy then.'

'Can you go and get Leon and Ramzi for me?'

'Sure thing, boss,' he replied and nearly fell out of his chair, regained his balance and swaggered back into the hotel.

Brampton chuckled. 'He really is such a sweetie. I so, so wish that his son hadn't died...'She paused. 'Did you know he had a daughter?'

'No.'

'He told me one evening. He and his wife had a daughter, which she'd always wanted.'

'A lovely woman, his wife,' Royce recalled. 'Did everything she could for us in Benghazi.'

Brampton said, 'Reading between the lines, she had trouble conceiving. So she was especially overjoyed with a daughter. But aged three, the child got an infection and died. Sinbad said there were no antibiotics because of Western sanctions against Libya.'

Royce nodded. 'Now they've lost Tareg, too.'

'God,' Brampton breathed, 'life can be so unfair.'

'If only we could rewrite history...' Royce agreed. 'Just sometimes.'

She held his gaze for a moment longer than she intended. 'Maybe we could have met at a different time.'

He looked at her curiously, unsure what she meant. 'And a different place.'

'Definitely.' She hesitated. 'Before Baghdad?'

The hotel door burst open and the two Libyan fighters emerged, arms around each other and singing in Arabic to the music wafting from the transistor radio. Their eyes were red and glazed, their faces slick with perspiration. The smell of marijuana on their breath was overpowering.

Ramzi struggled to make his mouth work properly. 'Mr James, Sinbad sends us,'

Royce stood up. 'That's enough, lads. It's time for bed. We'll be making an early start. Five o'clock.' He glanced at the Breitling on his wrist. Six hours to go. 'You two and I will take a two-hour stag each.

Looking at you, I'd better take the first one. You two go and get some sleep.' He frowned. 'NOW!'

The youngster jumped, shaken by Royce's change of tone. 'Yes, Mr James,' Leon said quickly, 'we go hit sack.'

As they hurried back inside Brampton asked, 'Would you like me to stay up with you?'

'Thanks for the offer, Jo, but it's probably best we're all as fresh as possible for tomorrow. It's likely to be a long hard day.'

'Okay,' she said resignedly and stood up. 'See you later.'

He watched her disappear into the hotel, his eyes lingering on the snug fit of her linen hipsters. Another time? Another place? If only, he thought harshly, and definitely before Baghdad.

Stubbing his cigar out on the decking, he went to the Range Rover, unlocked it and extracted the canvas gun-bag that contained his 9mm MP5K. He kept the bag on his lap, unzipped and ready for use, before he ordered a jug of fruit juice and ice and settled down for the wait.

As the minutes dragged into the first hour, men gradually stumbled out of the hotel and along the narrow main street, before disappearing into doorways or compound gates or down alleyways. Gas or candle light flickered on for a few minutes then went out. Finally the music in the hotel stopped. One by one the illumination in each room was extinguished. A hush descended over the settlement, broken only by the occasional baying of a dog. The nightscape took on an intense brilliance, ambient starlight surprisingly strong as Royce's eyes adjusted to the dark.

Yawning seconds slipped by on his watch-face, taking forever. How many times in his military career had he been on stags like this, wishing his life away? Too many, too many.

The hand finally touched 0100hours. Time to hit the sack. He left the chair and went inside the darkened hotel, where a single Tilley lamp hung from the ceiling in the hall, giving just enough light for him to find the room of the two fighters. Stepping inside, he shook Leon roughly awake.

'What? What?' the youngster asked groggily.

'Get up and get outside,' Royce ordered. 'Take your main weapon with you. Two hours, then call Ramzi. Right? If anyone comes into the village, any strangers, a car, a motor cycle, a bloody camel, let me know immediately.'

'Got you, boss.'

'DON'T fall a-fucking sleep!' He glared into the fighter's eyes. 'Got it?'

Leon nodded. Royce watched him go and returned to the room he was sharing with Brampton. He flashed his mini-torch to get his bearings, its beam picking up the curve of the woman's naked spine through the mosquito net and the back strap of her bra. Her sleeping bag gaped open to allow the still air to circulate as best it could.

He sat heavily on the bed, set his wristwatch-alarm for two hours, and lifted his feet up onto the bed. The gun-bag rested on his stomach. When he awoke, he would raise Ramzi and organise the stag changeover.

Instantly he was asleep.

It seemed that almost as quickly, he was wide awake again.

25

THE LIONS' DEN

The discordant sound of shouting voices broke into his dream, shattering its image like porcelain.

Royce opened his eyes to a world of darkness and flashing torch beams, criss-crossing like searchlights in the night sky. His disorientation was only momentary, his situation recall almost instant. The years of practise paid off and before the flimsy reed door was shoved in, he had the stockless MP5 out of its canvas bag.

A tall figure stood in the entrance to their room, outlined against the swinging Tilley lamp light in the hall. The turbaned head and AK47 was presented in crisp silhouette. As the barrel of the assault rifle came down into the firing position, Royce cracked off a double tap. Its punch blew the man back into the tribesman behind him. The smell of cordite filled the confined space. From outside came the shouts and screams of a madhouse as guests and staff awoke to find the hotel full of armed strangers.

Royce swung his feet off the cot and looked across to the opposite bunk bed where Brampton was sitting up, her sleeping bag gathered in both hands to her chest. There was no window, no alternative escape route from the cubicle. He reached over and ripped her mosquito net from its mountings.

'Come across!' he ordered. 'Get behind me!'

Her face pale and drawn, she kicked off the sleeping bag and crossed the gap, wearing just her white thong pants and lace bra. Royce reached across and pulled her in behind him, squeezing her between himself and the reed wall until he formed a human shield around her. He felt her warm breath on the back of his neck.

'I thought Leon was on stag?' she gulped.

'He was.' Terse. 'Blame myself, should have stayed up.'

The body of the dead Tuareg fighter had been left in the doorway as the other tribesmen hastily retreated, not wanting to meet the same fate. Shouting and yelling faded away to a general burble of excited conversation. Then footsteps were heard, moving tentatively along the corridor. Royce braced himself, feeling Brampton tense behind him, her body heat soaking into his back, causing perspiration to crawl down his spine.

Beyond the door, now hanging from its hinges, he could just determine a figure edging down the shadowy corridor towards them, back pressed hard up against the wall.

A distinctive female voice called out. 'Jo Brampton, is that you!?'

Brampton was uncertain. 'Ayana? Princess Ayana?'

'Come on out,' Ayana called back. 'You will not be hurt if you obey my instructions.'

'Please just leave us alone, Ayana,' Brampton returned. 'We are leaving in the morning. We are not a threat to you.'

There was a lightness of humour in the woman's voice. 'You are indeed no threat. But it is too late for that. C'mon out.'

'Please, just go away. We will leave.'

'Too late,' Ayana repeated. 'You've been sent for by Chief Mbobo. Therefore you must come.'

'And if we don't?'

'I am holding a hand grenade. Mbobo would prefer to have you alive, but I am sure he would not be that bothered if not. Do you want me to start counting?'

Options were racing through Royce's head. Apart from trying to rush out of the front entrance shooting, running into a bunch of armed Tuareg tribesmen, it didn't seem that there were any.

'What do we do?' Brampton breathed.

'We don't have a choice,' Royce decided. 'Keep talking and wait for an opportunity. Push the media interview angle, make them want us more alive than dead.'

'That's what I'm thinking,' Brampton replied. 'Massage some egos.'

'COME OUT!' Anger had crept into Ayana's voice, its volume rising. 'Ten seconds. Don't make me throw the grenade. One, two…'

'Okay, okay!' Royce called. 'There are two of us. We're coming out, one at a time…'

He moved forward to give Brampton room to stand. She took her blouse from the bedside hooks and struggled into it, snatched up her trousers and grabbed her boots.

'Hurry up!' Ayana snapped impatiently. 'Get out here!'

Royce followed, leaving his MP5 and automatic behind on the cot.

Ayana recognised him. 'Mr James? I see you again.'

He nodded. 'Unfortunately.' He indicated Brampton's bare legs. 'I think it best you let Jo put her trousers on. Don't want your lads getting too excited.'

She held his gaze. 'Of course, and not *just* my fighters.' She smiled, a private joke. 'Don't want her raped before she even meets with Mbobo.'

Royce didn't like the inference in her words. 'Nothing happens to Bram, Ayana, understand that. I hold you responsible.' He turned to Brampton. 'Get dressed, quick.'

Moments later they were hustled out into the hot night air. The T-junction was now filled with hardened Arab fighters and lit by the headlamps from an array of vehicles, including several pick-ups mounted with heavy weapons. Royce spotted a quad bike to the rear of the gathered force and guessed that could have been the scout who had first alerted Nazal's convoy to their presence. He also noted the two gendarmes, who were now keeping watch from beside their outpost.

The team's Range Rover and the Nissan had been commandeered by Tuareg tribesmen, the two crestfallen Libyan fighters standing bound and blindfolded beside them.

To Royce's surprise, Sinbad was not with them, but was standing beside the Tuareg hotel owner, who was dressed in his nightshirt, and watching on with members of his family and staff. It seemed that their fixer's happy knack of making friends had paid dividends once again. Royce just hoped that Ayana wouldn't spot him.

'We will travel in your vehicle,' the princess decided, turning to one of her henchmen. 'Bind their hands.'

Plasticuffs were slipped over their wrists and snapped closed, before they were pushed into the rear seats of the Range Rover, Ayana placing herself on the opposite side to Bram, keeping Royce squeezed into the middle. He was raging inside, angry with himself for allowing this to have happened. Why the hell hadn't he decided to travel back to Libya during the night? Why had he trusted Leon or Ramzi to stay awake for their shift? There was no answer that was acceptable to him. It was *his* fault again, like it always fucking was.

Armed Tuareg fighters climbed into the front of the vehicle and fired the engine. The driver stalled it, and tried again. It lurched forward uncertainly, joining up with the departing caravan of open-topped 4x4s and pick-ups.

'Where are you taking us?' Brampton demanded.

'To the next oasis,' Ayana replied. 'It is where Chief Mbobo has his camp, holds court. That is where Nazal Abu is in discussion and negotiation with him.'

'About what?'

Ayana stared at her. 'The future, what else?'

'There is no future for Nazal,' Royce interjected. 'Gaddafi's finished. It's all over.'

Brampton glared at him, but Ayana just shook her head sadly. 'You English do not begin to understand, do you?'

'What do you mean?' Brampton asked, but she was remembering Charlie Chingford's words before he died back at the villa.

'Nazal Abu is a deeply devout Sunni Muslim,' Ayana replied, almost a weariness in her voice. 'He believes in the new Caliphate. Abu has known and served Gaddafi for many, many years and always saw him as the Caliph, the only one who could make that happen.' The last feeble light of the village caught the side of Ayana's face, picked out the pout of her lips. 'But Gaddafi was too filled with himself, his Green Book, his own vision of things, not Sharia.' The interior of the car was plunged into full darkness as they sped out into open desert. 'Abu had just about given up on him, certain that now Gaddafi is too old to change, his brain too addled with venereal disease and drugs. That has always been the view of Abu's long-term mentor.'

'Who is that?' Brampton pressed, but she already knew the answer.

'He is known as al-Baghdadi,' Ayana replied. 'That is Abu-Bakr al-Baghdadi. Also has the nickname of the "invisible sheikh". He was a quiet cleric who became the leader of the Islamic Army formed to fight the American invasion of Iraq back in 2003.'

That name again. A feeling like ice water trickled down Royce's spine despite the warmth of the night. He shivered. 'I remember al-Baghdadi,' he said. 'Used a different name back then. The Yanks picked him up in Fallujah when I was there with a special Royal Marines team. That was about '04. He was interned at Camp Bucca. Since his release, the last I heard he'd become the leader of some other group.'

Ayana sounded annoyed. 'Not *any* other group, Mr James. It is the Islamic State of Iraq, also known by some as al-Qaeda in Iraq. But in truth it is more than that. It is the very embryo of the Caliphate itself.'

'Really,' Royce said, not bothering to hide his sarcasm. 'And how do you work that out?'

Brampton turned on him. 'Shut up, James, will you? I want to *know* about this?'

Ayana laughed lightly at seeing the two of them going for each other. 'And why do you want to know about it, Jo?'

'Because I'm a journalist, and it's my job.' A real anger had entered her voice. 'It's why we're here, why we're in this mess with you now. I want this story.'

The vehemence of Brampton's tone took the Somalian princess aback. Ayana considered for a moment, wanting to share what she knew, wanting to dent the smug sense of superiority these Western infidels always seemed to show. 'Well, I can tell you that Abu and his friends have helped to engineer this disruption of the so-called Arab Spring across the Middle East. It will be the catalyst that will make it all possible. Long established regimes will crumble, leaders will fall… here in Libya, maybe Egypt and Syria…even Saudi and the Gulf states. There will be political chaos, a vacuum which the true believers will stand ready to fill.' Her voice rose by an octave and the whites of her eyes glistened in the faint ambiance of the sun as it began lightening the eastern sky.

'That is what Nazal Abu believes,' she continued, 'along with his friend al-Baghdadi. Not just believing, but planning together. Not just here, but also a plot to sweep Islam into Europe that has not been seen for a thousand years. Even now the two of them are starting to put together a mighty army in Iraq that will become the core of a new Islamic State.'

An ominous and brooding silence fell between the passengers in the Range Rover. As the minutes dragged uneasily by, the dawn glow created an outline frieze of palm trees on the horizon. At the outskirts of the oasis settlement they began passing irrigated plots of cash crops and farmers' huts. An untamed camel vandalised the contents of a plastic roadside rubbish bin. Somewhere a cock crowed.

The procession of dusty cars and "technical" pick-ups meandered in between the shanty town buildings of mud-brick, reed and corrugated iron until they reached a central area that comprised a single-storey farmhouse bungalow. It looked on to a large adjoining corral made up of eucalyptus fencing. A giant tank stood on stilts in one corner, downpipes feeding a row of concrete water troughs. Ranks of lean-to structures like tall bike sheds flanked the corral on all sides to provide shade for the scrawny desert cattle during auctions.

But in the dim dawn light, it could be seen that the cattle sheds had been filled with another sort of animal, ones of steel and firepower. There were rows of wheeled armoured cars, light tanks and trucks of various sizes, dozens and dozens, even hundreds of them, depending how far back the rows of sheds stretched away from the oasis.

Just wash away the veneer of sand on each and, Royce guessed, you would find the almost pristine camouflage colours of the 32nd Khamis Brigade. So this was where Gaddafi's most prized army unit had vanished. No over-flying NATO aircraft, even if it ventured this far, would detect the brigade of vehicles hidden beneath sheets of corrugated iron that was part of a giant cattle farming project.

Their Range Rover pulled into the wide, dusty parking area in front of the sprawling farm house. A single, gnarled thorn tree stood at its centre with primitive reed and thatch huts flanking each side.

'Is that where we're going?' Brampton asked. 'The big house?'

'That is Chief Mbobo's residence,' Ayana replied. 'You'll be taken there...*If* he wants to see you. You'll be kept elsewhere.'

The driver managed to stall the car as he pulled up alongside one of the huts, before he climbed out and opened the door for Brampton to get out.

She was able to see him properly for the first time. Dirty robes hung on the emaciated body of a twenty-something fighter with an ammunition belt hung over his shoulder like some sort of fashion accessory. The face beneath the scruffy turban was thin and drawn with the dark glazed eyes of a heroin addict. His beard, without an accompanying moustache, looked somehow pathetic and incomplete as though it had been bought from a cheap joke shop. He waved an AK47 short in his right hand while grabbing her wrist with his left.

'Out of car, kafir whore!' he demanded, his dirty nails pinching her skin as he yanked her brutally from her seat.

Disturbed by the arrival of the vehicles, other fighters emerged sleepily from their living-quarters. They gathered inquisitively around the new arrivals as they made their way to one of the huts.

'Stand clear!' Ayana called. 'Don't touch my prisoners. They are not to be hurt.'

But her words were scarcely listened to, curiosity about a newly arrived white female proving too distracting.

'Is she Muslim?' someone asked in Arabic.

Brampton's anger flared and she turned on the man. 'No, I'm fucking not!'

'She English,' another voice observed. 'And no hijab. She is unbeliever, a spoil of war for us!'

She was suddenly aware of fingers grabbing at her breasts. Another man, bolder, managed to get his hand between her legs. She kicked out, forcing his grip to break.

Royce closed the gap behind her, his hands reaching forward to push her through the entrance into the gloom of the hut. Ayana followed, brushing aside the baying mob and slamming the door shut.

'Thank God,' Brampton breathed. 'That was close.'

'You were foolish to deny you were a Muslim,' Ayana said. 'They are now being told by controllers like Nazal Abu that if you rape infidel women ten times they will become Muslim by the will of Allah.' She smiled thinly. 'That idea appeals to horny young men more than making them blow themselves up to get twenty virgins.'

'How disgusting.'

'You are hardly one to judge,' Ayana retorted, and turned to their driver. 'Radi, I want you take care of my prisoners. Keep them safe and under guard. Give them food and drink. If you let any harm come to them, you will be fed to Nazal Abu's dogs. Do you understand me?'

Radi blanched. 'Yes, Princess Ayana. I understand.'

'Then get on with it.'

As their eyes accustomed to the increasing light coming through the windows, it became possible to define the layout of the hut. It was essentially a bunkhouse to accommodate the local workers or, as now, visiting fighters from Libya. Bed-stacks had been made from local timber as well as chairs and tables. In the far corner there was a collection of bulky, decorative cushions, spread around a hookah pipe where visitors could relax and talk.

It was only then that the two prisoners noticed the two holes that had been excavated into the dirt floor. Each was some six feet deep and six feet in length, and just about wide enough to take a couple of coffins side-by-side. Ornate wrought-iron gates had been adapted as make-shift cage lids. Radi reached down and lifted the nearest one open.

'Get in, kafir whore,' he commanded.

Brampton peered over the edge. All she could see was a bed of grubby straw and a galvanised bucket. The broken front half of a step ladder offered the only way down, propped against the side of the hole.

She turned to Ayana. 'Please don't make me go down there.'

There was a half-smile on the woman's lips. 'Sadly, Jo, we are little short on suitable accommodation just now. I'm sure you understand. Now please...'

Brampton realised the bodyguard was probably enjoying this, humiliating her. She dutifully knelt and edged herself over the ledge into the pit, and twisted herself around to climb down the steps. With her wrists bound together, it was difficult to manoeuvre herself without falling. There was a sudden scurrying noise from the straw below. She glimpsed shiny small eyes and the long, worm-like tail.

She was determined not to let Ayana see her weaken, and carried on down. As she reached the bottom, the rat sprang up, onto the steps, jumped and scrambled over her shoulder. She felt its claws grip her skin for a split second as it sprang up and away.

Brampton shrieked.

The rat scurried across the floor to the far side of the hut and disappeared into the shadows. Radi laughed and slammed the iron-gate shut, turning the padlock key. Brampton stood on the straw looking up, her jaw set, determined not to show weakness. Yet she was sure she was fooling no one. Both Ayana and the scrawny guard knew exactly how terrified she was.

Ayana turned to Royce. 'You next. Over there.'

Radi grabbed him by the arm and hauled him towards the second pit. Moments later he, too, was forced to climb down into his own open grave. The grating was locked above his head.

Ayana's parting words were, 'If you are lucky, you will both see me again.'

The door of the hut scraped shut as she and Radi left. A silence fell over the room. Virtually no light reached their two pits.

'Jo?'

'Yes.'

'Don't be scared. We'll get out of here.'

'Promise?'

'Sure.'

He'd barely answered when they heard the hut door open again. 'Hallo, remember me?'

Brampton recognised the voice and remembered Ayana's petite assistant. 'Amal?'

'Yes, I am here,' the voice replied gently. The smiling face looked down. 'I bring food and water. It is not much, some bread and dates.'

'That's fine. I'm not sure I'm hungry.'

Amal lowered a leather water bottle through a gap in the grating, then the loaf of unleavened bread. 'You must eat. I think you will need your strength.'

'What's going to happen to us?' Brampton asked.

'I really do not know,' Amal replied. 'They are discussing it, but I do not think a decision is made yet.'

She shuffled across the floor to Royce with a second water bottle and loaf. 'What are they discussing?' he asked.

'What is to become of you both, sir. I'm sorry that is all I know.'

'Can you help us?' he pressed.

She was hesitant. 'I don't know. I don't think so. I would like to, but

_'

At that moment the door of the hut scraped open again and Radi returned. 'Hurry up and eat!' he called down to them. 'Chief Mbobo wants to see you. You have fifteen minutes.'

Neither prisoner had much appetite, but both realised that they should eat and drink at each and any opportunity to preserve energy and strength for whenever it might be needed.

They barely had time to wash down the bread and dates with water than it was time to climb up out of their personal pits under the pointing barrels of AK47s being waved by Radi and two more of his Tuareg comrades.

Outside it was now full daylight, the air blissfully cool for the short time before the blistering sun cranked itself into a cloudless sky. There was tension in the air as dozens of the fighters stood around by their vehicles, expectantly smoking and drinking from cans and bottles, eager to learn the fate of the captives.

Royce noticed some of the men nudging each other and nodding towards Brampton. It was unusual to see her untidy, in grubby clothes, torn with buttons missing, her tangled curls in an untamed riot. For her part, she ignored the leering tribesmen. She kept her focus dead ahead, and walked tall with her shoulders back.

Princess Ayana awaited them at the foot of the steps up to the farm bungalow veranda. She'd taken time to freshen up and was immaculately turned out. Royce mused that even a British Army training sergeant would be hard pushed to find anything wrong with the camo fatigues, starched and ironed, and the jaunty tilt of her beret.

She sidled up to her prisoners. 'I don't wish either of you ill,' she said in a low voice. 'Show respect to Chief Mbobo if you know what is good for you. He is very young, just sixteen. He has only just been made tribal chief following the death of his father fighting as a mercenary for Gaddafi. He is looking to prove his power by example. Three fighters who disobeyed him were beheaded yesterday. Another two were disembowelled while still alive. Mbobo making his point.'

'Jesus,' Brampton reacted in a voice that was barely audible.

Ayana added, 'He is still a virgin and everyone knows it, jokes about it. His mother Basira is a marabout, a mystic and soothsayer. Her influence on him is powerful. She is weird, they say born in a cave in desert. Knowing what the tribe says about her son, she is keen for him to prove his manhood to them.'

Brampton frowned. 'What are you saying?'

'For your own safety, be careful.'

'Careful?'

'Go with the flow. And hold your tongue.'

'I don't understand.'

Ayana stepped away.

Two particularly tall and hefty Tuaregs in blue robes stood either side of the farmhouse doorway. The large ceremonial sabres strapped to their hips were intimidating enough, but they also held AK47 shorts at the ready and the expression on the sun-darkened faces suggested they would have no hesitation in using them.

The beaded fly-screen was abruptly brushed aside and Nazal Abu made his dramatic appearance. Gone was the usual Savile Row suit, replaced instead by a flowing *dishdasha* robe of brilliant white. Nazal was back to his roots, looking comfortable and at ease with himself, and wore no headdress to hide his lush white hair and handsome black-dyed goatee beard and eyebrows.

He looked down at Ayana. 'Chief Mbobo is ready. Bring them in.'

26

BIRTH OF THE CALIPHATE

Princess Ayana led the way, mounting the steps to the veranda. Radi poked Brampton in the small of her back with the tip of his AK47. He then swung it around to nudge Royce in the ribs. The two prisoners stepped forward.

The interior of the farmhouse was surprisingly large, an elegant entrance lobby in old colonial style with a number of timber doors running off it, each one edged with an ornate wooden frame. Clusters of senior Tuareg fighters stood around, chatting and smoking, but they fell suddenly silent as the prisoners entered.

Central was an ornately carved chair. Royce corrected himself, hardly a chair. This was more like someone's idea of a throne. Its high back, arms and legs were covered in finely-chiselled leaves and branches and animal heads. A lion here, a monkey there, and an elephant at the very top.

That in itself, under any other circumstances, would have amused him. Eerily less funny was the fact that the young man who sat upon it could hardly be described as anyone's idea of a monarch.

Although to be fair, Royce told himself, the young Tuareg did have a very distinctive look about him. He could have been scarcely sixteen with oily and neatly-barbered black hair. Short and plump, he'd have struggled to find any juvenile whiskers to shave in the mornings. But it was his choice of wardrobe that really set him apart, his rotund frame in a striking white suit of some exotic lightweight material – perhaps mohair or maybe silk – that had an expensive sheen. His shirt was black, setting off a wide pink tie that had been clumsily knotted at the throat. The slightly bizarre ensemble was finished off with a pair of crocodile skin shoes.

Royce glanced sideways at Brampton, knowing full well that his sartorial statement wouldn't be lost on her. But, in fact, she looked so drained and terrified he wondered if she'd actually noticed anything of the sort.

On the wall behind the throne was a stretched camel hide bearing a tribal brand in Arab hieroglyphics, with ornamental scimitar swords mounted on either side of it.

Perched on the arm of the throne, half draping herself over the uncomfortable-looking teenager was a skinny, wizened crone wearing long, ethnic- patterned skirts and a headscarf. It didn't take a genius to work out that this was Basira, the notorious mother of the new chief. She could have been a pantomime invention with a prominent Arabic nose and pointed chin, her skin shrivelled and sun-scorched like burnt toast. Unusually her eyes were the colour of jade, no doubt, he guessed, having helped to give rise to stories about her reputed psychic powers.

Mbobo kept his head bowed, Royce noted, as if unsure of himself, keen to avoid eye contact as the prisoners were marched in. Nazal Abu stood on the other side of the throne, in front of a timber punishment frame from which chains and leather belts with buckles hung ominously.

Behind him stood his bodyguard, the shaven-headed Nubian giant called Azziz. His huge muscles flexed and strained to control the two slavering Tosa Inus that were straining on their short leads.

Nazal jabbed his forefinger at the wooden frame. 'Strap them up,' he ordered Radi, who began his task with obvious relish, calling on another fighter to assist him. Nazal then turned to Princess Ayana.

To Royce's surprise, he spoke in English. 'Can you please explain to the Chief who these people are?'

'Of course.' Ayana stepped forward. 'If it pleases you, Chief Mbobo, the woman is a journalist from London.'

Another Tuareg took it upon himself to act as interpreter for the on-looking tribesmen.

Mbobo put on a grown-up face. 'London…Britain?'

He clearly understood English, and Royce wondered where he'd been educated.

'Quite so, Chief Mbobo.'

'Britain,' Nazal repeated. 'Land of the Unbelievers, launchers of the Crusades against Islam, slayer and torturer of Muslims.'

'A journalist,' Ayana repeated, aware that the two prisoners had now had their hands re-tied behind their backs and were being shackled to the frame. 'The woman Brampton works for a newspaper and a digital TV news channel.'

'And the fellow?' Mbobo asked in a very proper British accent that suggested maybe he'd been educated at some public school there.

Such were the privileges of political elites around the world, that it would not have surprised Royce.

'He is her security adviser, sir, her bodyguard.'

The boy giggled and said something under his breath to his mother in Arabic. He laughed at his own joke and the crone giggled with him, soul mates with her son.

Nazal translated, 'The Chief points out he clearly is not very good at his job. I understand it is said he was a Royal Marine in the Armed Forces. That is, again killing Muslims in both Iraq and Afghanistan in a modern-day Crusade against Muslims -' He let his accusation hang in the air while on-lookers waited for their English translation. A howl of anger and dissent rose and rippled through the gathering.

Royce felt his anger rise. 'I did not kill Muslims,' he said aloud, for the benefit of the mob. 'I protected unarmed Muslims against other Muslims who wanted to kill them -'

'Be quiet,' Nazal hissed. 'You will have a chance to answer questions soon enough.'

Brampton decided to follow Royce's example. 'I am a journalist.' She tried to make direct eye contact with the young leader, but he kept averting his gaze. 'Chief Mbobo, I came to your land here out of curiosity, nothing more. I learned that Nazal Abu had left Libya with remnants of the Khamis Brigade. I wanted to know where he was going and why?'

Mbobo finally allowed himself to look straight at her. 'I do not understand what reason you can have?'

'So that I can write about it in my newspaper – for the people in Britain.' She took a deep breath. 'I am a journalist. It is what I do. I need to tell the world about a brave new young leader and his tribe.'

Basira leaned over to whisper in Mbobo's ear, He listened carefully, then nodded. 'You smart woman, journalist. My friend here Nazal Abu can tell you what he tells me. Then I listen to your opinion.'

Royce didn't miss the quick daggers glare that Nazal threw at Mbobo's mother. But he covered it well, with a slightly fixed smile. 'Very well, Chief, I shall do so reluctantly because we do not know that this woman Brampton and her soldier friend are not really spies for NATO -'

Mbobo waved his protest aside, finding more confidence. 'Please just tell her what you tell me and my mother.'

Nazal took a deep breath. 'I tell Chief Mbobo that Gaddafi is finished. I tell him that there is a plan afoot for change across the entire world of Islam. They – Westerners like this shameful *kafir* reporter – have called the revolution here and in Tunisia, Egypt and Syria as an "Arab Spring". In truth it is students and terrorists with American values who want to abandon Islam for debauchery. But in that evil and turmoil, some like me have seen that there is a new Islamic World Order waiting to emerge.

'But I, Sheikh Nazal Abu, am not alone. To the south of here there is the true Islamic organisation of Boko Haram. I bring a gift of vehicles and weapons for the Chief that he can go to them, join them to form a new power base that – over time – can deliver the whole of western Africa to Allah – including the richest prize of all, Nigeria.'

'Very impressive,' Brampton said. Royce picked up the sarcasm in her voice, but he wasn't sure that Nazal had. 'That is what I want to write about, Chief Mbobo. How you and Mr Nazal are great new arising leaders in Africa. The world should know about you.'

Nazal wasn't very pleased with that. 'The least the world knows about the coming Caliphate, the better. Until it is too late.'

With Brampton's wrists now behind her back and straps around her armpits holding her rigidly in position, she complained, 'I find it hard to talk to you like this, Chief Mbobo. If you cut me down I can interview you properly for world television. Let them know that you are a new force to be reckoned with. I think the world will want to listen.'

Nazal was clearly irritated that the young man was listening to her with increasing interest. 'You realise, sir,' he repeated, 'that these two are most probably NATO spies, sent here to find out what happened to the Khamis Brigade?'

Basira leaned over and muttered in her son's ear. The boy chuckled. 'Mama thinks she does not look like a spy, or a journalist. More like a whore.'

It dawned on Royce that, although she did not speak in English, the marabout understood it well enough.

'If she is a kafir,' Nazal replied smoothly, deciding to change tack, 'then she is a whore. She is for you, Chief Mbobo, under the Sharia law of Islamic State under Allah. She belongs to you, a slave.'

Mbobo looked taken aback. 'For me?' He looked genuinely surprised and not a little frightened. 'Ugh, she is so old!'

Bizarrely, Brampton felt affronted and straightened her back.

Nazal saw his opportunity. 'Forgive me for asking, Chief Mbobo, but you are young. You are not married, have you ever known anyone but young boys?'

Basira gabbled something quickly, laughing oddly as she spoke.

'Women frighten him,' Ayana translated in Brampton's ear. 'He does not know what to do.' Their eyes met momentarily. 'It may not seem like it, Jo, but I am going to try and save your life.'

'What?' The word died on her lips.

'Please come here, sir,' Ayana invited with a broad smile. 'I will show you how to treat a slave, bend her to your will.'

Mbobo hesitated, drew back into his throne.

His mother cackled. 'Go, go!' she urged in Arabic, nudging him forward from his seat.

He rose reluctantly and took Ayana's outstretched hand. She grasped his fingers and pulled him very gently towards her. 'I know this woman, sir. Her name is Jo. She really is a journalist and now she is your slave. That means she is yours. She will do your bidding. Here, let me show you what I mean.'

Ayana took the teenager's pudgy hand and stretched it up towards Bram's chest. The journalist glanced down, realising even she could see the raised impression of her nipples through the thin stuff of her shirt.

'For God's sake, Ayana..!' she began in shock.

She felt the heat of the small, sweat-damp hand soak into her. 'D'you feel that, Chief? Stiffening under your palm?'

A ripple of chatter ran through the gathered tribesmen, some translating for others who spoke no English. There were some chuckles but mostly there was the tense silence of anticipation.

'That is *your* power over her.' She smiled down at him. He looked terrified, but forced a nervous smile. She added, 'Your power as a man over a woman, as a chief over a slave.'

His voice was barely a whisper. 'It gets hard.'

Brampton groaned in silent humiliation, cursing her own body.

'Now,' Ayana sad softly, 'let me guide you.'

She applied gentle pressure downward so his palm left her small right breast and picked up the contour of her belly. 'Under the waistband,' she commanded, her voice barely audible. 'It is your right as her master.'

Another ripple of excited whispers ran through the watching tribesmen.

'No!' Brampton protested.

Ayana's face pushed close into hers. 'Shut up, Jo! If you know what's good for you.'

Brampton shut her eyes as she felt the sweaty little fingers actually against her skin for the first time, their tips rimming the edge of her navel. His forefinger burrowed into it like an exploring little worm. She shut her eyes. Her navel was exceptionally deep. Anoushka had discoved that during their one time encounter. 'It is the gateway to your soul', she had announced erotically. And so it had seemed to her then.

Now was very different. Mbobo's pudgy hand was moving faster now, more confident, crawling across her pubis mound of soft hair.

She didn't follow the popular shaving practise, she wasn't sure why. Was it not wanting to appear like a pubescent girl child, she had asked herself, or some Californian porn starlet? Now, oddly, she wished she had. She didn't want Mbobo to touch her pubic hairs. Did Arab girls shave, she found herself thinking suddenly, and realised that she didn't know.

'Are you there?' Ayana hissed in the boy's ear. 'Have you reached her secret cave?'

Brampton gasped. Somehow she hadn't expected it, his finger on the hood of her clitoris, her moistening and opening to him, unbidden. Oh, shit, no, this couldn't be happening. She tossed her head from side to side, trying to shake her brains, her stupid mind out of her head. From side to side, side to side until it hurt, until her body obeyed her. But all she was aware of, all she could sense was the thud of a pulse between her legs, getting stronger and stronger. It was like a drum. Beating, beating somewhere within her womb.

'Stroke her, stroke her,' Ayana urged, her eyes fixed on Brampton's closed lids and her firmly clamped mouth, aware of the perspiration breaking out on her skin.

That was when the slow handclaps began, the gathered fighters realised what their new young chief was doing, coming of age, becoming a man before their eyes. The chanting rose to set a rhythm that seeped into Brampton's ears, into her head, travelled down her nerve ends, gathering and growing into a tight balloon of tension. The pain of it was unbearable, the shame of it. Knowing that everyone knew, knowing Ayana knew, even Royce knew. The whole fucking world knew, knew how she felt, how a man-child was taking her to the edge of humiliation and shame.

Anoushka was suddenly there, right in front of her. Her eyes penetrating, her voice rich and dark. 'Dah-ling, relax. They are enjoying watching you, so why not enjoy them enjoying you?' The words rang in her ears. Had her friend actually said that once, or was it her imagination? That posh hunt ball, when she'd drunk too much, and couldn't remember the next day. When Anoushka suspected someone had slipped her Rohypnol or some other substance. The Russian voice began to fade…'Humiliation only hurts because you let it, Jo. Embrace it…'

'Hard, hard.' Ayana's voice. 'Now. Hurt her, twist, twist.'

Her skin was taut as the blood pumped into her, threatening to split her open, and the electric wires connected, totally disobeying her. And then it happened.

It was not her scream, it was not her voice. It was some disembodied soul on the other side of the universe. She was aware, vaguely, of the liquid pulsing from her, over the fiddling little fingers. A pain of utter shame drilled into her temples like a physical thing. She jerked her shackled wrists against the straps, desperate, rocking the wooden frame. Her stomach contracted, hard, once, twice, involuntary, then again and again, as if someone was inserting a sparking cattle-prod into her, spasm after spasm. She became aware that her entire body was slick with sweat which was erupting from every pore of her skin, as one helpless orgasm followed another.

'For fuck's sake, Ayana!' Royce hissed, straining against his own shackles. 'Stop the little shit!'

The boy stopped then, a strange and knowing smile on his face, like someone who had made a great discovery. He held his wet hand up in front of his face, sniffed cautiously at it, licked it with his pink little reptilian tongue, then wiped his palm clean over Brampton's left breast. The erect impression of her nipple through the cheesecloth left no doubt in the mind of the audience that their new young chief had conquered the mind and body of his first slave.

The cheering, clapping and whooping of the tribesmen was spontaneous. Brampton's legs gave out on her, leaving her slumped and swinging by the straps, drained and spent.

'Are you alright?' Royce hissed.

She took a deep, breath, steadied herself. 'Christ…That was weird.'

'I'm sorry.'

'Thank God for Annie.'

'Who?'

She shook her head. 'It doesn't matter. Just don't talk about it.'

Ayana intervened. 'Silence, you two.'

Mbobo straightened his back and looked around the clapping audience of his fighters. No longer a child, he was the new warrior king, his confidence suddenly soaring. He turned slowly, with a new-found dignity, and waddled back to his throne.

Nazal Abu clearly saw an opportunity. 'Sir, if I may humbly suggest, you have had the slut for everyone to see. If you and your people decide to join me and Boko Haram and al-Baghdadi in Iraq in the new Caliphate, within its laws you can sell the prisoner. Indeed it will be the will of Allah that you do.'

A couple of the onlookers, who understood English, raised their hands. 'I will bid for the kafir whore!' one called called out in Arabic. 'I will rape her until she bleeds for Islam! I offer one hundred dollar!'

Royce was stunned as he managed to translate, and glanced at

Brampton. Thankfully it seemed her understanding of the language wasn't quite up to that.

'Two hundred dollar,' bid another.

The first bidder returned. 'Three hundred!'

It was then that Ayana intervened. 'I will pay one thousand for her.'

Her counter bidders remained glumly silent.

Nazal glanced sideways at her. 'You? What would you want with her?'

Ayana glared back at him. 'I need a new personal maid.'

'She is a journalist and a spy. I do not trust her.'

'You would have her put to death,' Ayana replied accusingly.

Nazal did not hesitate. 'Indeed I would.'

The old woman whispered in her son's ear again. He listened, thought for a moment, and then announced his decision. 'My mother suggests we let Allah decide on such an important issue. She says let the two women do combat.'

It took a moment for Brampton to absorb what she was hearing. 'Combat?' she echoed.

Mbobo laughed at the expression on her face. 'Like an English dual, but Arabic style. It is a long tradition in my tribe to settle disputes between families.'

Brampton was horrified. 'What sort of combat?'

Ayana leaned towards her, ran her fingertips along her arm. 'To the *death*!' she teased.

Mbobo saw Brampton's reaction and laughed. 'It is not usual... but it *can* happen.' With a new-found confidence, he added loudly so that the whole gathering could hear. 'If Princess Ayana is judged the winner, then my tribe shall go with Sheikh Nazal and join with Boko Haram and al-Baghdadi to create the new Caliphate. Should the whore win, then the portents are bad and I shall not.'

'What will I get out of that?' Brampton asked.

To her he suddenly seemed knowing beyond his years. 'To live, whore. And a story to tell if you are free to go.'

Nazal didn't like that. 'That is not a good idea, Chief –'

The boy raised his hand. 'Silence, Sheikh. My mother has advised me and I have decided what shall happen.'

'When, Chief?' Ayana asked.

'When the sun sets and the dogs bark.'

Sheikh Nazal Abu turned on her, clearly annoyed. 'Take them away, before anyone else has any more stupid ideas.'

'Yubba-dubba-do.' Stefan Seeff lowered his high-powered binoculars. From his concealed position on the plateau escarpment he could just pick out the white Range Rover, shimmering like a beacon in the light of the rising sun.

'What you got?' Parsons asked.

'They're in the village,' Seeff said, 'Or at least the Rover is. Parked outside one of the smaller huts.'

'Ah, yes, I see it!' Yves declared.

All three men were draped in blue and white Tuareg robes that Yves had purchased from a store in the last town they had passed through before crossing the border. His mastery of Arabic – spoken with a distinctive Algerian accent – had taken everyone by surprise, even his journalist client Rachel Starr. With his wild and curly black hair and beard, the Frenchman had transformed himself into a highly-authentic character from Central Casting. He had convincingly purchased a wardrobe of *dishdashas* and a *burqah* for the party from a small clothes shop and then cans of grey and brown paint from a vehicle body shop on the edge of the road running south.

Later, under cover of an abandoned and derelict homestead with a collapsed tin roof, they had hand-painted new camouflage colours on their Range Rover and Starr's BMW. A few disfiguring blows to the bodywork with a spider-wrench finished the effect of two cars that had seen better times. The sand had done the rest on the touch-dry finish.

'Any sign of Bram?' Starr asked anxiously.

Seeff shook his head. 'No, but something's going on at the main building. It could be an old farmhouse, a bungalow. A lot of people, tribesmen milling around outside.'

'Wait!'Yves grunted. 'People are coming out.'

'Got you,' Seeff agreed. 'That's Ayana.'

'You sure?' Starr demanded.

'Can't miss the lungs on that,' he replied emphatically. 'It's Princess Ayana alright.'

'And Nazal Abu behind her,' Yves added. 'Pompous prick.'

'Just look at him,' Seeff agreed. 'Thinks he's the dog's knob -'

'Ah!' Yves interrupted. 'That is them. I see Jo Brampton.'

Seeff gave a low whoop. 'And Rollo just behind her. Thank fuck for that.'

'Not so good, mon ami,' Yves drawled. 'They are both secured, tied. They are prisoners.'

'Got you,' Seeff said, now with less enthusiasm. 'Plasticuffs.'

'What are they?' Starr asked.

'You know, like giant freezer-ties, snap-tight,' he answered irritably.

'Oh, yes, I know.'

'Isn't that Sinbad?' Seeff asked. 'Just coming out the door now. Cool bastard.'

'Did he turn them in?' Parsons asked. 'Or has he just got lucky?'

'Bigger question than that,' Yves said, lowering his binoculars. 'What in the hell can we do now?'

27

ARENA OF ALLAH

She was not wearing any knickers, but no one seemed to notice.

However she was *very* aware of it as she ran through the winding streets of Porthleven. Her legs and feet were bare, but the locals – some who knew her and some who didn't – hardly spared her a glance. She was lucky that the cable-stitch sweater she wore was her father's, which meant it was large and long enough to keep her decent by half an inch. She knew it was his because she could smell him on it, his cologne and his pipe tobacco. But she couldn't remember why she was wearing it.

For that matter she couldn't remember why she was here in the fishing village at all, except that she was running from the wolf.

It had been following her since the moment she'd left her father's house – although it wasn't his house as she remembered it. The wolf had been waiting for her. It had a shaggy off-white coat and emotionless steel blue eyes. It didn't threaten, just watched. Unblinking and unnerving.

She had to find her father, warn him about the wolf. Although she had just left her father at his house, she knew she would only find him on the beach.

And the harder she ran, the more randy she became. What was that all about? She was sure everyone must know, because she could feel the moisture trickling down her thighs. People must see. It was so busy. Locals and tourists were everywhere, even though it was winter. Again, no one seemed to notice her.

She reached the quay where suddenly she was in the middle of an open-air fish market where Cornish fishermen in turbans and prayer-hats were at their stalls. They waved crabs and lobsters in their hands to attract buyers. She turned back. The wolf was still there; she glimpsed him, waiting and watching.

It really scared her, spurred her on and only moments later she was on the beach, like she had been last winter, before Royce was in her life, before Libya.

It was dark. The sand was white with a very hard frost, freezing her bare feet. It was under a full moon and steam was rising faintly off the warmer water as it shrugged onto the shore. There her father stood, staring out to sea, unaware. The wolf was behind him now.

'BRAM!'

She awoke with a start, in darkness, disorientated. Cold. 'Royce?'

'Bram, are you okay?' His voice was disembodied, far away.

Now she knew where she was. Back in her prison pit, in darkness, the only natural light through the rusting metal grille cover that was six feet above her head.

She realised Royce was shouting to her from his adjoining pit.

'I was asleep!' she called back. As she struggled to sit up, she remembered that her hands had been rebound in front of her at the wrists with plastic ties.

'Good. You'll need all your strength against Ayana.'

She shivered. 'God, I'm so cold. I can't believe it, in the desert.'

'Hot air rises,' he reminded. 'Cold air sinks. Have you got any food?'

She felt around her, fingertips in the damp straw. 'Some of that disgusting bread, I think.'

'Eat everything you can,' he advised.

She was surprised he was allowed to talk to her. 'Is that guard still here?'

'Radi went outside a couple of minutes ago. I've tried the grating over this hole. It's padlocked and the hinges are rock solid. Try yours.'

With difficulty, she clambered to her feet and managed to take a couple of steps up the ladder, raising her hands above her head. She grasped the wrought iron and pushed with all her strength. Nothing.

'No go, James,' she reported. 'Sorry.'

'Do you remember any of your unarmed combat training in the army?'

'Not much.'

'You'll need it if you're fighting Ayana. Think hard,' he advised. 'Remember what you can. Go for her eyes if you get the chance. Remember that your elbows are a powerful pair of weapons. And ribs are an easy open target. Not a vital organ, but a displaced rib can be crippling.'

'God, James, she might kill me.'

'Not if you kill her first.'

'It's not funny.'

'I wasn't joking.' He paused and added. 'I get the feeling she'd rather have you as a slave.'

'So do I,' she agreed. 'But I'm worried what else she might be ordered to do. Nazal and Mbobo – not to mention that witch of a mother of his – are pretty sick fucks.'

As she paused, they were both aware of the hut door opening and a shaft of light coming into the interior.

'Hey, Mr James? Are you here?' It was an unmistakable voice.

Royce could hardly believe it. 'Sinbad?'

'Oh, where are you? In this hole in the ground?' His head appeared over the edge, grinning down at him widely. 'I find you!'

There was no time to waste. 'You see the padlock? Is there a key somewhere?'

Sinbad looked around hurriedly. 'I cannot see…Ah! Some hooks by the door…' And he was gone. Seconds later he was back. 'Is this may be – Ah, someone is coming!'

The metal key shone momentarily in the light like a firefly then chimed against the wrought iron. Royce felt it bounce off his shoulder before vanishing into the straw matting.

'Who the fuck are you?' Radi's voice challenged in Arabic. 'What are you doing here?'

'I am sorry,' Sinbad replied apologetically. 'I am new here. I am looking for my friends from Makan Darar.'

'Fighters from there are on the other side of the corral,' Radi snarled. 'Now get out and don't come back.'

Sinbad scurried out of the hut and Radi walked over to Brampton's pit.

He looked down at her pale face staring up at him. 'You have about four hours before the sun goes down. You fight Gaddafi's whore. I put down twenty dollar that you die.' He spat the thick gob of phlegm so that it splatted onto her cheek, just missing her eye. 'You get sleep now, before you sleep forever.'

But now, as she wiped the disgusting goo from her face, sleep was the last thing on her mind. Over and over, she went through everything she had ever known about self-defence training. Desperately she tried recalling the martial arts courses, the instructors, the teachings and philosophies about bending like a willow, not snapping like a twig. Of using your opponent's strength to turn it back against them. All the memories of advice seemed to rush in at once to befuddle her brain.

Once she tried calling out to Royce, but Radi yelled at her to shut up and produced an electric cattle prod, waving it at her and threatening to use it if she spoke again.

She settled into silence and tried to focus on what Royce had spoken to her about unarmed combat on a few occasions, both in recent months and years ago when she'd long-forgotten he'd been the bad ass instructor who had failed her. In her mind she found herself focussing on his mouth, watching and listening to each word in that easy drawl of his, mesmerised.

'It is time!' The harsh voice of Radi cut into her edge-of-sleep drowsiness. 'Stand up!'

With her hands bound in front of her and unable to balance, she climbed awkwardly to her feet.

'Climb ladder!' Radi snapped. 'Quick, quick!'

'Okay, okay,' she answered. 'I can hardly see down here.' She rested her elbows on the stepladder to steady herself and began the climb carefully as her guard opened up the wrought-iron grille.

As she rose up into the hut, she glanced over to the second pit. There was no movement and no sound. Radi urged her towards the door, poking her in the thigh with the battery cattle-prod, the shock jabbing like the sharp stab of a knife.

'Jesus! Radi, do you have to -?' She stopped herself mid-sentence as she saw that he was grinning at her with yellowing teeth, enjoying every moment of her discomfort. She saved her breath and pushed open the door.

The warmth of the spice-laden, late afternoon air wrapped itself around her. A low, bright orange sun shone through the frieze of ragged palm trees, momentarily dazzling her. Her vision rapidly returned, now able to see the fenced corral in front of her. She was taken aback by the numbers of tribesmen, former Gaddafi fighters, Tuaregs, women and children of all ages gathered at the rails. She hadn't been expecting that. As the crowd realised that this was the female kafir combatant, the shouts of recognition, abuse and jeering rose. There was also some slow, hostile hand-clapping.

In that instant she saw in her head what they saw. A tanned white woman with long hair that was a wild black tangle of dirty curls, she stood tall with straight shoulders. She was bare-footed wearing thin, white linen trousers and sweat-stained matching shirt. A mess.

On the far side of the corral, by the farmhouse, was her opponent. Taller, black and proud was the magnificent warrior princess, Ayana. She stood in combat boots and wore the immaculate official fatigues of the Gaddafi Bodyguard. Her hair was scooped back into a ponytail that was held in place by a length of camouflage scrim.

Two huge vultures suddenly appeared out of the blinding sun, swooping on the summer thermals overheard, screeching, searching for some prey. It occurred to Brampton that if they came back in half-an-hour they might find a corpse that would satisfy their ravenous appetites for a week. Hers.

Mbobo's ornate wooden throne had been brought out of the bungalow and placed on the veranda. He sat there with his mother, who was again perched at his side, cackling and whispering in his ear. Next to him, stood Sheikh Nazal Abu, now in his traditional Qatari robes and head-dress. On the ground at the edge of the corral stood three people who Brampton realised she knew all too well.

The first were their Libyan rebel volunteers Leon and Ramzi, both blindfolded and both visibly trembling. Beside them was a slight, petite figure in a full, pale blue bourka that Brampton just knew was Tabina, the schoolgirl sex slave that months' ago she had so rashly promised to rescue. Those remembered words ringing in her head, sounded pretty hollow now. From that distance Brampton could not see the girl's eyes, but the defeated stance of her body language told the journalist all she needed to know. Standing a respectful couple of paces behind her was another, taller woman in black, waiting in attendance.

Nazal Abu stepped forward and raised both his hands. 'Chief Mbobo,' he pronounced in Arabic, 'his dear mother and tribal elders, and my own loyal warriors from Libya, I have some announcements to make.

'Great Chief Mbobo here made his decision this afternoon and is to offer the gift of his own and our loyal Libyan forces to Boko Haram in the south in a new partnership. This will consolidate the western and southern boundaries of the new Great Caliphate – the Muslim empire that the Prophet foresaw and promised us all those centuries ago. It will immediately bring much needed armour, heavy arms and battle experience to the fight.'

Nazal paused and cast his glance towards the diminutive figure of Tabina. 'In thanks and brotherhood, I offer my personal gift to Chief Mbobo of his first wife, who has been fully trained to serve her husband as he would wish.'

The faintest whimper of despair floated on the air, Brampton just catching it as Nazal Abu continued, 'I next bring to you a warning. What happens to those of you who do not follow the true faith of Allah or may be considering another path. If you are not with us, you are against us. These two fought for the rebels in Misrata, but in allegiance *against* the Muslim Brotherhood. Now they are assisting our infidel prisoners. This is the price they shall pay.' He lifted a hand in signal.

Brampton had not noticed the man in black. It was Nazal's bodyguard and dog-handler, the man alled Azziz. He was very tall and very broad. Black jumpsuit, black boots, black headband with white Arabic script imprinted on it. His beard, too, was black and bushy with flecks of white. But it was his eyes, she noticed most, also black but with the odd metallic gleam of ball-bearings that almost gave the impression that he was blind.

'Azziz,' Ayana whispered in her ear. 'The sheikh's right hand man and executioner. Do not ever cross him.'

Brampton swallowed hard. 'I've no intention,' she murmured.

It was then that she recognised one of the ornamental scimitars that she had seen earlier on the wall behind Mbobo's throne; it was now in the grip of Azziz's huge fist, held loosely by his side.

Two of Nazal's fighters stepped forward and pushed Leon and Ramzi in front of Azziz, kicking them in the back of their legs so that they fell to their knees. Both men had the blindfolds ripped from them. They glanced around, bewildered and scared.

'Look straight ahead!' Azziz shouted. 'Heads down!'

As they obeyed, the man swung up the scimitar that had been half-hidden at his side. Momentarily its burnished steel glinted in the light of the sinking sun. The twin handed power of its descent made a faint swishing noise as it displaced the hot desert air and sliced through the fragile bone and meat of Ramzi's neck.

The head thudded hard into the ground in front of its body. So quick, the skull so obscenely heavy that it made Brampton gasp with shock.

Leon, too, was startled. He turned his head only for his gaze to meet the blade coming down for the second time, on him. But it messed up the clean blow, the steel audibly hitting bone in a sickening noise as his body pitched forward. It took two more blows before the job was done. The detached head rolled away like an abandoned football, its eyes still unnervingly open.

Azziz threw the scimitar aside, reached forward, collected the runaway head and lifted the two grotesque trophies high by their hair, one in each huge fist.

The roar of approval from the onlookers gathered around the corral was deafening. 'ALLAH AKBAH!, ALLAH AKBA! ALLAH AKHBAR..!' Amongst the crowd, the blood lust was up and rising.

Nazal lifted his arms high and, by order of his unspoken command, silence fell immediately over the excited gathering.

'Finally,' he announced, 'we bring you an entertainment by the grace of Allah. Our captured *kafir* journalist and spy – whose newspaper in the West writes lies about all Muslims – is to fight for her very life before you now. She fights against my personal bodyguard and warrior, Princess Ayana of Somalia.

'Ayana may kill the woman or keep her as her slave and plaything -' He chuckled. 'I am not sure what would be worse for her.

'In the unlikely event that the Westerner wins – at the suggestion of Basira, beloved mother of your chief – she will be given two water-skins and allowed to leave in any direction that she wants at sunset. At dawn my attack dogs Pharaoh and Cerberus will be set after her...So meanwhile, let their battle commence!'

Brampton struggled to take in his words, their meaning. So all to play for, she thought grimly, her mind reeling. She still didn't really know what to expect, as Radi grabbed her arm roughly and pulled her towards the southern side of the corral.

Ayana was making her way towards the northern fence in the company of Amal, the younger guard who had always seemed so pleasant and cheerful.

It struck Brampton that if she played this right, she might at least escape with her life. If Ayana had to kill her to defeat her, then she was going to be in no position to enjoy her prize as a sex-slave or whatever else she had in mind, was she? But by the same token, Ayana was going to make bloody sure she won decisively and quickly. Or so she thought. Brampton was determined she was going to be no walkover. Besides, if she did lose there was no guarantee that some bastard like Nazal or Mbobo – or his sick fuck of a mother – might not intervene and decide another beheading might be a more appropriate end to proceedings.

As these conflicting thoughts careered through Brampton's brain, she gradually became aware that Radi was talking to her, giving her instructions. 'Listen, infidel bitch, Ayana is going to kill you. Spear you like a pig.' He handed her a long-handled lance with a wide, flat blade, its edges ground to a razor thinness that glinted wickedly in the dying sunlight. For the first time since she'd met him, Radi grinned. 'Unless you spear her first.'

She weighed the weapon in her hand. It was hand-crafted, she could see the individual whittling mark of the knife; it was surprisingly light and beautifully balanced.

'And this,' he added, thrusting the curve-bladed scimitar at her. She recognised it as one of the pair that had been on the wall behind Mbobo's throne earlier in the day. Some tribal relics, she guessed. She took it in her other hand. Unlike the spear, it felt heavy and awkward in her grasp.

'It has this with belt,' Radi added.

She noticed that he was actually staring at her chest as he spoke, and she guessed he was looking at the impression of her nipples. Momentarily her anger flared…but then an inner calmness washed over her. What the hell, he was little more than a teenager. Had probably never even seen a naked woman, even in a man's magazine or whatever they got out here in the desert. She straightened her back, perversely almost proud that she could prove so distracting to him.

'I will fight her for you,' she decided to say aloud. God, she thought even as the words escaped her mouth, where the hell did that come from?

He blinked and stared at her.

'I shall be your champion infidel whore,' she added, grinning at him defiantly.

Confused at her sarcasm, his stern face crumpled into an uncertain half-smile. 'Yes, you fight. Or you die.'

She lifted her arms. 'Fix the belt for me please.'

He regarded her oddly before moving in, with arms encircling her waist to fasten the belt, suddenly and obviously nervous that his hands might touch her body. She had to smile at that, but she now had other more important things on her mind.

The sunset was dimming fast and, as the twilight rapidly fell, hanging tar and camel dung-beacons that she hadn't previously noticed, were being lit at intervals around the edge of the corral.

The fitful flames cast long tongues of light and shadow lapping across the baked sand. At the far fence she could see Ayana surrounded by a few Amazon acolytes, including the diminutive Amal. She had stripped down to a green cutaway military vest which she wore with her regulation sage and black DPM trousers and combat boots. Brampton looked down. She was barefoot.

On the other side, Amal handed Ayana her own spear and scimitar – then something else. It was a length of netting.

Brampton was disconcerted. 'What the hell?' she breathed. Fishing net? She knew immediately, remembering something similar she'd seen in the movies long ago. Was it Spartacus, Gladiator, Ben Hur? Did it matter?

'Do I get a net?' she demanded of Radi.

The man shook his head and shrugged. 'I do not have.'

She noticed the combat knife on his belt and nodded towards it. 'Give me that.'

Taken aback, he shook his head again. 'It is not allowed.'

'Give me the fucking knife,' she demanded, gripping the haft of the scimitar on her hip, 'before I cut your shitting head off!'

He stepped back in shock at the vehemence of her snarl. Unsure, he drew it from its scabbard and handed it to her, blade first. 'Be careful. It very sharp.'

She glanced at him, and wondered if he realised just how stupid his words and actions were? Her skin touched his as she slid her hand over his fist to take the knife by its carbon handle. He finally looked, for a second, into her eyes, His fingers relaxed and she took the weapon. Deftly, she dropped it into the leg pocket of her thin linen cargo pants. Hopefully the knife's own weight wouldn't cut itself out through the material.

Just then a rapid burst of gunfire reverberated around the flame-lit arena. A gasp of consternation rose momentarily from the crowd until it was realised that someone had ordered that the giant water tank be holed. Its contents gushed out, in a waterfall that gulped its way to emptying all over the sand of the corral.

Royce's face flashed in Brampton's mind, hearing his dry laugh. 'Health and bloody safety at a time like this.' The scarce rainwater ebbed like a tide across the surface of the arena, turning the sand into a soft and sticky mud. Also making it dangerously slippery.

She looked around warily, not knowing what would happen next. Radi disappeared and Ayana's acolytes withdrew, scrambling between the eucalyptus bars of the opposite fence.

There was no starting shot, no gong or trumpet. Now it was just her and Ayana, the woman's tall, muscular frame slightly hunched, the light from the beacons glinting on her skin as she edged forward.

A hush of anticipation fell over the crowd. Brampton glanced to her right. Chief Mbobo was watching from his throne, his mother still perched by his side. Nazal Abu observed impassively, Brampton now knowing that his perverted mind would enjoy any indignity or horror that she or Ayana endured. Beside him stood a grim-faced executioner Azziz, now in control of his two Tosa Inu dogs that were straining and slobbering at the leash, clearly sensing sport was soon to be had.

It was then that Princess Ayana made her move.

28

INTO THE CRUCIBLE

They set off from the rocky plateau as the sun sunk into a sea of molten gold. Tension in the two vehicles was high as one followed the other, picking their way down the loose shale ridge to the desert floor. It formed a natural track caused by erosion over millennia. It may have been useful for mountain goats, but not much else. On one side the sheer drop fell away sharply into a two hundred foot void, and it was as though some prehistoric beast had taken bites out of the narrow ledge.

Seeff was in his element at the wheel of the leading Range Rover, humming inanely as he regularly changed gear; sitting beside him, Parsons had his eyes firmly shut. But in the rear, the Tasmanian-born Australian was unaware of the minute-by-minute danger as he swore and cursed at the atmospheric interference on their long-range radio as he tried to raise E Squadron HQ back in Libya.

In the following BMW, driver Yves and his boss Rachel Starr had a slightly less stressful time. He, in particular, could see each manoeuvre and decision that Seeff made. He could then follow him exactly or make an adjustment of his own to gear selection, speed or steering.

After a final bump-and-jar crossing of the screed at the bottom of the plateau that tested the suspension to the point of near destruction, the Range Rover finally reached the level desert. It now stretched out before them towards the distant oasis. The flat and featureless terrain offered up an achingly open sky that appeared to go on for eternity. It was a vast indigo dome, fading away under the creep of darkness as nearer or larger stars made their first shy appearance of the night. Not for the first time, Seeff had one of his rare private moments of wonder when he recalled it being explained at school how sometimes he was looking at stars that had died hundreds of years before. He was witnessing light that was still travelling from them, they were that far away. Still he found it hard getting his head around that one.

He hated air-con – even when it worked – and had all the windows open. The evening air that rushed in was still warm and cloying, but just cooler enough to be comfortable, allowing for mild exertion without sweating. It carried with it the sweet, faintly aromatic slipstream of the desert.

Seeff kept his headlights off. There was just enough ambient light to allow him to avoid the occasional rocky outcrop and pick up the outline of the main track into the settlement. Its presence ahead of them was marked by a faint halo of flickering light. Strange, Seeff thought, finding himself reminded of tribal torch-lit ceremonies back home in his native South Africa.

He slipped down a gear and cruised to a halt. The nearest crude buildings were now only a couple of hundred metres distant, their inky outlines clearly defined along with the shaggy-headed palm trees. He strained to hear something. It was the dying tones of a hypnotic call to prayers. The voice was scratchy, played on some old tape-recorder from another era.

As that noise died away, it was replaced by another. It sounded like a crowd.

'Football,' Parsons said, now with his eyes open and feeling wide awake. 'Could be Millwall at home.'

'Some excitement,' Seeff agreed. He declutched, shifted into gear and moved on.

They edged slowly into the outskirts of the settlements. There were very few substantial structures of breezeblock with corrugated iron roofs. Most were of mud-brick or rattan-wall , or else made of refugee plastic and sacking materials. The noise of cheering and jeering grew louder as they approached. Amazingly there was no one about.

Suddenly Tremain announced, 'I'm through! I've picked up HQ!'

Seeff hit the brakes. In the back, Tremain began his spiel, 'Hello, Tango Sierra Five to X-ray, do you read me..?'

Contact with base was essential, so Seeff curbed in his natural impatience and took in his surroundings. One thing that he had already considered was any exit plan from this settlement. Would they be lucky enough to find Royce and Brampton? What condition would they be in? Would they be bringing back colleagues or corpses? Or injured? And was Sinbad still with them? Would there be others?

These considerations were tumbling through his mind when he saw the ancient French army 4 x 4 truck. He was sure it dated back to the 50s. It was parked in a narrow alley between two ramshackle sheds.

He pulled over and the BMW stopped behind him. There appeared to be no one around in the dimming twilight.

'Let me take a look at this,' he said to Parsons and opened the driver's door. Yves had also seen the lorry and climbed out to join him.

'Mon Dieu,' the Frenchman observed. 'An old Berliet 380. Two-door version. Takes me back. Not seen one of them in a while.'

The design lines of its cab were modern and minimalist, but now somewhat spoiled by sun-faded paintwork, a cracked windscreen and one gaping headlamp socket like a missing eye. Its rear cargo body sported a khaki tarpaulin cover that had seen better days.

Seeff sprang on the foothold and tested the handle. The door was unlocked and opened stiffly. He scrambled in. 'Yubba, dubbah, doo!' he declared triumphantly. 'Ignition keys are in.'

He started the engine. It spluttered and coughed a couple of times, then fired. The sound was reasonable. 'Fuel three-quarters full,' he noted and then switched off. 'Surprised they left the keys in.'

'Saves losing them,' Yves observed. 'And I doubt many of these nomad fuckwits can ride a camel, let alone drive. We should take the keys. Might need the extra capacity.'

'My thoughts exactly,' the South African agreed, extracting the keys and jumping back down. 'Or stop them from following us.'

'Good point.'

He turned and peered through the mini-rear window of the cab to see what was in the cargo hold. After a low whistle, he said, 'Looks like a GPMG and ammo belt. Not British.'

'What?' Yves was surprised and evidently overjoyed. He ran along to the tailgate. The heavy general-purpose machine gun was mounted on a tripod in the back with a belt-feed of ammunition and ready to go. 'A PKM,' he confirmed with a grin, happy at the prospects of some serious kit in their arsenal.

He and Seeff nodded, both satisfied with their find.

The two men returned to their vehicles. Seeff opened the driver's door of the Range Rover and slipped in.

'…You're fading,' Tremain was saying, talking on the long-range radio in the back. 'Can you get in touch with the French in Niger? Do you read..? – Oh, for fuck's sake! I finally get through and it's some fuckwit from Brum, I can't understand a fuckin' word he says. And he can't understand me.'

'I always wonder how the hell the Americans manage,' Parsons added. 'Never could understand a word in them Vietnam War movies or their recent War on Terror crap.'

Tremain ignored that. 'I've given the co-ordinates for this place,' he announced. 'Says they'll get back with confirmation – or any other news. I'm guessing any messages will go the scenic route through NATO.'

'Can't do more than your best, bud,' Parsons soothed, then turned to Seeff. 'What's with the truck?'

The South African held up the keys. 'Extra capacity if we need it. And an HMG in the back. Might come in handy.'

'I'm not fucking Lawrence of Arabia, Stefan,' he protested. 'I'm not looking to start a war.'

Seeff turned on the engine of the Range Rover. 'You might want to stop one from starting.'

It was barely another fifty metres to what appeared to be the main part of the settlement that, in addition to primitive accommodation, was mostly made up of basic livestock shelters to protect animals from the sun. But, now they were able to confirm what they suspected through their distant surveillance from the plateau.

The animals in these rows and rows of auction stalls were made of steel, not flesh and blood: dozens and dozens of armoured cars, personnel carriers and armed pick-ups hidden from view. All carried the livery of the Libyan 32nd Brigade.

At the rear of the stalls – in readiness for a quick getaway – the Range Rover and the BMW were reversed in alongside the tatty rows of parked tribal vehicles. Each in the team took a sub machine-gun short and an automatic, which they hid beneath their Arab robes. The exception was Rachel Starr, who carried just a pistol stuffed in the waistband of her jeans, which she wore beneath her suffocating black bourka.

As the crew of the Range Rover met with her in front of the two cars, a figure in black battle fatigues detached itself from the shadows and ambled towards them.

Seeff spotted the armed Libyan fighter first. 'Trouble,' he hissed as the man approached slowly. Fuck, he thought, where was Yves when you wanted him, their only really fluent Arabic speaker?

'You come to see the fun?' the Libyan look-out began in Arabic, his sub machine-gun hanging loosely on a sling in front of him. 'It has begun.'

'Allah akbur!' Parsons offered, doing his best. The accent was atrocious.

The Libyan guard looked bemused. 'You are from around here?' He tilted his head, trying to get a better view of Parsons' face, which was partly hidden by the drape of his head-dress.

'What do you want?' The new voice in Arabic was stern and demanding.

Yves really looked the part, appearing behind the Libyan guard. 'Oh, what? Ah, that accent?'

'I am from Algeria,' Yves said.

'Ah,' the Libyan turned and said slowly, 'perhaps that explains it...' But his tone and his action suggested that he was rapidly becoming suspicious of these new-arrivals. Both hands grasped his SMG and he attempted to swing it up into the firing-position. That was when Seeff swooped in from behind the man.

In one deft movement he jerked the head back hard with his left forearm, smothering the man's mouth and nose, exposing his throat. With his right, Seeff stabbed his combat knife into the side of the man's neck as far as it would go. He then pushed the blade forward to take out the trachea. It was that quick.

Seeff continued to hold the look-out tight as blood spurted down the front of his combat shirt. The dying man convulsed violently for a second or two, before falling suddenly still. His body twitched spookily a couple of times.

'Halal,' Seeff said flatly. He let the body drop in a heap to the ground, then stooped and wiped the blade of his knife clean on the sleeve of the corpse.

'For God's sake, Stefan,' Parsons protested, 'was that really necessary?'

'I think so.'

Parsons grunted irritably. 'We need to get rid of the body.'

Without emotion, Yves jabbed his thumb in the direction of a pile of rubbish that had collected behind one of the stalls, mostly cardboard boxes, crates and an old mattress.

Seeff nodded. Kicking aside the look-out's sub machine-gun, he lifted the body beneath its armpits while Yves clasped the ankles. Together they carried it to its temporary resting place, leaving a glistening crimson trail in its wake. They dumped it in the pile and covered it with the mattress.

They returned to the others, gathered in front of their two vehicles. Seeff picked up the dead man's sub machine-gun and inspected it with an expression of disgust. 'Filthy. More danger to him that anyone he shoots.' He pulled out the magazine and tossed the weapon itself through the rear open window of the Range Rover.

A roar of excited voices went up from beyond the stalls.

'Someone's scored a goal,' Seeff mused.

Starr turned her head. 'What the hell *is* going on over there?'

Yves squinted toward the flickering light of the corral. 'Time we find out.'

'What do we do next?' Parsons asked.

Seeff wasn't used to making all the decisions. He tried to think what Royce would have said, had he been in their position. First, secure base and escape route.

He said decisively, 'I think Iain should stay with our main vehicle, the Rover, to protect it and maintain communication with our people in Libya. Rachel stays with him.'

'I wanna come with you guys,' the journalist protested.

Seeff shook his head. 'Absolutely not. If anything goes wrong, you can use a gun or drive either vehicle. No damn argument, okay?'

Her face paled at the vehemence of his response. 'Okay, keep your Y-fronts on.'

'The remaining three of us stick together,' Seeff added. 'We're all armed, so we can cover each other, but keep your weapons well out of sight. Walk and act as if we have every right to be here. Let Yves do the talking. If any of us get separated, we use our short-range radios.'

'Agreed,' Parsons concluded. 'What actually happens, depends on what we find.'

Starr touched his arm. 'I just hope they're all okay, that we find them alive.'

The man nodded. 'So do I.'

Yves said impatiently, 'Let's go.'

Princess Ayana edged forward. It was almost dark now, the arena of the fenced corral lit only by the fitful light of the burning beacons that cast long shadows over the wet sand. She was stood slightly hunched, her spear held prone in a double-handed grasp, the small net cast over her shoulder.

Brampton stood her ground, bouncing lightly on her bare toes. Words of instruction that Royce had once given her echoed in her head. *Use your opponent's strengths against them.* Ayana wore army fatigue trousers and combat boots. She, on the other hand, was wearing skimpy light linen and no shoes. She would use agility and speed, she decided.

Ayana was skirting cautiously around her. Bram turned on the balls of her feet, keeping the encircling Ayana fully in her line-of-vision at all times. Light played on the blade of Ayana's spear where the steel had been hammered and ground to a wafer thin edge. She winced at the thought of it slicing into flesh, especially hers. They had danced a full three sixty degrees. Then, without warning, Ayana lunged.

Although she'd been expecting it, waiting for it, Brampton's reaction was slow. Ayana moved with the speed and power of an athlete. Brampton danced away, but too late. The point of the spear must have been aimed at her navel. In fact it cut through the thin stuff of her shirt, its razor blade burning the thin tyre of flesh above her waistband. Blood exploded in a tiny starburst on the linen material.

The first strike wasn't missed by the crowd who were watching intently. They gasped in unison. Then a cry went up and obscenities were yelled in Arabic. Their communal blood lust was rising to a new level.

Brampton spun away in a pirouette that would have made Anoushka proud of her. Ayana moved heavily in an attempt to follow her, hampered by the weight of her boots. Now Brampton had the advantage, faced with Ayana's body offered in unprotected profile. Flickering light played on the silky black skin of the offered ribcage as her top rode up. A successful strike would slice into her opponent's kidney, she knew. Was that why she hesitated for a split second too long? She thrust the spear with all the speed and energy she could muster.

Ayana stumbled backward but the blade of Brampton's spear kept coming. It wasn't as honed as her own blade and it just grazed the skin rather than pierced it. Nevertheless, blood trickled as a dark crimson stain on the ebony flesh. Another howl of approval went up from the onlookers.

It was then, while Brampton's reach was fully extended and her spear on the ground, that Ayana made her move. She snatched the net from her shoulder and flung it in the air. Momentarily it blossomed, opening like a flower. Brampton was crouched on one knee, retrieving her spear. The net fell on her.

'Oh, fuck!' she cursed. The one thing she had imagined, had feared, was actually happening.

It closed in all around her as Ayana yanked the net hard and tight. It closed on Brampton's arms, pinning them to her sides. It forced her head down. If she chose, at any moment now, Ayana could stab the helpless bundle with her spear or do something unspeakable with the scimitar at her side.

Brampton realised at this second that she really was fighting for her life. She scrabbled for the leg pocket of her cargo pants, her fingers finding… nothing. Oh shit, had Radi's combat knife fallen out? In terror she looked around her on the ground. She could see nothing, but her eyes were watering with grit and smoke from the beacons, unable to focus.

Then her fingertips touched the carbon haft of the knife. Thank fuck! she thought savagely and grasped it with demonic determination. She lashed out like a wild thing. There was no forethought or precision to it. She just sliced and hacked, hacked and sliced wherever she felt the netting cords. A couple of times she felt resistance, knew she'd hit Ayana, but didn't stop. She was in a frenzy to escape, a fly trapped in a spider's web.

All of a sudden she was free. As she gasped, filling her lungs with air, she saw that Ayana had stepped back. She, too, was winded, at bay. Slightly crouched, she was breathing heavily with blood dripping like dew from a variety of light stab wounds, her thighs, her belly and her breasts. There was even a small incision on her right cheek. She wiped it with the back of her hand, tasted the stuff with her tongue. Blood and damp sand stuck to her face like war-paint.

It was then that Brampton saw that Ayana's sword lay abandoned in the mud. She realised it was now or never. Without pausing for thought she reached for her scimitar with her free left hand and drew it from the scabbard. It was heavy and unwieldy, but she persevered. She lifted it high and brought it down with as much force as she could, slicing the shaft of Ayana's spear just below the neck of the blade. It went clean through.

If Brampton thought she had gained the upper hand, she was in for a sudden and unexpected surprise.

It occurred to her that Nazal Abu might have also seen the result of the gladiatorial combat going the wrong way. Perhaps it was just tribal tradition or the bright idea of Mbobo's old crone of a mother, but at that moment a skinny old man in a ragged turban and short robes scurried into the arena. He carried a hessian sack that contained something that was visibly moving.

Momentarily both women were distracted. The bare-footed man pranced around them, opening up his bag of treasures and spilling the wriggling serpents onto the sand just a few feet away from them.

'For the sake of Allah!' Ayana screamed, stepping back. Adding in Arabic, 'The accursed snake-man.'

29

DOGS OF DEATH

As soon as he heard Brampton leave the shack with the guard Radi, Royce had got to work in earnest. He'd begun formulating a plan from almost the moment the two of them had been designated their separate cell pits. With his hands bound by strong plastic freezer ties in front of him, he'd surreptitiously begun unpicking the laces from his boots in the darkness. He had to be cautious because the slightest movement rustled the dry straw, and at any moment Radi could have peered over the edge and shone down a torch.

Now that he was alone Royce was able to finish the task in double quick time and tie the two long laces together at both ends to form a large loop, the top end passing over the plastic tie. He leaned his back against the earthen wall of the pit and placed the other end of the lace loop around his boots. By drawing his fists up and down, the laces would become like a very blunt band-saw, eating away at the plastic tie. It was a technique that he'd been shown on an Escape and Evasion course once. He realised it was going to be a long and painful process, but at least he knew that it would work – eventually.

Soon his biceps and triceps were starting to burn. Although fit he was hardly in peak condition and hadn't seen the inside of a gym since he'd left England. But concentration on the muscular pain was blunted by his focus on what might be happening to Brampton outside. There were howls of excitement and whoops of approval coming spasmodically from a crowd of spectators. That was followed by a united gasp of shock that sent a chill down his spine. He wasn't sure why, but there was something about the abrupt silence that was profoundly disturbing.

Still he kept sawing. Sawing, sawing, sawing. He couldn't bear to even squint to see what progress his laces were making in wearing through the plastic. At this rate it would take forever. Then, suddenly, it happened when he least expected it. He fell back, laughing, remembering the old Chinese proverb, *The drip wears the stone*. The relentless sawing motion of the tough laces had worn through the plastic with a combination of friction, wear and heat.

He'd lost count of the time, but now vigorously rubbed the circulation back into his wrists. Once the sensation returned, he felt about in the straw for the padlock key that Sinbad had thrown down to him earlier. It took longer than he'd anticipated to actually locate it. Once he had it, he mounted the step-ladder and thrust his hand through the iron grille lid to his pit. It was an awkward manoeuvre to twist his hand to insert the key. His muscles were burning and his fingers had grown numb with temporary peripheral neuropathy. He could not believe it when the key fell out of his hand. It clinked musically on the earthen floor. He climbed higher up the steps until his face pressed hard against the metal as he stretched out his hand as far as it would go. The key remained tantalisingly out of reach.

That was when he heard the noise, from somewhere in the shed above him. But what was it? Who was there? It sounded like crackling plastic. Then there was the noise of breaking crockery – followed by a curse in Arabic?

Did he recognise that voice? 'Sinbad?'

'SSSHH, BOSS!'

Royce waited impatiently in silence for what seemed an eternity. In fact it was scarcely a minute before Sinbad's grinning face appeared above him. 'Sorry, I so long, boss. That bloody guard Radi is outside your front door.'

'The key,' Royce said, pointing at the floor. 'Can you open the padlock?'

Sinbad obeyed, turned the key and lifted the metal lid to the pit. Royce sprang out and looked around him. He saw where the clear polythene had been ripped from the window aperture and the remains of the earthenware pot beneath it. Looking the other way, he registered the second empty pit where Brampton had been held.

'Has the fight started yet?' he asked as he glanced around the stacks of bunk beds, realising he couldn't wander outside in western clothes.

Sinbad wore a fixed smile on his face, not wanting to give bad news. 'Not yet, boss. Them bastards just execute our friends.'

It took a second for the words to sink in. Royce stared at him. 'What?'

'Them execute Ramzi and Leon.' Sinbad motioned with a flat hand. 'Chop, chop.'

'Oh, Christ, I don't believe it.' Royce looked away, sickened. 'Poor bastards. I wasn't expecting that.'

'I do not know why they do that,' Sinbad muttered. 'I think it is to rule by fear.'

'That's usually how it works,' Royce agreed, still finding it hard to assimilate that it had actually happened, that he would never see the two cheery youngsters again.

It was then that he spotted a grubby brown cotton robe hanging from a clothes hook. He snatched it up, slipping his arms into the baggy sleeves. It stank of body odour, which he fought to ignore. Then he rapidly turned his own *shamag*, which he often used as a scarf with his travel vest, into a head-dress with its cotton cord to fix it in place. The transformation took only seconds but, with the addition of his tanned skin and several days' growth of beard, it looked convincing enough.

Sinbad was becoming anxious. 'We must go now,' he said, moving back towards the window where he had broken in. 'I think it is not good for Miss Jo, boss. I think she will be in big trouble.'

'Back out the window?' Royce asked.

'Yes, boss. Quickly, please.'

Brampton stared in disbelief at the skinny snake-man as he danced around carrying the sack at arm's length.

'Shit!' she said aloud. This was someone's idea of a joke. The contest had become too boring or predictable for some sicko. Her guess it was Ayana's lover, who appeared to have abandoned her for his new cause. From what she had learned, this would be typical of Nazal Abu. Upping the ante, giving his new boy-king friend a taste of adult pleasures to come. Saying how this should liven things up a bit.

Now she wished she hadn't had the bright idea of not wearing shoes or boots. Desperately she tried to remember what Royce had said about snakes. He'd given one of his interminable safety briefings way back when she'd first met him in Tripoli. 'The only venomous snakes likely to be encountered in the dunes,' he had said. What was it Rachel had jokingly called them? Horny bastards?

She stared at the wriggling knot as they untied themselves. Two types, she thought. Three of them seemed to be the same, they moved away from the dropped sack in a quick crab-like motion. Like American sidewinders, she remembered suddenly, twelve or thirteen different toxins in their venom. Very painful bites, but not necessarily lethal to humans. It finally came to her. Horned vipers, that was it. And now she could actually see the tiny but distinctive fleshy horn-like feature above each eye.

As the snake-man withdrew, she noticed that Ayana had frozen, mesmerised by the other two snakes. They were smaller, barely two feet long, but somehow scarier than the others. It was the noise they made, angrily rasping their scales together, and their short, darting movements, seemingly irritated and unpredictable. That sound? Like a wood saw. Was it Saw Scaled snakes? Among the most dangerous in the world.

Brampton made a snap decision. She lunged with her spear, scooping the blade under one of the serpents and flicking it up in the air towards Ayana. The princess screamed aloud and jumped back. Spiralling in mid-air, the creature tried to sink its fangs into her, but just bit onto the hot night air. It brushed against the perspiring ebony skin before hitting the ground with a thud. Brampton had missed her target by a fraction of an inch.

She decided she had one more chance. Again she scooped the blade under the second rasping viper and tossed it upward. But Ayana was ready this time, and jumped back. With her spear now rendered useless, she drew the scimitar from its scabbard. Overcoming her obvious phobia, she lunged madly at the two snakes as they started moving towards her with deadly intent.

In a frenzy she bladed the head off each snake in rapid succession, their separated bodies twitching and turning like live ropes as their neuro systems kept them sparking with redundant life.

Brampton felt the bile rise in her stomach, then remembered the other snakes. She turned quickly in panic. Were they creeping up behind her? Was she about to step on one?

She saw them with a sense of blessed relief. The horny bastards were in no mood for a fight, the three of them wriggling away to safety and darkness at the edges of the corral. Their owner scampered after them with his sack, to try and save them for another day and another arena where they might fare better.

Brampton swung round with her spear to confront Ayana, who was approaching cautiously with the scimitar held loosely in her right hand. The journalist lifted the tip of her blade, holding it steady and pointing directly at Ayana's abdomen.

'If we go on like this, Jo,' Ayana said. 'One of us will get killed or maimed.'

Brampton was confused. 'What are you suggesting?'

'That you surrender now.'

'Piss off!'

Ayana smiled thinly. 'That we discard the weapons. And wrestle to surrender. The men won't care if one of us is killed, we're just sport to them. Nazal Abu is a bastard.'

'You've changed your tune.'

'No. He was always a bastard, but he was *my* bastard. Now, he doesn't care, his mind is on bigger things, bigger fantasies to rule the world with al-Baghdadi.'

Thoughts were racing through Brampton's mind, but in the heat of the moment, with her adrenalin pumping, it was hard to reason and think straight. Only one of those thoughts kept shouting at her through her confusion, and that was to get rid of the weaponry that could kill or cut.

'Okay,' she agreed. 'Together?'

Royce jumped down from the window to land in the narrow alleyway between the two huts.

Sinbad was waiting anxiously. 'You okay, boss?' He gestured to the front of the building to the illuminated quadrangle at one end of the corral. 'That is the farmhouse, where you and Miss Jo was taken this morning.'

Royce nodded grimly. 'I remember.' He thought for a moment. 'Is our Range Rover still parked there, at the front of the prison hut?'

'Yes, boss, but bastards strip everything out.'

He recalled that their Range Rover had been parked in a row alongside other vehicles that Mbobo and Nazal's people used regularly, mostly pick-ups and 4x4 runabouts.

Cautiously he edged his way towards the firelight and rowdy noise. Beyond the immediate row of parked vehicles were the quadrangle and farmhouse, outside which sat Mbobo and Nazal with their respective entourages, watching the proceedings.

There were tribesmen and fighters everywhere, including some women and children. Thankfully everyone had their back to him and Sinbad, all intent on watching the fight between the two women. Royce had a narrow view between two bystanders of Brampton and Ayana circling each other cautiously in the middle of the corral.

'Sinbad?'

The sound of Seeff's voice made both men jump. They turned abruptly to be confronted by three smartly-dressed Arabs.

Seeff spoke again. 'Fuck me, Rollo, is that you?'

Royce quickly overcame his own shock at their unexpected arrival. 'Sshh!' he hissed. 'Follow me.'

He edged his way back into the cramped alleyway. When far enough away from anyone in the quadrangle being able to overhear them, he said, 'Bram's fighting with Ayana. It's some weird idea by Nazal to impress the local chief.'

'Seems to be working,' Seeff observed. 'Like a fucking remake of Spartacus.'

Royce ignored that. 'We need to get her out of here. You got wheels?'

'We have our second Range Rover,' the South African replied. 'It's round the back – and Rachel Starr's BMW.'

'What?' Royce could hardly believe it. 'And the whole bloody Press corps?'

Seeff grinned. 'No, just Rach. And Yves, here with us.'

Royce recognised the Frenchman for the first time and inclined his head in acknowledgement. 'Bugger me, Stef. We need a plan, and quick.'

'Together,' Ayana agreed as Brampton drew out her own scimitar and held it in her other hand.

'We put them down...' Brampton said softly, bending towards the ground. 'Now...'

'And that knife of yours,' Ayana added.

Brampton pulled it from her trouser pocket. Its steel blade chimed against the scimitar as it landed in the mud.

It was then that Ayana made her sudden move, catching Brampton off guard. She lunged forward, head-butting hard into her belly, knocking the breath out of her and sending her flying backwards. She hit the ground hard, but the watered sand thankfully softened the shock to her spine. Immediately Ayana was on her, astride her waist, her thighs pinning her to the ground and her hands around her throat.

Ayana may have been considerably heavier, but she lacked Brampton's suppleness from regular yoga. Her legs were quickly up behind Ayana's back, one calf managing to hook around the offered neck. It was an untidy manoeuvre, but she managed to pull back and kick the Somalian woman off to one side.

Brampton was still on her back as Ayana staggered to her feet, breathing heavily in the cloying warm air. Noise of the cicadas began to rise from the surrounding oasis undergrowth. She was now sweating profusely as she moved in again on Brampton, looking down on her prey, deciding where to put her attack in.

But long-forgotten memories were coming back to Brampton. Once on your back, circle round to keep your enemy always in front of you, your legs and feet always ready to repel them. Something else Royce or one of the other Selection staff had taught her. Also good in common assault or rape attempts, someone else had cheerfully added at the time. However, with Ayana now hunched over her, and her own feet bare, Brampton wasn't so sure.

For several moments, Ayana circled her, looking for a way in, a way past the long, waving legs. At last she made an unexpected sideways lunge, then back the other way to confound Brampton. She succeeded and dived in, receiving a knee hard in her flank before she landed. Both women were suddenly entangled, their faces close. Ayana again had her fingers around the other's throat, squeezing her into submission, cutting off the air supply. Brampton heard Royce's voice screaming in her ear again. 'Make a fist! Protrude your knuckle! Punch into the bicep.'

Her knuckle-punch went in, hard, into the black girl's toned muscle, deep and sharp. An animal yelp escaped Ayana's lips and her grip loosened momentarily. Just relaxed a fraction, but it was enough.

It gave Brampton sufficient space to use her elbow, to jam it hard into the other's rib-cage. She was sure she felt a bone give, actually heard it fracture. Ayana screamed. At that moment, Brampton managed to bend her elbows and, with her fists together, thrust upwards between Ayana's arms to force them apart and break the grip on her neck.

Brampton threw herself to the left, rolling away as fast as she could.

For a moment there was a lull, both women winded and wounded. Both dragged themselves up onto one knee, regarding each other, scowling and breathing heavily. Their shirts had buttons torn off, material ripped and stained with damp sand. Perspiration shone like lacquer on their skin in the humid, heavy air.

Ayana was first to her feet, straightening her back and shoulders, absorbing the pain in her ribs, trying but unable to fill her lungs fully. Brampton struggled to find the strength to stand and struggled to think clearly, to come up with any sort of strategy.

That was when Ayana took her by surprise again, diving first to her left. Brampton parried, moving to match and meet her. But before she could, Ayana diverted back to her right. She flew beside Brampton with an outstretched arm to scoop around her waist and pull her backward onto the arena floor.

Before Brampton realised what was happening, Ayana was sitting astride her, the heat of her thighs and crutch burning into her abdomen. The journalist knew what would happen next. Again the warrior princess would have those strong fingers at her throat, squeezing the surrender out of her. And Brampton knew full well that she no longer had the strength to counter it, to fight back. Unless she acted immediately, her fate was sealed.

To surprise Ayana, she formed the first two fingers of her left hand into a Churchillian salute and, with all the strength she could muster, aimed for the other's eyes. She struck with force. Ayana, screaming and blinded, fell back, clutching at her face.

Brampton lifted her buttock, forcing off the weight of the black woman, spilling her sideways onto the ground. Then she was up, finding energy from some deep reserve she didn't even know she had.

She stood, legs astride, looking around. Ayana was curled at her feet, gasping and sobbing, hands to her face. What happened now?

Clearly the victor, Brampton was aware of the blur of faces in the flickering firelight of the hanging beacons. Voices were raised in cheers and jeers and shouts of rage.

Turning, she looked towards the farm where her judges sat. Chief Mbobo and his mother were with the gifted slave Tabina by his side, his bride to be. Next to them was Sheikh Nazal Abu, an impassive expression on his face, his eyes hidden behind Rayban shades. As always he was protected by the mighty Azziz with his two Tosa Inu attack dogs, Pharaoh and Cerberus, even now snapping and straining at their leashes, tails wagging furiously, eager to be let off.

What the hell should she do? She vividly recalled the promise that had been made, that if she won she could walk free. Overnight at least. Whether or not that would actually be allowed to happen, she had doubts. But, sod it, nothing tried nothing gained.

She reached down and picked up her fallen scimitar. With a loud cry of victory she raised both hands above her head.

There was a moment of silence, of anti-climax. Then the booing and jeering began. She lowered her arms and glanced anxiously towards the farmhouse. Mbobo, his mother and Nazal were in a huddle, their heads together. It was then that Nazal turned to Azziz and said something. The big man nodded his understanding, looked towards her, then bent over to release the fighting dogs.

Pharaoh was slightly younger and slightly bigger than the other Tosa. He was away first, making a beeline straight towards her, saliva streaming from his giant open jaws. Cerberus was hard on his heels, determined to catch up.

She stared at them, paralysed with terror, as they approached at speed.

30

BATS OUT OF HELL

Normally she would never harm an animal, but this time her reaction was instinctive as the snarling jaws of Pharaoh were on her, yellowed teeth gnashing.

She brought the scimitar down awkwardly across its shoulder as it leapt at her. Stumbling backwards, she threw her left hand up to defend herself. Teeth snatched at her forearm as she was a lost in a maelstrom of claws and fur and blood. The animal howled as the momentum of its attack threw her back onto the ground. She hacked out again blindly with the scimitar, striking again and again.

The heavy weight of the Tosa went suddenly slack, and she pushed the body off her, only to see the second animal Cerberus standing, waiting, looking directly into her eyes. She knew exactly what it was thinking. It made its move.

A single shot cracked out, silencing the crowd in a nanosecond of surprise. Cerberus stopped in mid-flight, its legs collapsing under it and the impact of the bullet toppling it over into the sand.

As realisation happened – that someone had shot the dog – a woman screamed. People started shouting.

Seeff bent and released the stun-grenade into the corral with all the gentle grace of a bowls player on a green. It rolled smoothly and slowly to the centre of the area, stopped and blew off. Its flash was retina-scorching in its brightness and the screeching noise hurt the eardrums as it detonated. The yells of fear from the crowd almost matched its ferocity, the audience of fighters and militiamen turning and running for their lives. They were dispersing as fast as their legs would carry them into the safety of the maze of cattle stalls all filled with military vehicles.

Royce now swung the smoking automatic that Seeff had given him earlier towards the prison hut. The guard called Radi was recovering from his state of shock like everyone else and attempting to get his sub machine-gun into a firing position. He didn't know that the tribesman in the dirty brown robe was his Englishman prisoner, didn't know that he was his very own personal angel of death. The double-tap from the Sig Sauer took him down, two rounds thudding into his chest barely millimetres apart.

At the far end of the quadrangle, Azziz and the bodyguards of Chief Mbobo were springing into action. He and Nazal Abu were already being roughly bundled into the safety of the farmhouse.

Brampton was now on her knees tending to Ayana as Royce approached. 'Jo, it's me.'

She looked up, confused, her hair awry and clotted with wet sand. 'James! Oh, thank God, what's happening? I don't understand.'

'Our friends have come,' he said tersely. 'We're getting out of here.'

'I can't leave her. I've blinded her.'

'Ayana?' Royce asked, incredulous. 'C'mon, we must go now.'

'I can't,'

'NOW!'

Yves had stepped into the centre of the quadrangle, producing a sub machine-run from beneath his robe. He opened fire on the row of parked vehicles, including the stripped Range Rover. He swung his aim as he fired in short bursts, blowing out the tyres of each in turn.

Brampton had helped Ayana to her feet.

'Okay,' Royce agreed with reluctance. 'Bring her with you. But let's

GO!'

He ushered her forward, past the prison hut to where the others in their group waited.

'Hiya, Curly!' Seeff greeted warmly as he led the way down the side alley and through the rows of cattle stalls to where the second Range Rover and Starr's BMW awaited. Tremain and Starr emerged to greet them, the journalist waving frantically. 'Over here, Bram, over here! Thank God you're okay!'

Ayana had begun to recover, and now walked with her head bowed and a handkerchief pressed to her eyes, still barely able to see.

'We've got the two vehicles,' Seeff said, 'But they're stuffed full of kit.'

'Eight of us,' Royce said, doing the calculations. 'It's tight.'

It was then that the slender figure in the pale blue bourka appeared as if from nowhere.

Brampton knew instinctively who it was. 'Tabina?'

'You remember me?'

The journalist reached out for her. 'Oh, yes, sweetheart. How could I forget? I've never stopped thinking about you.'

'I hoped I'd find you, too,' the girl said. 'I got away in all the confusion. If Sheikh Nazal finds me...I think it is a mistake. God knows what he will do to me.'

'Not a mistake,' Brampton assured. 'You're safe now.' She hugged her tightly. 'We'll look after you.'

'I am sorry what happened here. I thought my Pharaoh was going to eat you.'

'*Your* dog?'

'Sheikh Nazal says in eyes of Allah, Pharaoh and I live together as man and wife -'

'Tabina! That is so sick...' Brampton's voice trailed away as she suddenly became aware of the old woman in a black bourka standing in the shadows behind the slave girl.

'Oh my God, who's that?' In the darkness all Brampton could

make out were the frightened hazel eyes and the heavy application of mascara.

Tabina turned. 'Sorry, it is only Mona. She is my new ladies'-maid.'

Ayana heard the conversation and stepped closer, still pressing the handkerchief to her face. 'Tabina has taken pity on Mona. She is destitute. As a teenager she refused an arranged marriage to an old man.'

'A friend of her father,' Tabina explained.

'The father threw acid in her face so no one else would ever want her,' Ayana said. 'No one has…until now.'

But Royce was concerned. 'I'm not sure we'll have room for her.'

Seeff intervened. 'It's okay, boss, there's a truck we can use. It's got a French HMG that Yves knows. Over there. It's fuelled and ready to go.'

'You're a genius,' Royce decided. 'I'll take it with Yves and the women. They can nurse Ayana – more than she bloody deserves.'

'We'd better go,' Seeff urged, 'before the Tuaregs realise what is happening.'

The group divided rapidly, with Sinbad joining Starr who was driving the BMW and Seeff taking the wheel of the Range Rover with Tremain and Parsons. Seconds later the two light vehicles burst into life and were being driven away into the desert. Royce coaxed the aging Berliet to fire up while Brampton, Tabina and Mona assisted Ayana over the tailgate. They sorted out the sacking to make the injured woman more comfortable, while Yves fed a fresh ammunition belt into the mouth of the rear HMG.

Royce spoke into his short-range radio, using their hastily-decided call-signs. 'Big Bugger, calling. I'm rolling. On my way.'

He reversed out rapidly in a wide sweep. In the wing mirrors he could see that tribesmen were emerging from the maze of cattle stalls behind them. 'Yves, think we need to get rid of those vehicles. We don't want anyone following.'

The Frenchman's voice crackled in his ear. *'Consider it done, mon ami.'*

Royce changed gear and the Berliet began to tremble as Yves opened up with the HMG, gobbling up the belt as he hosed along the line of pick-ups and four-wheel drives. Windows disintegrated; rear hatches shattered and metal panels detached themselves like reluctant strippers. A couple of petrol tanks exploded with eye-scorching gusto.

The lorry gathered strength and they speeded up, out into the open desert. Some of the tribesmen loosed off rounds at them, a couple of bullets ricocheting off the tailgate.

Slowly the light and brightness of the settlement shrank away in the side-mirrors. Silence closed in around them, along with the humid tropical warmth. After a few miles, Royce found the Range Rover and the BMW stopped, waiting for them to catch up.

His radio crackled. It was Seeff. *'Boss, we're thinking of returning to an OP we've been using on this plateau till daylight. Push on then?'*

'Roger that,' he agreed. 'Sounds good to me.'

Minutes later, he'd changed his mind as he followed the two smaller vehicles up the narrow shale track. It was a hair-raising hour before he was able to pull up on a substantial flat rock shelf and apply the brake. It was there that they settled down for the night, rolling out sleeping bags, getting a brew on and cooking military rations.

After a while Tremain announced, 'I got a sort of confirmation from MOD London. Confirms French Air Force detachment in Niger has acknowledged receipt of our request. I think that's as good as it'll get.'

After eating, they all settled in for the night. Royce, Seeff and Yves arranged two-hour shifts with night-vision sights to watch over the settlement.

Nothing was discernible until shortly before dawn. It was Seeff's shift and he shook Royce awake. 'Rollo, something's going on. What d'you think?'

He handed the night-vision binoculars to his boss. Royce studied the scene for several minutes before commenting. 'Nazal Abu is pulling out,' he said flatly, not disguising the disappointment in his voice. 'A hundred and fifty miles over the border and they'll be in the Boko Haram stronghold of Maiduguri. According to intel that Ollie has, they've also got hideouts scattered all across the Sambisa forest. These Libyan vehicles will never be found there.'

Yves had woken and joined them. He shrugged, 'As always, we are too late.'

Although Royce managed to get back to sleep, it was light and disturbed by vivid dreams. Suddenly Yves was shaking him awake, a black sweet coffee thrust into his hands.

The sky was lightening, another wondrously fresh desert dawn that lifted the spirits with a promise that was impossible to deliver. It was almost an analogy of the Middle East itself. So much potential that was somehow never quite realised.

He checked with the women. Brampton was delighted that Princess Ayana's vision was virtually restored. Her eyes remained sore and in need of proper medical attention, while Tabina was exploring her new freedom by abandoning her bourka and shaking free her long black hair. Mona sat behind her, stroking through it with a pearl-handled brush.

The pair of French jet fighters came in from the west, flying fast and very low, one behind the other. If you'd been waiting for them with hand-held SAMs, they'd have been over you and gone again before you knew it.

'Mirages,' Yves declared.

They'd come and crossed over the target in the blink of an eye and had banked steeply some miles to the east. Now they were returning. The two fighter bombers screeched towards them, afterburners full on, the first attacking and his wingman protecting.

Ordnance tumbled like dark faeces from the lead aircraft. At that distance it looked as though the entire settlement was being blown to hell. After the dazzling pulses of brilliant light, black and white smoke belched rapidly into the sky to hang in a lingering pall. Job done. The two pilots didn't even bother to return to take photographs of their work.

But, of course, Royce and his team knew the job wasn't done. The attack had mostly destroyed empty cattle shelters and possibly left a few dead and injured tribespeople who had been in the wrong place at the wrong time. It looked as though the farmhouse had taken a direct hit, but it was difficult to tell at that distance. Besides, there was no knowing if either Chief Mbobo or Sheikh Nazal Abu were in there or had left with the convoy earlier. Royce was well aware that the devil, it seemed, really did look after his own and bless them with his own good luck.

Everyone was eager to press on and get back to Tripoli. After a quick breakfast of army rations and biscuits, they were on the move again as the sun began arcing into a white hot sky. The three vehicle convoy rattled its way along another goat trail until it finally reached the desert floor and gathered speed towards the border with Libya.

Passengers were redistributed between the vehicles. Parsons took the opportunity to invite Ayana to be his passenger with Tremain so he could mount a major charm offensive. It was clear to Royce his intention was not only an unofficial debrief but to also to persuade her to become an agent for him. The princess insisted on keeping Mona by her side, which didn't cramp Parsons's style as she clearly understood no English.

Yves drove Starr's BMW, which allowed Sinbad to do a wonderful agony uncle act with Tabina. It had become clear from the things she said to everyone that she was on the verge of becoming a mental – and possibly physical – basket case. Gaddafi and Nazal between them had completely messed up the young girl's head. It was heart-breaking.

That left Stefan Seeff happily driving the old Berliet truck and found Brampton and Royce alone for the first time in the cargo hold since they'd escaped the settlement. The temperature cranked steadily up, the indistinctive dun-coloured lunar landscape rolled by like a fixed loop video.

Brampton ventured, 'Glad you got rid of that awful brown robe you were wearing yesterday.'

'Sorry, it was a bit honking,' Royce said, settling down next to her. 'All I could find in my wardrobe at the time.'

'Mind you, I can't exactly be smelling of roses.'

Royce had noticed there were buttons missing on her shirt and caught himself watching as her breasts, in the soft lace bra, rose and fell freely with each bump in the track.

He laughed. 'Can't beat the aroma of honest girlie perspiration.'

Her eyes widened. 'God, James! That sounds like one of Stefan's chat-up lines.'

'Dammit, it does, doesn't it?' He feigned a look of horror. 'I wouldn't wish that on any woman. I'm sorry.'

She giggled. 'You're forgiven. You were there for me when it mattered.'

'It didn't feel like it.'

'For me it did.' They were seated side by side on the empty sacks and, for the first time, she looked directly at him. 'I felt I knew what you were thinking, that you understood…when Mbobo started touching me up…'

'Look, Jo, you don't have to…'

She shook her head vehemently. 'I know that, I know that. But you were there, you saw what happened. I think you're the only one who could ever understand. You know what I mean?'

'You actually enjoyed it.' It was a statement, spoken softly.

'No, I didn't!' Sharp.

'But your body did. That's what I meant.' He added, 'It's the human condition, like it or not. You can't do a thing about it.'

She stared at him. 'You sound like Anoushka.'

'Your friend? *Really*?'

She waved that aside. 'What do you mean?'

'A mother is bathing her child. A bird flies in from outside. The mother – who is terrified of birds – runs out of the bathroom, screaming. That child is forever scared of birds.'

Brampton nodded. 'True enough.'

'A boy or girl is spanked at school and becomes aroused. Unexplained, but it stays with them, in their psyche forever. Part of the human condition...'

She shook her head. 'But Mbobo, that little shit – and everyone realising what I was feeling...He didn't know what he was doing, but he nearly gave me an orgasm. Can you imagine how humiliating that is?'

'It was unnatural, unexpected – and bizarre. That's exactly why it turned you on.' Royce said. 'Don't beat yourself up about it. It just proves you're normal.'

She thought about his words, tried to absorb them. The featureless landscape continued by, the constant jolting less rhythmic than a train but almost as mesmerising. He hugged her reassuringly.

Suddenly she said, 'God, I need a fuck.'

'What?'

'Oh, sorry. Did I really say that? God, I'm sorry.'

'It's nothing. It happens. You think you're going to die. Really think. And then you don't. Hormones kick in.'

'What?'

'High dopamine levels in women after danger. Triggers a need to reproduce while you can. It's similar in men.'

She stared at him. 'I've never felt like this before. Have you?'

'Yes.'

'Do you now?'

'After that...what do you think?'

'I want...you know? With you. Do?'

'Shut up.'

He put his hand over her mouth. She bit him, hard. He slapped her face, with enough force to make her cheek colour. Her mouth found his, her hand behind his head turning a self-defence technique upside down, forcing their lips and tongues together. Her fingers clawed into his back, as he shifted position and moved onto her.

'Fuck you,' she said.

'Fuck you,' he returned .

She threw her arms around him, pushing her mouth onto his. He slid the shirt from her shoulders and unclasped her light mesh brassiere. It fell away to reveal the nipples that had been at the centre of so much boyish speculation. They did not disappoint. They stiffened and grew as his incisors sunk into them and his finger and thumb twisted harshly. Her teeth sunk into his earlobe in retaliation, really hard, drawing blood. He punched her lightly in her belly and she went ballistic.

'Get your pants off,' he snarled.

The next few minutes seemed like an hour, the lovemaking was harsh and tender at the same time, a yin and yang of unbridled passion. It was pure, unadulterated human lust. They fell back, panting, dripping in sweat.

Brampton said, 'I want a cigarette.'

'I've given up.'

'So have I.'

'Since when? Well, I was going to.' She frowned. 'Those little cigars of yours?'

'One or two a week. If I deserve them.'

'Who decides that?'

'Me.' He fished in his pocket. 'A tin of Café Cremes. Didn't even know I had them.'

'Sod, James, they'll do.'

He lit them both.

After a while Brampton exhaled her final inhalation and looked sideways at Royce. 'Never again. Right? Never.'

'Never,' he agreed.

31

HIDDEN IN PLAIN SIGHT

In the early afternoon, the little convoy pulled round into a rough, protective three-vehicle circle, like an old Wild West wagon train in the desert wilderness. But the only living thing interested in them was a vulture swooping high in the white hot sky. In the narrow shade of the truck the group stretched their legs, made a brew and shared some meagre army rations between themselves.

It was then that Ayana finally found a signal on her Libyan Army radio. She wandered off, gabbling excitedly in Arabic, until she was out of earshot.

She was smiling broadly when she returned. 'I have good news for us all,' she announced. 'I have friends in Tajarhi. They say we can stay there tonight.'

'Tajarhi?' Parsons repeated.

'It's the southern-most settlement in the Fezzan region,' Royce reminded. 'We bypassed it on the way down. It straddles some of the historic trading routes.'

'Bugger all ther,e though,' Seeff added. 'Except an airstrip on its southern edge.'

'We will get food and shelter,' Ayana said, irritated at the lack of enthusiasm. 'And water to bathe.'

'Now that would be nice,' Brampton said with feeling.

The convoy took off again, heading north. When they finally arrived at the sprawling desert village of Tajarhi, the sun was setting the western horizon ablaze, backlighting a frieze of date palms, the landscape dimming rapidly.

They came to a halt beside a large compound of neatly-rendered mud walls. Whoever owned the place clearly wasn't short of a dinar or two. Royce had barely dropped down from the back of the truck, when one of the bare metal gates of the compound swung open. Two AK-armed females were dressed in the camo uniforms of Gaddafi's personal bodyguard.

Ayana, now wearing oversized designer sunglasses, stepped out of her car and waved at them. 'Good to see you again, ladies,' she greeted in Arabic.

The girl soldiers replied in kind. 'Everything is ready for you, boss,' one added.

Turning to Royce, Ayana said, 'We'll park inside the compound. It will be safe enough in there.'

As she turned away, Royce caught the aroma of wood smoke and cooking in the still air. Then he heard the distant sound of a private aircraft, like the faint hum of a mosquito, getting louder as it headed towards the landing-strip to arrive in the last vestiges of daylight.

It had been a long, eventful day and he was glad it was over. He put his weight behind the second gate, pushing it wide open to allow Seeff to drive the truck into the dusty courtyard. The South African found himself parking in front of an expansive mud-brick villa bungalow with a veranda and an Italian-style terracotta tile roof. It was what passed for a top-end luxury dwelling in this part of the desert, confirmed by the comforting hum a large generator hidden somewhere in the surrounding garden.

The gates were closed after the two cars drove in and the passengers started to disembark. The female soldiers then began leading everyone to their allotted quarters with marked efficiency. Royce realised then that the building was actually the size of a small hotel, probably owned by a local official in the Gaddafi government. Everyone was paired off into twin-bedded rooms: Royce with Seeff, Brampton and Starr, Parsons and Tremain together, Yves with Sinbad, while Ayana led Tabina away with Mona to another room away at the front of the building.

When they were called to supper an hour later, each had taken a welcome hot shower and changed into fresh clothes. Ayana and all the other Libyan women were missing, apparently eating together somewhere else in the bungalow.

The meal was simple, a Berber dish called *f'tet*, thin strips of bread with chickpeas and lamb chunks in a tomato and onion sauce. It had just been thrown together by the girl soldiers who were looking after the place, but to the famished escapees it was a dish so delicious it would be remembered forever.

They all sat at a large rustic table, while Brampton spooned the stew from a big earthenware pot into individual bowls.

'I'm glad to be out of that bloody car,' Tremain said.

'Air con playing up again?' Royce asked.

Tremain shook his head. 'The smell of bad eggs. Or farm manure. Almost the whole time.'

Parsons explained. 'Tabina's new maid. Seemed to never stop farting.'

'What?' Starr asked, taken aback.

'Poor love,' Brampton said. 'You heard what happened to her? God knows what we *don't* know about what happened to her.'

'Please!' Tremain complained. 'I'm trying to eat.'

'Fuckin' Sharia law,' Seeff swore. 'I bet we see it in the UK before long.'

That seemed to remind Parsons. 'By the way, Princess Ayana has told me she will be coming back to the UK – immediately or very soon.'

For a moment Royce thought Parsons was forgetting his cover as a

BBC World Service producer. But then the man added, 'So you news hounds might want to make sure you've got contact numbers for her.'

Brampton glanced around the table. 'And Tabina? What about her?'

'If she agree, I take to my home.' Sinbad looked scared that he would be over ruled. 'If you allow – my wife, I think she will take care of her.'

Brampton suddenly felt overwhelmed. 'Oh, Sinbad, what a brilliant idea! That would be wonderful.'

Parsons wasn't really listening. He had the prize he wanted, had clearly landed Ayana for MI6. He raised his glass of lemon water. 'I think we can safely say Mission Accomplished. Cheers, everyone!'

They then all left the table, exhausted after the days of strain, long hours on the road and a fulsome meal. Royce exchanged a long and lingering look with Brampton. She pursed her lips momentarily. But she didn't smile before turning abruptly away to follow Starr into their shared bedroom.

The three close protection operators agreed on successive two-hour stags, Royce volunteering for the first. Although he was now packing his favoured CZ85 in a belt holster, he also collected a 9mm MP5K short from the truck before settling down on the front terrace. Seated on the timber balustrade, it gave him an enhanced view of the star-lit horizon beyond the compound walls and the vast indigo sky overhead.

He fought hard to concentrate, to keep his mind from wandering to thoughts of Brampton, the wild and animal passion they'd shared, all too short-lived and bitter sweet. Somehow he guessed it would never happen again. Probably *should* never happen again.

Both the villa and the settlement of Tajarhi had long fallen silent, except for the incessant faraway yapping of a small dog and the background trilling of cicadas. He then thought he could hear a car approaching, but then the sound faded abruptly. No headlights had made an appearance at the front of the villa.

He glanced down at his Breitling. The long hand nudged midnight plus one.

That was when he suddenly became aware of voices. Female, excited. A lamp came on at an open window to his left, projecting an illuminated square onto the surface of the courtyard. He recognised Princess Ayana's voice, hushing the others to be quite.

Quickly he remembered it was her bedroom, shared with Tabina and Mona.

At ease, he dropped his shoulders, lowered the MP5K. Another half hour and he was due to be relieved by Seeff, who would take on the next two-hour stag.

And that was when he heard the male voice for the first time, gruff and low. It was crazy. He knew there were no men at the villa. Ayana had told him that the property was a secret security outpost run by Colonel Gaddafi's female bodyguards, where members of the leader's extended family could stay safely when required with full military protection. Such properties were scattered throughout the land. Was it the voice of a visiting local official? At this time of night? Royce was mystified.

He slipped from his seat on the balustrade and re-entered the villa. Out of curiosity he first moved some forty metres down the hallway to the rear of the building.

Backing against a well, he peered around an ornamental arch. To his surprise, he found a rear door to the building guarded by two more female bodyguards he had not seen before. Moreover he could hear the gentle tick-over of an automobile engine. He berated himself for trusting in Ayana's hospitality just because Ollie Parson's had.

Carefully he edged back into the hallway and returned swiftly to the front of the villa.

He saw the bar of light from beneath the bedroom door of Ayana, Tabina and her ladies'-maid. Again he became aware of the deeper tone of a male voice amongst those of women talking.

He didn't recognise it. Speaking Arabic, but he was certain it wasn't Yves or Seeff or Parsons – or even Sinbad.

He rapped on the door. 'Ayana, what's going on?' he demanded and reached for the handle. 'I'm coming in.'

Then he heard Ayana. 'No, do not!' Her voice raised an octave in warning.

He pushed the door roughly open – only to come face to face with the snout of a heavy 9mm automatic.

'What the – ?'

Ayana waved the gun. 'Come in. Give that weapon to Amal. And keep your hands out where I can see them.'

Royce immediately took in the scene, a lifetime of training kicking in.

But the main light was off and the single standard lamp cast as much shadow as it did illumination.

Apart from Ayana standing behind the door, the cheerful small bodyguard named Amal, whom he had met before at Nazal Abu's villa in Tripoli, had appeared from nowhere and was now disarming him. Apart from the sub-machine gun, she also found and removed the Czech automatic from his belt holster.

'Have you just arrived?' he asked Amal, remembering the private aircraft he'd seen coming in at last light.

Amal was quick to smile, and nodded. 'Yes, Mr James. I was flown in a bit earlier.'

Tabina was seated on the edge of her bed, dressed in a silk dressing gown, watching proceedings impassively. It occurred to Royce how "out-of-it" she seemed, almost zombie-like, as though spaced out on drugs or away in some world of her own.

In that instant he found himself searching the shadows in the room, looking for the old woman called Mona.

He turned to Ayana. 'I heard a man in here,' he accused.

She did not answer.

The answer came from a chair in the furthest dark corner of the room. 'You did. It is me.'

Royce was aware of Ayana closing the door behind him. He was stunned. Suddenly he knew that voice, knew it from the impassioned radio speeches, from the television broadcasts. Colonel Muammar

Gaddafi. At that precise moment, the most wanted man in the world.

The Libyan leader leaned forward in the armchair and the lamplight caught his features, the heavily-pocked face, rough shaven and with a head that had been hastily shorn of its familiar tangled locks. His body was draped in a black bourka, it head-dress fallen to the floor by his feet.

The stench of bad eggs was overwhelming.

'Sir, this is the man they call Rollo,' Ayana said in English. 'I told you about him. He works for the BBC spy.'

The heavy mascara around Gaddafi's eyes made him look like a pantomime dame. 'Rollo,' he repeated. 'A soldier, brave man.'

Still in shock, Royce muttered, 'Just trying to do my job, keeping my people safe.'

Gaddafi nodded his understanding. 'Like me,' he said and farted, apparently unaware of what he was doing. That was when Royce recalled the stories of those journalists who had interviewed the man. 'I tell my friend Tony Blair. When this trouble starts – back in beginning of the year – I speak on telephone to him. Twice. I beg help. I tell him it is not my people rising up against me, it is terrorists. Tell your government, I say to him.'

Royce tried to make sense of the rambling voice. '*Not* a people's revolution?' he ventured, trying to be clear. His utter shock giving way to curiosity.

Gaddafi was contemptuous. 'Of course, not! It is jihadists – *al-Qaedi* and others, they are everywhere now. They breed in Misrata. A nest of vipers. My own friend is leading them. Nazal Abu has the virus. I warn Mr Blair and I plead with him to tell David Cameron, to tell Mr Obama.'

'And what did your friend – Blair – say?' Royce asked.

The Libyan looked forlorn. 'He tells me to leave, to go for my own good. Blair betrays me, tells me to call Mugabe. Let me stay there in exile.' He shook his head. 'No way, no way will I desert my people.'

'But you've just gone away in disguise with Princess Ayana. In Nazal

Abu's convoy,' Royce challenged. 'To join up with Boko Haram?'

Gaddafi shook his head. 'You don't understand. I can trust no one now. Only Ayana. Everyone in my family is doing deals. It was only option of the moment. It is her idea for me. Hide in plain sight, she says.'

Ayana spoke for the first time. 'I am thinking that maybe our Leader can find sanctuary with Boko Haram,' she explained. 'Our Leader could – after all – take his place at the head of the Caliphate.'

'And Nazal Abu had no idea?'

'Absolutely not.'

Royce could believe that Nazal Abu would not have given the old crone a first glance, let alone a second.

Now he regarded the Libyan leader more closely. He did not look like a well man. 'Can I ask – what changed your mind?'

Gaddafi snorted, and farted again at the same time. 'That is easy. At the farm. The public beheadings of those two young men. Young rebels, they remind me of me when I was their age. Misguided by this uprising, yes. But full of honour, full of bravery. That decides me. I will go home to Sirte and place my life in the hands of Allah. And my people.'

'And do you think you will survive?'

The Libyan laughed, and farted and phlegm caught in his throat. He cleared it and spat on the floor. 'Not if the Americans can help it. Even though my people want me, they will have me dead.'

Royce frowned. 'I thought you'd been reconciled nowadays?' It was true that the governments of the West and the media no longer vilified Gaddafi as they had a couple of decades before.

Gaddafi snorted. 'Not since Washington knows about my Gold Dinar.'

'Gold Dinar? A currency?'

'No one tells you, Mr Rollo.' Again he chuckled throatily. 'What a surprise. The Americans and English don't care yet about the jihadists in Libya. They care about me and the Gold Dinar.'

Ayana said, 'One hundred and fifty tons of Libyan gold and a similar amount of silver. With Tunisia and Egypt, our Leader has planned to create a new oil currency alliance to make us independent of Wall Street and the City. Piss on their worthless petro-dollar bills.'

'That, my friend,' Gaddafi added, 'is the *real* reason the Americans encourage the so-called Arab Spring. And it is why they suddenly decide now that they want me dead.'

Ayana stepped in. 'Forgive me, Sir, but I think we have talked long enough. I know our pilot will be anxious to be off and to get to our destination under cover of darkness.'

Gaddafi nodded, picked up the bourka head-dress and rose to his feet. 'Goodbye, Mr Rollo,' he held out his hand. 'You tell your BBC spy boss that he is wrong. London and Washington will one day pay big price for this mistake.'

Royce found himself shaking the man's hand.

'You tell them,' Gaddafi repeated and moved towards the door.

Ayana waved her automatic. 'Sit down, Mr Rollo. Stay here with Amal and Tabina for the next hour. Don't be fooled by Amal's pretty smile. If you try to leave, she will shoot you dead.'

To prove the point, Amal already had her own pistol out and at the ready as Colonel Gaddafi slipped passed her and into the hallway.

Royce said, 'My job is to protect my clients, nothing more.'

Ayana hesitated by the door. 'When you do see your BBC spy boss, Mr Oliver, tell him I will keep my word. I shall call him when I am in London. It will not be long.'

With that she was gone, and the smell of bad eggs faded away.

Royce sat down in the chair vacated by Gaddafi and stared at the closed door. Just what the hell, he wondered, would Parsons make about this bizarre and extraordinary meeting when he told him about it in the morning?

He heard the faint sound of a car starting through the open window and listened as it faded into the distance and the noise of the cicadas closed in.

The small convoy of vehicles arrived back at the Golden Palms hotel two days' later.

Royce had not told Parsons the full story of what had happened that night in Tajarhi. Only that Princess Ayana had left with Mona and had promised that she would soon in touch with Parsons in London. There seemed little point in saying more, in complicating things. Although clearly irritated, that had seemed to satisfy the MI6 officer well enough.

By now the entire world was recognising that the regime of Colonel Gaddafi was finally over, although the man himself appeared to have vanished from the face of the earth. There was much speculation that he had been spirited away by his friends, his enemies or even the Western allies and given sanctuary in some despotic desert kingdom or with his old pal President Mugabe of Zimbabwe.

It had been just a few days that they'd been away, but the whole mood and atmosphere at the place had changed. Low-grade politicians and profiteers had quickly moved in with their big money and antennae for opportunity and fast bucks.

On the journey, Brampton had written up notes in draft for an article on her big adventure to Niger and a short script for a piece to camera. She decided she should do it while she was still dishevelled and bloodied, her hair matted with sand and sweat from the journey. Royce was persuaded to go with her to the rooftop, to help her film the account against a backdrop of Tripoli and the Mediterranean.

A couple of times, while he was crouched over the camera, he noticed that she had flinched visibly and they'd have to do a retake. He was puzzled, because it wasn't timed with any of the spasmodic gunfire that still occurred from time to time. At last they had it in the can.

'Are you okay?' he asked.

She looked embarrassed and lowered her voice. Other television reporters were having similar ideas and setting up cameras and sound equipment on the hotel roof. 'They're are still *so* tender,' she whispered. 'Just my shirt rubbing, like jogger's... No one's ever twisted and bitten them like that before.'

He looked slightly abashed. 'Sorry.'

She placed her hand on his bicep. 'Don't be. They've never felt so alive, in a permanent state of excitement. I just have to get used to it.'

He raised an eyebrow. 'We said never again, remember.'

There was a mischievous glint in her eye. 'Right. Never.'

Brampton's joy at getting her film report done was short-lived when she returned to the hotel lobby after a lengthy hair wash and bath in lukewarm water. The first person she spotted was young Chesney Sykes, who was talking to Rachel Starr with all the blasé and extravagant hand gestures of a five-star war correspondent. What the hell was he doing here, she thought savagely? Without a second's hesitation, she diverted her course towards the zebra-skin sofa where Parsons sat talking with Royce and Seeff.

'Hi.guys. Mind if I join you?'

'Ah, just the girl,' Parsons said.

'Where's Iain?'

'Where he's happiest, playing with his airwaves. Upstairs trying to contact our bosses in London.'

She sat down next to Royce. 'And Ayana?'

'At the Corinthia apparently,' he replied, raising his eyebrows. 'A bit more her style than here, apparently. But she will be joining me back in the UK soon.'

'The BBC?'

Parson realised his error. 'Er..?'

She touched his knee. 'It's okay, Ollie. I think I know you wear more than one hat. Landing her will be good for your career.'

'I'm not sure about that.' He laughed. 'And you, you've scrubbed up well, if I might say.'

'Best cold water bath I've ever had.'

Seeff's eyes were on her chest. 'I can see that.'

She ignored him. 'I just want to eat a proper meal. Then write my story up tonight to file it in time for this Sunday's edition.'

'Ah, Jo,' Parsons said, 'I shouldn't be in too much of a rush.'

'What do you mean? It's a fantastic story, my fight with Ayana. It'll knock the smug smile off Alex Crawfie's face.'

Parsons lowered his voice. 'Only it's unlikely ever to see the light of day.'

'Why ever not?' Royce asked.

'Because No.10,' Parsons said slowly, 'isn't too keen on telling the entire world how it allowed a core element of Gaddafi's armed force to escape into the desert to join up with Islamic militants.'

'It'll come back to haunt them,' Royce said, 'I'm sure of that.'

Seeff said, 'I guess Prime Minister Cameron and judo Judy Hague want to wallow in the glory of ousting Gaddafi.'

'My editor may have another view,' Brampton pressed defiantly.

'I've already spoken to him, Jo,' Parsons interjected. 'Russ Carver is here now with your replacement.'

'What?' she was shocked. She'd clocked Sykes but didn't know her editor was also in the building. 'Have *you* had a hand in this, Ollie? Do I just know too much?'

Parsons shrugged and held his hands out, palms up. 'Nothing to do with me, Jo. Sorry.'

'I don't believe you.'

At that moment Iain Tremain made one of his fairly rare appearances.

Parsons looked up, immediately sensing something was amiss. His friend looked unusually glum. He stood back, and beckoned Parsons with an inclination of his head. A sense of concern fell over the small group as Tremain was joined by Parsons and the two of them drifted away in an urgent huddle.

'Bloody hell,' Seeff said, 'has the Queen died?'

Brampton punched him on the arm, hard. 'Stefan, don't! That's not nice.'

'Maybe Cameron, then,' he suggested.

She chuckled. 'Run through by the Queen, perhaps.'

The two MI6 spooks re-joined them.

Parsons said, 'Iain's got some news. It's not good.'

Tremain looked directly at Brampton. 'Jo, I understand your Dad was soon to publish a book about Vladimir Putin of Russia?'

Her heart skipped a beat. 'Yes, early next year. A prediction of what is going to happen. He's got a deal with Simon and Schuster here and in the States.'

'Your Dad went to a meeting in Brussels,' Tremain explained, 'to arrange an extra pan-European deal with a new publisher there.'

Brampton suddenly realised what Tremain had said earlier. 'You said my Dad *was* going to publish a book?'

Tremain took a deep breath. 'I'm afraid there's no easy way to tell you this. After a lunch with the publisher, your father was taken very ill with food poisoning and died. The Belgian police have discovered that the publisher does not exist.'

Parsons added, 'They suspect foul play.'

Epilogue

IN MEMORIAM

Timeline: London, early November 2011

'I didn't think you'd make it,' Brampton said.

He kissed her hard on the mouth, bruising her lips. 'I moved heaven and earth,' Royce said. 'Have you missed me?'

'No.'

'I'm sorry I couldn't make the funeral. Too short notice.'

'I understand. That was okay. Anoushka and Adrian came to Cornwall. Even Maxim Petchkin managed to attend, which was sweet of him. Dad would have liked that.'

Royce looked around. 'This is altogether different.'

She said, 'I admit I didn't realise he was so widely read and respected.'

The Memorial Service for Boris Bramberg was in another league. Held at St Martin's-in-the-Field, a church situated off Trafalgar Square, three months' later, it had attracted an amazing number of his readers and devotees from around the world. They included a number of Russian oligarchs resident in London, distinguishable as much as anything by their bulky, black-suited bodyguards with radio earplugs and bulging underarms. Many foreign correspondents had come too. Brampton had already spotted big names like Colvin, Lamb, Bowen, Urban and Crawford amongst them. What really surprised her was that so many by-line journalists had travelled so far and taken the trouble and time, often at personal expense, to attend this service. It made her heart swell with pride.

It was a shame that London's weather could not have held off, but the bruised November clouds wept cold tears over the mourners who gathered to pay their respects. For Brampton the service was made all the more poignant and personal to her that, after a long hiatus, Colonel Gaddafi had only just finally been found – and then killed by his captors a few weeks earlier.

It reminded her. 'I got a text message from Sinbad a couple of days ago.'

Royce was surprised. 'How's he doing?'

Brampton looked overjoyed. 'The text was a bit all over the place. Remember he took Tabina back to Benghazi? Seems she and his wife are getting on fine – like the daughter she had who died. She's teaching Tabina hair-dressing.'

'Good to have a happy ending,' Royce said with a smile.

Organ music swelled from within the church.

'We'd better go in,' Brampton said. 'I saw Ollie and Iain earlier.'

'I'm sorry your story was spiked.'

Her eyes hardened a fraction. 'I've moved on, James.'

It was clear he'd do well to move on too. He said, 'Stefan said he was coming. But he was on a promise in Brighton last night.'

'I'm sure he'll do his best.'

'And your Dad's book on Putin?'

'Delayed. The bastards did a thorough job. They hacked his laptop and wiped everything. But his agent and publishers both had parts of earlier drafts – and I had a lot of his notes hidden in my freezer – thanks to you.'

'And so?'

She turned her face to the chill north wind. 'I'm going to finish what he started. What else can I do?'

Royce felt a cold shiver. 'Winter's on the way.' He looked towards the church. 'It'll be good to get inside.'

Across the street from the church, Viktor Volkov raised his hand as he sat at the table outside the coffee-house. The waitress smiled and scurried across to him.

'Yes, sir?'

'A straight black coffee, full strength.' He frowned. 'That accent? Are you Russian?'

She smiled. 'I am from Ukraine.'

AUTHOR'S NOTE

The opening chapters of this book feature my fictionalised version of real events in Libya when two Chinook helicopters of the British Army arrived carrying a Secret Intelligence Service (SIS or MI6) team, protected by members of E Squadron SAS.

This sequence tallies accurately within all other published newspaper accounts that I have read.

While I was writing this book the world lost two fearless British female frontline journalists. Marie Colvin of the *Sunday Times* was believed to have been the deliberate target of a sniper in Syria, while courageous loner Sue Lloyd Roberts – renowned for her work in Bosnia – sadly succumbed to cancer on the home front.

It seems that worldwide respect for the impartiality of the broadcast media and the press has diminished, making the lives of those seeking the truth on our behalf ever more at risk.

I am especially grateful to SKY News reporter Alex Crawford and her account of the Libyan uprising in her book *Colonel Gaddafi's Hat* (Collins) and Annick Cojean for her shocking revelations in *Gaddafi's Harem* (Grove Press UK).

As the "Arab Spring" was taking hold throughout the Middle East in February 2011, Colonel Gaddafi had two telephone conversations with his old friend, former Prime Minister of Britain, Tony Blair. In them – according to transcripts – the Colonel insisted he was not fighting rebels but "jihadists", who wanted to control the Mediterranean and then attack Europe.

'We are not fighting them,' Gaddafi said, 'they are attacking us. I want to tell you the truth…The story is simply this: an organisation has laid down sleeping cells in North Africa. Called the al-Qaeda Organisation in North Africa…The sleeping cells in Libya are similar to the dormant cells in America before 9/11.'

However much may have been supposition at the time, Gaddafi's prophetic warning came to pass. Libya collapsed following his overthrow and murder. In the vacuum that followed much of the country came under the control of the jihadist extremists of the Islamic State in Iraq and the Levant (ISAL), the successors to al-Qaeda.

My regular team of advisers this time included Neil, Mat, Barney, Leslie and Geoff Harkness who stoically drove miles into the desert for me on Google Earth.

A special welcome goes to newcomer Dee Bee, who gave so generously of his "close protection" experience and expertise that covers both Iraq and Libya. He did his best to take all the danger out of my characters' adventures and kill my best laughs. Happily he failed in both, but anyway kept most of them pretty safe – for which I am deeply appreciative!

TERENCE STRONG

LONDON, 2017